Between the Waves

ALSO BY HILARY TAILOR

The Vanishing Tide

Where Water Lies

Between the Waves

HILARY TAILOR

LAKE UNION
PUBLISHING

Between the Waves

HILARY TAILOR

LAKE UNION
PUBLISHING

Text copyright © 2025 by Hilary Tailor
All rights reserved.

Published by Lake Union Publishing, Seattle

www.apub.com

Amazon, the Amazon logo, and Lake Union Publishing are trademarks of Amazon.com, Inc., or its affiliates.

EU Product Safety contact:
Amazon Publishing, Amazon Media EU S.à r.l.
38, avenue John F. Kennedy, L-1855 Luxembourg
amazonpublishing-gpsr@amazon.com

ISBN-13: 9781662526787
eISBN: 9781662526794

Cover design by Emma Rogers
Cover images: © chaossart © Alexey Seafarer © Bastian Kienitz / Shutterstock; © David Cheshire / Arcangel

Printed in the United States of America

For my father, Christopher.

It is easy to imagine a wave. But what about the space in between where the sea draws its breath, the moment of stillness before action is taken? Nobody talks about that liminal place, where a line waits to be crossed and nothing returns to the way it was.

Sunrise

Memories are slippery. Like oil in water, they scatter into fragments and form their own shapes. Sometimes, Roz tries very hard to remember the events of that morning, in the order that they played out, but all she can bring to mind are dream-like sensations, jumbled up and hard to place. She remembers the air, rinsed with salt water, the cool breeze thickening her hair as she climbed the narrow path, three steps behind Catrin, up to the top of the cliff in the lifting darkness. She can recall the sound of her own breath as she neared the old stone cairn, the soft *thunk* every time Catrin's bag swung away and fell back to her hip. Roz remembers the shudder of the mercury sea as it hurled itself against the rocks below them, the click and wind of Catrin's old-fashioned camera, capturing the thin seam of colour that flooded the horizon.

That morning had been the best of Roz's life. On holiday, with her two closest friends; thirteen years old and she had never witnessed the sun rise. Standing there, on top of the cliff, on a Welsh island measuring two miles by one, she felt she had the world at her feet. Her only regret was not waking her sister to share it, the promise to Hazel she had broken.

Whenever Roz thinks of Hazel, which is often, she is always wearing red paisley pyjamas and clutching her favourite toy, Goggin. Goggin had been patched and stitched over and over. He was a confusing bundle of knitted limbs. Nobody could remember what animal he was originally supposed to be and nobody, apart from Roz and her parents, understood the great affection Hazel had for him. At eleven, she was supposed to have grown out of things like that, but Hazel was still a baby in so many ways.

Was it after Catrin climbed down to the cove below that Roz felt she was being watched? She remembers the long shadow of the cairn, the meaning of those stones, old as centuries, one for each of Catrins' relatives that had passed away. She can still feel the ground tilting below her feet as she ran back down to the house, the sensation of being observed clinging to her, like nausea. The night before, when things were normal, they had all sat around a fire and Catrin's father had told them of the cold-eyed fairy folk that lived in the holes of the ragged cliffs. As she raced down the cliff path that morning, she imagined them flying after her, their arms outstretched, their fingernails trying to catch her hair.

Roz can remember all of these details with a clarity that hurts, but they are jumbled up in her head. She can recall the relief that flooded through her like a dam-burst when she reached the house, her hand on the door, the paint still slick with salted dew. It is only at this point, when the door opens wide to the smell of toast and coffee, and she enters the kitchen where her parents are, that her memory resolves itself into a coherent, terrible chain of events.

'Where have you been?' her father asked. 'We've been worried.'

'Just up to the cliff. Catrin and I wanted to watch the sunrise.'

Her father frowned. 'That was irresponsible, Rosalind. Out on the cliff path in the middle of the night . . .'

'It wasn't the middle of the night.'

'. . . taking Hazel with you, without telling us.'

'I didn't take Hazel with me.'

'Catrin, then,' said her mother. 'She must be with Catrin.'

Roz's words faltered. 'Hazel didn't . . . come with us.'

Her father, her mother, became very still. The three of them looked at one another, and Roz saw their faces change from irritation to fear.

'Then where is she?' her mother demanded.

'She's . . .' The words dried up in Roz's mouth. She left the kitchen, her heart thumping hard, and ran up the stairs to her parents' room. Hazel's bed was unmade, the duvet thrown back. Goggin wasn't there. Roz had been sweaty from the run back to the house, but now she felt cold. A horrible shiver ran right through her body, her throat constricted. Swallowing hard, Roz opened the door to the room she shared with Nina and Catrin. Catrin hadn't returned and Nina was still asleep.

'Nina, wake up,' said Roz with urgency. 'Did Hazel come in here?'

The lump on the bed didn't move.

'Nina!' urged Roz, half shouting, half crying.

The lump shifted, curls poked up above the line of the sleeping bag. 'I told you I'm not coming. I'm tired.' Nina sounded annoyed.

Roz could hear the terror in her mother's voice rising through the house, the clattering of footsteps as the adults began to look. 'Hazel doesn't like being alone. If she didn't go with Roz, where has she gone?'

Roz remembers hovering at the top of the stairs. A bad feeling descending upon her, like a curtain at the end of a play. Somehow, she knew she had to hold herself together, that if she gave in to fear, it would make everything real. So she stood on her tiptoes and looked out of the picture window that gave a view across the small island to the headland. The path that snaked up to the top of the cliff was a wandering, crooked line. She could see the seam of gorse and the field that lay beyond it, sloping down towards the house. She could see the edge of the cliff cut into the pale blue of the sky. But she couldn't see her sister. Hazel wasn't there.

Later, much later, when the house had emptied of volunteers and the police were still out searching the island by torchlight, somebody gave her mother a sleeping pill. The silence that enveloped the house, then, felt suffocating. Roz had sat on the top of the stairs, knees drawn up to her chin, in the darkness, wondering when she would be fed. The tip of her tongue found her bare knees, and she tasted the sea. She didn't know if the salt came from the air, or if she was tasting her tears.

Chapter One

It is hard to get out of bed. It is always hard on this particular date. But this year, Willow, Roz's daughter, turned eleven. For some reason, it has made every angle of Roz's grief come back into painful focus. Since her daughter became the age her sister never moved beyond, almost everything about Willow brings Roz face to face with what losing Hazel means. Every time Willow discovers something thrilling and new, Roz could weep because it's one more thing Hazel never got to see.

And the guilt. The guilt never leaves her. It is a hum of white noise, the soundtrack of her life.

Roz eventually gets out of bed, her legs heavy. She knocks on Willow's door, telling her to get up. As she sets out the breakfast things, she remembers doing this for Hazel, when they were little: the good-natured squabbling over a treasured Peter Rabbit plate; Hazel's deep love of apricot jam; her dislike of crusts and warm milk. These are the details that Roz recalls, the minutiae of her life with a sister who never grew up. Twenty years, to the day, and Roz is still waiting for the happiness to creep into these memories. She wants to remember her sister with a smile. It hasn't happened yet.

Roz looks at her watch and beats on the bathroom door. 'Willow?' she calls, her irritation rising. 'It's nearly eight.'

Willow doesn't answer, even though Roz knows she can hear her. When Roz booked it at the beginning of August, she thought a holiday club would be something Willow would enjoy. Now she steels herself for the same argument, the same hot rush of frustration.

'Willow!' she shouts, hating the way she sounds. 'You're going to be late.'

The bathroom door opens, and Willow pushes past her, a grim look on her face. 'I don't want to go to stupid holiday club every single day. I don't know why I can't be at home during the holidays.'

'It's better for you there, it's supervised.' Roz glances into the chaos of the bathroom and picks up Willow's pyjamas from the floor. 'Besides,' – Roz reaches over and strokes Willow's hair – 'it's nice to spend the day having fun with kids your own age, isn't it?'

Willow shakes her hand off as if it is cursed. 'Melissa's allowed to have friends over. Her brother's at home to look after her, and he's sixteen.'

Roz imagines Melissa's house, a teenage boy in his room, plugged into a PlayStation: a gang of eleven-year-olds in the kitchen making lunch, the front door swinging wide open because they haven't latched it properly. 'No,' says Roz. 'We've already talked about this.'

'Dad wouldn't mind,' Willow says under her breath. She gulps down a glass of milk, picks up the toast that Roz has buttered and goes to find her bag.

Roz bites her tongue. 'Just get in the car, yeah?'

'Dad said I could live with him if I wanted to.'

The words sink into Roz like knives. 'You can't live with him. You live with me.' She is aware of treading a high wire between wanting to court Willow's favour and wanting to pick her up physically and bundle her into the car, strapping her down with a five-point safety harness like she used to do when she was a toddler.

'Yeah, but it doesn't have to be a . . .' Here, Willow pauses, trying to parrot her father's words. '. . . *permanent arrangement*. I can live with him in the holidays when there's no school.'

Roz wonders if any of this will ever get easier, if the feeling of exhaustion will ever pass. 'Get into the car, Willow. Please. For me. Just do this thing for me.'

Willow sits on the bottom stair and slowly puts her shoes on, struggling with the laces. Roz kneels down to help her daughter. As she makes a bow and ties it tight, Roz has a vivid memory of doing this for Hazel when she was four years old. She can feel Hazel's chubby fingers patting her gently on the head, her warm, sweet breath as she whispered damply in her ear: *Fank you, Woz*.

A hot, fat tear slides down Roz's cheek. 'Get in the car,' she says quietly, wiping it away.

When she drops Willow off, Roz signs the register and before she puts the pen down Willow has found a friend and is disappearing with him into a large sports hall. 'Bye, Willow,' Roz calls, a note of desperation in her voice. She wills her daughter to turn around and give her one last acknowledgement. Willow turns slightly and waves her arm, absent-mindedly, their argument forgotten. She looks so much like Hazel. For a moment, Roz considers changing her mind and telling Willow she made a mistake, that they can spend the day together instead. But the further away her daughter gets, the more the knot in her stomach loosens, and she feels the familiar pull and push of wanting to keep Willow safe and wanting to give her freedom.

She would like to talk to someone about how she is feeling. Someone who understands what happened to her. But all the friends she made when Willow started school have drifted away into their own little cliques. She remembers these women rolling their eyes when she hung over Willow in the playground, choosing instead to huddle together on a bench in the park, happy to let their children get on with it, relieved to have some adult company for a change. But Roz could never tear herself away from Willow, and over the years she lost the chance to explain why. It is Nina or Catrin she would like to talk to, she realises. When they were little, having Nina and Catrin at her side felt like having a security blanket permanently wrapped around her; they were the only people who truly understood. But Roz isn't sure where Catrin is. They lost touch so long ago, it got so bitter. And Nina is a different person now.

They'd met on the very first day of school, the three of them in the playground, not knowing what to do. She had noticed Nina immediately. She'd been wearing the kind of shiny patent leather shoes that Roz wasn't allowed to have because they were too grown-up. Roz's jealousy must have overcome her anxiety, because when she had sidled up to get a closer look, she saw, to her astonishment, that the shoes also had a small heel.

'You can try them on if you want,' Nina had said, cementing their friendship, 'but only if you share those sweets with me.' In Roz's eyes, it was a fair swap. Much later, she learnt that Nina wasn't allowed to eat sweets, and that Roz could have worn those shoes all afternoon if she'd asked. Catrin, on the other hand, had turned up for school dressed in her brother's hand-me-downs. The first person to tease her about it, a boy built like a barrel, was the last. Catrin floored him before he had finished talking. Impressed, and a little afraid, Nina and Roz found themselves drawn to her. Before the week was out, their circle was complete.

When Roz gets back into the car, she catches her reflection in the rear-view mirror. Her shoulder-length hair, neither blonde nor brown, falls in a way that is neither curly nor straight. Her skin is washed out, as if the colour has been drained from it. She was a blonde baby with delicate freckles. When did they disappear? Roz looks away from the face that stares back at her. The more the years pass, the more she seems to lose definition. She rummages for her phone in her bag, thinking about the what-ifs. Would she be calling Hazel now, sharing her worries about Willow, comparing notes on motherhood? Would Hazel have understood? Or would they have drifted apart, as Roz had with her oldest friends? She doesn't think so. Hazel had stuck to her, limpet-like, since she could walk. To be loved like that, looked up to and venerated, the strength of Hazel's unquestioning loyalty was once both an honour and a burden. Now, it is guilt that weighs down Roz's life.

Roz presses the buttons to make the call. It is a yearly ritual, something she never talks about to other people. She's stopped trying to understand why her parents will not share their lives with anyone but each other, why the contact she has with them is brief and widely spaced. Birthdays, Christmas and Hazel's anniversary. These are the days when she calls her parents. Each one feels like she is running a marathon. She takes a deep breath, steels her resolve, and dials the number.

Her mother picks up.

'Hi, Mum,' says Roz.

'I've been up since five. I can never sleep. It's the same every year.'

'I know. I'm sorry.' Roz slumps in the car seat, suddenly without strength, and gives herself in to grief.

Her mother's voice trembles. 'I sit at the kitchen table, remembering that day, and I watch the clock. I'm just waiting for it to happen, all over again, that realisation she was gone when you came back without her. Everything about that morning . . . it just goes around in my head.'

'I'm sorry, Mum.' Roz's eyes itch with salt water. It is all she can say, and she says it every year.

'We trusted you with her. You should never have taken her up there,' her mother sobs.

'I didn't take her,' Roz says quietly.

'Maybe we should talk to the police again.'

Roz pictures the hallway in her parents' house. The box files and folders stacked up against the wall containing police reports, press reports, lists and timelines. The table in the sitting room covered in paperwork littered with sticky notes. A mug filled with highlighter pens and old plastic biros. The large legal dictionary that led them through a labyrinth of language.

'Please, Mum, that won't help. It won't bring her back.'

'That man, Catrin's father, always so confident nothing could go wrong, letting Catrin run around that island without a care in the world. No fences on the cliff path. Telling us nobody else could possibly land a boat there. He made us feel stupid – stupid for wanting to keep you both close on that holiday. And then people started saying he might have had something to do with it all—'

'People who weren't there and didn't know us, Mum. People who just wanted to stir up trouble.' Roz feels the beginning of a headache and she massages her temples with her free hand.

'They could do one of those pictures of what she might look like now,' continues her mother. 'She'll be thirty-one now. She might have children of her own. I might have passed her in the street.'

Roz tries to swallow the words down, but she can't. 'She's dead, Mum. That's what we were told. That's what we have to believe.'

'You don't know that,' her mother snaps. 'Nobody knows that. There's *no* evidence.'

'There's no evidence she was taken, either,' Roz says gently.

The conversation rumbles on. Always the same. Roz will never be able to provide the answers her mother is looking for. And nothing, *nothing* will bring Hazel back.

Chapter Two

Roz

The house bears the residue of their frantic departure. Roz bends down to pair up several shoes Willow discarded on the hall floor. She looks at her watch. It's not nine o'clock yet. She hesitates and feels a flush of shame. This is becoming a ritual, after she has packed Willow off to school, but she can't help it. Ever since it was announced that Nina Lewis was the new agony aunt on *Rise*, TV's newest breakfast show, Roz hasn't been able to look away. She goes into the sitting room, digs the remote control out from a pile of washing she's left on the sofa, and catches the last ten minutes of the show. Nina, who has adopted her mother's maiden name, is just finishing her slot. She's seated on a bright orange sofa, with two other presenters. All three of them have impossibly white teeth.

'We've got time for one last letter,' says Nina, in an English accent Roz doesn't recognise. 'This one is from Yvonne, in Ashbourne, Derbyshire.' She clears her throat and, with a perfectly manicured index finger, tucks her straightened hair behind her left ear. 'Dear Nina, I lost my husband last year and I can't seem to get over it. I've tried joining clubs, exercising, you name it. We had a good marriage, and I just can't move on.'

Nina looks directly at the camera, and her gaze envelops Roz with an intensity she remembers, making her feel like Nina is talking to her personally. Her eyes are a strange grey. Catrin once said they were the colour of sea glass, and they haven't lost that ethereal, magical quality.

'Well, I'm going to go against the grain here and say I don't blame you for not moving on,' Nina says. 'Why should you? You've had a terrible, terrible shock and you need time to get over it. My advice is this: don't push yourself into anything you're not comfortable doing. Look after yourself and – it's very important, this – let *others* look after *you*.' Nina cocks her head on one side for a moment, as if she has just had a bright idea. 'If it's companionship you miss, have you thought about getting a dog? Or borrowing a neighbour's?' The camera pans away and a discussion begins in the studio, in which Nina and her colleagues chat on the sofa about the pros and cons of dog ownership for the bereaved.

Roz drinks Nina in. Every time she watches her, she still cannot equate her with the girl she grew up with. All her curls are gone. They have been erased by some kind of chemical process. Her fingernails are long and painted, when Roz knows Nina used to bite them. She wonders if she has had cosmetic surgery. Her lips look bigger. It gives her a strange feeling, watching someone she knew so intimately through the gloss of television.

Hazel's disappearance flung them all in different directions. If her mum and dad hadn't tried to involve a lawyer, would they still be friends? Would Nina have moved away to London and ended up as this version of herself? Would Roz be spending this day supported by her two oldest friends instead of seeking comfort through a screen?

She turns to the pile of laundry and attempts to fold it, to bring some kind of order to her thoughts. She made a terrible mistake that day with Hazel, not looking after her properly, and the mark of that mistake has bled into every area of her life. She can't afford to fail with Willow. It is better that she is looked after by others. She is safer at holiday club, where the teachers are trained and properly qualified. When Willow grows up, she will understand, and she will, Roz hopes, forgive her.

Sadness and shame make a terrible potion. It binds a person to silence. Roz hasn't told Willow about Hazel. She still can't bring herself to talk about what happened.

The resemblance between Willow and Hazel is not just in her own head. Roz's parents find it hard to look at their granddaughter, another reason they rarely meet. It is a hurdle, a feeling between pleasure and pain, that Roz has to navigate every day. Sometimes, she wills Hazel to show herself in Willow's face, or a gesture she makes. But other times, when Hazel appears in her daughter without warning, it is like being punched.

Roz sighs, the washing forgotten, staring through the screen and into the past. Her memories of that holiday are muddled and incomplete, they reveal themselves in abstract snatches, like the open doors of a surreal advent calendar. She sees the black of the water, the hard brutal cold of it. The rocks, splintered and sharp, rising like teeth. She sees a tall stone cairn, casting a long, cold shadow. The feeling she is being watched. But most of all, when she allows herself, she remembers those strange symbols, scratched into the doorways in The Old House: repeated circular marks, like the hooves of an animal stamping the ground, and inside some of them patterns like flower petals, pointed and sharp, scored with such force that Roz wondered what had compelled those long-ago people to make them. Even now, she can picture the indents of the symbols, etched into the stonework, the feel of them under her fingertips.

Witches' marks, Catrin had called them, carved by ancestors to protect the inhabitants of the house. Catrin had spent every summer on that tiny island, and those marks meant nothing to her. Generations of her family had lived and died in that house. It was part of her DNA. But on that first and only visit, Roz had noticed those symbols, the hoof marks, and the petals, on every entrance to every room.

They were supposed to protect, Catrin said. What she didn't say was from what.

Roz pulls herself back into the present, switches off the television and gathers her work bag, laying everything out on the kitchen table. The sketchbook is empty, her pencils still sharp. It is only her notebook that shows signs of industry, a scribble of words to get to grips with a brief she was given a week ago. It's a good job, the kind of children's book most illustrators would kill for. But Roz has always found it painful to draw children. In fact, she has actively avoided it, until her separation from Simon at the beginning of the year. Now she can't afford to be so picky.

As if her thoughts have conjured him up, her phone lights up with Simon's name.

'The school just called me. Willow wanted to talk.'

Roz's heartbeat quickens. 'Is she OK?'

'Yes, she's fine. She asked me if she could skip the last week or so and come here.'

Her relief dissolves into irritation. 'But you're at work all day. There would be nobody to look after her.'

'She's miserable there, Roz. She needs a break from school.'

Roz feels the insinuation, embedding itself into his words. 'It's not school. She plays sport and gets some fresh air with kids her own age. It's better than being here, with me. Anyway, I'm working flat out on a project right now.' She glances at the blank sketchbook on the table in the kitchen, glad they are not having this conversation face to face.

'Well, what about this friend of hers who has an older brother to look after her? Couldn't she go there?' Simon uses his patient voice, a tone he sometimes uses on Willow. It is a voice she hears more and more these days.

'Are you telling me you'd be happy to send her off to a family you don't know, to be looked after by a sixteen-year-old boy?'

'Well, I guess not, if you put it like that. Willow gave me the impression you knew them.'

'No, I don't know them that well. Why can't you take some time off work? You could look after her.'

'It's a busy time at work . . .'

Roz hears a well-worn list of reasons why Simon can't take responsibility for Willow. She feels the old resentment well up, lets her mind drift off, waiting for Simon to realise he won't win this argument unless he's willing to supervise her himself.

'The arrangement that we have can't last forever,' he concludes.

'What arrangement?' she says, landing back into the present.

'The house, Roz,' Simon says with a note of exasperation. 'When Willow starts her new school next month, you need to sell it, like we agreed. I don't want to be in this flat any longer than I have to. I need the cash from the sale.'

Roz bites her lip, can't think of what to say.

'You *have* been looking for somewhere else to live, haven't you?' She hears the suspicion in his voice.

'Yes, of course,' she lies. 'It's just a bit difficult right now. The estate agent said the market is slow.'

'Roz, if you don't start seriously looking, I can't keep up the payments on the mortgage. I'm haemorrhaging money here, paying for two places.'

'It's just taking a bit of time to get more work in. It's been a bit . . . difficult,' she admits.

'Then get a regular job, if freelancing isn't working. I can't support you forever, and when we divorce I won't be supporting you at all. Just Willow.'

Roz looks around the house she has occupied for most of her adult life. She knows Simon has been generous, letting her stay here while he moved out. The agreement was to stay until Willow is in her new school, then Roz can move out of the catchment area, somewhere cheaper. It all makes sense, she knows it does. But she can't bring herself to look for anywhere else. This is the house her baby has grown up in. It has kept Willow safe for eleven years. Apart from her and Simon agreeing their marriage had run its course, nothing bad has happened here. Roz can't imagine living somewhere new. The spell that has kept her child free from harm might be broken. But she can't afford to buy Simon out. She can barely afford the heating bill.

'Call the estate agent today, Roz. Before you have to go and pick up Willow. Get yourself registered with as many as you can. It doesn't take long.'

Roz feels herself drowning under a sea of things she doesn't want to do. 'I can't. Not today,' she says weakly. Her voice hitches and gives her away.

There is a pause, and then a small groan as Simon realises what day it is. 'Shit. Sorry. I just realised. I forgot the date. I'm sorry, Roz.'

She doesn't tell him it's OK. She is too tired to tell him that.

'Have you mentioned it to Willow?' Simon asks, his voice contrite.

'No.'

'Maybe it's time, Roz. She's old enough to understand.'

'She's got enough to deal with. She's only just getting used to the idea of us living apart.'

'She's fine. You have to start treating her like a young adult.'

'She's eleven!'

'She's pulling away from you because you don't trust her. And you're keeping this huge thing that happened to you from her. It's not good for you. Either of you.'

Roz is silent.

Simon makes a small noise of frustration. 'How can you expect to get over Hazel if you won't talk about her?'

And there it is – the reason she will not talk about Hazel to people who don't understand. How can she explain to Simon, to Willow – to anyone, really – that she doesn't want to *get over* Hazel? She wants Hazel here, by her side, like she used to be.

Chapter Three

NINA

Nina is called into the director's office before she can escape. The early starts have been murderous, and she is longing to get home, wash her make-up off and go back to bed for a couple of hours. She walks off the set, picking her way over camera and monitor cables in her high-heeled shoes, desperate to take them off, desperate to slip into something she can sit down in without sacrificing her blood supply.

'You've settled in well, Nina,' says Curtis, the director, seated behind his desk, leaning back on an expensive leather chair that tilts to accommodate a body that has spent hours being perfected in a gym. *It's probably got the word executive in it*, she thinks to herself drily. *Executive. Office. Chair.*

'It feels like a good fit,' she says, recycling words she has heard other younger people say.

'Viewers love you . . . mostly. But they're hungry for detail.'

Nina absorbs the criticism and puts on her brightest smile. 'OK,' she says, waiting for him to get to the point. It's a thing she's noticed about people who work here. If it takes five minutes to say something that only takes one, they'll do it. Just to hear the sound of their own voice. Nina says nothing, allowing his words to circle until, eventually, his point lands.

Curtis puts his hands behind his head in a way, she is sure, is calculated to show off his pectoral muscles under that thin T-shirt. 'I'm always looking for ways to increase ratings, increase the visibility of the show. I'm wondering if we should make you a bit more . . .' He moves his hands back in front of his face and waggles them in an indistinct, confusing way.

'A bit more what?' Nina frowns and then immediately corrects herself. She has noticed lines on her forehead recently. She wonders if she needs to book another trip to the clinic.

'We'd like to see a little more of you. We want to bring an element of confession into the show.'

'Confession?' Nina says, an uneasy note in her voice.

'You know, it would be nice to hear you talk about your own personal experiences.'

'Are you talking about my divorce?' she asks, narrowing her eyes.

'Yes,' he nods, and shrugs. 'Howard is a celebrity. Divorce is a topic that's delivered regularly to your inbox. People like to hear you've been through the same thing as them. And if your ex happens to be more famous than you are . . . it's a bonus, really.'

Nina ignores the comparison. 'That feels cheap and tawdry, Curtis. I thought this was supposed to be a classy show.'

'It is. Look at you. Look at Howard. You're both very sophisticated people. Which makes the fact you got divorced very compelling. It makes you intriguing, Nina.' He cocks his head to one side, as if he is noticing something about her for the first time.

'I don't care. I'm not going to talk about my very public divorce on this show. If the viewers want to find out about it, all they have to do is look it up on the internet. Anyway, we both signed a non-disclosure, so even if I wanted to, I can't talk about him.'

'Well, OK,' he says, nodding. 'But isn't that your job? To talk about things?' He cocks his head to the other side, and it infuriates her.

'Other people's lives, yes. Not my own. What is this, Curtis?'

Curtis shrugs again. 'It's what our viewers want. You're more relatable if you talk about your own problems too.'

'And what if I don't want to talk about my own problems?'

'We have you on a six-month trial period, yeah?'

Nina laughs, incredulous. 'Are you serious? I'm only just getting off the ground here.'

He sighs. 'I like you very much, Nina, but you can sometimes come across as a little aloof. We want people to relate to you. Feel like they know you. We need them to be confident about exposing their problems on live television. It's a very delicate business. You are in a position of great trust.'

'I know all of this.' In her mind's eye, Nina sees herself taking off a spiky-heeled shoe and flinging it at this man's head.

'What I mean to say is, you're quite a formidable person, Nina. Our audience needs to feel that you're one of them.'

'You just told me they love me.'

'And then I said *mostly*. Nina . . . we just want to keep it real.'

She thinks about the make-up that is caked on every morning over her face, the straightener that is applied to her hair. The underwear that flattens her stomach. The shoes she is itching to take off. She tries to maintain a neutral face. 'I'll have a think about it,' she says.

'Think about what you want,' he says. 'And then think about what I need.'

When Nina returns home it is lunchtime, and her decree absolute is waiting for her on the doormat. She opens the drawer in the study and puts it there, trying hard not to feel like a failure. Years of practice have taught her not to give in to weakness, but when she goes into the kitchen to look for something to cheer her up, she feels more like a glass of wine than the crab salad waiting for her in the fridge. She reasons with herself as she reaches for a long-stemmed glass. She's been up since 3 a.m. Her body thinks the sun is over the yard arm.

She opens the wine fridge and selects a bottle of white. She reads the label and pours herself a small measure, swirling it around the bowl of the glass. The legs slowly arch and fall back into the honeyed liquid. She dips her nose into the mouth of the glass and inhales, noticing the character profile, separating out the different aromas. As she finally allows herself a sip, she lets the flavour fill her mouth, and her eyes travel across the expansive walls of her kitchen, the huge picture windows that showcase the garden, the collection of Giacometti drawings that litter the walls. Before she met Howard, she knew nothing about wine or art. If she is going to take a positive from their divorce, it is an impressive collection of modern masters and a sophisticated understanding of fine wine.

Her cat, who has tired of waiting to be served his lunch, now jumps on to the kitchen countertop to purr loudly in her ear. He winds his fluffy white body around her arms, his tail tickling her cheek. As she reaches into the fridge for his food, she hears the theme tune from *The Twilight Zone* coming from her bag and knows before she pulls the phone out that it is her mother.

'Mum.'

'Nina, darling.' Her voice has a low, growling quality and Nina is reminded of the cat, who is outraged she has deviated her attention from him. 'I'm just wondering about that shirt. It's lovely, I'm not saying it's not, I just thought it made you look a little . . .'

Nina looks down at her shirt.

21

'The colour's *great*. Though I always thought yellow was rather . . . You looked a little pale, I thought. That's all.'

Nina liked the shirt when she put it on this morning, she felt good in it. Now she's not so sure. She looks at herself in the mirror on her kitchen wall. Does she look pale?

'Why don't I take you shopping?' her mother asks. 'We can make a day of it. You look fabulous in red. We could pick out a nice . . .'

'I can't wear red, Mum, it clashes with the sofa, on the set. And before you ask, no, they won't change the sofa.'

Her mother makes a noise of disapproval. 'I'm sure we can find something else. There's a little boutique I haven't shown you yet. They have the most divine dresses.'

'I have to wear high-street stuff, Mum, so the viewers can get the same look.'

'Whatever happened to aspiration?'

The cat raises his voice and fixes Nina with an animal stare.

'Listen, Mum, I have to go, I . . .' She tucks the phone between her ear and shoulder, forks the cat food into a dish.

'Do something about that shirt. We need you in blue if you can't wear red. Something that enhances your beautiful eyes.'

'I have something blue,' says Nina, feeling relieved.

'The silk, with the pussycat bow . . .'

'Yes, that one.'

'Wear it tomorrow. Promise?'

'I promise.'

'I'll be watching, Nina. You know how proud I am of you.'

Nina ends the call, feeling a familiar cocktail of love and frustration. She owes her acting career and everything that followed to her mother. There was a time, after Hazel, after her father died, when everything was so awful there didn't seem to be a way out. When Roz's parents had turned on Catrin's family and Hazel's disappearance hung over everyone like a spectre, Nina's mother, newly single and bitter, decided a new start was in order and moved them both to London. Nina hadn't taken much persuading. Her friendship with Roz and Catrin was in tatters, she knew it wouldn't recover. She didn't take much persuading when her mother enrolled her in acting classes, either. The humming anxiety Nina felt in the aftermath of Hazel's death vanished when she pretended to be someone she wasn't. To her credit, her mother turned a terrible situation into something good.

Yes. Nina owes her mother everything. But lately, she can't help feeling exhausted by it all. She contemplates her reflection in the kitchen mirror. There are mirrors all over the house, she is never far from herself. There are lines of age waiting in the corners of her eyes. She does look tired, a little drawn. There will come a time when the silky blue shirt with the pussycat bow won't be enough. And then what will happen? She looks away, unable to hold her own gaze, only to catch herself in another, larger mirror on the opposite wall. Perhaps it is the 3 a.m. wake-up calls. Perhaps she needs more attention at the clinic. But really, deep down, she knows the early starts have nothing to do with this feeling that has begun to follow her around like a hungry dog. The feeling she is playing with people. That she is a fraud.

Every day, into a dedicated email account, a river of misery pours from broken hearts and lonely souls. Every afternoon, an assistant goes through that account and forwards on the most suitable problems for next morning's show. Nina knows she can't help those people any more than they can help themselves. She is no more genuine than the silk eyelashes she is itching to peel off her Botoxed face. What has surprised her, though, is how good she is at it. She was a mediocre actress, she can admit to that. But when she masquerades as someone who cares and understands the problems of others, she knows she is a convincing liar.

She wishes she could tell someone how she is feeling. She thinks about Catrin and Roz, often, but doesn't dare seek them out. They are intertwined with that time in her life when things were uncomplicated and fun. Her parents were still together. She was the apple of her father's eye. And her two best friends understood her and accepted her in a way nobody has since.

True, she hadn't taken to Catrin at first. She'd seemed rough and unpredictable, but from day one she'd not only showed up the meanest boy in school, she'd made Nina laugh so hard her face ached. Catrin could do repulsive things like turn her eyelids inside out, or burp the national anthem. Things Nina knew were wrong, ugly and bad, but every time Catrin did them Nina squealed until she thought she might wet herself. She had never met a girl like Catrin before, a girl that behaved like a boy and got away with it. The playdates her mother arranged were with girls just like her: neat and biddable children in the right sort of clothes. From that first day of meeting Roz and Catrin, Nina had been prepared to defend their friendship from her mother's disapproval, but when she'd mentioned Catrin's name, Nina's mother leapt upon it like a cat upon a mouse.

Roz and Nina had assumed Catrin was just like them, but Nina's mother knew all about Chapel Farm and the Morgan family. The bottles of apple juice sold in the local delicatessen had their name stamped on the fancy labels. There was butter and cream, too. The fields and woodland that bordered the village belonged to the Chapel Farm estate, which was hidden behind tall iron gates and a high wall that seemed to go on forever.

It took a long time for Nina and Roz to be invited to Chapel Farm. When they turned ten and were deemed old enough to walk the short distance back from school on their own, they had always gone to Nina's house, to leaf through her mother's *Vogue* magazines. But one afternoon, for reasons Nina cannot remember now, their routine changed. They left the school gates and walked along a quiet country lane in single file. When the pavement ran out, Nina couldn't understand. 'Where are you taking us? There aren't any houses here. It's just fields.'

'There are houses. Well, a house,' sighed Catrin, as she stopped at a pair of huge iron gates. She fiddled with a key, and it opened a smaller, person-sized hole cut into the left-hand gate.

'Oh my God, Catrin, you live here? In this massive house? Why didn't you say anything before?' Nina screamed, taking in the sweeping drive and the enormous building at the end of it.

'It's our family business.'

'Are you rich?' Nina pressed.

'I'm not sure,' said Catrin, looking down at her clothes, which were too small for her, at the school shoes she had inherited from her brother. 'My brother says we're asset rich and cash poor, whatever that means.'

In the space of two years, between the ages of eleven and thirteen, Nina and Roz became intimately acquainted with Chapel Farm – the way the house never reached a high enough temperature to feel warm, that the furniture and carpets were heirlooms and antiques. Nothing was new, but everything had a story behind it. Catrin's mother had died when Catrin was a baby, and her father seemed gruff and unwelcoming at first, but as Nina grew older she realised that he was, in fact, just busy. But none of that had mattered to Nina and Roz back then, because it was the kind of place where you could escape, undisturbed, for hours.

They'd turned the attic space into their den. Once, Nina found some silk scarves in an old crate and had pretended to conduct a seance, calling on dead celebrities, creating a makeshift Ouija board from an old Scrabble game. In the candlelight, with scarves tied around their heads, the *tick tick tick* of the rain falling on the roof slates, the smell of joss sticks heavy in the air, they'd told each other the sort of things you only confess to your very best friends.

Nina thinks back to that girls-in-the-attic space, and knows without a doubt she was the most vibrant, the most passionate, the most honest version of herself then. Since that holiday at the age of thirteen, when Hazel left her bed and never came back, all Nina has been doing is pretending.

Chapter Four

Roz

Roz is staring into the fridge for inspiration when her phone rings. She isn't a confident cook, which makes it doubly hard to feed Willow, who is going through a picky phase. She closes the fridge door, glad to be able to put off a decision about dinner for another few minutes, and walks over to where her phone is charging, just catching the call before it is dropped.

'Hi,' says a friendly voice. 'Is that Rosalind? Rosalind Richardson?'

Roz frowns. Not many people know her maiden name and her separation isn't common knowledge.

'Yes?' she enquires, circumspect.

'My name is Stella Cox. I'm a journalist.'

'A . . . what?' Roz wonders if she is the subject of a prank call, or something Willow has set up.

'An investigative reporter. I make a podcast called *The Forgotten*, perhaps you've heard of it?'

'I'm sorry, I think you've got the wrong number.'

'Your parents gave me this number. Tony and Eileen? I spoke to them just now.'

Roz's head begins to swim. 'I don't understand,' she says.

'Your sister, Hazel. I've been doing some research . . .'

Her name, the shock of a stranger saying it, stings Roz like a wasp. She can feel her face heat up. 'What?' She turns around in her kitchen, feeling winded, half expecting someone to be there, watching her, recording the conversation.

'I'm sorry,' says Stella. 'I know this is a difficult subject for you. For all of you. I'd like to make a programme about Hazel to honour her memory.'

Roz gathers herself. It is a physical effort. 'I don't know what kind of sick joke this is, but it's not funny. If you ring this number again, I'll call the police.'

'Please, Rosalind. I don't mean to upset you, that's the last thing I want to do, but your parents thought I should talk to you.'

'Talk to me about what?'

'I have some information about Hazel's disappearance I'd like to share with you. Some new evidence.'

Now the anger comes. The hot, sweet feeling of it rolling over her, giving her strength. 'Hazel is dead,' Roz declares in a clear voice. 'She's been dead for twenty years.'

'Nobody knows that for sure, though, do they?' Stella says gently.

'My parents are vulnerable people. How dare you contact them and bring all of this up again?'

'They seem very keen to explore all the possibilities of what happened that day. And the twenty-year anniversary . . . it's today, isn't it? It must be very difficult—'

'Hazel was swept out to sea. That's what we were told.'

'Your parents don't believe that, though.'

'My parents are desperate to hang on to any information that helps them believe she's alive. You're exploiting them by doing that, because Hazel is not alive, she's dead.'

'I hope you don't think I'm overstepping the mark by asking you why you seem so sure about that?'

Roz takes a deep breath. 'They scoured that island. For days. There was no sign of her. The only way off the island was by boat. The boat was still there. Everybody who was staying in The Old House was still there. Hazel couldn't have – wouldn't have – left the island alone.'

'What about somebody sailing over that morning, someone that wasn't part of your holiday group?'

'The only two people that could make that journey were Adam and his father, Arvis, who ran the boatyard in Eider. The police interviewed them. They were on the mainland when Hazel disappeared. There were witnesses.'

'There was some talk about Catrin's father being involved.'

'That was a vicious rumour, started by the press.'

'That your parents didn't refute, I think?'

Roz feels sick, thinking about that time. 'My parents were out of their minds with grief.'

'Somebody else, perhaps?'

Roz wants to scream but controls her voice. 'Little Auger is surrounded by a rock formation that makes it almost impossible to steer a boat through. Nobody else could land a boat there.'

'Well, I managed it,' says the voice down the phone.

'Wh . . . what?' says Roz weakly. She slaps her hand down on the surface of the kitchen countertop in an effort to ground herself.

'I'll admit it's not easy, but it's doable. I've been visiting the island for several weeks.'

'They've let you do that. The owners?' Roz feels the floor shift beneath her.

'Well . . .'

'So you've been trespassing.' Suddenly, Roz finds firmer ground.

'Yes, I suppose I have.'

'Do you know how many cranks we've had to deal with over the years? How many false narratives and spiteful busybodies?'

'I can imagine, and I am not one of those. I simply want—'

'What about what I want?' Roz has to stop herself shouting down the phone.

'What do you want, Rosalind?' Stella replies kindly.

There is a silence that expands in the evening air, while Roz gropes for an answer. 'I want people like you to leave me alone,' she says slowly, in a fearful whisper. 'To leave Hazel alone. I lost a sister, and my parents lost a child. Why won't you let us grieve in peace?'

Roz ends the call, her hands shaking. She walks to the sink, fills up a glass with water from the tap and drinks it in one go, forcing the lump in her throat down, down, into her stomach. She wipes her mouth with the back of her hand, keeping it there for a second in case the sob she can feel in her ribcage escapes into the air.

'Mum?'

Roz spins around, sees Willow at the foot of the stairs. And for a moment, it is Hazel standing there, dressed in a hoodie and shorts, her fingers untangling the split ends in her hair. An image flashes into Roz's mind. Their last summer together. Sitting on the steps that led into the back garden. Roz above, Hazel below her, using Roz's knees like an armchair.

Roz took a length of Hazel's long hair. It felt warm and slippery in the sunshine. She noticed that the strands were all different colours. Not a mousy brown, like hers, but shades of chestnut and ochre that became golden towards the tips of her curls.

Look at all these split ends, she'd said as she ran her fingers through like a makeshift comb. *Shall I trim them? It'll only take a minute.*

No, said Hazel, gathering her hair and pulling it around her shoulder, out of Roz's reach. *Don't hurt my hair.*

Roz laughed. *It won't hurt. Hair is dead. It doesn't have feelings. Mine does*, said Hazel quietly. *It likes being long.*

The memory hurts Roz as it sears through her consciousness, the fact she will never be able to touch Hazel again, run her fingers through her hair and feel her warm skin next to hers.

'Who was that on the phone?' Willow asks, frowning.

'One of those horrible cold callers, trying to sell me something,' Roz says, trying to make her voice light.

'It sounded like you knew them.'

'I didn't know them. Her,' Roz says, her voice becoming stronger with the truth.

'Who was it?' Willow persists.

'Nobody.'

'You were arguing with her.'

'I wasn't arguing.'

Willow throws her arms in the air. 'You never tell me what's going on! You're always hiding something.'

Roz can feel herself growing hot with the onset of tears. She rushes forward and embraces her daughter, who stands in her arms, rigid and unyielding. 'I'm sorry,' Roz says. 'I'm just trying my best.' She pulls away, trying to give Willow her most reassuring smile.

But Willow has a defiant look on her face that Roz doesn't like. 'Mum . . .' she says in a quiet voice, 'who's Hazel?'

Roz thinks quickly, her stomach plummeting. 'The name of the woman on the phone.'

When Willow meets her eyes, she can see she has failed a test. 'You said you wanted the woman on the phone to leave Hazel alone.'

'I didn't say that.' Roz shakes her head slowly, aware she is entering dangerous territory.

31

Willow doesn't look away. 'And then something about a sister,' she presses. 'You don't have a sister.'

'No, I don't,' says Roz, and the pain of the lie slices her in two.

It is only later, when they have both eaten a lacklustre meal in near silence, that Roz realises she never asked that woman, Stella, what new evidence she had found. She contemplates calling her parents again, but she cannot make herself do it. She is not feeling strong enough to absorb the blame, always simmering under the surface of every conversation. Not twice in one day.

She wishes she could remember everything that happened the morning Hazel disappeared. When she was a student, she began to see clairvoyants – women in darkened rooms, giving her messages from Hazel. But none of them could say what had really happened to her. Roz has tried Reiki, meditation, hypnosis. The relief is temporary, but she still can't recall that day in any meaningful detail. It is a blur of sound and shape, a circular narrative with no end and no beginning.

When Willow has gone up to her room, their truce delicate and uneasy, Roz pulls out her phone and searches Stella Cox's name. She has won awards for her work. Roz hates the name of her podcast, *The Forgotten.* Nobody forgets about their loved ones. She clicks back and looks at the last call. Stella Cox's number has been logged on her phone, and almost without thought she presses it, gently. The screen changes immediately, and the distant sound of ringing comes from the speaker. As if someone else is guiding her hands, she pulls the phone up to her ear and waits.

'Stella Cox.' She doesn't answer the phone like other women do, as if they are asking a question. Stella declares her name, her voice steady and reassuring.

'It's Roz,' she responds. 'You called me earlier.' Her own voice sounds small in comparison.

'I'm so glad you called me back, Roz. Can I call you that? Roz?'

'I haven't changed my mind. I just want to know what it was you found.'

There is a small beat. 'I'm sorry, Roz. I can't tell you that.'

'W . . . why?'

'Look. I'm going to be very honest with you, because I think it's the best way for you to understand my position.'

'What position?'

'I found something that, really, I think I should probably give to the police. And I will do that, of course I will, eventually. But right now I have a very small window of opportunity where I can record some interviews, before the authorities get involved and finding out the truth becomes much more difficult. Do you understand what I'm saying?'

'No. No I don't.'

'Basically, I really think Hazel's story would make a wonderful podcast. Your parents are hopeful it will bring her case into the public consciousness once more. In order to make the podcast the absolute best it can be, I need to get the people who were there with her that day on the recording. Your mum and dad have both agreed, but I'll be honest with you, Roz, it's really you, Nina and Catrin I want to talk to. You were there together that morning, and from what I understand from your parents, you were inseparable. I need your involvement to make the story really compelling.'

'But I already told you. I don't want to get involved.'

'That's understandable.' Stella's voice shifts from businesslike to caring. 'I know how hard this must be.'

'So tell me what you found.'

'Of course I'll do that. But first I need to record the interviews. I've scheduled something for August bank holiday Monday, if that suits? It's Tuesday today, so just less than a week.'

'As soon as you tell my parents, I'll find out anyway what this evidence is, so you may as well tell me now.'

'It's not your parents I'm going to interview. It's Catrin.'

Roz feels wrong-footed. 'Catrin? You've been in touch with Catrin?'

'Yes.'

'And she's agreed to take part? Why?'

'Because she wants to know what happened. She wants the truth.'

Roz doesn't know what to say. After twenty years of thinking about Catrin, wondering what she's been doing, how she's been getting on, this woman has just effortlessly summoned her into the present.

'Roz,' says Stella gently, as if she is talking to a child, 'don't you want to know what happened to Hazel?'

'Hazel died,' Roz tells her, but it sounds pathetic, like something she's been told to say.

'Why do you think she died, Roz? Why don't you think she's out there, somewhere?'

'Because . . .' How can she put it into words? Because believing your sister is dead is so much easier than believing she is still alive.

Chapter Five

NINA

It is a warm evening. The low hum of the air conditioning breaks into Nina's consciousness as she stares out of her window on to the garden she rarely uses. She has often joked with the man who comes to look after it that he spends more time there than she does. Being indoors is a preference she and her mother share. There is something about being in nature that Nina doesn't like. She has come to understand this about herself. It was an education that began on Little Auger.

She had a vague idea of what an island holiday might be like – she had been abroad with her parents once or twice, and her memories consisted of sandy beaches and endless sunshine. The forecast was warm, according to her father, and Catrin had spoken of picnics and walks. Nina took this to mean it would be brilliantly sunny, all the time. What she didn't understand was that the Welsh coast is always colder, a Welsh island colder still.

When they arrived at the boatyard, after nearly three hours in the car, Nina was surprised that the weather was overcast, and the island itself half hidden behind a veil of mist. It looked more like something out of *Jurassic Park* than *Swept Away*. The only bright spark was a boy in the boatyard who piqued her interest. He was a little older than she was, maybe sixteen. He worked alongside his father; both of them moved with purpose, their bodies tanned and lean. The father was called Arvis, a strange name she had never heard before, with an accent she couldn't place. The boy was called Adam, and she couldn't take her eyes off him. He was the one who readied the boat that would take them over the water, hauling their bags with ease and efficiency. She willed him to notice her, but gradually he gave himself away when she caught him stealing glances at an oblivious Roz.

Catrin had leapt on board without any assistance, helping her father stack the bags. When Adam reached out to help Nina into the boat, telling her where to sit to balance out the weight, she thought she'd felt a swoop of desire and wondered if he felt the same. The journey was less than half an hour, but once they cast off Nina found that the motion of the boat made her nauseous. She looked down into the sea as they cut through the waves, terrified of throwing up, hoping Adam didn't notice how green her face must be. She'd imagined the water would be a beautiful azure blue, or an emerald green, but all she saw was black. Leaning over the side, she wetted her fingers and pulled her hand back in shock. It was freezing. When she looked more carefully, her vision moved beyond the skin of the surface to what lay below. Rising up towards her from the floor of the sea was the top of a mountain range, it seemed, and for a moment she felt the sweep of vertigo as she looked down into an unknown world. As they neared the island, the sea changed colour; it churned and frothed over the ragged edges of the rocks, making it milky and opaque.

'Keep your hands inside the boat,' Adam warned. To her dismay, he'd spoken without looking at her, concentrating instead on the rocks ahead of him, rocks that clawed their way above the water and into the sticky air. The words stung her, smarting her eyes more than the salty spray that the boat kicked up, adding to her misery.

Nina remembers looking over at Catrin, who was talking with her father about the strength of the current. Roz and Hazel were sitting close with their mum and dad, who were tightly holding on to their children. She was the only one who hadn't come with a parent. Her mum and dad were at home, arguing with one another. Nina had been made to pick sides fairly early on – she knew her father had committed an unforgivable transgression. She was made to feel the humiliation just as keenly as her mother did. Surely, a holiday here would be better than spending the summer in a house that was rapidly filling with a cold, impenetrable silence.

The rocks became taller, and they changed from claws to teeth. Some of them towered over the boat, and Nina felt they could be swallowed up without warning. There was something cruel about them that reminded her of creatures she had seen in the zoo, safely behind glass. She looked over to Catrin. Her face was alight with anticipation.

When they moored up in a small, secluded cove, Nina finally wobbled off the boat, grabbing Adam's outstretched hand, reluctant to let it go. The cove was filled with stones, slick with moisture. They made a dull clacking sound under Nina's feet and the noise reminded her of slow, sarcastic applause.

'Remind me to leave you a copy of the tide timetable,' she heard Adam telling Catrin's father. 'At the moment, high tide is late morning and late evening, so realistically you only have one chance a day to get on and off the island, if you don't want to sail in the dark.' He spoke to Catrin's father as if they were equals, as if he was a man, and Catrin's father treated him as such.

'What do you mean?' she asked Adam, breaking into their conversation. 'What do you mean that we can only get one chance a day?'

'You can only reach the island during high tide, otherwise the boat can't get over the rocks,' he explained. 'High tide occurs around every twelve hours. You can't just leave when you want to.'

Adam was the first boy she properly fell in love with. It was unrequited, something Nina has never had to experience again. But she remembers that feeling, of being destabilised, not just by Adam and the way she felt about him but by understanding she was trapped on that island, that there were things beyond her control. That feeling never left her, all the time she was there. She was at the mercy of nature. It granted you life, and it took it away.

Her phone rings, and her mind is still on Little Auger when she answers.

'I hope this is a good time to talk, I know you have a crazy sleep schedule right now. It's not too late, is it?'

'Who is this?' Nina looks at the phone screen, sees it is a number she does not recognise.

'Oh, sorry, it's Stella, Stella Cox. We met briefly through your agent, Verity Walsh? It was a couple of years ago, at a party.'

'Verity's birthday,' Nina remembers. 'You do that podcast, don't you?'

'Yes. *The Forgotten*. I've been on *Rise* actually, talking about it, but it was before you started working there. I'm a huge fan, by the way.'

Even though Nina knows she probably doesn't mean it, it's nice to hear. She tucks her hair behind her ear, straightens her back, and smiles to the empty room, wondering if she is about to be offered an opportunity.

'Well, I'm just going to get straight into it, because I know how unbelievably busy you are. I'm making a podcast about the disappearance of Hazel Richardson. It's the twenty-year anniversary of her disappearance, and a great time to bring her back into the public consciousness, don't you think?'

Nina's mouth opens to reply before she can process what Stella just said. For a wild moment, she wonders if she has conjured up this woman by thinking about Little Auger. The way she said Hazel's name . . . lightly, swiftly, as if it didn't carry that dreadful weight. Nina's mouth freezes, lips parted, her mind scrabbling for a reply.

'Sorry,' says Stella into the silence. 'It must be a bit of a shock, to talk about her. I know how these things can catch us out. It's been a long time.'

Caught out. Yes. She shakes her head, as if there is something lodged in there. 'Well,' she says. 'I wasn't expecting . . .'

'I didn't realise you were on Little Auger when she disappeared. It's not something that's ever come up in my research. It wasn't until I spoke to Rosalind Richardson and her parents that I—'

'Wait . . . what? You've spoken to the Richardsons? To Roz as well?'

'To all of them. They're keen to get involved.'

The floor begins to tilt, and Nina sits, heavily, on a stool at the breakfast bar in her kitchen. 'Involved in what, exactly?'

'I found something, Nina. I think it might be an important clue to Hazel's disappearance.'

'What did you find?' says Nina, trying to keep her voice steady.

'I can't talk about that now, but I'd like—'

'Hang on. Hang on. What is this? Seriously? You call to tell me you found something, but you can't talk about it? So why call in the first place?' Nina realises, too late, that she is being manipulated by this woman. She's probably recording their conversation.

'I just want to talk to you about that holiday you took together. No big deal. Catrin's on board as well. You're the last piece of the puzzle.'

'Catrin?' Nina echoes. Her name is like an incantation. Nina remembers her as a thirteen-year-old, a camera slung around her neck, her face freckled with sunshine. She knows what she looks like now, because she has googled her, of course she has. She has googled all of them.

Stella says, conspiratorially, 'I actually think this might be great for you. I can't believe you've managed to keep this connection to Hazel Richardson so quiet.'

A hot wash of anger rises up in Nina. 'Don't you dare. Don't you dare leak that out. It's private.'

'Nina, I have no intention of doing that. My work is based on trust. I couldn't do my job if people didn't trust me.'

Nina bites down hard on her cheek, drawing blood. She can taste it in her mouth. 'If you have the other two on board, you don't need me. I was asleep, anyway, that morning. The others went without me.' Even now, to say she was left behind, it makes her feel thirteen again, anxious about missing out.

'It's not just about that morning though, is it?'

'What do you mean?' says Nina, swallowing blood.

'It's about the relationship between the three of you after it happened, the way it affected you all. You moved to London because of it, didn't you?'

Nina is disoriented, she doesn't know what answer Stella is looking for. 'I . . . my mum moved here when she split with my dad.'

'Look, I'll be honest with you, Nina – this could work without you, but it won't be as good. It's going to come out anyway, that you were there, and you knew these girls, with or without your involvement. Or you could be part of the story. You could help shape it. I'm absolutely not pushing you to do this, not at all.'

But you are, though, aren't you? Nina thinks.

'Come back to the island with me,' urges Stella. 'Just for a day. That's all I need. A day of your time to walk me through what happened and how it's affected your life.'

The conversation Nina had this morning rises to the surface of Nina's mind. Curtis would love her to do this. He would love her connection to Hazel, and that dreadful time. He would love her regret, that she didn't get up and go with Roz and Catrin that morning, that it all might have turned out differently if they'd all stuck together. He would love to see her tears.

Chapter Six

Catrin

Catrin looks out of the tiny window on to a celestial expanse of cloud, the morning light so clear and bright it doesn't feel like the country she remembers. She holds her breath as the plane sinks into a fog of white, dimming the light in the cabin, and she ignores a pinch of regret that she forgot to reply to her brother's last text. She had meant to let him know she was coming today, but she's been operating on her own timetable for so long, she has lost her manners.

She points her camera through the window and takes a few shots. When she sees the familiar coastline, the white cliffs of Dover, she feels an urge to cry at the sight of it, even though this has not been home for nearly half of her life. The alcohol she has drunk now curdles in her stomach, making her maudlin. She pictures her father, thinks back to their last conversation at Chapel Farm, and she wonders if he will agree to take her in. Apologies were never her forte. It is action she admires. And if this trip goes the way she wants, she will force her father to understand.

The landing gear opens and the plane tips forward, slowing down to a speed she cannot begin to guess. She sees the Thames snaking its way ahead of her, the water brown and heavy with silt, carrying flat barges loaded with shipping containers, colour-coded like Lego blocks. And then touchdown. The jolt of it making her bones ache.

Hot air and diesel fumes still stinging in her nostrils, her head aching, she enters the arrivals area and looks for the trains. The time it will take her to travel west and then make her way to Chapel Farm will be as long as the journey she has just taken. The passage out of London passes in a blur of interrupted sleep and vivid dreams. She sleepwalks from one train to another, the route embedded deep within her subconscious. It is dark and raining when she disembarks. She climbs into a taxi, even though she doesn't have the money. When the buildings become sparse and the walls become hedgerows, she falls asleep once more, her head on her pack, her camera bag still slung around her neck.

She is woken by the taxi driver, idling outside the gate, the windscreen wipers playing a steady beat against the rain. The noise is soporific, and the interior is warm. There is a faint scent of pine. She wishes she could kick her boots off and curl up on the back seat, sleep here for the night instead.

'Are you sure this is the place?' the taxi driver asks, his voice full of doubt.

'Yes,' she mumbles. Her mouth is dry. She knows she must smell. 'There's an intercom on the wall. Press it and the gate should open.'

The path is inky black, and the ancient lime trees bordering it tower over the car as it passes below them, the headlights illuminating their branches from beneath. She sees it through the eyes of the driver, the long sweep of driveway, the house at the end, the fields beyond. It looks impressive in the dark.

Her father is waiting with her brother, James; she sees his face through the misted glass. It's been a few years since they spoke. The time gap makes any small talk shrivel up in her mouth. She gropes for the button that winds down the window.

'Catrin,' he says, his voice full of astonishment.

'Hi, Dad,' she replies, deciding on breezy familiarity, as if nothing bad has happened between them. 'Can you pay the driver for me? I don't have any money left.'

He turns away and walks around the fountain, back into the house, his gait a little slower than she remembers. He must hate that, not being able to stride around the estate. She notices a stick in his right hand, and it suits him, she thinks. She imagines him swinging it around, barking orders, banging it for emphasis.

Her brother takes her rucksack. 'I can't believe you came back,' he says, giving her a hug. 'It takes a complete stranger to bring you home.'

'This is your home, not mine,' replies Catrin, hugging him back, the camera bag caught between them.

'It will always be your home,' James says kindly, taking in her dirty face, her unwashed hair. 'But doing this podcast isn't going to help matters. Dad is dead against it. He thinks it'll affect the business again.'

'Finding out what happened to Hazel is more important than his precious reputation.'

'Just go easy on him, OK?' James asks.

'Like he has with me?' Catrin asks, shaking her head, feeling her breeziness disappear. 'What about you?' she says. 'Are you fretting about Chapel Farm's reputation too?'

'Let's not have an argument before you've stepped into the house,' replies James, grinning at her.

For a moment, she wonders if this is their mother in him, speaking to her, and it melts Catrin. James's kindness and easy-going nature were all her mother's traits. He even looks like her photographs, now he is the same age as she was when she passed away. 'I missed you,' Catrin says, reaching for him, catching him in another hug.

'Mmm,' he replies, hugging her back. 'When was the last time you had a shower? I put the water on, just in case.'

The shower is a luxury compared to what she has been used to and she allows herself a moment of appreciation for hot water and an endless supply of soap. When she eventually emerges, a towel wrapped around her damp hair, it is late, and her father needs to sleep, but Catrin has woken up.

'Nightcap?' she asks James, looking hopeful.

James groans. 'I have to be up at six.' He sees Catrin's face, her bottom lip jutting out. 'A quick one, then,' he says, ushering her into the sitting room. She looks around the room, at its dark wooden furniture and oak panelling. The old leather sofa is gritty from dust brought in by the dogs. The Welsh blankets thrown over the arms, hand-woven by great aunts and grandmothers, are covered in their hair, and the hair of every dog that came before them. The whole room smells of Labrador, and it brings Catrin a deep and simple comfort, to sit between them, accepting their heads on to her lap as if she has known them forever. Catrin's father has always had Labradors. Even though these two have replaced the dogs she grew up with, they are part of the continuity that is the lifeblood of Chapel Farm. They even have the same names.

James pours her a brandy. 'This is all we have, and it's been open for years.'

She drinks, enjoying the fire that envelops her throat, her other hand stroking the dogs.

'How have you been?' he asks. 'Are you still Of No Fixed Abode? We still get the odd letter for you. I never know what to do with it.'

'I have a postbox in Harare. Just send everything there.'

'I thought you moved out of Zimbabwe.'

'I'm back and forth. Where the work takes me.' She nods, tipping her glass to catch the light.

'I don't know how you stand it, not having a proper home to go to.' He sounds like their father. He is a man now, she realises, not the boy she left behind. She looks at him, his legs crossed in an armchair, sipping brandy, looking every inch to the manor born.

'You should try it,' she says. 'It's freeing.'

'I might not have a choice if this podcast happens. We lost a lot of business after Hazel disappeared. Those allegations, about Dad, that the Richardsons did nothing to dispute.' James pauses, too polite to spell it out.

'I made a mistake, back then,' Catrin confesses. 'That's partly why I've decided to come back.'

'You made a mistake? What – you think that Dad isn't to blame after all? That he didn't have something to do with Hazel's death?'

'I never said that. The papers implied that. Not me.'

'Your silence spoke volumes.'

'I was very young.' Catrin feels caught out, she is used to being the interrogator. She'd forgotten her brother's ability to cut straight to the point.

'You have old shoulders on your head, Cat. You left this house aged sixteen and have barely been back since. You've always been very good at fighting your own corner. It's a shame you couldn't do the same for Dad.'

Catrin reasons with him. 'I'll make up for it, with this podcast, I promise. It will make everything better.'

'They tried to sue us, the Richardsons, did you know that? They let people say what they wanted, and people stopped supporting Chapel Farm. *No smoke without fire*, is what everyone thought.'

'The journalist behind the podcast has a good reputation. If Hazel is still alive, she might hear it and come forward.'

James leans forward in his chair. 'Do you really believe that? That she's out there somewhere?'

Catrin puts her glass down and cracks her knuckles, one by one, a habit formed in her early teens, something she had forgotten until now. 'I spent a long time thinking Hazel was dead – of course I did, it's the most obvious explanation,' she begins. 'But over the years, some of the things I've seen . . . I would never have believed it if someone had just told me. I've taken pictures of the most extraordinary, the most outlandish, the most unbelievable situations. When Stella Cox called me and told me what she'd found, it was enough to have me jump on a flight and come over here.'

'What has she found?'

'She's found a way to get on to Little Auger without the help of Adam or Arvis, number one.' Catrin counts off on her fingers. 'Number two, she's managed to do this, several times, without anybody noticing, which makes me wonder if we were all a bit too certain Little Auger was the impenetrable fortress we believed it to be.'

'So? She got lucky.'

'Number three,' says Catrin, holding up her fingers to him, 'she found some piece of evidence she feels is important on Little Auger. She told me it would completely change the narrative.'

'What has she found?'

'She wouldn't tell me.'

'That's convenient.'

'She's a good journalist, James. I don't think she would lie about this. She wants all three of us – me, Roz and Nina – on Little Auger to talk about the effect it has had on the rest of our lives. And perhaps to find out what really happened that morning.'

'How can you solve what nobody could all those years ago?'

'Nobody spoke to us, James. Apart from an initial chat about where we all were, nobody wanted to talk to us kids. We were overlooked. And when we got home, we never spoke to one another about it. Stella is doing what should have happened twenty years ago. She's talking to the people who knew Hazel best. The people who were there.'

James uncrosses his legs and leans forward in his chair. 'Please stay for a bit this time, Cat. Don't run away again.'

Catrin acknowledges the implication, but can't bring herself to meet his eyes, even though she wants to. 'That right . . . I was angry. I mean . . . I was sixteen, James. He'd just announced you were going to inherit Chapel Farm—'

'Cat, we both knew that was always on the cards.'

'Yes, I know . . .' Even saying it now hurts, not just her pride, but somewhere deep down that always felt Chapel Farm belonged to her as well. 'Mum . . .' – to say her name out loud causes her throat to constrict – 'Mum ran this farm, side by side with Dad. When he gave it all to you, it felt as if he was giving you everything that was left of her.' Catrin swallows hard and looks at James, willing him to understand. 'I never thought he would do it. I thought he might change his mind.'

'You know how archaic his family is. How archaic he can be. You know I would share anything I inherited from him with you.' James finishes his drink and places the glass carefully on a little side table with barley-sugar legs.

Catrin looks away once more, hears the ticking of the grandfather clock. 'That's not the point, James. When your own parent doesn't want to leave you with anything . . .' She stops talking, unable to tell him it made her feel ashamed.

'Look,' says James, 'Roz and her family put us through hell after Hazel died. And it sounds to me like it's going to happen all over again. Chapel Farm isn't just a business. This is my home, Cat. It might not mean much to you, but it's everything to me. It's our family, our heritage. I won't lose it.'

Catrin feels the cold fist of regret squeezing her conscience. 'James, I'm sorry. I wish I could change the situation, make it all go away.'

'Then don't do the podcast. Tell this Stella woman to get lost.'

Catrin shakes her head, miserably. 'I can't do that, James. I need to know the truth.'

Chapter Seven

ROZ

Roz can sense heat on her eyelids, a signal that Mercy is cupping her palms close to Roz's face, that the session is coming to an end. It feels like she has been asleep for most of the hour, and she's not sure if this is a good thing because it's brought her a deep sense of relaxation, or if she's missing out on the benefit by being unconscious. Her sitting room smells of lavender oil, and the air is filled with the song of calling birds. The birdsong was Mercy's idea. She has invested in a little speaker that connects to her phone so her clients can have a choice of background music. From Roz's forehead to her groin, Mercy has placed a line of stones. An amethyst, some rose quartz, and other crystals Roz can't identify. She feels the weight of them, pressing her down into the massage bed. Her knees have a small cylindrical cushion under them, and she is cocooned in a blanket. She feels cosseted, looked after, safe. And she wonders if this is part of it, that it's not the process of realigning chakras or whatever it is that Mercy is doing above her, but just the fact that one human being is looking after her, caring for her, showing her concern.

By the time Roz has opened the curtains and gone to find her purse, Mercy has packed up her bed, crystals, blanket and pillows and is ready to go to her next client.

'Make sure you drink plenty of water for the rest of the day,' says Mercy. 'I've released a lot of toxins. You need to flush them out.'

'I will, I promise,' says Roz, handing over some cash.

'How do you feel?' asks Mercy, tucking the notes into the back pocket of her shorts.

Roz checks herself. 'Relaxed. Yeah. Good, thanks.'

'Believe in yourself, Roz,' says Mercy. 'There's a lot of doubt in there.' She touches Roz's head briefly, and her touch feels like a butterfly, beautiful and fleeting. 'Don't forget the water, I mean it,' Mercy reminds her as she leaves the house, weighed down by her equipment. She is a small woman, but she carries everything lightly, her muscles visible in her arms and legs.

Roz closes the front door and turns to the kitchen to get herself a glass of water. The house is still. Roz frowns. Usually, Willow puts music on in her room when Mercy comes.

'Willow?' Roz calls, standing in the hallway, her hands on her hips. 'Willow?' She looks in the kitchen, wondering if Willow is raiding the fridge. But there is nobody there. Roz goes up the stairs, pushing the bathroom door open when she reaches the top. Willow's bedroom door is ajar, and Roz puts her fingertip to it so it opens gently, not wanting to disturb her daughter. Everything is as it should be, but Willow is not there. Roz is just about to panic when she sees her own bedroom door is shut. She is sure she left it open this morning.

'Willow? What are you doing in here?' she asks, as she pushes the door open. Willow doesn't answer. She is sitting on the floor next to Roz's wardrobe, a large photo album on her lap, a sketchbook, open, on the carpet next to her.

51

Roz stops as if she has hit a wall. 'What are you doing?' she repeats, although she doesn't need to ask. Willow has snuck into her wardrobe and found Hazel's things: a photo album with all the pictures Roz could salvage from her parents when she left home, and the sketchbook she filled with her likeness before she disappeared. Seeing her daughter with them, the sketchbook flung open, the album on her knees, the page bending painfully under Willow's hands, it shocks her, the careless way Willow is treating her memories.

Roz had imagined, over and over, showing these books to Willow. In her mind's eye, she had seen herself explain, gently, to a much older Willow, who Hazel was, how much she was loved, how much she is missed. She had imagined bringing the books down, laying them reverently on a clean kitchen table so they could look at them together, when she was ready. Not like this.

'Who is this?' says Willow, indicating the photographs that Roz has laid out so carefully, labelling them in her best handwriting. Willow jabs her finger on to Hazel's face and Roz winces.

'Give me the book, Willow. You had no right to go into my things . . .' Roz reaches out with her arms, but Willow snaps the album shut and pulls it to her chest. 'She looks just like me. Is she my twin? How come I never met her?'

The eager way Willow throws this out does nothing to steady Roz's fraying emotions. Everything about Hazel feels fragile, and Willow is taking her memory and trampling over it. 'She's not your twin,' replies Roz in a high voice, disliking the way Willow is making it about herself. 'Those pictures are more than twenty years old.'

'Then who is she?'

Willow is still sitting on the floor, the album wrapped in her arms. Roz is looking down at her but, for some reason, they both know it is Willow who has the upper hand. Hazel's name is written all over that book, there is no escaping the truth now.

Roz feels as if a spring has been wound, very tightly, inside her chest. 'She's my sister,' she says in a strangled voice.

'I knew it! I knew you lied to me when you got that phone call. Is she dead, then?'

Roz is winded by Willow's question; her prurient curiosity feels poisonous. 'Yes,' says Roz, aiming for calm. 'She died.'

'What of?' Willow says, a note of disinterest in her voice. But – is Roz imagining it? – is there a look of triumph in her eyes? They sweep over Roz with disdain, making her feel like a bad mother, a bad sister.

She feels weak, disoriented by the conversation. She can't find a way through it. 'Those are my private things. I don't snoop around your bedroom looking through your things.'

'Yes you do.'

'That's called cleaning.'

'Why didn't you say anything about her? Why didn't you tell me I had an auntie who looks just like me. It's so cool.'

The word breaks Roz. '*Cool?* You think it's cool to have a sister that died, do you? You think it's cool I'm so upset about it I can't bring myself to talk about it? You have absolutely no idea.'

Roz's words, her obvious anger, should shock Willow into contrition, but they have the opposite effect. Willow is like Simon and doesn't like being wrong. She lights up with defiance, like a spark that has just caught a breeze.

'You said you didn't have a sister! You kept this from me, and she's *my* aunt. And this . . .' Willow picks up the sketchbook. 'You've *never* drawn me. Even though I've asked you so many times. But here . . .' She flicks through the book, and a cascade of Hazels, drawn in pencil, watercolour, charcoal, flutter in and out of Roz's vision. 'Hazel asleep,' she reads in a tearful voice. 'Hazel on the sofa. Hazel with Goggin. Who's Goggin?'

'Stop it!' Roz lunges for the sketchbook and grabs at it.

'Ow,' says Willow, examining her arm where Roz has accidentally scratched it.

Roz uses the opportunity to take the album too. She carefully folds the pages back, smoothing out the wrinkles. 'Get out of my room,' she says, her voice ragged with emotion.

'You care more about your sister than me,' claims Willow, half shouting, half crying.

'Don't you dare speak to me like that.'

'At least I'm not a liar.'

Willow sobs and leaves the room, and Roz can hear her using the landline downstairs. She hears her go into her bedroom and hears her come out again. She listens, motionless, as her daughter's feet meet the stairs. She holds her breath, it seems, until she hears the purr of Simon's car draw up, the front door open, and slam, loudly, the door opening again and Simon calling up the stairs. Then she sinks to the floor, cradling the memories of her sister, and weeps into the silence of the house.

Chapter Eight

NINA

Sylvia is early, but Nina's mother is always early. The doorbell rings as Nina runs a brush through her hair, cursing that she hasn't had a chance to put her make-up on. This morning, she went back to bed after work and forgot to set the alarm. She opens the front door and her mother offers up her left cheek. She looks impeccable in a floral wrap dress that manages to be both sexy and demure at the same time. Her hair is styled and set. She is wearing Gucci sunglasses, and a small, tasteful clutch bag is trapped between her firm body and a tanned forearm. For the millionth time, Nina feels a mixture of pride and insecurity. She will never be as glamorous as Sylvia Lewis. It is a skill that cannot be wholly learnt.

Her mother holds her at arm's length, giving her a customary appraisal. 'You look a bit peaky, Nina, is everything all right?'

Nina swallows her irritation. 'You're early. I haven't had time to do my face. I only just got out of the shower.'

Sylvia frowns. 'Don't be grumpy, darling.'

'I'm not,' says Nina, putting on a bright smile. 'I don't feel like going out for lunch, though. Can we just eat here instead?'

'Of course, you must be tired. You go and do your face, and I'll whizz something up.'

Nina's irritation melts away as she gives in to being mothered. When she returns to the kitchen, she feels much better. Sylvia has made a nice-looking salad, and she is pouring out a glass of wine for them both. 'Thanks, Mum, you're a marvel.'

'I am,' Sylvia says smoothly. 'Sit down and eat. And tell me what the matter is.'

Nina groans. 'Work stuff. They want me to . . .' She screws her face up. 'They want me to talk about myself on the show.'

'I don't understand.' Sylvia sits opposite her at the table and passes her a knife and fork.

'Curtis, the director, wants to bring an element of confession into the slot . . .'

'Urgh . . .'

'He thinks I'm not relatable enough. He wants me to talk about my own problems.'

Sylvia shakes her head faintly and tuts. 'That sounds awful. Absolutely dreadful.'

'I know.'

'I hope you told him where to go,' Sylvia says, frowning, unfolding a napkin and smoothing it on to her knees.

'Yes, I did,' says Nina, sipping her wine.

'That's my girl.'

'But my trial period is coming to an end and he hinted he might not make everything official.'

'He can't do that, surely?'

Nina waves her fork in the air. 'I have no idea. I need to talk to my agent about it, but I can't seem to get hold of her. Curtis can do what he wants, I suppose. It's not my show.'

'I don't understand this fashion for getting everything off your chest in public. It's so tawdry,' says Sylvia, forking a tomato out of her salad.

Nina smiles. 'That's the exact same word I used. Tawdry.'

'Problems should be dealt with privately,' Sylvia remarks.

'Well,' Nina laughs, 'I suppose if we all followed that logic, I'd be out of a job.'

But Sylvia isn't laughing. 'When I was having all that difficulty with your father, did I run around telling all and sundry he was having an affair with that awful woman? No, I did not. I kept it to myself and carried on as normal, and my friends privately thanked me for it, I'm sure.'

'Don't you think it might have helped to talk to someone, though? Just one person?' Nina remembers how miserable her mother was, the terrible atmosphere in the house. But she doesn't remember any friends. Her mother has never had any friends as far as Nina can remember. All she remembers was the relief she'd felt going to Little Auger without her bickering parents. She hadn't really thought about what was happening at home, though, in her absence. It must have been awful for her mother.

'Why should I talk to anyone?' Sylvia asks. 'Nobody likes a cry-baby, Nina. It's most unattractive.'

'I didn't mean that,' says Nina. 'I just meant having a chat, sharing a problem. It does help sometimes, I think. Look at how many people write in to me. They need a listening ear. It makes them feel better.'

'In my experience, a problem shared is a problem doubled. I've always taught you that, darling, and it has stood you in good stead.'

Nina clears her throat. 'Is that why we didn't go to Dad's funeral?'

'We didn't go to his funeral because he died when he was working in Hong Kong, and I didn't find out about it until his wife thought to tell us. Nina, what's brought all this up? You never talk about your father.'

Nina sits back on her chair and puts her fork down. 'I don't know,' she says. 'I suppose I've been thinking about that time in my life. Before everything . . .' Nina cannot finish the sentence.

Sylvia puts her fork down too, and her lips pucker with concern. 'I knew you looked out of sorts, as soon as I set eyes on you today. What's really going on, Nina?'

'I've been contacted by someone. They want to talk about Hazel.'

'What sort of someone?' asks Sylvia.

'A podcaster.'

'A what-caster?'

Nina giggles. 'A podcaster, Mum. Someone who records programmes. Like radio programmes, but for the internet. It's a thing.'

'Well, it doesn't sound like my sort of thing,' Sylvia says dismissively. 'Why do they want to talk to you about Hazel?'

'They want to talk to all of us. Stella – the podcaster – says she's found something on the island, but I think it's just a ploy to get us back there together and talk about the fallout of what happened.'

Sylvia looks concerned. 'You're not going to do it, are you?'

'I did wonder about it, especially in light of what Curtis said. He could give me a new contract if I dangle that over his head.'

'Bringing you to London, putting some distance between you and that awful situation, was the best thing we did. The death of that little girl would have defined you for the rest of your life. Don't go back there, digging it all up again.'

'Believe me, I don't want to. But . . .'

'What? But what, Nina?'

'What if this podcaster has found something?'

Sylvia dabs her mouth with her napkin and lays it on the table. 'Listen to me. There'll be no going back if you get involved. You can't unsay things, Nina. And the things you do say could get twisted into something they're not. You need to forge your own way, darling, set your own agenda. Don't get caught up in someone else's story.'

'Yeah, no. You're right.'

Sylvia leans over the breakfast bar and holds Nina in a level gaze. 'Look at me, Nina. People like Curtis are full of it. I bet you he'll renew that contract whether you talk or don't. They're lucky to have you on that sofa. And as far as this podcaster goes, they'll lose interest if you refuse to do it. They're probably on a . . . what's it called? A fishing expedition. They're probably poking around to see if they get a response. Don't give them one. And stop looking backwards. The past can't be changed, but the future can.'

This is one of the things Nina loves about her mother. Her absolute, unwavering certainty. But Little Auger is a splinter that settled under Nina's skin long ago, and she wonders if it can ever be pulled out. Since Stella Cox rang her up, she cannot help but think about that summer. She should have known Sylvia wouldn't want to discuss it, but that doesn't stop the memories flooding back.

Nina arrived on Little Auger wrestling with a tangle of emotions: misery, because of what she had left behind, relief at being able to get away from it, and guilt for feeling both of these things. Her father had been sleeping on the sofa. He had asked her, very sweetly, if it would be all right if he used her room while she was gone. To think about him, curled up underneath her Barbie duvet cover with matching pillowcases, made her eyes prick with tears. She'd wanted to talk about it, to tell Roz and Catrin, just to say it all out loud, but Sylvia had been very clear with her that she was not to talk about what was going on at home. She had made Nina swear on her guinea pig's life that she wouldn't say a word to anyone on Little Auger. Keeping that promise ate away at her, until Roz provided a solution of sorts. On the first day of the holiday, she asked Nina what was going on. She could see something wasn't right.

'I can't talk about it, Mum won't let me,' said Nina miserably. She tried to focus on unpacking her bag neatly in the room that would be theirs for the week.

'If you can't tell me, then I think you should make a journal,' suggested Roz, who was a big believer in keeping promises. 'That way, you can talk about it without actually telling anyone. Hazel and I use them all the time. You can have one of mine, if you like. I couldn't decide which one to bring, so I have a spare.'

'What's a journal?'

'It's like a diary, but you don't have to write in it every day, just when you feel like it. And nobody is allowed to read it, unless you want them to, so you can write what you like without getting into trouble.'

Nina liked the sound of that, plus she felt certain it didn't break any of her promises to her mother. When Roz handed her a slim book with neat, ruled lines, the emptiness of it spoke of possibility, freedom, and hope. She wrote in it almost immediately, spilling her troubles across its pages. The thoughts that had been swirling around her head began to filter out. Her embarrassment at having parents that didn't get on. Her mother's constant desire for perfection and her failure to maintain her own marriage. The deep shame this brought upon Sylvia seemed to roll off her like a heady scent and it surrounded Nina, infusing her life, too, with a sense of failure.

As Nina waves her mother goodbye, she wonders whether it might have helped her in some way with Howard, had Sylvia been a bit more open. It's taken her a long time to admit it, but she didn't know how to hold her own marriage together.

'I always feel I'm getting about eighty per cent of you,' Howard said to Nina once. 'Like you're hiding little bits of yourself. Where's the other twenty per cent?'

'Aren't I allowed to have a private life?' she'd replied testily.

'I never really know what you're thinking, I suppose that's what I mean.'

Nina remembers the fury she felt when she discovered Howard had read her journal. It was the only place she felt safe enough to open herself up. She'd kicked him out and changed the locks the very next day. She'd never confided in her mother about what had led to the divorce, and Sylvia had been delighted to get her daughter back. Nina had dealt with her break-up alone, as Sylvia had done. But a little part of her wonders if her mother is sometimes wrong.

Nina has a vision of Howard, his face poking through the letterbox, pleading with her to let him in. He had shouted into the hallway that he had loved her more when he read her diary. It had made him feel closer to her. But Nina couldn't shake off the feeling she had been caught out, that he now knew a part of her that was shameful. She had put the television on, very loudly, until the shouting had stopped.

Her phone pings in her pocket, and she is dismayed to see it is a message from Stella. How are you fixed for bank holiday Monday? I'm planning to go to Little Auger to interview Catrin and Roz. I can give you a lift?

Nina spends the rest of the day trying to compose a reply, before deciding not to reply at all. By the time she is ready for bed, there is only one place she feels safe enough to talk about Little Auger and the short time she spent there. She still writes in a journal; it is a habit she cannot break. This evening, she uses it to separate the tangle of thoughts that Stella's text has brought about.

Little Auger wasn't the perfect holiday she'd hoped it would be. Even the friendship she'd formed with Nina and Roz felt strained, sometimes, because of Hazel.

When I think about Hazel, Nina writes, *I remember how protective she was about the smallest of things. She was always rescuing insects, chasing after moths and ladybirds. She was never as nice to us as she was to animals. I think she was jealous of our friendship with Roz, it took Roz away from her, and she didn't like that. I wonder what would have happened to her at secondary school. What would have happened, had she lived, if she would have naturally separated from Roz. If she would have found friends of her own.*

Nobody tells you how hard it is to make friends when you're older. My friendship with Roz and Catrin, felt like a perfect circle on a clean sheet of paper. I have never experienced that here, in London, even after I dropped the Welsh accent. The only person who has been a constant friend in my life is my mother, and what does that say about me?

Chapter Nine

It is not often warm in Chapel Farm but this morning, it is. When Catrin remembers growing up here, she thinks of ice flowers blooming on the inside of her bedroom window in winter, the creak of the antiquated heating system failing to heat the house. She thinks of draughts snaking through the rooms, wandering the hallways like wraiths in purgatory. All the windows are single glazed, little diamond-shaped panes of glass held in place by strips of dark-grey lead. Sometimes the lead would shrink or crack, finally giving in to age, and the glass would simply fall out, unnoticed, until the temperature of the room told them something was amiss. As a schoolgirl, Catrin thought nothing of putting her uniform into bed with her, so it was warm to dress into the next morning. She nearly did it last night, until she took out her phone and saw the temperature would be tolerable. She wonders if Chapel Farm is the reason she moved to Africa, where the cold only visits at night and becomes a welcome respite from the heat.

She looks around her bedroom, at the same bed she slept in as a child. In fact, her room has not altered much since she left here, aged sixteen. The wallpaper has an abstract, bubbling pattern that is detailed by a three-dimensional foamy texture. Above the bed, just below the windowsill, the paper is bald, the texture picked off by adolescent, unthinking fingers. Catrin looks out through her window, expecting to see the same expanse of grass, clipped and green, surrounding the flower beds, rolling down the hill to the lake below. But instead, she sees that the herbaceous borders her father was so fond of have been overtaken by weeds. The lake is obscured by thickset trees that have grown taller, wider. She remembers her father planting those trees, slim silver birches that reflected the moonlight like sentries on duty. Now the trunks have fattened and split with age. Through their youthful smoothness there are rough and blackened wounds. She knows that her father and James have had better things to do than repurpose her room, but it seems that the whole estate has slumped into decline.

Catrin grabs her camera and leaves her room to go and find her father, every creak and groan of floorboard under threadbare carpet as intimate to her as the voices of her family. The walls are covered in the kind of patterned wallpaper that disguises the many acts of damage she and her brother inflicted over the years. Above her head, the ghosts of hunting trophies can still be seen, now scorch marks on the paper. Forcing her father to remove them was a small victory in her adolescence, but now she thinks about it, it was probably James who persuaded him, in an attempt to keep the peace. She descends the huge staircase, the carved wooden dragons that top the balustrade familiar under her palm. The front door is wide open and a chilly breeze bustles in, even though it is a sunny day. She can see a flurry of wet paw prints that tell her the dogs have been in the lake. She glances out of the door, past the crumbling fountain and down the gravelled driveway that gives out to the long corridor of lime trees that lead to the gate. When she has finished taking pictures, she walks through the house to the back.

She wanders through the kitchen, noting the large oak table, the ancient Aga, the Sheila Maid above her head. It is the same as she remembers, more tired and rundown, but when she opens the back door, she sees that changes have been made to the estate. The flower and herb garden that her mother dug out has been expanded into a large walled affair, the raised beds divided into neat oblongs where vegetables now grow. Catrin walks past climbers winding themselves up tall bamboo structures, their pods heavy and ripe to pick. She pushes a door set into the wall at the furthest end and it opens to a less glamorous area, where at least two dozen chickens scratch and strut. Her father is collecting eggs from the coop – she takes a sly, candid shot of him – and as she approaches, he hands her a large basket lined with an old towel. With a jolt, she recognises the basket. She knew it belonged to her mother, who used it to collect flowers from the kitchen garden when it was solely hers. Catrin frowns. She can't recall seeing any flowers when she passed through. Catrin had always taken pleasure knowing the blooms she collected as a child were planted by her mother. It was a connection between them, a way of keeping her memory alive to fill a jug with gladioli or daffodils she had put into the earth before Catrin was born.

'So you have chickens now?' Catrin begins, securing her camera around her neck, trying to find something uncontroversial to say.

'Since last year,' replies her father, nodding for her to bring the basket nearer so he can transfer the eggs.

'What's happened to Mum's garden?'

'The soil's good there. We expanded the vegetable patch and sell to local restaurants now.'

'What happened to her flowers?' Catrin shifts the eggs in the basket, feels the warmth of them against her fingers.

'Flowers don't pay the bills. Vegetables do.' Her father deposits more eggs into the basket. His fingers are quick, despite his age.

Catrin struggles to digest this information. She knows she has nothing to do with the running of Chapel Farm, that she hasn't come here to argue with her father. But it seems callous, somehow, this indifference to her mother's legacy. 'There are fields out back you could have used,' she remarks, trying to maintain an even voice. 'You didn't need to dig up her garden.'

'The fields are rented out now, for grazing.'

Catrin is surprised. 'All of them?'

He nods, briefly. 'We only have two left. We sold the rest off.'

'Maybe it's a good thing to downsize,' she observes. 'James says you're working too hard.'

Her father pauses and sighs, as if she has missed his point. 'It's not my choice to sell, Catrin. But there it is. Business has slowed since Brexit. We'd just built everything back up again and then they had to go and leave the European Union. It would help if you didn't speak to this journalist. I wasn't in favour of passing the message on, but James went and did it anyway.'

'It might be helpful, to involve someone with fresh eyes.'

'Fresh eyes?' he says in a gruff voice. 'Greedy eyes, more like. She wants this for herself, not to help us.'

'Aren't you curious what happened to Hazel?'

'I know what happened to that little girl. She wandered off and got swept out to sea.'

'We can't be sure.'

'Yes we can. You're making this into something it's not. It's what your lot are always doing.'

'My lot?' Catrin feels her face heat up.

'The press. Always twisting other people's words, looking for a story.'

'I don't deal with words. I deal in pictures,' she says, trying to defend herself.

'It's not just words that get manipulated these days.'

'It doesn't mean we shouldn't try and get to the truth.'

'It will bring all that upset back to that family, and to ours. People boycotted Chapel Farm produce when they thought . . .' His voice trails off. 'Now see what'll happen with social media. It'll be a disaster for the business.'

'She'll make this podcast with or without my help. I may as well be there to make sure it's done properly. We can well and truly clear your name.'

Her father gives a hollow laugh that makes her feel stupid. 'My name was clear before that little girl disappeared. My name has always been clear. It's only you that seems to doubt it.'

'Dad . . . I . . .' Catrin wants to tell him that the uncertainty over Hazel's disappearance permeated her subconscious, that her feelings at the time got muddled up – she didn't know who or what to believe. She missed having a mother so keenly that summer. She would have sat Catrin down, talked to her in a quiet moment about what was going on, Catrin was certain of it. But when they returned from Little Auger, her father picked up his tools and spent the next ten days digging drainage for the fields.

'Catrin, you've always gone your own way, no matter what I say.' He closes the coop. 'Take the basket into the kitchen, will you, and put them into boxes with the others. They'll be collected this afternoon.'

When she has finished stacking the eggs in their boxes, Catrin finds James fixing a fence that borders the grazing fields. There are skylarks singing above her head and she can hear the comforting call of sheep. The air is thick with the moist smell of grass and earth. She takes some shots of the landscape, the sweeping, open sky crossed with feathery vapour trails and flocking birds. She never appreciated any of this when she was a child, but now, after documenting how other poorer people live, she suddenly appreciates the great bubble of privilege she has grown up in.

'So you've spoken to Dad, then?' James asks, motioning to her to pass him a box of galvanised staples.

'How can you tell?' Catrin replies. As children, she and James used to complain bitterly about being given a job as soon as they went anywhere near their father, but now James seems to have developed the same skill.

'I can tell by the look on your face,' he smiles, as he takes a handful of staples and puts them in the top pocket of his shirt.

'He's taken over Mum's garden. There's nothing of her here any more,' Catrin complains, sitting down on the grass beside him, putting the box on her lap.

James stops hammering and sits on his haunches. 'He's not doing it to piss you off, Cat. We need to run at a profit. And at the moment, that profit is very small. You haven't been here to see it. It gets harder every year.'

'Why don't you pack it in, then?'

'This piece of land is all I know. What I say and what I want aren't always the same thing.'

Catrin puts her head on one side. 'And here's me thinking men weren't self-aware.'

'We just pretend to be emotional vacuums, so women don't ask us any tricky questions.'

Catrin laughs. 'I see you still don't have a ring on your finger. I thought you would have been snapped up by now, a handsome landowner like you.'

'No time for that, I'm afraid,' he says ruefully.

'You know you don't have to go out and socialise, don't you?' Catrin teases. 'There are dating apps for that sort of thing.'

'Unlike you, I like to take people to dinner before I take them to bed.' He glances over at her own hands. 'There's no ring on your finger either.'

'And there never will be. I don't stay in the same place for long enough. It suits me.'

'Try it. You might like it.' And then, as an afterthought, as he looks into the distance, 'It would be nice to have some company for a while.'

Catrin looks at her brother, and wonders what would happen if she hung around here for a month or two. If it would make things better or worse. The distance between them when she arrived has narrowed. She has missed this easy conversation, she realises. She has missed having an ally. And he reminds her of the mother she didn't get to know.

'Do you ever hear anything from them? From Roz and Nina, I mean?' she asks, feeling a small wave of disquiet. Catrin looks out across the field to the sky beyond it, thinking what a relief she'd felt not to have to carry on that friendship under the weight of Hazel's death. Everything about sharing a space with Roz and Nina had seemed wrong. Catrin remembers becoming intensely aware of her own body at the age of thirteen, and what it did in front of her friends. Wondering if she was behaving respectfully enough with Roz, if she had used the wrong tone in her voice, the wrong facial expression. She found she couldn't do anything without a constant, internal narrative on her own behaviour. It was exhausting. Consequently, she didn't refer to Hazel's death. Instead, she shuffled around it awkwardly until she couldn't wait to get away from her friends and be herself once more. Catrin has often thought that if it had happened when they were older, their friendship might have survived. Nobody teaches children how to grieve until it's too late.

'Roz went to live in England and never returned,' says James, rummaging in his shirt pocket for another staple. 'I heard she married young. Her parents still live here, though, unfortunately.'

'They used to be such good friends with Dad.'

'Only because you were so friendly with Roz. The main reason they came on holiday to Little Auger with you that time was because they didn't trust him to look after their precious daughter.'

'Looks like they were right.'

'It wasn't his fault, Cat.'

'I know. I know that. Sorry,' she says.

Several curious sheep saunter cautiously towards them. They stop a few metres away, unblinking. Shearing season is over and they are now growing their winter wool, their bodies becoming fatter with warmth. They stand together, shoulder to shoulder, their black jaws chewing the grass, their heads motionless, ears up, as they monitor the incursion into their territory. James ignores them and rolls out the next section of wire mesh, pulling it taut between two wooden posts.

'What about Nina's father?' Catrin asks, passing James more staples. 'He stuck around, didn't he, after Nina and Sylvia left for London?'

James fixes the mesh with three swift blows of the hammer. 'Not for long. I think he moved away after he remarried. But Nina is very visible – or perhaps you don't know.' James pauses and explains Nina's rise to minor fame and her slot on morning television. It leaves Catrin with a funny feeling.

'She doesn't even have a Welsh accent any more,' sniffs James, twirling the hammer in his hands.

'I suppose she's lived in London longer than she lived here,' replies Catrin, sitting down next to the fence post, near to a large bottle of water.

'Well, you've managed to keep yours. It's fainter, mind. But it's there.'

'I wonder what Roz is up to?' Catrin muses, pulling a handful of grass out of a tussock next to her and throwing it into the breeze. She can smell it in the air, soft and sweet.

'Hopefully having a happy life without her awful parents,' replies James smartly. 'Give me that bottle of water, will you? I need a break.'

James sits next to her, his back against the mesh he has just hammered in. They pass the water back and forth.

'Did you ever go back to Little Auger after Hazel died?' Catrin asks.

'I've been a few times, yes,' he says. 'I think because I wasn't there when it happened, it didn't seem real. For a while, there were groups of idiots who tried to land on there to see if they could find Hazel. But no one ever managed. Adam and his dad did quite well for a while, towing them back and patching up their boats.'

Catrin sits up. 'Adam? I haven't thought about Adam for years. I wonder what he's doing now.'

'Running the boatyard in Eider, I think. Arvis had a heart attack and retired early. Adam took over, last I heard.'

Catrin looks into the distance. 'I still think of him as a teenager, but I guess he'll be in his thirties now, like me. I can't imagine him running that place alone. When I picture him, I remember a teenager, mooning after Roz.'

'Poor Adam. Roz probably didn't realise.'

'Does he know about the podcaster? Adam, I mean,' Catrin asks.

'No idea. Ask him. I take it you're going to Little Auger today?'

'I want to leave tomorrow morning. I'd like to spend today taking pictures of the estate. The light is so perfect right now.' She leans back, pulls her camera to her eye and snaps an image of James looking down the valley to the house. His profile is handsome.

He has a Roman nose; his short curls are defined by sweat. The shadows on his face make him look like a sculpture. James shoves the camera gently away, giving her a dark look. 'Can I borrow the Land Rover?' she asks, laughing. 'I need to tow the boat to Eider.'

'You don't ask for much, do you.'

'It's Friday tomorrow. I'll be back by Tuesday, latest. I'll only be gone a few days.'

'A few days?'

'I want to go over there, by myself, before Stella comes up from London on Monday. It's a bank holiday weekend, so it's not like you'll be visiting suppliers, will you?'

'Go on then.' James gets up, puts the cap back on the water bottle and looks for the hammer.

'Has The Old House changed?' asks Catrin, still seated. She reaches over for the hammer, which has hidden itself in the grass.

'Are you kidding me? Nothing changes in this family. Things just . . . disintegrate. It's a millstone if you ask me, Little Auger and that house. I talked to Dad about selling the lot last year, but he won't have anything said about it.'

Catrin offers James the hammer and when he takes it, she holds on to the handle and pulls herself up to standing. 'Why would you want to sell it?' she asks, dusting the grass off her combat pants.

'It's not like it used to be. We don't go there all the time.' He gestures to the fields that slope down to the house. 'I had an idea about planting a vineyard, making our own wine on Chapel Farm, but it needs investment and selling the island seemed like a good way to raise the cash. But Dad said no, so there you go.'

'Well, we don't agree on much but I'm with Dad on this one. It's been in our family for centuries.'

James looks at her with amusement. 'Cat, you don't even live on this continent. It doesn't look as if I'll ever have a family of my own. Nobody uses it. And it's been bad luck for us.'

'You don't believe all that, do you, James?'

Her brother's face changes. The amusement disappears. 'We nearly lost the business after Hazel died. It took us years to get back on our feet. If you go making this podcast, you're only going to make things worse for us. So yes, I believe in bad luck.'

Chapter Ten

ROZ

After one night and a morning without speaking to Willow, Roz calls Simon once more.

'How is she?' Roz asks.

'Quiet,' says Simon.

'So you didn't take her into holiday club this morning?'

Simon sighs. 'Roz, I think it might be for the best if Willow stays with me for the rest of the holidays.'

'You think it's better that she spends the whole day, alone, in your flat than being supervised at holiday club, having fun with her friends?'

'Look, it's Thursday. The bank holiday is coming up. I can work some flexitime, and my neighbour has a girl the same age as Willow. They've met before, they like each other. She's offered to have her when I need to be in the office.'

'You seriously think Willow is better off with a complete stranger?'

'She's not a complete stranger.' Simon makes a noise of exasperation. 'This is what I find very difficult about you, Roz, you put up hurdles at every turn. You want Willow with you, but you don't want to have her in the house when you're working, you want her at school, which is the very place she doesn't want to be.'

'It's a *holiday club*, she's mixing with kids all day, running around . . .'

'. . . but it's stifling her. She's desperate for a bit of freedom. She wants to feel like a grown-up. Don't you see that?'

'She needs supervising . . .' says Roz weakly.

'Roz, when are you going to get over this?'

Roz feels her hackles rise. 'What?'

'I thought it was just when she was a baby, calling a doctor as soon as she had a sniffle . . .'

'That's not—'

'Calling me at work, every thirty minutes. And now she's older, she feels it, Roz.'

'Feels what?'

'This thing you do, not letting her run free. Wrapping her in cotton wool.'

'I don't do that! She's been at holiday club all week.' Roz feels the injustice keenly.

'An organised scheme, managed by over-qualified people.'

'What's wrong with that?'

'And the secrecy. Not telling her about Hazel. It's not good for anyone. I found it so compelling when we were both seventeen, the mysterious-girl vibe, but it gets old, Roz. Willow feels it now. You shut her out of a big part of your life and she's beginning to notice.'

'You can't just take her away like this, because you think I'm distant.'

Simon sighs loudly. 'I didn't say that, Roz. Anyway, I'm not taking her away, she wants a break. She's very hurt by what she saw. I told you that you should have mentioned Hazel sooner than this. She's asking me questions and I have no way of answering them because you barely told me anything about her when we were together, and your parents were even worse.'

The subject is too big for Roz to respond, too ugly to examine. Out of habit, she clams up and waits for the silence between them to push the conversation into a different territory. Sure enough, Simon relents and calls for Willow to come and talk.

When the call ends, Roz is still unable to make her peace with Willow, who refuses to speak to her. She looks around her house. It feels tainted, now, by their argument. She tries to recall the pleasure of buying it, of doing it up, preparing Willow's room for her when she was just a bump. The feeling that finally, *finally*, Roz would be looked after by a family who loved her, a family who put her first. And then a thought settles in her head. Maybe Willow is best off without her. A slow, hot tear makes its way down her cheek. She is ruining everything, and she can't help herself. She can see it happening, like a car rolling towards a cliff.

Her phone vibrates and she looks at the screen.

Hi, Roz, it's Stella. I'm going to be in Eider on Monday. It would be great if we could talk. I really think you need to see what I've found.

Roz tries to guess, for the thousandth time, what evidence Stella Cox has found on that island. It can't be Hazel's body – the thought makes her sick – even a hungry podcaster wouldn't withhold that from the police. If she could just go back to Little Auger . . . Maybe going back would help her untangle the mess her life is in. Perhaps meeting Stella, talking to her, would be a help. Once again, the urge to talk to someone who knows floods through her.

Then, Roz remembers Adam.

She doesn't think about Adam often, but when she does, she still remembers the connection they made. It was because of Hazel's absence, this thing that existed between them, but even so, it felt real for those few short days.

Several hours after Hazel disappeared, she found herself alone at The Old House. Somebody had to be there in case Hazel came back, it may as well be her. Adam and his father had brought the police and a few volunteers as soon as the tide allowed, as many as they could fit into the boat. While the villagers fanned out to search the island, Adam had come to see how she was.

He had found her sitting outside the house, scanning the headland, hoping that every dark shadow moving on the hill was her sister. She hadn't seen him approach. He just sat next to her and started to talk. Roz remembers that he didn't refer to what had happened, exactly, but everything he said, the way he said it, implied concern. When the conversation lapsed into silence, he dug into his pockets and pulled out two pieces of twine, one the colour of butter and the other the colour of sky.

'Do you know how to tie knots?' he asked her, a question she had never been asked before and has never been asked since. He took the two pieces of twine and looped them around one another, a delicate, writhing dance, until the two pieces slipped together and became one, like fingers in a glove. 'It's called a fisherman's knot.' He placed it carefully upon her knee.

The symmetry of it pleased her, and for a few seconds she forgot her sister had gone. She forgot her parents blamed her for it. As she picked up the twine, she let the weight of guilt slip away, just for a minute, while she tried to figure out how to tie one for herself.

She has always remembered this kindness; it has stayed with her for the past twenty years. And sometimes – not often – when she finds herself with two pieces of string, she replicates this knot, just to see if she can remember. It is a skill she has never had to put to work in her own small life, but for reasons she can't explain, it is one she hasn't forgotten.

On her phone, Roz searches for boatyards in Eider. There is only one. She dials it before she can stop herself.

'AA Boatyard? Hello?'

'Sorry,' she begins. 'I was wondering if it would be possible . . . to talk to Adam. I'm not sure if he works there any more – his father used to own the boatyard.'

'What's your name?'

'Er, Roz. Roz Richardson.' She uses her maiden name, she doesn't know why.

'Roz?' There is a pause. 'Hazel's sister.' Not a question, but an understanding.

'Adam? Is that you? Oh my God, Adam.'

'Roz. There's a blast from the past.' He sounds caught out, uncertain of himself. It makes her feel uncertain, too.

'I didn't think – I guess I thought you wouldn't . . .'

'Still be here?' He laughs.

'Yes. No, I didn't mean . . .'

'I'm joking.'

'. . . How's your dad?'

'Living the life of Riley. He's retired. I run this place now. It's good to hear from you.'

Roz hesitates, not sure how to progress. 'I got a phone call, from someone making a podcast about Hazel. They've been visiting Little Auger.'

'What? How?'

'They found a way to get over there. I thought it was impossible.'

In her mind's eye, she pictures Adam scratching the back of his neck where his hair was shortest. She remembers the sandy colour of it, the way it seemed flecked with gold. She wonders if he still has his hair, if the colour is the same.

'Nothing's impossible, I suppose,' says Adam. 'But usually people who don't know how to navigate the island get caught on the rocks and have to get rescued. He must've got very lucky, I guess.'

'She. It's a woman. Stella Cox. And she's been several times. Or so she says.'

'Stella?' Adam swears under his breath.

'Do you know her?'

'No. Yes. Not really. I met a woman called Stella a few weeks ago. She was in the pub. We got talking. We drank. A lot. She kept buying me rounds. Shit. She asked me about Little Auger and how hard it was to get over there. I ended up boasting I could do it, like a macho prick. She quizzed me about it pretty hard. I thought she was . . . well. I thought she was interested in me, not the island. What an idiot.'

Roz nods to herself. 'So she has been over there, she managed it.'

'Looks that way, yeah. Sorry, Roz. That's my bad. Is she causing trouble? She looked like trouble when I met her.'

'She says she's found something, connected to Hazel's disappearance. I thought perhaps she was lying, but she's obviously been over there.'

'What did she find?'

'Well, that's the problem, she won't tell me, unless I come to Little Auger and do an interview with her.'

'What a bitch.'

'My thoughts exactly.' For some reason, Roz is absurdly happy at how this conversation is going. She thought it would be awkward, talking to Adam after so long, that he might not remember her. Her words come out easily, they chase after his own, following them close behind.

'Just call the police, they'll deal with her,' says Adam. 'They'll have grounds.'

'I thought about that, but . . .'

'What?'

'Is she still there?' Roz asks. 'Stella Cox?'

'Uh-uh. No. I would know if she was. She rented a boat from me and brought it back last week.'

The thought that occurred to Roz earlier solidifies in her mind and sits there, like a stone. She deleted the text she had from Stella, asking to meet in Eider on Monday, but she hasn't forgotten it. 'Adam, I want to go back. Just to look around. It might help me decide whether I want to do this podcast or not. I can't remember those final days very well. It's all a jumble. That time . . . it was so . . .'

'I know, I know,' says Adam softly. 'I get it.'

She remembers how the minutes stretched into hours, and when day turned to night, and Hazel still hadn't been found, it was Adam and his father who continued to search and call her name. She remembers Adam holding her shoulders as she hiccupped with fear, telling her that his dad knew the island like the back of his hand, and that if Hazel was there he would find her.

'The thing is, Adam,' Roz says, taking a deep breath, 'I lost touch with Catrin. And my parents made life difficult for her family. I'm not sure they'd want me there.'

She hears Adam consider the implication. He blows out a breath of air and the sound reaches Roz's ear, distorted by the miles between them. It reminds her of the sea. 'Well, Catrin doesn't live here, and her family don't come here much any more. So I'm guessing they won't care. Not if we don't tell them.'

A wave of gratitude courses through her. 'Thanks. I mean it. I owe you.'

'No you don't,' he says simply. 'It will be good to see you.'

As soon as she has rung off, she begins to pack.

Chapter Eleven

CATRIN

Catrin has borrowed her brother's Land Rover so she can tow the boat to Eider. She drives slowly, unused to the weight of it pulling at odds with the car when she turns, the density of traffic on the motorway a world away from the dusty tracks she is used to navigating. The driving in this country surprises her, it is much more aggressive than she is used to. She spends the journey with both hands glued to the wheel, her teeth gritted so hard it gives her a headache. When the motorway thins out and the flat, grey landscape gives way to undulating green, she should feel relieved, but instead she feels a further swell of apprehension. She used to love this place. She associated it with innocence and fun. Now it feels tainted with sorrow and regret.

Her disappointment increases when she finds out Adam is not at the boatyard. She should have called him to say she was coming. A wordless teenager working his summer job fills the tank with fuel and helps her launch the boat. It is only when she is finally out on the water that she turns her back on the mainland, and, as always, she is captivated by the sight of Little Auger. Since she was little, she has known the locals called it Little Anger, that there are rumours and stories associated with that name. But Catrin refuses to call it that. Little Auger is a protected space, the place where her happiest memories were made. Not the place of folklore and scary stories, used as a tool to keep people away. When she gazed upon it, as she is doing now, from the perspective of a boat, she always thought it looked wild and exciting. An adventure waiting to happen. Her memories of the island are so closely linked with her mother, she cannot think about Little Auger without thinking about her. Although she died when Catrin was a baby, she has grown up with the same traditions her mother started: picnics on the shingle beach, walks along the headland in the evening to watch the lights of Eider blink on at sundown. The universe above her head every night as she sat with James around a fire and listened to her father tell ghost stories. Little Auger was the place her mother came alive again, the only place her father relaxed enough to talk about her freely. It was more than magical, better than beautiful. It was a liminal place where ordinary life paused and held its breath. She knows these memories of her mother are not her own. But the stories of her, told by her father and James, repeated over and over time, have become the only memories she has of her.

Now, as she approaches the wet, black rocks that protect the island, her memories are coloured by a darker lens. She cannot resist getting out her camera, even though she knows the movement of the boat won't help. She captures the lowering clouds massing above it, the inky sea that moves restlessly around it, and Little Auger breaking out of the water like the snout of an animal testing the air. As she approaches and slows the boat, the texture of the rocks becomes apparent. Some of them are covered in tiny barnacles, and they remind Catrin of seed pearls, stitched into the bodice of a dress. As she moves through a path carved into her memory, they rise in front of her, ancient and reptilian, their summits covered in white guano. Lower down, a sulphurous lichen stains them yellow.

As the rocks descend through the waterline, they are black, where the light begins to fade, and nothing grows. Catrin feels the swell of the waves underneath her, the strength of the current feeling the shape of the boat, moving it around as if deciding what to do with her. She knows she could be turfed out and on to the rocks should the island decide it. She does something she hasn't done before: she offers a small prayer for safe passage, as she angles the boat and moves it, gingerly, through the pattern of the rocks, exactly as her father taught her to do.

The narrow, convoluted passageway eventually opens into a wider cove, where there is a large flat black rock jutting out horizontally, making a natural jetty. Several rusted mooring rings are embedded into the side of the rock, making it easy to tether the boat. Catrin clambers out, feeling relieved she made it. She shoulders her backpack and picks up a bag of provisions she bought in a service station on the way. She only intends to stay a few nights. James can't do without the Land Rover for long. She walks across the oily black stones and they clack wetly under her feet, destabilising her, pulling her down. A narrow, sandy goat path that leads out of the cove opens out to a wider track, lined with twisted scrub. It looks like a tunnel from a fairy tale, and at the end of it, the house.

The Old House is whitewashed, in contrast to everything but the cloud-filled sky. The sight of it is an anchor in her uncertainty. She can feel the grounding force of it as she approaches, pushing the front door open, not needing a key. There has never been cause to lock the door. The house has a symmetry to it; the hallway bisects the ground floor. To the left is the kitchen door, to the right is a parlour that has been repurposed into a small library and map room. At the back, a set of stairs reaches up to the bedrooms, and in the apex of the roof on the landing, a triangular picture window has been added in, giving a view from the top of the stairs on to the path running up to the cliff.

It is dark inside the ground floor because the windows are small and smeared with salt water. The air smells undisturbed, briny, and cold. Catrin walks into the hallway, sand on her shoes, and is conscious of her footsteps rasping on the stone floor. The door to the little library is ajar, and she can see a weak shaft of sunlight illuminating a thick layer of dust on the table in there. She moves into the kitchen and takes stock of the room. The same stove her mother cooked on is positioned under the original chimney. At the end of the room is a wood burner, the only concession to comfort. Catrin remembers coming down in the mornings to warm herself in front of it, pressing her cold hands on to the cast iron, still hot with last night's embers. She walks to the table in the centre of the room, touches the scratched and scored surface. Cut from a single piece of Welsh oak, it has been in the house for more than a hundred years, too big to pass through the door.

The last time she saw this room, it was filled with people. Her father, Roz's parents, the police, and volunteers. The chairs are frozen, pushed back from the table as if the room is expecting their return, as if there is unfinished business to be done.

Catrin turns on the kitchen tap, and nothing comes out. She goes back into the hallway and pulls open the lid of the control box that is bolted to the wall. One by one, she flips all the little plastic switches on, and she begins to hear the refrigerator, the water pump, hum into life. The light in the hallway comes on, buzzing like an angry fly, and she quickly switches it off. The water supply rarely runs dry here, it rains so much, but the electricity operates on solar power and she's not sure how the generator works if it runs out. After a few minutes of running the tap to get the stale water out of the pipes, Catrin fills the kettle and clears out the wood-burning stove, laying it with fresh paper and sticks. She must make sure she can light a fire. Fire is the only source of heat here, and although it is a warm day, this is a house that always seems cold, just like Chapel Farm. There is still time to go back to the mainland if she needs anything, but the tide will turn, eventually, so she needs to check now. There is a large pile of logs and kindling to the side of the stove, but she can't find any matches. Cursing herself for forgetting to bring some with her, she begins to scour the shelves, opening every drawer and cupboard, knowing there must be some matches or a lighter somewhere.

Eventually, she opens a deep drawer in the bottom of the Welsh dresser standing in the back of the kitchen, near the wood burner. She uses the light on her phone to illuminate the interior of the drawer, and sees there are several boxes of matches, lighters and candles. She reaches for the matches, her phone still switched on, and there is something else, something familiar, tucked in the back. She pulls it out, a smooth black cylinder that slides into the palm of her hand with such familiarity it quickens her heartbeat. The weight of it tells her it is not empty. She peels off the lid and looks inside, shaking the film roll out on to her palm. This is the same roll of film she took that summer, finished off on the morning Hazel disappeared. Left here, on the kitchen table, in that casual way that teenagers strew their belongings around, and thrown in this drawer by an adult, no doubt, to clear space for the search party. How could she have forgotten this specific roll of film? The fallout of Hazel tipped everything upside down. Her art teacher didn't ask her for her holiday project when she returned to school, and she wasn't in her right mind to remember it. For twenty years this little roll of film has been sitting in this drawer, like an unexploded bomb. She has been led straight to it within ten minutes of landing here, as if she has been guided by invisible hands.

Catrin looks at her watch. The tide has not yet turned, there is still plenty of time to make the journey to Eider village. If she got this roll of film into a developer before it closed, she could see those images tonight, or in the morning. She could book herself into the Bed and Breakfast, sleep there instead and come back here tomorrow. Before she has thought everything through, her body is moving, making the decision for her, her arms gathering her rucksack, her hands sliding the film canister into her trouser pocket, her fingers flicking the switches on the control box in the hallway.

It is vanity, she knows this. Catrin can't wait to see what kind of an eye she took those pictures with twenty years ago. She knows she is a good photographer, but she wants to know how much of her skill was unschooled, how much of it has been learnt over the years. There is also something else. That hard part of her she has developed over the years, that journalistic instinct for a good picture, is going into overdrive. There are images of Hazel on that undeveloped film. And these images will be filled with such tension and pathos, the power of them calling to her is more than she can resist. These are the images of a holiday, before it went disastrously wrong. It doesn't matter what she thought she was recording when she took these pictures, Catrin knows there will be other, hidden perspectives, things she could not or did not see with youthful eyes, things that are coloured by what happened next.

Chapter Twelve

NINA

Nina arrives at the restaurant first and orders a bottle of sparkling water as she slides on to the leather banquette. It is not long before Verity appears, like an MC in a cabaret show, striding across the floor towards her.

Verity does not suit her name. Before Nina met her, she had imagined someone petite. Teeny tiny, with a high, squeaking voice. But Verity is the polar opposite and carries it well. For any woman who inhabits the world of TV and film, it is easy to be convinced you are not thin enough, tall enough, pretty enough, white enough. Verity is none of these things and she is the most attractive person Nina has ever met. The way she dresses – in deep, saturated colour or bold large-scale prints, an armful of jewellery that announces her presence as she walks – tells the world she gives not a fig about other people's opinions. Her laugh is too loud, the gap in between her front teeth is huge. And after the chemo ruined her hair, and she discovered she had a beautifully shaped head, she chose to keep it short and shaves it herself, with her husband's beard trimmer. Eyes turn towards her as she crosses the floor, her shoes, always high, striking the marble, her reconstructed breasts back to their magnificent pre-cancer perkiness. People stare at her, assuming she is famous, ignoring Nina, who is waiting patiently for the floor show to end.

'Hello, my lovely, I'm not late, am I?' Verity stretches her arms wide before she reaches the table. Nina steps out of the banquette and accepts her embrace. To be hugged by Verity is to experience all that is right with the world. It is a warm, soft experience that smells of musky, sexy perfume. Nina smiles at the contrast with her own mother, who thinks Verity is coarse.

'It's so good to see you,' breathes Nina, feeling blessed.

'Please tell me we're not drinking water for lunch, it's Friday. Let's have something much nicer, shall we?' says Verity, handing Nina the wine list. 'Choose something expensive but not extravagant. And not red. It gives me a headache.'

Nina chooses a bottle of Sancerre from a vineyard she is familiar with in the Loire Valley, while Verity orders lunch.

'Now tell me how you're getting on with *Rise*,' says Verity. 'You look good on that sofa, but I heard that Curtis is being his usual dickish self.'

Nina wonders who she has heard that from. This is the thing about Verity. You are lulled into thinking you are her favourite, but she represents other people who think they are her favourite too. Being wined and dined like this, it is a flattering experience, until you learn that she took someone else out to a better restaurant last week. Nina debriefs Verity, going over the conversation she had with Curtis and her resistance to opening up about herself on the show.

'He does so love a drama, that boy. How did he end the conversation?'

The words are still imprinted on to her memory. 'He said I should think about what I want, and then I should think about what he needs. Can he fire me for not spilling the beans about myself?'

'Of course he can't. But he can make up some bullshit and not renew the contract. You're still on probation there. It's within his rights. What do you want, Nina? He's got a point. If you don't want the same thing, it's not going to work. Curtis might lack subtlety but he's good at what he does, and he knows what audiences like. You should have a good think about where you want your career to go. It's going to be hard getting you acting jobs again when people get used to you in this kind of environment. But not impossible, especially if you pull out early.'

'There is something else. Your friend, Stella Cox?'

Verity sits back, frowning. 'Stella-the-podcaster Stella?' she asks. 'She isn't my friend. I thought she was yours.'

'I met her at your fortieth birthday party. She told me you were old friends.'

'That's exactly what she told me about you a couple of days ago! She called me, saying something about having her phone nicked and she had to cancel a lunch date with you, but she didn't have your number. So I . . .' Verity trails off, the truth dawning on her.

'So you gave my number to her.'

'Well yes, I . . . oh no.' The realisation makes Verity's eyes pop, and she pulls a grotesque, comical face of contrition. 'She was so genuine. What a talent. No wonder she's so successful. I wonder if she likes her agent?'

'Verity!'

'Sorry. What did she want with you, anyway?'

Nina has thought carefully about what to say about her past. Despite Verity's outgoing personality and taste for gossip, she is discreet when she needs to be. 'She's doing a podcast about the disappearance of a little girl.'

'Which little girl? Do I know her?'

'It happened twenty years ago on a small Welsh island.'

Verity screws up her face in concentration. 'Oh! I remember that. Didn't they suspect the father? Or some guy who was staying with them?'

'There was something about that in the press but no, they weren't suspects.'

'Right . . . and where do you get involved?'

Nina swallows a large, fortifying swig of wine. 'I was there. When she disappeared. I knew her. I knew the family. We were all on holiday together. I . . . I was only thirteen.'

Verity is silent for a few long seconds. She reaches out and encloses Nina's hand in hers. 'Dearest girl, how awful. I had no idea you lived with such tragedy.'

The tears are completely unexpected. They rise up inside Nina and spill over on to her cheeks. She is mortified and, for once, wishes they were in a cheaper restaurant where the napkins are paper. The white linen she has on her lap doesn't seem to soak them up. 'Oh my God, I'm so sorry,' she gulps.

'No need to be sorry. What a dreadful thing.' Verity reaches into her handbag and pulls out a large pack of scented tissues. 'Take them all,' she says generously.

Verity's kindness, and the comforting smell of lavender, sets Nina off again. 'I don't know what's wrong with me,' she sniffs, swallowing hard. But she does know. Verity is the first person who has ever shown her compassion for what she has gone through, because, apart from her mother, Verity is the first person she has told about Hazel. It is unfamiliar, it knocks her off balance.

'Tell me about Stella's podcast. You don't need to tell me about the little girl. I can see it's too upsetting for you.'

Nina tries to compose herself, hoping her nose hasn't turned red. 'She called me to say she'd found something. Some sort of evidence that might be important. I don't know if she's lying or not.'

'Why would you think she's lying?'

'Because nobody found anything at the time. And nothing has been found since. She wants me and the girls from the other families to go back so she can do some kind of interview on the island. Either she's lying or she's planning some kind of big reveal. Either way, it'll be horrible.'

'That just sent a shiver down my spine, I don't mind telling you,' Verity says in a low voice. 'I can see why you're upset by it. But maybe . . .'

The hesitation in her voice is enough for Nina to stop crying and raise her head. 'You think I should do it, don't you?'

Verity's face softens. 'Well, I think we should look at the facts. What about the other girls? Are they doing it?'

'I think so.'

'So the podcast will go ahead with or without you being there.'

'I guess.'

'If you did this, several things would happen. You'd get exposure through an award-winning journalist, that can't be a bad thing. Curtis would be happy – again, not a bad thing. And if you didn't want to carry on working with Curtis, you'd have another avenue open for work, if the podcast was successful. Maybe you could help present the podcast, for example. Do you like the idea of presenting?'

'Verity . . . I don't want to do it at all. This just feels like too much.'

'So let's look at the other end of it. If you didn't do it, what would happen?'

Nina doesn't want to think about that. She just feels wretched.

'I'm your agent, Nina. It's my job to be honest with you. Your divorce from Howard has hurt your career. Without a famous actor by your side, you're not the hot ticket you once were. On top of that, you're not getting any younger. I don't need to tell you how women fare in this business.'

'Let me down gently, why don't you . . .' says Nina miserably.

'The best generals go into battle knowing who and what their adversaries are. I'm a fucking amazing general, Nina. And I will go into battle with you, but you need to be up for it. I can't represent someone who is half-hearted about their career. I know it sounds harsh, but I don't need to tell you how many other women would sell their children to swap places with you. Curtis knows that as well as we do.'

'Is it that bad?' asks Nina.

'No, not yet.' Verity pats her hand. 'You have time. I hate to say it, but sneaky Stella is right. Your connection to this disappearance will make you interesting and desirable.'

'But I don't want . . .'

'If Stella has really found something, her narrative is going to play out if you are part of it or not. Are you still friends with the other people involved – the women she has been in touch with?'

'No, not any more,' says Nina quietly.

'Then you must think of the fallout that might be created in your absence. Especially if the people involved don't have your best interests at heart. I've done my share of damage limitation, and celebrities always come out better when they have a good relationship with the journalist who is writing their story. If you can control the narrative, you have power, Nina. And power is something you could do with, right now.'

Nina acknowledges her lack of power. She feels the wisdom of Verity's words, the thinly dressed-up threat that she will be dropped from the books if Nina doesn't try harder. And later that day, when she writes in her journal, Verity's words are still in her head.

Power is important, she writes. *But I was just a girl.*

She stops writing and pictures herself, a teenager on a small island, unable to leave, no allies to help her on the worst day of her life. She pictures herself and Roz sitting together in the evenings, scribbling in their journals before they went to sleep. She wonders if Roz still does it. If the habit she instilled in Nina still burns as brightly in her.

What little power I have, I need to use it to protect that girl, to rescue her from whatever Stella Cox is going to say.

Chapter Thirteen

ROZ

Roz gets off the train, crowded with Friday bank holiday travellers, and walks through the village of Eider towards the coast. Eider is prettier than she remembers, the doors and window frames of the cottages picked out in pastel shades against whitewashed render. The smaller streets are still cobbled and the houses lean close together, convivial and cosy. When Roz sees the sign for the boatyard, she does not anticipate the little jump her heart makes. She is nervous. The sixteen-year-old boy she remembers is now a thirty-six-year-old man.

The boatyard has high stone walls and tall chain-link gates, which are flung open, exposing the interior. Roz walks towards a line of boats that are raised on to wheeled trailers, some of them covered in tarpaulin. Beyond them, the narrow slipway runs into the sea, and piles of lobster pots, coils of rope and plastic crates line up like a haphazard jumble sale. Roz looks around and sees a tall three-sided corrugated iron building, the end nearest to her open to the elements. She can see a boat inside it, hoisted up high to expose the hull. Rock music plays out from the interior, and Roz walks towards it, assuming the office must be further in. She has yet to enter the building when a voice behind her shouts her name. She spins around, and a man-version of Adam-the-boy walks towards her, his slow, easy stride strangely familiar to her, even after all these years. He is wearing loose-fitting combat shorts that fall off his hips, steel-toe-capped boots, and an orange polo shirt with *AA Boatyard* embroidered on the pocket. His sandy hair is pushed out of his eyes by a baseball cap, the peak darkened with oil. He takes off the hat to get a better look at her, pushes his hair back with the other hand. His face is as tanned as his arms and legs. When he smiles, his teeth are a bright, faultless white.

He stops in front of her and says, 'I'd give you a hug, but I'm covered in oil and that's a clean white T-shirt you have on there.'

She is relieved he has told her what is not going to happen. She smiles at him, clutching on to her backpack, feeling like an idiot, and a small laugh escapes her. 'You look the same, but with stubble,' she says. 'So weird.'

'You look the same, too. No stubble though. How was the journey?'

'OK. The train was late. But I managed to get my connection.'

He looks at her, really looks at her in a way she hasn't been looked at of late. 'How have you been, Roz?' he asks gently.

She shrugs, shakes her head, swallows down the ache in her throat. 'That's a hard question to answer.'

He nods. 'I get that, yeah. Look, I feel partly responsible for all of this. If I hadn't told Stella, she might not have made it on to the island.'

'Maybe it's a good thing,' Roz says, looking away. 'I don't know. I guess that's why I've come. Because I don't know what else to do. I can't sit around at home any more, that's for sure.' She thinks about the empty house, the silence from Willow, the driving need to get away from an environment so saturated by the memory of their argument. 'Coming here seemed like the least-worst thing to do,' she says.

Adam looks at his watch. 'It's getting a bit late to catch the tide. But if you really wanted to, we could go right now. Or you can stay here for the night and go tomorrow.'

'No, I don't want to do that. Let's go now.'

'OK. You need to give me a minute. Wait by the dock, over there. I'll just grab a few things and get the lads to finish up here.'

Roz makes her way across the boatyard and finds herself on the dock, where she has a grandstand view of Little Auger. In her memory, Little Auger is a faraway country, but here, she is confronted by the reality of it – a dark mound, rising out of the sea like the hump of a much larger creature sleeping under the waves.

Roz turns away, waiting for Adam to come. She had expected to feel awkward in front of him. People who know about her sister make her feel like this, sometimes, as if she needs to perform a tragic role. Occasionally, she sees a flicker of disappointment when she doesn't live up to it. She wonders if the easiness comes from the fact that Adam has lived through it too. Roz looks at the ropes coiled around the dock, and she sees that some of them have hag stones tied to them with twine. She crouches down to touch one, its surface worn to a bone-like smoothness, and a memory swims up of that holiday and Adam, appearing like a genie on Little Auger, emerging from behind the rocks or walking through the long grasses, his arms laden with milk and bread, the morning newspapers for the grown-ups. And sometimes, a gift for Hazel.

The first day, he brought her a stone with a hole in it. 'It's a Glain Neidr,' he explained, handing it to her. Hazel and Roz didn't speak Welsh. They both looked at him, not understanding. 'The English have many names for it: hag stone, serpent's egg, witch stone.'

'A witch stone?' Roz asked, thinking about the marks in the house.

'Yeah. They're supposed to protect against witches. And nightmares, if you tie one above your bed. There's some fishermen who believe they give a good haul.'

Hazel had taken the stone from him, holding it up to the sky so she could see through it. She laughed in delight when a gull flew across her view.

'I'll bring you a length of twine tomorrow so you can put it above your bed. Or you could tie it around your neck, if you like?'

He looked at Roz as he said this. Hazel was absorbed in the stone. It was white in colour but where the hole was made, it exposed a black interior. 'She'd like that,' said Roz, smiling at him. 'Thanks.'

The next day, he came with twine and tied the stone for Hazel. 'Lift up your hair,' he said, standing behind her, and he lowered the stone slowly over her head, like a queen at coronation. Then a strange look came over his face. Roz saw it, because she was watching him. Hazel was oblivious. 'What's that?' he asked, touching the back of Hazel's neck with his thumb.

'It's a birthmark,' said Roz.

'It looks . . .' Adam didn't finish the sentence. Roz drew near him and looked at Hazel's neck. The similarity between the crescent-shaped mark on her sister's skin and the marks scored into the stone of the house was obvious. Roz hadn't realised until now. 'Maybe you're the chosen one,' he laughed. 'Marked by the fairies as one of their own.'

Hazel was entranced with this explanation, and with the stone. 'Maybe I need a fairy name?' she asked him.

'I think Hazel is just fine,' he smiled. 'It's a very auspicious name.'

Hazel frowned, not understanding the word.

'Hazel wood is the wood of wisdom,' said Adam. 'It's used for finding water,' he said, 'and it's used for witches' wands, or so they say.'

'How does it find water?' asked Roz, intrigued.

'Have you never used divining rods? To find water underground?'

Both girls shook their heads.

Adam rolled his eyes in mock disbelief. 'It's not just the wood that's clever. The hazelnut is full of knowledge. There's a folk tale about a pool with nine hazel trees growing around it. When the nuts dropped into the water, the salmon ate the nuts and took all the wisdom. Until the biggest salmon was fished out and cooked for someone's supper. A druid, actually, who wanted the wisdom for himself, you see.'

'Did it work?' asked Hazel.

'Sort of. The kitchen boy that cooked the fish licked his thumb when he touched the salmon. So he ended up the clever one. Not his master.'

It was often like this with Adam. A chance remark would unravel into a story. When he left, his presence lingered in Roz's mind, and she replayed these stories in her head. Both visits to the island, he had found her and Hazel, alone. Both times, he had looked at her more than her sister. On the third day, when she watched him leave after giving Hazel a piece of smooth green sea glass, Roz wondered if the gifts were a way of talking to her. If he had given her the hag stone, it would have seemed odd. But to bring these things to her little sister, to make Hazel gasp with delight, it felt natural, easy. To please Hazel was to please her. Perhaps, she wondered, that was his real intention.

Adam's voice pulls her into the present. 'Oi, you'll bring me bad luck if you take that.' He is approaching with a rucksack. He has put a waterproof jacket on over his shirt and wears a pair of sunglasses on top of his head instead of the baseball cap.

'I remember you finding one of these for Hazel,' says Roz.

'I probably shouldn't have given it to her,' Adam says. 'The magic only works for the person who finds it. They say that the stones find you, not the other way round.'

'Why are they supposed to be so lucky?' Roz asks.

Adam puts the rucksack down and runs his hand through his hair. 'Well, the thinking goes that magic can't work on moving water, and because the hole is made by the sea it forms a kind of lasting protection. That's why fishermen tie them to their ropes. Bad luck is too big to pass through the hole, it gets stuck.'

'I want to find one. Can I? Before we go?'

'Sure, take a look on the shore here. I need to do a couple more things before we go. But we have to leave in the next ten minutes to catch the tide.'

Roz leaves her bag behind and jumps from the jetty on to the pebbles. It isn't easy. She spends a couple of minutes combing the shore, until she realises that the sea sorts through the objects that pass through it, and it deposits them, in some kind of order, on to the land. The hag stones tied to the ropes are the size of chestnuts, so she finds the line of small- and medium-sized stones. And then it is just as Adam described – a stone presents itself to her, white on the outside, a black cylinder where the hole passes through from one side to the other. She looks at it for a minute, the world she can see through the hole, feels the weight of it in her palm, and considers this coming together of opposites that she can see in her hand. The air and the earth, the dark and the light, a presence and absence, all bound up in a single object. Roz squeezes the stone. She hopes it will bring her luck. She hopes it will help her get the answers to questions she hasn't had the courage to face.

Chapter Fourteen

Roz

'What have you found there?' asks a voice. Roz spins around and there is a pensioner, walking towards her on the shore, carrying a bin bag full of rubbish, a plastic grabber in his hand. He is bent and wrinkled but his body moves quickly, like a much younger man.

Roz shows him the hag stone.

'That's a good one,' he says, nodding. 'They bring luck, you know. Some people say you will always return to the place you found your Glain Neidr.'

'Adam told me, yes,' she says, gesturing to the jetty, where Adam is packing the boat.

'Visiting, are you? You're not local.'

'I'm going to the island, over there.' Roz points to Little Auger, unable to bring herself to say its name.

As Roz tells him this, Adam calls her name from the jetty. 'Two more minutes, Roz, then we have to go,' he shouts.

The man looks at her properly, and then over to Adam, a spark of understanding in his eyes. 'You're Hazel's sister,' the man declares. 'I should have recognised you.'

'Do we know each other?' asks Roz, surprised.

'I was part of the search party,' he says, his voice full of sorrow. 'A terrible business. We all lost Hazel, that day. We all grieved. The village hasn't forgotten, you know. I'm surprised you're going back to Little Anger though.'

Little Anger. Roz is reminded of the other name the island sometimes goes by. The papers were full of it when Hazel disappeared, but her parents wouldn't let her read the stories. They kept the pages, though, labelling them carefully and filing them away like treasured family photographs.

'Why do you call the island that name?' she asks.

The man looks at her, surprised. 'Everybody calls it that. The people of Eider, I mean. The villagers.' Then he looks away, considers what he has said. 'Maybe not in front of tourists, though.'

'Why?' asks Roz.

'It's not a nice story. I probably shouldn't tell you if you're about to spend the night there. Especially because of what happened to Hazel.'

'Well, you can't say that and then leave me here, hanging,' remarks Roz, in what she hopes is a light-hearted voice. 'Maybe I should know *because* of what happened to Hazel?'

The man puts down his bag of rubbish and leans his weight on the grabber. He glances over to the island and then back at Roz. 'Little Auger was originally named after the auger shell. See how it rises up and then tapers into the sea, like a shell lying on its side? But the island has always been known as Little Anger around here ever since I can remember. It's possible the letter *u* was written upside down, once. A mistake that never got corrected.' He shrugs and kicks a stone. 'But the other explanation is far more juicy, so most people prefer to stick with the folklore. It's a gruesome story, are you sure you want to hear it?'

'Yes,' says Roz, unable to contain her curiosity. 'Tell me.'

He looks up above him, to the wheeling gulls, as if drawing his knowledge from the sky. 'There were two families – clans, I suppose you would call them, the Sallows and the Thorps. This was hundreds of years ago, mind. They lived in or around Eider and had a long-standing dislike of one another. The Thorps seemed to be the most well regarded, or perhaps they were more feared, because when they banished the Sallows to live on Little Anger, there is no evidence the rest of the village objected. Maybe the Sallows were troublesome, and it was a blessing when they were hounded off the mainland. Maybe the rest of the villagers were too scared to intervene. But something happened between those two families, and as a result, each and every Sallow was sent across the water to Little Anger and told never to return.'

'How did they survive over there?' asks Roz.

'Little Anger has an aquifer in the centre of the island. The rock, you see, it holds fresh water, but not enough to sustain livestock too. Island life was hard, because of that. Every now and again, the Sallows sent a party over to the mainland to raid the Thorps' livestock. There's only so many fish a man wants to eat.' He gives Roz a grin. 'Anyway, one night they sent over several men to take some sheep from the Thorps' flock, and they killed one of the Thorp boys – on purpose, or an accident, we will never know. So the Thorps took their revenge.'

'How?' asks Roz.

'Well, the Thorps were clever. They waited. They bided their time. Until one night, when there wasn't a moon, they sailed over to the island and slaughtered every man, woman and child they could find.'

Roz shudders. 'And that's why the island is called Little Anger?'

'No.' The man shakes his head. 'That was just the beginning.'

'The beginning of what?'

102

'The thinking goes . . . well, if you imagine what it must have been like, that night, the soil on the island took on a lot of blood. When the killing was over, there was no family to gather their kin. The bodies were left where they lay, as a warning, and nobody touched the place. Nobody wanted to. There's an old folk song about the birds coming for miles, a great black swooping cloud over the centre of the island. What the birds didn't eat, well, that went back into the land eventually.' The man scratches his chin thoughtfully. 'When that much blood seeps into the earth it gets a taste for it, you see. It can't stop itself.'

'What do you mean by that?' asks Roz, a feeling of revulsion rippling over her.

'It was believed that Little Anger got a liking for the dead. There were shipwrecks, always have been. The rocks around there are treacherous. Many survivors thought they could swim to Little Anger, for safety. But nobody can swim there and stay alive. Little Anger makes sure of that. My grandmother used to say it's no place for the living. It's an island that gathers souls. I've lived in Eider all my life. There's been death associated with that place for as long as I can remember.'

The optimism of the day has suddenly vanished, and Roz is left with an uneasy feeling.

'That's not to say you could have done anything to prevent Hazel's death,' the man says kindly. 'What will happen, will happen. The land will take back what it nurtures, in time. And sometimes, it takes it back sooner than we'd like.' He sighs heavily. 'It's always a terrible thing, though, for the people left behind. But those souls are free now. My grandmother swore you could see them at sunset, running wild over the cliffs on Little Anger.'

Roz pictures the cold-eyed fairy folk that Catrin's father had told them about, and wonders if that story is linked to this one somehow.

103

Adam calls to her, 'It's now or never, Roz.'

'I'd better go,' she says, relieved to have an excuse to leave.

The man gives her a nod and gathers up his rubbish bag, waving the grabber side to side over the shingle like a metal detector. Roz makes her way back to the jetty.

'What was old Dylan saying?' asks Adam, when she returns.

Roz watches Dylan grabbing a stray flip-flop and putting it deftly into his rubbish bag. 'He just told me the history of the name, Little Anger. I knew there was some kind of folklore attached to the island, but I had no idea it was so bloody.'

Adam looks annoyed. 'Trust him to spill the beans just as you were about to stay there. I could slaughter him myself.'

'Adam . . .'

'Sorry.'

'Why didn't you tell me?'

'And why would I have done that? I made a big effort not to talk to you about stuff like that, back then. We were all under strict orders not to mention it. We thought it would upset your family. So we decided not to say anything.'

'Yeah, no. You're right.' Roz looks out, over the sea, to the island in front of her.

'Roz, if you want my opinion, what happened to you, to Hazel, it was a terrible thing. It doesn't mean the island is a bad place. You don't believe it, do you?'

'No, I guess not,' she begins.

'Don't let other people's stories colour your time there. Little Anger is a special place. A beautiful place.'

'A cursed place, if you listen to Dylan,' Roz says, trying to make a joke of it.

'Then don't,' says Adam firmly, throwing her backpack into the boat.

Chapter Fifteen

ROZ

Before Adam leaves Roz on Little Auger, he goes through their arrangement.

'I'll pick you up here, at exactly the same time tomorrow afternoon. Wait for me if I'm late. If there's an emergency, there are flares in the house. You'll find them in the little room with all the books in, in a metal box. Let them off on the eastern cliff, facing the village, if you can. Anybody will come out if they see that. No matter what time.'

Adam assures her the house will be open, tells her how to switch on the electricity and, as a final flourish, presents her with a large bottle of water, a lighter and a pack of sausage rolls.

'I have food and water in my backpack,' she protests. 'I'm not staying long.'

'Doesn't hurt to have a back-up sausage roll,' he replies with mock solemnity. 'And the water in the tank, there. It's rainwater. I'd boil it first before you drink it.'

She stands in the cove and watches him manoeuvre the boat back through the rocks and out of sight. Suddenly, she feels very alone, and the enormity of where she is begins to sink in. She turns towards the house, but when she gets near it, the memory of waiting there all day, in vain, for Hazel to come back makes her feel claustrophobic, so she opts to walk the island: the perimeter of it, first. She leaves the large water bottle on the doorstep and looks around her, trying to figure out which way to go.

She instinctively avoids going straight to the stone cairn and walks the other way round, knowing she will eventually come to it last. The cliff path around the island is narrow and when it strays too far towards the sea, newer, alternative paths further inland have been carved out over the years by Catrin's family. The terrain, though rocky, is covered in vegetation, and there are sweeping areas of wiry grassland dotted with little yellow flowers that grow close to the ground, low enough to escape the relentless wind. She remembers an afternoon making chains with these flowers. It had been an unsatisfying task, because the stalks were not as pliable as the traditional daisy, but Hazel had been remarkably adept. Roz had put it down to her having smaller fingers, and they had argued about it good-naturedly in the sunshine. Roz waits for the pain that usually follows a memory like this, and it comes, but it is tempered by the warm air and blue sky above her head.

Roz passes clumps of gorse, all of it in flower. She recalls the smell – vanilla, and coconut – and it makes her heart race to remember that morning, climbing up to watch the sunrise with Catrin. She stops for a drink from her water bottle and takes out one of Adam's sausage rolls, sitting on the grass and looking out to sea. All around her, she hears the constant, restless murmur of it, and when she looks beyond the cliff, she sees rings of white foam circling every rock that breaks the surface of the water. It is a cruel thing, she thinks, that Hazel's body has never been found.

Roz remembers overhearing a policewoman talking with Arvis, Adam's father, about it. They were in the library, bent over a map of the area. Everyone else was outside, shouting Hazel's name. Roz had stopped in the hallway when she heard them talking. Any piece of information was golden to her. None of the grown-ups would tell her anything, so she had resorted to eavesdropping instead.

'Where could we expect to find her if she drifts?' the policewoman asked Arvis.

Roz could hear the rustle of the map, the soft stabbing bounce of Arvis's finger marking a spot. 'Here,' he said. 'I would look here first, but she'll take time to get there. She might not show up for a day or two. She might not be caught in a current, mind,' he finished thoughtfully.

'What do you mean?'

'If she went in this direction, went over the cliff *here* and the tide was further out, she may have found herself *here*.' Again, Roz could hear that dull stabbing sound of skin on paper.

'Then what, Arvis?' the policewoman asked.

Arvis sighed. 'Then she'll be trapped. The rocks . . . It's like being caught in the jaws of something. Her body won't move. If that's the case, we won't be able to get to her. You can't get a boat anywhere near there.'

'Perhaps we could fly a chopper over there.' There was a hesitation. 'We need to justify the expense, though. The thing is, Arvis . . .' Here, the policewoman paused, unwilling to say the words. 'If she fell, would there be any chance she'd survive it? Is this search and rescue or . . . or are we talking retrieval?'

Arvis's voice dropped, but Roz could still hear what he said next. 'If she fell here, you're looking for a body. You won't need the chopper, either, to know where she is. You just need to watch the birds.'

'Birds?' The policewoman sounded as confused as Roz felt.

'The gulls. Large flocks, fighting with one another,' he said quietly. 'Then you'll know she's down there.'

These snatched conversations, exchanged looks, and the silence when she came into a room, these are the things Roz remembers. Her mind is so lost in the past as she wanders the path, she isn't prepared for the shape of the stone cairn to resolve itself so swiftly as she nears the ridge of the easterly cliffs. She stops, unable to go any further for a moment, and she walks slowly, as if approaching an unpredictable animal, never taking her eyes off the tower of stones, every one of them bearing the weight of the dead.

Before she left home, Roz wondered what she could do to mark Hazel's life. She had wanted to plant a hazel tree here, as she has done in her own garden, but knew it would be too stony to dig a decent hole, too exposed. So she has done the next best thing. She brings out a hazelnut from her trouser pocket, and pushes it into the earth at the foot of the cairn. It is a nut from her own tree, slightly under-ripe, but it feels symbolic and satisfying, leaving a little piece of her own garden here for Hazel.

When she has finished, Roz mumbles some words she has prepared. It doesn't feel silly, it feels meaningful, and as she does this, she feels – or does she imagine it? – a shift in the atmosphere. The wind seems to drop, the sigh of it breathing through the grasses suddenly stills. Even the gulls stop shrieking and all she can hear is the rhythm of the waves, like a muffled heartbeat. Roz waits for something else to happen, but nothing does, and she slowly makes her way down the hill.

When she is halfway down, she is overcome by the feeling she is not alone. But it isn't a bad feeling, like the one she felt the day Hazel disappeared; it is a feeling infused with warmth and her mind fills with the memory of her sister, everything that was good about her. It is the first time she has felt close to Hazel, that whatever part of her has been left behind is here with her on the cliff path, right now. Roz looks around her, taking in the landscape. It is not a pretty place, but there is something darkly compelling about it.

Roz doesn't know if it's got something to do with the marks in the house, the hag stones on the beach, or the stories that surround this place. *Something is here*, she thinks to herself, *something powerful, and I need to find out what it is.*

'Hazel?' she calls on impulse. 'Are you there?'

The wind stirs the grasses once more, as if by answer.

'Hazel?' Roz pleads. 'Let me know you can hear me.'

Once more, the wind picks up, and as Roz scans the landscape, alert as any wild animal, she sees a movement behind a wall of scrub. Heart beating violently, she moves slowly towards the tangle of vegetation, which is too dense to get past. There is a gap further down, and she passes through it, realising she is now on the old cliff path, which has been screened off by hedging, presumably to encourage walkers to use the new one. She remembers being told not to use the original path, but it was easy to stray on to it. Even now, twenty years later, there is still a clear, narrow strip between the scrub where nothing grows. The edge of the cliff is lined by low-growing gorse, the roots of which serve to stop the earth from crumbling and falling into the sea. Roz traces her steps back towards the movement she thought she saw. When she draws level, she tries talking to Hazel again, her voice growing stronger the more she hears it. The feeling that something is here, with her, grows inside her. The fact she is alone in a place that has brought Hazel closer to her in a single afternoon gives her confidence in her own voice.

'Hazel. I'm here. Are you here too? Give me a sign. Anything.'

A gust of wind rattles the gorse, and their branches nod to one another as if they understand. And then among the yellow is a flash of red. A slim ribbon tied to a branch, its long ends flapping in the breeze like an exotic insect. Roz touches the ribbon, wonders who has put it here. It doesn't look weathered and old, and there are creases in it that tell her it has been used to tie something else. For a wild moment, she wonders if this is a sign from Hazel. But Hazel never wore her hair up, it was always loose. She looks around to see if there is anything else, any more bits of ribbon, but there are none. Frustrated at her own lack of understanding, and mindful the sun is beginning to set, Roz decides it is time to turn back. She looks for a break in the scrub and crosses back on to the new cliff path, following the same steps down to the house she took the morning Hazel disappeared. As she approaches the house, she notices the first of the witches' marks carved into the stone above the front door. She has, in idle moments over the years, googled *witches' marks*.

> Apotropaic marks were often carved into points of entry such as doorways, windows and fireplaces, to prevent evil spirits from entering. The daisy wheel, or hexafoil, comprises a continuous, endless line, designed to confuse and trap evil spirits.

She has found many examples like the ones in The Old House, marks that look as if someone has taken a glass, turned it upside down and made several urgent impressions with the rim. She remembers thinking these were hoof marks as a child, and she can see why as she looks at them now, above the doorway of the house.

The Old House is well over two hundred years old. Roz wonders who built it and what made them stay in a place where so many souls had perished before them. Were they desperate, or just foolhardy? For the first time, the marks on the doorway provide Roz with some comfort. She pushes the door open and, as Adam has instructed, she opens the mains consumer unit and flicks down all the little switches. A distant hum in the kitchen tells her the electricity is working, and she busies herself lighting a fire before the light goes out of the evening sky and it begins to get cold.

The kitchen is dominated by a large range cooker, and at the end of the room is a wood-burning stove. The stove looks clean, and there is kindling and paper stacked to one side. When Roz opens the glass door to the burner, she sees it is already laid with dry paper and sticks, as if somebody was just about to light it, and it seems odd, this detail, until she supposes it is good practice, or tradition, to have a fire laid out, ready to be lit. She sits back on her haunches and looks at the stack of paper next to the stove. She cannot help herself, she flicks through the pile of newsprint until she sees the dates rewind to twenty years ago. Towards the bottom of the pile, there is a newspaper dated one week before Hazel disappeared. She puts it on the kitchen table, knowing she will torture herself later by reading what was happening in the world before it all came crashing down. Then she lights the stove, fills the kettle that sits on the top, and waits for everything to warm up.

It is only when she has pulled out a bowl of pasta salad she prepared last night at home that she realises she hasn't thought about Willow all day. The notion shocks her. Willow occupies most of her daily thoughts, but since she arrived at the boatyard she has crossed some kind of line into her pre-Willow past, a place where there are no reminders of her, a world in which Willow never existed. She pulls out her mobile phone, even though Adam has warned her she might not have reception, and sure enough the call to Simon doesn't go through. Roz frowns and switches her phone off to save battery. Not to think about Willow for a whole day, it is unprecedented. Her mind is filled with Hazel instead.

Can she not think of one child without forgetting the other? She can't seem to hold them both in her head at the same time. Perhaps this place has cast a spell on her, and she can only think about the past here. She looks down at the kitchen table where her

111

mother stacked toast in a slim silver rack, preparing breakfast for a waking house. She sits down in the same chair her father occupied when she came back, alone, and they asked her where Hazel was. It is as if time has been suspended here, that this is a place where breath is held, where a stillness exists, a lull in motion. She looks out of the door and sees the stairs, recalling her younger self, sitting on the top step, wondering what she should do while she listened to her mother wail.

Losing someone in the way they lost Hazel happens by degrees. It is like being lowered into water, very slowly. At first, Hazel was simply not there. Then she was missing. Then she was in danger. Then she was dead. Before they knew it, the whole family was submerged, the realisation closing over their heads, until nobody could breathe any more.

Roz wonders if the stories are true, if Little Anger gathers souls and Hazel's is here, running wild in the cliffs. She recalls the feeling she was not alone on the headland, the answering sigh of the grasses when she called for her sister. From a very young age, they both made fairy houses at the bottom of the garden with cut grass and twigs. They both believed in a world that was not their own, a world that existed deep underground or high in the trees. A world that sometimes overlapped and stumbled into theirs. A nagging thought she had as a child steps out of the shadows of her memory.

What if there is something, on the island, that took Hazel from this world into another, and she's still here?

Superstition, ritual, and lore. These are things that have lasted millennia. These are the stories that have survived generations. The man on the beach, telling her about Little Anger. The look on Adam's face when he saw Hazel's birthmark.

Stories survive for a reason, Roz thinks to herself. *Who's to say they aren't true?*

She is so absorbed in her own thoughts, she doesn't notice the sun go down. The kitchen dances in the firelight, the shadows creep across the floor. She has a sudden urge to draw, something she has not experienced for a long time. She pulls a little sketch pad and pencil out of her bag. As she begins to make sketches of Hazel, her feet nudge the bag of groceries that Catrin left under the table, but Roz is too immersed in a different world to notice.

Chapter Sixteen

CATRIN

Catrin knows there is a little place to moor up near to the shops in Eider, so instead of heading back to the boatyard, she points the boat towards the village. She runs to the chemist, relieved that they close late on a Friday, and begs the manager to develop the film, printing on the largest paper he has in stock. He shakes his head, they don't have that facility, the village is too small. She will have to go to the nearest big town, a forty-five-minute drive from here, to get a one-hour service.

Catrin sprints down the road, picks up the Land Rover and drives as fast as she dares, the film canister burning a hole in her pocket. Her phone tells her a big retail park on the outskirts of the town is the best place, and she pulls the car in and runs to the counter. While she is waiting, she marks time by eating a terrible meal in a plastic restaurant, noting the sun's progress, knowing she has missed her chance to go back to Little Auger tonight. She calls the bed and breakfast in Eider to beg them for a room. Exactly one hour later, she returns to the counter.

'They're just coming out of the machine,' the shop assistant tells her. 'Won't be a minute.' He disappears into the back and Catrin paces the floor near to the till.

'Can I have the negatives too?' she calls out, knowing she will want to print her own copies at some point.

'We always give the negatives back,' the shop assistant says, emerging once more, a flat parcel in his hand. Her photographs. She can see a clear plastic window showing the top print. It is all she can do to restrain herself from ripping the parcel from his hands so she can see what it is that she found so interesting she had to capture it twenty years ago, aged thirteen. But she holds it together, thanks him for working so quickly, and pays him what she owes. When she shuts the door behind her, she looks up and down the street of the retail park, engulfed by a familiar moment of hesitation.

Now she has what she wants, there is a small part of her that begins to doubt. This is a familiar tussle, it happens always when she views a collection of her photographs for the first time. She knows she can't go back and retake whatever it is that this parcel holds, she can only immerse herself in that singular moment in history. She will never capture that moment again, it is gone forever, miraculously preserved for eternity – if she chooses to keep it. Catrin is always critical of her work, she always sees something she could have done better. She doesn't want to be too hard on her previous self, but she also knows she will look at these images and hold them up to the same level of judgement she uses on her present-day self. She decides to delay, to drive back to Eider, settle herself in the Bed and Breakfast so she can look at the photos undisturbed.

The parcel seems to grow in her hands as she ascends the stairs to her room at the very top of the guest house. When she has unlocked the door, she shakes off her jacket, removes the pillows and duvet from the double bed and smooths the sheet underneath so it is as flat as possible. Fighting the urge to devour every photograph as quickly as possible, she instead takes out one piece of paper at a time, giving herself over completely to the image before she places it down, carefully, on the bed. The first few images are unremarkable; she lines them up in a row. Some shots of Little Auger taken from the boatyard while they waited for Adam and Arvis to load up the boat that would take them all over. Next, there is a nice shot of The Old House. She has crouched down into the grass and the perspective makes the house loom above the camera lens. Catrin feels a sense of pride in her thirteen-year-old self, that she took that shot, instinctively, and it paid off.

The next photograph is of Roz, Hazel and Nina, sitting on the rocks in a cove. Catrin spends a lot of time looking at this shot, trying not to weigh the image down with everything that followed. Nina looks self-conscious. Her curly hair is blowing in the wind, obscuring some of her face. Her smile isn't as wide as it could be and her knees are drawn together, tucked under her chin, her arms wrapped around her legs. It is then that Catrin remembers Nina's parents were in the process of splitting up at that time, something Nina did not mention all week. Roz and Hazel are sitting close together. They both have beaming smiles, pleased to be on holiday, happy to be together. Catrin feels a dull pain in her chest as she lays the image down next to the others on the bed, and this increases when there are more images of her friends, documenting their holiday before it suddenly ended. Some of them are lovely portraits, taken when Catrin was experimenting with different lenses or light exposure. But the images are all suffused in pathos, simply because of what came next.

The next few photographs are the beginning of her sunrise project. They are all fairly similar, some nice shots of the changing light, but nothing terribly original. Then she comes to the sequence taken on the morning of Hazel's disappearance. There is a shot of the path in front of them, emerging through the half-light, winding up to the cliff. It is atmospheric. She has, by accident or design, got the exposure just right for the low-light conditions. Catrin must have turned around at that point to look behind her because there is a nice candid shot of Roz climbing the path a little way down, grinning up to the lens, her hair unbrushed, a hoodie over her pyjamas, completely unstaged. At the top of the cliff there is a shot of the cairn, some views to Eider, but, again, nothing original about the sunrise she had so badly wanted to capture. Catrin puts the photographs carefully on the bed, lining them all up so they display in a neat grid. The packet is now thin, there are only a few photographs left. She takes out the next image, and sees it is when she decided to climb down to the shoreline. Here, she has employed that same perspective she used at The Old House, taking shots underneath the cliff, which looms above her. There is a sense of power and dominance that she approves of, the early morning light illuminating the different textures and qualities in an eerie pink glow. She can see the rock strata, the deep shades in layers made over time, contrasted by a bright line of yellow gorse running at the top. And above that, a coral sky.

Catrin looks at the image for a long time. She was lucky with the light. It looks as if she has taken the photograph with a modern digital filter. Because the rocks are damp, they reflect the warmth of the new sun, and it gives them a metallic quality. She pulls out one of the few remaining photographs and it is a similar image. Her eyes travel up from the base of the cliff, dark and wet, to the top, where the line of gorse is in bloom.

Then she sees it. Two standing figures, silhouetted against the sky. They stand behind a line of gorse, visible from head to midriff. Catrin brings the paper close to her eyes, but no matter how hard she tries, she cannot make out who they are. She reaches into the packet and pulls out another image. In this one, the figures have moved, and there is a gap in the gorse, so one of them can be seen almost head to toe. Catrin looks at it for a very long time. She empties out the packet and looks at the remaining photographs, greedy for more information, but now she has moved to a different spot, and these are a series of views over the sea.

Catrin cannot believe she didn't notice the figures on the cliff when she took this picture. She must have been preoccupied with another aspect of the shot. She cannot take her eyes away from them. Who could they be? Catrin's mind turns to Stella, who has been travelling back and forth to the island. If that's the case, it could be anyone. But realistically, it is more likely, at that hour, to be someone she knew. Her memory reaches back down the cliff path to the adults in the house. They were all up when Roz returned. Any of them could have been out that morning, but Catrin knows they all told the police they were not.

Catrin is overcome by a need to talk to someone about this. She cannot work out if she is seeing something easily explained, or something sinister. Either way, it feels too big to keep to herself. She thinks about calling James, but she hesitates. It's not him she wants to talk to, really. He wasn't even there. And her father . . . the doubt she thought had gone resurfaces once more. Could this be him? With somebody else? The only other people who would possibly understand are Roz and Nina.

Roz always maintained she was alone after Catrin left her, and that when she returned to the house, Nina was still asleep. As far as Catrin knows, Roz stayed by the cairn for a while before returning to the house. But how long was she up there for? And who else was there?

Chapter Seventeen

NINA

Nina is woken up by her phone ringing. It is only ten o'clock at night, but she has had a long week and lunch with Verity has given her a hangover. She groans, annoyed with herself for forgetting to turn it off. She gropes blindly for it on the bedside table, feeling like a snail being wrenched from its shell. At least it's Saturday tomorrow, and then the bank holiday. She has a long weekend to relax.

'Hello?' she answers, still half asleep.

'Nina? Is that you?'

'Who is this?' Nina asks, sitting up in bed. There is something about the voice, the Welsh accent.

'Catrin. It's Catrin.'

'Catrin?' Despite writing about it in the safety of her journal, Nina is not ready to confront the past. Not by a long shot. 'How did you get my number?'

'Stella Cox gave it to me.'

Nina is too confused to feel angry with Stella. She just feels numb. Her tongue is slow and thick in her mouth.

'It's been a long time,' Catrin begins. She sounds as if they spoke last year. Not two decades ago.

Don't you think this is weird? Nina wants to say. *Are you as freaked out as I am?* But instead she replies 'Yes,' in a strangled voice, feeling exposed in her pyjamas, pulling the rumpled duvet around her to protect herself.

'How have you been?'

The question seems ridiculous. How do you fill in the last twenty years in a single sentence? 'I'm fine,' Nina replies dumbly. 'How about you?'

Catrin takes a big breath and blows it out across the miles, into Nina's ear. 'I don't know, really. It's weird, being back in Wales. Dad's driving me mad. It's great to see James. And I'm reminded of Mum, even now. Lots of different emotions all rolled into one. I've taken some lovely shots of Chapel Farm, though.'

Nina is reminded of Catrin's unchecked honesty, a quality she always liked about her when they were little. A quality that disappeared before Nina left for London. She feels a tug of affection for the old Catrin.

'Stella said you'd agreed to do the podcast,' Catrin concludes.

'Well, I haven't yet,' replies Nina. 'She told me you were doing it, though. Is it true?'

'Yes. I want to get involved. I think there are things we don't know about that morning. She's got a great reputation . . .'

'Lying and trespassing?' Nina scoffs. 'A great reputation, sure. I think she's about as trustworthy as a viper.'

'But she might be able to find out what happened to Hazel. Don't you want to know?'

'I haven't thought about that day for years,' lies Nina. 'That part of my life is something I left behind when I came to London.'

'Well, I think about her.' Catrin pauses for a moment, and Nina doesn't know how to help her fill in the blanks. 'I came back

120

to Little Auger this afternoon,' Catrin continues, 'and I found something weird.'

Nina takes a deep breath. 'What did you find, Catrin?'

'I took some photographs from underneath the headland at the time Hazel disappeared, and there are two figures there. They're too small to make out, but it means that someone has been lying about that morning, or someone made it on to the island and made it off again without us knowing.'

'How do you work that out? That someone was lying?' asks Nina, feeling she is inching into a body of water that might be too deep.

'Roz was the only person up there that I know of. But she says she never saw Hazel. So either she's telling the truth and it's two other people up on the headland, or she's not telling the truth at all.'

Nina feels as if the situation is unravelling before her, and she just can't catch the tail of it. 'Is this the thing that Stella is talking about? The evidence she's found? A photograph?'

'No. Stella has found something different.'

'Do you know what it is?'

Catrin laughs. 'Of course not, she's using it for leverage, to get us all back on to Little Auger. She wants us to meet her there on Monday. She said she sent you a message about it. It would be great if you came too.'

Nina remembers the text from Stella that she never replied to. 'And you're happy to play along with this, are you? She's shady, Catrin, come on.'

'No more shady than some of the things I've done,' says Catrin, and Nina can hear the smile in her voice.

'You admire her, don't you,' says Nina.

'I do. She's a fine journalist. The awards she's won had stiff competition. She got into podcasting when it was still a fringe thing in the corners of the internet. Now she sells her shows to outfits like the BBC before she's even started making them.'

'But she's messing with our lives, Catrin. She's creating a story about something she knows nothing about. If we all told her we wanted no part in this, she'd probably go away, and we can all go back to living our lives.'

'Look,' Catrin says. 'These two people, on the headland that morning, don't you want to know who they were?'

'What if it's your dad, Catrin? Have you thought about that? People still remember the rumours about him and his involvement. Or strangers who made it on to the island while we were sleeping? Or what if there's actually an innocent explanation for these two people being there, but it all spirals into something awful because of this podcast?'

'If there's an innocent explanation, then I want to hear it. Don't you? I didn't do enough to support my father when those accusations nearly ruined our family. But I can do something now. I can find out who these people are and put a stop to those rumours once and for all.'

Nina suddenly understands that this will never go away, that now Catrin has the bit between her teeth she won't be stopped. She thinks back to the conversation she had with Verity over lunch. She feels powerless.

'Come on, Nina,' presses Catrin. 'Don't tell me this isn't interesting or important. Nobody ever found out what happened to Hazel. The Richardsons did nothing to defend my family from the accusations that were flung around. If I can prove it wasn't my family's fault, once and for all, then everybody wins, don't they?'

'Catrin, if Hazel wandered over the cliff edge, which is what we were told, her body is long gone. We will never be able to prove that she died because of an accident. But an absence of evidence is evidence itself—'

'There isn't an absence of evidence now, though, is there? We have two things. This photograph and whatever Stella has found. Nina, we really need you. I need you. I need an ally in this. Stella isn't one of us.'

Nina has a sense she is about to enter into something she cannot return from, that she is about to cross a line. But the pull of Catrin's words, the enveloping comfort of them. *One of us.* 'What do you want me to do?' Nina says, feeling her reserves crumble. She can't remember the last time she felt in cahoots with anybody, apart from Sylvia.

'You were always closer to Roz than I was. Are you still in touch?'

'I wasn't closer to Roz. What makes you think I was?'

Catrin sighs and it is like hearing a gust of wind down the phone. 'Childhood paranoia? I don't know. Isn't it the fate of a trio to always have one person at odds with the other two?'

'I haven't spoken to her since we were kids. Same as you.'

'I don't think she wants to come here to work with Stella. But maybe you could persuade her? If I wade in, I'll say something to upset her.'

'What can I say that would help? Hazel was her sister. You can't make her come and confront that if she doesn't want to.'

'Roz is part of the answer. I think we need to try.'

'I don't know, Catrin . . .'

'You're part of the answer, too, Nina. I've missed you. And I need to know what the hell happened to your accent. Maybe that can be Stella's next podcast.' Catrin puts on a hokey American twang. '*The Mysterious Disappearance of Nina's Welsh Accent.*'

Nina giggles. The sound surprises her.

'OK. How about this,' says Catrin. 'You come up here, we spend some time together on Little Auger, just the two of us. If you don't want to be a part of it, you can leave before Stella arrives

123

on Monday. It's the bank holiday, the weather isn't awful . . . you'd have a twenty-four-hour window to make a decision before Stella rolls into town. And if you decide to stay, you can persuade Roz to come and join us.'

Nina thinks about it. It could help her, to go there. And be gone before Stella arrives if she changes her mind.

'How soon can you get here?' says Catrin, as if she is reading Nina's mind.

'Tomorrow. I'll come tomorrow. I can leave early and be there late morning.'

'I'm at the Bed and Breakfast in Eider. Call me as soon as you arrive. We'll stay in The Old House tomorrow night, but we need to talk to Adam first – do you remember him? His father owned the boatyard. Then we'll go over to the island. See if we can pick up some clues.'

Nina laughs. 'You sound like George from the Famous Five. *Adventure on Little Auger.*'

'Well, it will be, won't it?' Catrin pauses. 'Listen, Nina. I don't know what happened between us. Well, I do, I suppose, if I'm honest. But I always regretted not keeping in touch. It just got so messy with Roz and her family.'

'I know. I'm sorry.'

'Well anyway. This has been nice. Talking, I mean.'

'Yeah,' Nina agrees. 'It has. See you tomorrow.'

When she puts the phone down, Nina tries to go back to sleep, but she can't. She feels a pull of kinship she cannot resist. The feeling she is needed by a person she once loved, and who once loved her back.

Chapter Eighteen

NINA

Before she leaves for Eider, Nina calls her mother.

'Why would you do that, Nina?' demands Sylvia. 'Why would you go back there?'

'Verity thinks I should go so I can steer the narrative.'

'Verity.' Sylvia spits her name out like a swear word. 'I took you away from those girls for a very good reason.'

'I need to do this if I want to keep my career.' A fleeting image of the library in The Old House fills her mind. The worn Turkish rug on the floor. The floorboards that squeaked when you walked on them. Nina wonders if the house has changed. She has a hunch it will be exactly as it was the day they all left.

As she drives to the village of Eider, Nina has plenty of time to think about that summer. She remembers a feeling that she somehow carried a mark upon her, a mark that told everyone her family was disintegrating. But nobody mentioned it, and she felt herself relaxing as the week went by. When she stared into the rock pools at low tide, clear as glass and containing a wealth of creatures she hadn't noticed before, she felt herself slip off her old skin, like the seal women Catrin's father spoke about when they sat around the campfire at night. She remembers sitting next to Roz at bedtime, both of them scribbling away, and although they were silent, it made her feel less alone to talk like this, secretly, with someone who wouldn't tell others.

Nina looks into the rear-view mirror to change lanes on the motorway, and she can see herself, sitting next to Catrin in the car on the way up to Eider, on this very stretch of road, the two of them humming with anticipation. As if in response to the memory, she feels her own body begin to hum, looking forward to seeing Catrin again, perhaps repairing a friendship she thought might be lost. She doesn't want to think about the journey back, twenty years ago, but her mind is spooling uncontrollably into the past, and she can't do much to stop it.

Roz and her parents had stayed behind in Eider waiting for news of Hazel, so it was Catrin's father who drove Nina back home at the end of the week. She and Catrin had sat side by side, but barely exchanged a word the whole journey. Nina left a silent car and entered a silent house. Letting herself in through the front door, she'd listened for some kind of noise. An argument, perhaps, or the slamming of a door. But when she clicked the front door shut behind her, the atmosphere was different. It had changed in a way Nina couldn't grasp. She walked through to the kitchen, afraid to call out, but knowing there was somebody there. Her mother was sitting at the table, looking into the distance, a fixed stare on her face as if she had been frozen in time.

'Where's Dad?' she asked her mother, looking around. Perhaps they had made up while she was away. Perhaps they had realised what a colossal mistake they were making, and everything would go back to normal.

Her mother shook herself out of her reverie, clearly caught out by Nina's arrival, and she stood up and wrapped her arms tightly around herself. 'Darling, I need you to be brave,' her mother said. 'I need you to be strong.'

'Where's Dad?' Nina repeated, dropping her bag and going to look in her bedroom. The bed was made, neatly, and there was no sign of her father's things. Anywhere.

Sylvia had followed her in. She was close enough that Nina could smell her perfume, hear her sharp intake of breath, as if she was a player preparing to deliver a line she'd been rehearsing. 'He's gone, Nina. He left us to be with that awful woman. I'm sorry to tell you this on top of the Hazel business. Neither of us could have predicted . . . and I can't change any of that, anyway. I know it sounds dreadful, but in the long term I think it's for the best. We can both make a fresh start. I thought about London. We could move there together, Nina, find a lovely new flat. We can become city girls. Wouldn't that be exciting?'

But Nina didn't hear what her mother was saying. All that stuck out was the words she had used to describe the terrible thing that had happened: *The Hazel Business*. She had hated her mother in that moment. It was brief, the feeling, because soon after that, things shifted below Nina's feet so swiftly, her mother was the only person who was a constant, sure-footed presence in her life. Her father kept away. There had been an incident in the night, a few weeks later, when she had been disturbed by his voice and a prolonged, violent banging on the front door, but by the time she had woken properly, it had stopped, and the next morning she wondered if it had been a dream.

When the new school term started in September, she looked out for her friends with trepidation. It had only been a couple of weeks since they left Little Auger, but Roz was unrecognisable. She had turned into a ghost, speechless and pale. Her parents had already threatened legal action against Catrin's family, and without making any reference to it, which was odd in itself, Catrin had quietly turned her back on both of them. Watching Catrin that morning in the playground, Nina realised she'd already found new friends – friends who hadn't suffered tragedy over the summer holiday. Friends who were carefree and uncomplicated.

It was the first time in her life that Nina felt like she was drowning, stuck in the middle of a wide river with no means of reaching dry land. She should have fought for Catrin, she should have been loyal to Roz. But her reserves had already been worn down by the events of that summer. Things were better at home if Nina didn't mention her father. So she didn't. An estate agent came to value the house. Her belongings were packed up into tall brown boxes, her guinea pig given away. By Christmas, she had a new life in a new city, and Sylvia was the only person left. Nina hung on to her mother as tightly as her mother hung on to her.

Her mother has been a rock in her life, without doubt; she was the person who dragged Nina out of that river and ferried her to dry land. Sylvia has always told Nina they are best friends, and every time she says it, Nina feels a small, sad ache that this is true. How has she reached her thirties and the two most reliable things in her life are her journal and her mother? She has never found friends again like Roz and Catrin. Nina has made mistakes in the past, she knows she has, and she lost the two most important people in her life. But coming back here, to confront those mistakes, she might just give herself a second chance.

When Nina pulls into the car park of the Bed and Breakfast in Eider, she knows she is returning to an area of her past that was bleak and dark, but her overriding feeling, as she turns the ignition off and reaches for her phone, is one of quiet optimism. She remembers the time before everything went wrong, when Nina cared less about what she looked like, about what others thought. She had friends who loved her whether she had bitten nails or not. She had forgotten that feeling of unselfconsciousness, the feeling of being unfettered and free. Now she remembers its delicious existence, she wonders what it would be like to have it back.

Chapter Nineteen

CATRIN

Catrin comes down to the car park as Nina is getting out of her car. Nina is a completely different creature to the girl she remembers and Catrin would not have recognised her, were it not for those cool grey eyes. She is glamorous, polished. Although her clothes are casual, they look expensive and tailored to her worryingly slender frame.

What's the phrase people use? Catrin thinks to herself. *She looks well put together.* And that hair. Catrin cannot get over her hair.

'Where have your beautiful curls gone?' she gasps, as she looks Nina up and down, feeling grubby and underdressed. When they were younger, Catrin was always the leader, but the woman before her looks superior, totally in control. Catrin suddenly realises she doesn't know Nina at all. She didn't even sound Welsh on the phone.

Nina touches her hair self-consciously. 'Oh, it's just easier to style this way, that's all. I have to get up really early, and . . . well.'

Catrin clutches her forehead with her hand. 'There I go. I didn't mean . . .'

'It's OK . . .'

'It wasn't a criticism. Honestly. You look great. More than great. Amazing.' Suddenly, Catrin doesn't know what to do with her arms, they feel heavy and stiff. She thought she might hug Nina when she saw her, but her arms stay put.

'Thanks,' says Nina, her eyes sliding away around the car park. Her fingers are neatly laced together in front of her. The way she stands reminds Catrin of their first day at school. She is relieved to see something of the Nina she once knew in the playground. The muscle memory of a child that still exists inside the woman.

'It's just so completely bonkers to see you,' she blurts out.

Nina's face breaks into a relieved smile. 'I know. It's weird.'

'Yeah. Totally. But good-weird, right?' Catrin's arms are suddenly released from their spell, and she opens them to Nina. They hug, briefly, but Catrin feels the strength of it, the warmth in it. 'Let's go to the pub,' she says. 'We can grab something to eat before we go and talk to Adam.'

'Adam.' Nina's eyes widen. 'I had *such* a huge crush on him. He was gorgeous. I was livid when he fancied Roz.'

'Well, I'm sure he'll be full of regret when he sees you today. You look amazing. Do you have to go to fashion school to learn how to look like that or is it a natural skill?'

'Stylists have nifty tricks, and they tell you after a while, if they like you.'

'Well, you can't tear me away from combat pants and army T-shirts,' declares Catrin, looking down at her own uniform that has served her well over the past decade.

They take a seat in the pub and Catrin shows Nina the photograph while they are waiting for their lunch.

'I've been staring at it all morning. I still can't figure out who it is,' Catrin says, pouring sugar into her black coffee.

Nina takes the print and studies it for a long time, an inscrutable expression on her face. 'It's impossible to tell if it's adults or children.' She continues to stare at the picture. 'What about someone who landed on the island without us knowing? There's plenty of people who'd want to crash the place, and as long as they stayed away from the house, they wouldn't be noticed. I know it's difficult, but Stella obviously managed it. It's not Fort Knox.'

'I think that's why we need to talk to Adam,' says Catrin. 'Maybe he knew all along that other people could reach the island, but he and his father didn't mention it? It would have shattered our happy family illusion that we were impenetrable. That we were safe.'

'And then what?' says Nina, sipping a tonic water. 'He tells us it's possible and we begin to think Hazel's been abducted? Living another life somewhere with a new family?'

'I don't know.' Catrin shakes her head, feeling the complexity of the situation. 'Maybe.'

'Come on. The most likely explanation is she wandered around, she fell, her body was swept out to sea and never found.'

'That may be true. But I still want to know who these two people are. And I hate to say it, but the most likely explanation for that is that one of them is Roz. A houseful of witnesses say you were asleep. So that rules you out.'

'Well, thanks,' Nina mumbles, frowning at the figures. She touches them lightly with a long, manicured fingernail, and Catrin is reminded of the smooth pink seashells that sometimes wash up on the shore of Eider.

Catrin shuffles her bar stool closer to Nina to get a better look. 'It can't have been me, because I took this picture,' she says thoughtfully. 'So the only people left are the adults in the house, or Roz. Roz's parents were with one another the whole morning. My dad was with them too, after he woke up. He left the house to call the police and Arvis on his mobile phone. He couldn't get reception inside. He was only gone a short while and it was after the alarm was raised, despite what the papers printed. Only Roz was alone, with no one to back up her story. It's Occam's razor.'

'It's what?' says Nina, looking up quizzically.

'Occam's razor,' Catrin supplies. 'A theory that if you have different reasons to explain something, the simplest explanation is the most likely. She was there, Nina. She was there on that cliff, around the time I took that picture. One of these people must be her.'

Nina nods slowly, still considering the photograph. 'But why would Roz lie about not seeing anyone else that morning until she got back to the house? Why would she lie about Hazel going missing? They were as close as any two sisters I've ever seen. Roz loved her. You can't be suggesting . . .'

'I'm not suggesting anything. I'm not saying Roz did anything wrong.'

'Then what?'

'Something happened that morning that we can't explain. This photograph tells me there were others on the island, or somebody lied. I just want to find out which one it is, that's all.'

The boatyard is a short walk from the pub. They pass down the high street and there's a queue of people waiting cheerfully outside the ice cream shop, craning their necks to look at the flavours inside. The old-fashioned pharmacy next to it has its door flung open, welcoming in the sunshine on to the varnished wooden floor. Catrin and Nina weave their way around panting dogs pulling on leads, and small children clutching buckets for crabbing, holding tightly on to the hands of mothers in loose sundresses. Along the way, Catrin tells Nina about what she has been doing with her life for the past twenty years, and then about the decline of Chapel Farm.

'So you've come back for good? Or are you just taking a sabbatical?' Nina asks, momentarily drawn by the window of a fancy gift shop.

'I don't know. I don't feel like I belong here any more, but I think James is struggling and it's been really nice to see him again.'

'And how's your dad?'

Catrin rolls her eyes. 'Exactly the same. You'd think we were still in the 1950s. He's winding down, though.' Catrin thinks about how frail her father had suddenly seemed, something she thought she'd never see. 'What about your dad? I heard he remarried and had another kid.'

'And then he died.' Nina gives Catrin a grim-faced smile.

'Oh shit, Nina, I'm so sorry. Me and my big mouth. When did that happen?'

'Not long after we moved to London. He got a job in Hong Kong and died when he was out there.'

'Have you kept in touch with his other family?'

'Nope.'

'Did he have a boy or a girl?'

'A girl.'

'So she would be – what – late teens?'

'I suppose so.'

'And you don't feel curious about what she's like?'

'No,' replies Nina in a tired voice.

'Fair enough.' Catrin senses it's time to stop asking questions when, thankfully, the boatyard comes into view. 'Here we are.'

The boatyard is open, the metal sign *AA Boatyard* arching over the open gates. They walk past a stack of kayaks and life jackets, almost in the same spot as they were twenty years ago, Catrin thinks. She scans the yard and spots a group of men in boots and yellow waterproof dungarees standing underneath a boat hoisted above their heads. They are pointing at something on the hull that Catrin can't see, but she knows one of the men must be Adam.

'Adam,' Catrin calls, but they are too far away. Then she puts two fingers in her mouth and lets out a loud, shrill whistle. All the men stop what they are doing and one of them breaks away.

'Catrin. What on earth are you doing here?' Adam looks completely taken aback.

'Surprise!' she replies, grinning at him. 'You could look more pleased to see me.'

Adam laughs and runs his hand through his hair as he walks towards them. 'I am, I am. I'm just . . . wow. I thought you lived abroad.'

'Well, I'm back for a bit.' Catrin steps forward and gives Adam a backslapping hug. 'This is Nina, do you remember her?'

'Uh, yes, I think so,' says Adam, nodding at her. Catrin wonders if she detects a blush underneath that suntanned stubble. 'What is this then, a reunion?' he asks, taking off his baseball cap and scratching the back of his neck.

'Sort of,' says Catrin.

'Are you going over to Little Anger? Today?'

All three of them look over to the black smudge settled between the sea and the sky.

'When the tide's ready, yes,' Catrin answers, putting her hands in the front pockets of her pants.

'Why don't you both stop here for the night? Go tomorrow. We can have dinner or something and catch up.'

Catrin shrugs, says, 'I was here last night. Shame I missed you. I tried to find you yesterday, actually, but chatty boy over there told me you had the afternoon off.' Catrin waves over at the teenager who filled her boat up and helped her launch it.

'Uh, I had to go and see to Dad.'

'How is he?' Catrin asks, remembering the giant of a man who had always been there for her family over the years.

'Good, actually,' Adam says, and then smiles to himself, 'but he needs reining in. He wants to sail over to Ireland and tour the coast, but I don't think he should do it alone, with his heart condition. So we're trying to figure out who could take the ten-day trip without killing him,' he laughs.

'Not you or your mum then?'

'You wouldn't catch Mum on the water, and I have to supervise this lot.' He jerks his thumb behind him at the men standing under the boat, who are continuing their discussion.

Catrin smiles. She doesn't remember Adam having much of a sense of humour, but it looks like some things have changed. 'James tells me the yard is doing very well.'

'It is, it is.' Adam nods. 'I'm not the only one, though,' he grins. 'I hear you're some kind of hotshot photographer, dodging bullets for a living. Impressive, considering what a little shrimp you were.'

'Watch yourself, Adam. I can still take you in an arm wrestle.' Catrin playfully punches him in the arm.

'That was a one-off, and you caught me by surprise,' Adam scoffs.

They laugh together, and Catrin is suddenly conscious that Nina is there, watching them both goof about.

'Listen, Adam,' says Catrin, remembering why she is there. 'Someone's been in touch with me. A podcaster who says she's been able to access the island, alone. Have you heard anything about that?'

The shift in Adam's demeanour is swift. The smile vanishes and a serious look crosses his face. 'Er . . . no.'

'I'm surprised somebody's been able to slip past you . . .'

'This place has been like a madhouse over the summer. Boats I don't recognise everywhere. People renting kayaks. I can't keep my eyes on the sea twenty-four seven.'

'Well, anyway,' says Catrin, noting the defensive tone in his voice, 'it got me thinking. Twenty years ago. Is it possible someone could have landed on the island without us knowing about it?'

Adam looks worried. 'Why, has somebody said something?'

'No, what I mean is, could somebody have landed a boat and left the island that morning without us knowing?'

Adam draws breath, thinking. 'Well, I suppose anything is possible. You might bash your boat up doing it, but it's possible, I guess, yeah.'

'Did you see anything that morning? Any boats coming in very early, or going out?'

'My dad went through this a million times with the police. We didn't see anything unusual, but we were busy, you know? I worked here all summer with Dad. We both saw a few of the fishermen first thing, but no boats going near the island. It's too rocky around there, anyway. People give it a wide berth, a good catch isn't worth losing your engine for.' He pauses, gazing out to sea. Catrin wonders if he is as lost in the past as she has been over the last few days. 'So you're going over there at high tide, are you?' he asks, returning to the present.

'Yeah. I'd invite you over, but you look busy.' Catrin nods to the group of men standing under the hull, who have finished their discussion and are waiting for him to return.

'Maybe I should come with you on my boat? Give you a hand if you need it? It's been a while since you made that crossing.'

'I made it yesterday, remember? We'll be fine,' Catrin reassures him when he frowns with concern. 'Let's catch up when we get back.'

'Are you staying overnight?' he asks.

'Yes. One or two nights. Don't look so worried. We'll be fine,' she repeats. 'I'm a big girl now.'

'Yeah, sure. Well, OK. If you don't need my help, I'd best get on.' Adam rakes his hair with both hands, nods and walks back to the boat. 'Good to see you, Catrin,' he calls.

Catrin turns to Nina. 'Are you going to tell me that wasn't weird?'

'He did seem a bit . . . distracted, I suppose,' says Nina.

'Something's rattled his cage,' says Catrin, unable to contain a smile. She watches Adam as he rejoins the men, her eyes narrowed into a thoughtful gaze. 'It makes me think he might know something we don't.'

Chapter Twenty

NINA

Catrin and Nina load some extra provisions from Eider's only supermarket on to the boat and Catrin guns the engine. The boat traces a wide arc through the black water as it turns towards Little Auger and Nina feels a lurch in her stomach, hoping the journey over won't make her feel sick this time. She finds she doesn't want to look at the crouched black mass ahead of her, which seems like the back of a creature rising out of the waves. Instead, she turns her gaze to the water beneath them. As Catrin navigates out of the shallows, Nina can see seaweed and kelp rising in columns below her, grabbing at the boat. She shudders as they pass a particularly dense patch, green tentacles with large, leprous pustules bubbling up from the deep. When they make it out of the harbour, they are finally free of it, but now she sees a mountain range of rocks rising up, the sharp peaks dangerously close to the hull of the boat. Her body remembers the feeling of vertigo from twenty years ago as the boat skims over them.

Catrin shouts to Nina as she steers the boat. 'Something's up. Adam didn't look delighted to see us.'

'Maybe he has other things on his mind,' replies Nina, trying to keep her hair out of her face. She can feel the blunt ends whipping her skin and hopes it won't give her a rash. 'This is ruining my blow-dry.'

'Do you think he was weird about us going to Little Auger?'

'I don't know,' says Nina, wishing the topic of conversation would change.

'And as far as his alibi goes, Arvis would have been busy at the yard that morning, he wouldn't have noticed if Adam left for a while. It's a big place. In fact, Adam could have left with a friend.'

'Why does Hazel's death have to be someone's fault?' Nina says under her breath. 'Can't it just be an accident?'

They stop talking as they approach Little Auger and the journey passes without any more conversation. Nina feels the land rise up in front of her like an adversary, the rocks arranged like enormous prehistoric scales. It is beautiful and frightening at the same time.

'It's OK,' Catrin reassures her, misunderstanding her expression. 'I did this yesterday so I'm a real pro now.'

They enter the corridor of rocks that leads to the cove and the boat takes on the swell of the current, making Nina feel nauseous. 'I can't believe your father let you do this when you were so young. I remember going back and forth with you to Eider for the fun of it and nobody batted an eye.'

Catrin grins, looking ahead for danger, and Nina observes her with the luxury of not being noticed. Catrin stands, feet apart, like a man, her body taut with muscle, her skin tanned from years of sun exposure. Nina remembers why she liked her so much. She was fearless, unaffected, she didn't care what people thought about her. She was everything that Nina wasn't.

I bet she's never worn a scrap of make-up, thinks Nina to herself, and she wonders at the freedom of it, to wake each morning and stride out of the house without so much as a glance at a mirror.

Catrin always navigated school on her own terms. She has probably done the same with the rest of her life. Nina wonders if losing a parent has freed Catrin in some way, allowing her to be herself, unburdened. Losing a parent for Nina has only bound her more tightly to her mother.

They haul their bags out of the boat when it is secured, and Nina looks around the little cove. Suddenly, her legs give way, and she's not sure if it's the movement of the boat or the enormity of being back here. 'I need to sit for a while,' she says, lowering herself on to a smooth-looking rock. 'Just for a moment.'

They watch the push of the tide soak through the pebbles on the shore, they listen to the sound, like erratic applause, echo around them. The air is heavy with salt water. She remembers how her hair became stiff with it, how it curled into ringlets and lost its frizz. She runs her fingers through to the ends and draws up a fistful. It doesn't look straight any more, even after so short a time. The wind on the journey over here and the salt are already undoing all her hard work. She wonders how a little piece of land can change a person both inside and out.

'You know,' says Catrin, cutting into her thoughts, 'Adam really had a thing for Roz. He might be covering up for her. They spent a lot of time together after Hazel disappeared. She was more or less relegated to the house by her parents while everyone was out looking. What if he knows Roz was involved somehow? And he's protecting her?'

Nina sighs. 'They did spend a lot of time together, it's true. She was here for a while after we went back home, wasn't she?'

'The Richardsons moved into Adam's house. They were there for another week at least while the search for Hazel continued. Plenty of time to build up a rapport.'

Nina pulls out her phone and frowns. 'Can you get reception on here?'

'Only with certain networks, and even then it dips in and out.' Catrin leans over to Nina's phone, looking at the screen. 'Use my phone if you want to. It usually works. But we need to be on higher ground.'

Nina pockets her phone. 'Actually, I won't bother. It'll be nice to have a break from it. Let's go, I feel better now.'

They make their way over the pebbles and rocks to the winding goat track that leads to the house. The track is lined with scrub either side, bent at an angle that tells of its struggle against the wind. Nina sees the branches are thick with lichen, making them look mouldy and decayed. Then suddenly, as they round the last corner, the house is revealed to them, the front door facing them square on, its whitewashed walls, the texture of porridge, peeling from the weather. They both look up at the roof. There are a few slipped and broken slates. There is smoke spooling out of the chimney.

'What the . . .' Catrin drops her bags.

Nina looks at the smoke. 'Could it be Stella?' she asks, feeling slightly afraid.

Catrin shakes her head. 'Stella's in London,' she says in a low voice, 'and there wasn't a boat in the cove.' She turns to Nina and puts her finger to her lips. Nina drops her bags, quietly, on the grass and follows Catrin as she slowly approaches the front door. Catrin pushes it open gently and they both step into the hallway, listening intently. The house smells of wood smoke and burnt coffee. It is warm and stuffy, as if the fire has been burning for a long time. Nina gets the sense she is in a fairy tale, that she and Catrin are the bears coming back to find their breakfast has been eaten. By whom, though? There is nobody in the library, she can see by the dust in there it hasn't been touched for years. The kitchen, then, where the fire is dying; the coffee pot has long boiled dry. The door is wide open, the kitchen table is covered in pages and pages filled with scribbles. And among it all, fast asleep, her head on the table, her arms folded around herself, is Roz.

Chapter
Twenty-One

Roz

Roz wakes with a start and is assaulted by a paralysing pain running down the side of her neck. How long has she been asleep for? She moves her head, gingerly, massaging the muscle that is complaining bitterly at being stretched out for so long. She has drool seeping out of the side of her mouth, and as she lifts her head she can see the sketches she made last night and early this morning. After a few tentative attempts to draw Hazel and Goggin, or the essence of them, she'd felt a surge of recognition as to how it could be done, and she'd begun to draw them from memory. She has filled page after page of her sketchbook, driven on by something she has yet to understand.

When they were younger, Hazel sometimes posed for her, and Roz became good at drawing her sister, often making small caricatures to amuse her. But Roz has not been able to draw Hazel since she died. She's tried, several times, but it was so painful not to be able to capture her, to do her justice, that eventually she stopped trying. But last night, she produced sketch after sketch of something that pleased her, something that didn't look like Hazel exactly, but captured her spirit.

She reaches out and begins to gather up the pieces of paper carefully, assembling them into some kind of order. She will think about what they mean when she gets home.

'Roz?'

A voice breaks into her reverie, and she can't place who it is. The voice calls her name once more, and Roz realises it is not the remnants of a dream but someone in the same room as her. She turns around at the sound, causing a ricochet of pain down her neck. At first, she thinks she is seeing ghosts. But the two women standing at the doorway of the kitchen are not made of memories, they are here, in the present. Nina she recognises slowly, she is just as strangely unfamiliar as she is on the television. But Catrin hasn't changed at all. And then Roz realises what she has done, whose house she is in. How this must look. And another thought crowds into her head: *Why are Catrin and Nina together?*

Catrin stands over her, and Roz tries to get up. She begins to stammer an apology. 'I'm sorry, I . . . I . . .'

'What the hell is going on? How did you get over here?' Catrin demands.

Catrin picks up a sketch, and Roz reflexively tries to snatch it back. 'Don't . . .'

'*Don't?*' Catrin questions in a mocking voice. 'What are you doing? Using this place as an art studio? How long have you been here?'

'I . . . sorry. Sorry.' Roz can see Catrin's eyes taking in the details, the empty coffee cup, the remains of a meal.

'I don't understand. When did you get here? Who brought you over?' Catrin asks. 'It looks like you moved in.'

'No, no, not that at all. I just . . . I wanted to . . .' Her voice halts, and no more words come out. Because, really, Roz isn't sure what she is doing here. She still doesn't know what it is she wants, but she knows she is nearer to finding out. 'Adam brought me here, yesterday.'

'Adam,' Catrin repeats. It is a conclusion, not a question. Catrin throws a look at Nina and some kind of shared realisation unfurls between the two women.

'That's why he was so shifty,' mutters Catrin to Nina. 'He knew she was here.'

Roz doesn't like the way she is being spoken about, as if she isn't in the room. As if they have been discussing her, the two of them. And a memory unfolds, of this feeling, the same feeling, when she was a teenager, of being left out of knowing conversations between the two of them, a camaraderie she didn't feel a part of. She knows some of this was due to Hazel. She looked after her little sister willingly when she was asked to, but she knew that Nina and Catrin thought Hazel a drag. Too often, plans they had made mysteriously fell through when they knew she had to come with them.

The three of them stand quietly for a moment, Catrin and Nina facing Roz like a couple of disappointed parents. Did they pick up their friendship years ago, deciding not to let her in? Have they met one another over the years for cosy lunches, exchanged news about their children? Do they have children? Perhaps their children are friends. Her mind races on, leaping from one paranoid narrative to the next, all of which exclude her.

She clears her throat. 'I wanted to ask your permission first, Catrin, but I was afraid. After what Mum and Dad put your family through.'

'I wouldn't have denied you that,' says Catrin, her voice softer now, but still nettled. 'You have a right to visit the place your sister disappeared. It's polite to ask, though.'

'I know, I'm sorry. I was going to go back today, anyway.' Roz looks from Catrin to Nina. 'What are you doing here?'

Once more, they exchange a look that Roz doesn't understand.

'I'm just here for the ride,' Nina replies vaguely, and Roz recognises the lie. She fights down the desire to demand to know what is going on between them. She knows she doesn't have the right to ask.

'What have you been doing here?' asks Catrin.

'Well,' Roz begins, 'I got a call from a podcaster.'

'Stella. Yes, we know about her,' nods Catrin, crossing her arms and surveying Roz with interest.

'I wasn't sure I wanted to have anything to do with it, but she's got my parents on board, and she said you were both involved . . .'

Again, a look passes between Nina and Catrin.

Roz continues, 'So I thought, if I could just come here, by myself, see how I felt about being back without everyone watching me . . . it sounds silly.'

'No, it doesn't,' says Catrin.

'I just wanted to see if she was here,' Roz says simply.

'Who? Stella?' asks Catrin.

'No. Hazel.'

'You think she might be alive?'

'I don't know. We were told nobody unfamiliar with the island could possibly land on it. We were told Hazel was dead. But my parents always believed . . . and now Stella. I don't know what to think any more. That's why I wanted to come back here. To get my head straight.'

'How long have you been here for?'

'I came yesterday. I should get going. Adam will be here soon.'

'You can't go. We've barely spoken. You should stay another night.'

'No, no. I'll get out of your way. You clearly have plans.'

They both turn to Nina, who says nothing, observing the two of them silently from the doorway.

'No, I don't want that,' says Catrin, softening. 'Please stay. Let's spend a couple of nights here, together.' She sounds conciliatory.

'What about Adam . . .'

'I'll call him now, tell him he doesn't need to collect you.' Catrin pulls out her mobile, sounding businesslike. 'There's a place at the back where I should be able to get reception.' She disappears out of the house for several minutes.

Roz stands awkwardly, stealing glances at Nina, who has now moved into the room and looks as uncomfortable as Roz feels. They finally exchange a few meaningless words and Roz tries to see the girl she once knew under the veneer of the woman before her. Her hair has more curl than on the TV. As for the rest of her childhood friend, it is impossible to locate her. After a few minutes, Catrin blows back into the house and suddenly Roz feels an impulse to get out from under her gaze.

'Can I use your phone?' Roz asks. 'Mine doesn't get any reception.' As instructed, she walks out of the house, where the walls are too thick to make calls, and climbs up a hummock a little way away. As she stands on the knoll, she can see the shape of the island, narrowing down to its tail, and beyond that, the unforgiving sea. The wind gusts around her, snatching the warmth out of the August sun. She pulls her coat around her more snugly and stands facing the wind, so her hair blows away from her face. Instead of calling Simon, she looks at the list of recent calls and sees the word *Boatyard* is at the top, above a number with no name. The name feels like a life ring in a deep swell. She jabs at it, and Adam picks up immediately.

'Catrin?' he asks. He sounds apprehensive.

'No, it's Roz.' The relief she feels is palpable in her voice. 'My phone doesn't get any reception here.' She doesn't even know why she called him.

He makes a noise of relief. 'She's just given me a right telling-off. I didn't know what to say when she told me she was going over there. She's pretty annoyed with me.'

'Don't worry. She'll be fine.'

'I didn't tell her about me and Stella. In the pub. I thought it might be another nail in my coffin.'

'Your secret's safe with me.'

'Thanks, Roz. I knew I could trust you. She'd kill me if she knew.'

Roz feels a drop of happiness spread over her. Catrin and Nina might not trust her, but Adam does. At least, it feels as if he does. She's glad she acted on that impulse to call him, she's so relieved to hear a friendly voice.

'How was it yesterday?' Adam asks gently, as if he just read her mind. 'Did it help, being there?'

Roz remembers the moment when she felt Hazel was right there with her on the cliff path, the sense of kinship she felt. 'Yeah. It did. It's weird. I should feel sad, but I don't. I want to be here, even though what happened was awful. There's something about this place that makes me feel closer to Hazel. I was able to sketch her face for the first time in twenty years.'

'My grandma used to say that when you're part of a tragedy, you leave something of yourself behind. And that's why you feel drawn to return to places of great sadness. You have to, because your body, or your spirit – or whatever it was that was split apart – it wants to be reunited with the piece that was lost.'

'Do you think that's true?' ponders Roz.

'How should I know?' Adam says with a laugh. 'Maybe we just need to go back to remind ourselves that we survived.'

'It makes me feel guilty, surviving,' Roz admits, but admitting it to Adam feels good.

'Surviving is overrated. I hear that living is much better.'

They end the call, after Roz agrees to find Adam in the boatyard to say goodbye before she goes home. For a moment, she looks out over the island, tracing the cliff path as it snakes to the cairn. Then she dials Simon's number.

'Hello?' Simon answers in a suspicious voice.

'It's me,' she replies. 'I don't have any reception here, I've borrowed Catrin's phone.'

'Catrin?'

Roz realises she hasn't told Simon where she is, because she came here on a whim. 'I'm actually in Eider, working on some landscapes that I've been commissioned to do,' she lies. 'I bumped into Catrin – my old friend from school? – and she asked me to stay with her for a day or two.'

'When are you coming back?' It isn't a demand. He seems happy she is away.

Roz doesn't know the answer to this question because she is confused by her willingness to be away from Willow, the pull she feels for this place. She doesn't want to race back home. Not just yet. 'A couple of days? Hopefully, Willow will have forgiven me by then,' she says, grimacing. 'How is she?'

'She's great. She's discovered my old Star Wars Lego sets and is building the Millennium Falcon as we speak.'

'What's that?'

'It's Han Solo's ship. He co-piloted it with Chewbacca. You're obviously not down with the kids like I am. She's been at it all morning. Hasn't even turned the TV on.'

Roz tries to feel pleased, but she feels wrong-footed, somehow. Willow has never shown any interest in Lego, she can't picture it. 'Can I speak to her?' she asks, suddenly desperate to claw back some ownership.

Simon puts the phone down and Roz can hear the push and pull of their words, indistinct, but Roz can sense the shift as Willow wins the battle.

'Sorry,' says Simon. 'She'll come round. Maybe a couple of days apart will help. By the way, did you contact any estate agents yet? About selling the house?'

'No, I . . .'

'Well, I can do that today. Willow is excited at the idea of moving.'

'You *told* her?'

'Yes. She gets it. I explained we need to sell the big house to get two small ones.'

'But Simon . . .' Roz's head is spinning, she's not sure how the conversation got away from her so fast.

'It's not fair, Roz. I need more space.'

'But you told her we were going to sell her home?'

'Uh-huh,' Simon says casually. 'We're not the first parents to divorce in her friendship group. If we involve her from the start, she'll be on board. It's exciting for her. She's going to have two houses, two bedrooms. What kid doesn't want two bedrooms?'

'I just can't think about this right now,' says Roz, shutting her eyes tightly. 'It's too much.'

'Well, look. There is an alternative.'

'What?' A small surge of hope springs up in Roz.

'You can take over the whole mortgage and the bills. You can buy me out. You get to keep the house, and I'll have a chunk of change to move out of this place.'

Roz's heart sinks. 'You know I can't afford that.'

'I thought you said work was going well.'

Roz sighs, and wonders when she became such a liar. 'It is . . . it's just . . . I don't think I can afford that.'

'Then something has to give. We agreed to be amicable, for Willow's sake.'

'I know, I know.' But Roz doesn't feel amicable. She ends the call but doesn't want to go back into the house. She sits on the hummock, looking out to sea, wondering what is happening to her. She is again aware of a finely tuned equilibrium tilting off kilter. That when she gains a piece of Hazel, she loses a part of Willow, and the weight of the shift tips her off balance. Maybe she should go back home. She should call Adam and tell him to pick her up before the tide turns. But if she does that, she knows the little piece of Hazel she has found here will be lost.

Chapter Twenty-Two

CATRIN

'Are you going to show Roz that photograph?' Nina asks, arms folded, watching for Roz's return through the kitchen window. 'Is that why you want her to stay?'

'Not just yet. I want to talk to her first. There's something odd about her, something not right,' says Catrin, as she feeds the wood burner.

'She's distracted,' says Nina. 'It must be hard, coming back here. She's probably dealing with a lot of . . . I don't know . . . stuff.'

Catrin feels a racing wind chase through the house as she hears the door swing open, announcing Roz's return. 'Did you get through?' she asks, holding her hand out for her phone.

'Yes,' answers Roz, cheeks pink from the wind. 'Actually . . . I spoke to Adam. He's worried you're angry with him.'

Catrin takes her phone, frowning. 'I had no idea you were that friendly with Adam. I already told you I'd call him.'

'I just wanted to . . . He's been kind to me.'

Catrin sits down at the table. 'I don't know what's going on with you. We don't know each other any more. We haven't spoken for twenty years. Maybe it's time we started. What do you think?'

Roz nods and sits down at the oak table, etched with the marks of a thousand mealtimes. Nina remains standing, leaning with her back against the kitchen countertop, her hands gripping the wood behind her as if to steady herself.

'You're right. I'll start with what's happened since I got to Eider,' Roz begins. 'Just before I came to the island I was talking to one of the villagers, who told me about the other name for the island. He told me about the massacre that happened here—'

'Years ago, Roz . . .' interrupts Catrin.

'He said that Little Anger – what everyone who lives here calls it – Little Anger is a place that gathers souls.'

'This is just folklore,' Catrin sighs. 'Fairy tales and warnings passed down through the generations, so kids don't take it upon themselves to sail over here. It's a dangerous place because the rocks that surround it are treacherous. Not because of some ancient magic and hearsay.'

'I just think,' continues Roz, her eyes almost glassy and faraway, 'like any story that has survived over the years, there must be some truth in it. Adam told me he thinks people leave a piece of themselves behind in a place of tragedy. That sometimes, survivors feel an urge to go back because their body misses it. I think there is a piece of Hazel here. A little bit of her spirit or something. And then I think of all those people that got murdered here. And I wonder what happened to them all. Their bones might still be here, in the earth. Maybe they left behind something else. A trace of themselves. Otherwise, why would there be all these marks over the house?' Roz gestures to the window in the kitchen, the doorframe.

'You mean the witches' marks?'

'Yes. Did you know that Hazel had a birthmark very similar? On her neck?'

'A coincidence,' Catrin says dismissively.

'Then why would somebody do that? Make those marks in this house?'

Catrin shakes her head. 'Superstition, tradition. People do stuff without even thinking about it. They just repeat what's been done before. I don't even notice them any more.'

'We don't notice *enough*, these days. We've lost those instincts, where we connect with nature, we're so bound up with technology. But when I walked to the headland, I knew there was something of Hazel here, I can feel it. I know how it sounds, how all of this woo-woo makes me look. But I've never felt this close to Hazel since she died. There's something here and it's connected with me.' She touches her chest with her fingertips when she says this.

'Well, of course,' says Catrin, a note of exasperation in her voice. 'This place is full of her memory.'

'It's more than that,' says Roz stubbornly. 'I wonder if her birthmark was a sign, that she was marked for a purpose. I know that sounds ridiculous . . .'

'Roz . . .' says Catrin, trying to sound patient.

'Don't.' Roz's voice is tearful, accusing. Her hand closes into a fist. 'You're just like my ex and my daughter. Talking to me like I'm a child. I'm not a child—'

'You have a daughter?' Catrin interrupts, hoping to change the direction of the conversation before it tips into an argument.

'Willow.' Roz's face brightens, and then clouds over. 'Eleven years old. She looks so much like Hazel . . .'

'Do you have a picture?' Catrin asks.

Roz finds her phone, powers it up and hands it to Catrin.

'Wow, she really does look like Hazel. Nina, do you want a look?'

Nina, who has been watching them both throughout this exchange, comes forward to see the picture. She takes the phone from Roz's hands and holds it, transfixed. 'Why are you here, Roz?' she asks eventually, still not looking up from the photograph. 'Chasing ghosts? When you have a family . . .'

Roz looks lost and confused. 'The truth is, Willow would rather be with her father right now. I haven't . . . I haven't done a very good job with her. Turns out I'm a bit of a dead loss at parenting.'

'I remember how carefully you looked after Hazel. There is no way you could be a bad parent. I don't believe it,' counters Nina.

'Well, I am. I can't trust her. I can't trust myself to look after her. She's at the age where she wants some independence, and I just can't give it to her. My marriage ended because of it. Simon said I stopped being fun when I had Willow.'

'He sounds like a bastard,' says Catrin darkly.

'He's not. Not really. He's right.' Roz sighs. 'I don't think I was ever fun. He fell in love with me because he thought I was mysterious. He told me once that I was a puzzle he wanted to unlock. I wanted to get married because I needed someone to love me. I just wanted to be looked after, not unlocked. He felt very rejected when I wouldn't open up about Hazel—'

'It takes two to end a marriage, Roz,' interrupts Catrin.

'Now I'm losing Willow, and that will be my fault too,' Roz says, her voice full of misery.

'So why come here?' asks Nina once more.

'I don't know. I suppose I've lost my husband, and I need to sort myself out before I lose Willow too. I have never been able to talk about Hazel. It's too painful. I made a promise to her, and I broke it. I promised I would wake her and take her with me to watch the sunrise, but I didn't. She must have heard me leaving and followed me.'

'If that's true, you can't change any of that, can you?' Catrin asks gently.

'That morning, after you left me to take photographs from the shoreline, I got the feeling I was being watched. I don't think I *was* alone up there. I think there was someone, or something, there.' Roz shivers and then looks up, almost hopeful. 'Unless it was you. Did you come back up?'

'No, of course I didn't. I was taking photographs.'

'Of me?'

'Of the cliffs,' says Catrin simply.

Roz lets out a breath. 'Sorry. It's just that I got the same feeling yesterday when I was out on the old cliff path. Then I saw . . . oh, it sounds silly now, but I asked for a sign, and I saw a red ribbon tied to the gorse on the clifftop. And I thought, *What if it's Hazel? Trying to tell me something?*

Catrin looks over to Nina. She knows Nina is thinking about the photographs, but she has no intention of dropping that bomb just yet.

'Look,' Catrin says. 'I've arranged for Stella Cox to come here tomorrow. If there is anything to figure out, she's the woman to do it.'

'What?' Nina's voice is like ice. 'When did you arrange that? You said she was coming on Monday.'

Catrin's sense of purpose falters when she hears the edge in Nina's voice. 'I called her just now,' she explains delicately. 'She's on her way up from London and she'll be here tomorrow afternoon. This is the right thing to do, I'm sure of it.'

'You lied to me!' says Nina. 'You got me up here, letting me think it was just the two of us and—'

'Honestly, I didn't think about it until I saw Roz and then it seemed too good an opportunity to miss. We can make sense of it all with someone whose job it is to investigate disappearances. A

155

professional. We can learn the truth together.' She opens her arms as she says this, for emphasis. But Roz and Nina don't seem to be on board.

'For Christ's sake, Catrin!' says Nina. 'Stella Cox is doing this for entertainment! Not for any of our benefits. Don't you get that?'

'She says she's found something here and I believe her,' Catrin says smoothly, dropping her arms. 'Roz is clearly affected by her time here. And we haven't spoken properly to one another about this, ever. Don't you think it's time we did?'

'We're talking about it now!' snaps Nina. 'We don't need a stranger in the room recording our conversations and airing them out to all and sundry! I thought you were less naive than this, Catrin. Don't you know how the media works in this country? It's a shark tank.' Nina turns to Roz. 'Surely you don't want some journalist poking her nose into your business. She could say all sorts about Hazel.'

'It's already been said,' says Roz miserably. 'And she's going to do it anyway, with or without our help.'

'That is just what she wants you to think!' Nina is half shouting now. 'I can't believe you did this, Catrin. You told me it would just be the two of us.'

'You don't have to get involved . . .' Catrin feels Nina's anger, but she can't stop it. It is the right thing to do. It's time they found out the truth.

'How can I not get involved? I'm here, aren't I. You have me captive,' Nina spits back.

'Look. Just meet her. See what she has to say. If you still don't want anything to do with it, I'll take you back myself.'

'I'd forgotten this about you,' says Nina in a sullen voice. 'You only care about what you want, what you feel. You don't have the capacity to put yourself in other people's shoes.'

'That's not fair—'

'Actually, it is,' interrupts Roz, standing up, leaning her hands on the table and staring down at Catrin. 'I remember when we all went back to school, and you virtually ignored me. When I asked you what the problem was, you said it was because you couldn't cope with the weirdness of it all. *The weirdness of it all!* That's how you described it.'

'Look. It was a terrible time, no doubt about that. But Stella might have a clue.' Catrin feels Nina and Roz closing ranks. 'And it might help. Don't tell me you don't want to know what evidence she found, Roz. It could change everything. It could give you answers.'

'Of course I want to know . . . but I agree with Nina. I don't see why we have to do everything on *her* terms. Why can't we just go to the police?'

'And say what?' asks Nina in a resigned voice. 'There's a woman who says she's found something, but we don't know what it is?' Nina pauses, thinks it through carefully. 'We could make her tell us by refusing to do the interviews, I suppose . . .'

'She won't do that,' says Catrin. 'She'll make you do the work first, and then she'll give us what we want.' Catrin looks from Nina to Roz, and back to Nina once more. 'Look. I understand why you're both reluctant. The question here is, what is it that *we* want? When we pinpoint that, we can try and get it with or without the help of Stella. I'll go first, shall I? I want the truth. I want to know what happened to Hazel. Roz? What about you?'

Roz shrugs. 'I want to know what happened to Hazel too. I can't remember that morning clearly. I'd like some closure. That's what I want, really. Some sense of peace.'

Catrin turns to Nina. 'Nina? What do you want?'

Nina's face is like thunder. 'I want to stop being manipulated by people like you and Stella Cox. And I want to get off this miserable little island and go home.'

Chapter Twenty-Three

NINA

Nina sits down at the kitchen table, next to Roz. 'This is so typical of you, Catrin,' says Nina bitterly. 'It's just like that time when we were twelve and you enrolled us all into the Brownies without asking, just because *you* wanted to go. That was a whole year of Wednesday evenings I never got back.'

'Look, if I could take you back to Eider right now, I would.' Catrin looks at her watch. 'But the tide has already turned and it's too late.'

'Why do I get the feeling you're just saying that because there's no way I can prove otherwise?' Nina looks around the kitchen. 'Is there anything to drink in this place besides coffee?'

'I brought something from the supermarket,' says Catrin. 'Roz? Do you want a drink?'

'No,' says Roz, getting up. 'I'm going out again, see if I can find Hazel.'

'Stay for a minute, please, Roz,' says Catrin, and Nina wonders if she can hear a note of regret in her voice for steamrolling over their wishes in favour of Stella's. 'Before Stella gets here, I think we need to talk about the events of that morning. We never really did go over it together. We were just . . . plunged into looking for Hazel and then we left the island.'

Nina has an urge to point out to Catrin that they could have talked together at school, if Catrin had been more interested in being with them, but she bites her tongue because there is enough bad feeling in this room already.

'Be my guest,' Roz says, with a hint of petulance. 'You were out the longest. And you saw nothing? Nothing at all?'

'I . . .' Catrin glances at Nina, but Nina ignores her. Any camaraderie they'd rekindled this morning has gone in the face of Catrin's selfish pursuit of the truth. 'All I remember is leaving you to take some shots of the cliff, and then returning to the house and it was in chaos. Do you remember anything about being up there, alone? You were worried about leaving Hazel behind, not letting her know we were going . . . did you stay up there for long?'

Roz stares, aghast, at Catrin. '*You* were the one who said not to try and wake her, that my parents would hear, and they'd stop us from going! I should never have listened to you. I should have woken her up and brought her with us.'

Catrin shrugs. 'You seemed glad to have a break from her, Roz. You said that morning, it was nice not to have to look after her all the time. Your parents babied her, didn't they? They made you baby her too. You said so yourself.'

'Is that why you and Nina didn't like her?' asks Roz with suspicion. 'You were always ducking out of being with her—'

'We did like her!' interrupts Nina. 'She could just be a bit . . .'

'She was only two years younger, but the age gap felt a lot wider,' says Catrin gently. 'Our friendship was with you, Roz. Not Hazel. We liked Hazel. But we loved you.'

'Then why invite us all to the island?' Roz says in frustration.

'If you recall, I didn't,' says Catrin. 'But your parents wouldn't let you come alone, and Hazel didn't want to be left behind. Before I knew it, the rest of your family had invited themselves.'

Nina sees the expression on Roz's face. 'I don't think this conversation is helping,' she says quietly.

Roz sits back down at the table, next to Nina, and puts her head in her hands. 'You're right. Hazel was babied, and I was just as bad as my parents. They made me look after her all the time. That's one of the reasons I loved being friends with you two so much. I could look up to you.' Roz looks up and smiles at the memory. 'Both of you, you always seemed to know what to do, you always had a plan on the go. I just . . . followed. It was a really nice feeling, letting go of responsibility.' Roz pauses, momentarily lost in thought. 'I suppose that's why I wanted to be loved by Simon so badly. I thought, after Hazel died, that things would settle . . . that my parents might start thinking about me. But things never settled. They focused on Hazel even more. Her absence eclipsed everything in that house when I was growing up. Everything. Every conversation, every decision . . .'

'It must have been awful,' acknowledges Nina, reaching over and giving Roz's hand a brief squeeze. Roz's skin feels natural, familiar, under her touch.

'Why did you like me?' says Roz, sounding so small and defeated that Nina's heart breaks a little. 'What on earth did I bring to our friendship?'

'That's easy,' says Catrin with a grin. 'I was always on the lookout for a mother figure. Someone soft and warm. You listened to me, Roz, took me seriously. And, yes, I admit, I enjoyed bossing you both about. I know I could be like that, sometimes.'

'Just a bit,' laughs Nina, before she can stop herself. It is hard to remain angry in the face of Catrin's honesty.

'What about you, Nina? The girl who had everything. What did you see in us?' asks Catrin.

Nina doesn't have to think. She knows, has always known, the size of the hole Roz and Catrin left behind in her life. 'It sounds stupid, to say it out loud,' she begins.

'Tell us,' says Roz, reaching back over the space between them, taking Nina's hand this time. 'It won't sound stupid. Not at all.'

'That . . .' says Nina faintly, feeling the prick of tears at the back of her eyes, looking at her hand in Roz's. 'That's exactly what I mean. To be believed, to be told I wasn't doing anything wrong . . . it's so hard to explain, because my mum is amazing, incredibly supportive, it sounds so ungrateful to say anything against her. She was perfect. *Is* perfect. But she expected me to be the same as her. All those ironed dresses she made me wear, when really, sometimes, I just wanted to be in jeans like you two.'

'I was *so* jealous of those dresses!' exclaims Roz.

Nina turns to Roz, feeling shy. 'And to be touched. You were always so cuddly, Roz. Always giving me a hug or taking my arm. You taught me there was another way to show affection.'

Roz squeezes Nina's hand even harder.

'And you, Catrin,' continues Nina. 'Oh my God! You made me laugh so much. Do you remember the time we were all wondering how you got a love bite from a boy? And then you just lunged forward and gave me one on my neck . . . like a vampire.'

'And it took *ages* to disappear . . .' says Roz, clapping her hands to her face.

'. . . and my mum asked me what it was when we came back home . . .' laughs Nina, '. . . and Catrin said it was a bruise before I could think of what to say.'

'Her face! It was a picture,' agrees Catrin, smiling at the memory. 'She didn't know whether to believe me or not.'

'Sometimes,' Nina says, 'I would wake up the next morning with a stomach ache because my muscles were so sore from laughing at the stuff you came up with. Remember playing knock-down-ginger?'

'And shoplifting nail polish from the chemist?' remarks Catrin.

'Awful.' Roz shakes her head. 'We were awful children.'

'Roz returned that nail polish the next day, because she felt so guilty,' remembers Catrin.

'I did.' Roz nods sagely. 'It was the right thing to do.'

'Liar!' Catrin says. 'You only did that because Hazel found out and she thought you'd go to prison.'

'Oh! I'd forgotten about that!' laughs Roz. 'She was terrified. I had a hell of a job putting it back without being caught by Mrs Evans.'

'Didn't Nina distract her at the counter by asking if she would order some blue mascara for her?'

'Yes!' says Nina, remembering. 'And she told me off because she said I was far too young and only ladies of the night wore blue mascara.'

'And nobody had a clue what that even *meant*.'

The memories take on significance when they are retold, proof of how strong their friendship was. But eventually, their supply runs out. When the words begin to fade, so does the tentative bond that briefly held them together. Nina feels it loosen and collapse in the silence that follows, where everyone reaches around for something else to say.

'Anyway. I think I'm going to go out . . .' mumbles Roz. 'There might be . . .' She doesn't finish the sentence. She shuffles past Catrin, awkwardly, to get out of the room.

Nina and Catrin watch her leave and they both wait until the door has shut before they speak.

'Are you going to tell her about the photograph?' presses Nina.

Catrin looks thoughtful. 'Don't you think she could be putting on all of this fragile-girl thing? To hide something? It feels like an act.'

Nina shakes her head, her frustration returning. 'No. She just seems sad, like she's struggling with life. She's trying to find an explanation for Hazel's death.'

'What – spooks and witches?'

Nina hears the derision in Catrin's voice. 'Are you sure you aren't influenced by what her parents did to your family? You must feel some resentment there.'

'Wouldn't you?'

'Not towards Roz. Her parents were awful, remember? You above anybody know how tough it can be to have a parent you don't agree with. You aren't responsible for your father's actions any more than Roz is responsible for her parents'. You have more in common than I think you'd like to admit.'

Catrin's shoulders drop.

'And she has a point about this house,' Nina continues, indicating the marks at the window. The grooves in the stone windowsill have gathered a century's worth of dust. There are symbols in there she can't make out, but they have been carved into the stone with such force, such passion, it gives Nina the creeps. 'What were they trying to keep out, these long-ago ancestors of yours?' she says. 'People have been seeing ghosts, talking to spirits, for millennia. Doesn't Roz have a point? If there's no truth in a story, it wouldn't have legs, would it? It wouldn't be passed down through generation after generation, would it?'

But Catrin is defiant. 'Lies can be inherited just as easily as the truth. This is all tangled up in her relationship with her daughter, if you ask me. It's more about the living than the dead.'

'Don't you ever wonder what would have happened to us if Hazel hadn't died? I wouldn't have been taken away to London, your family business would be successful and the three of us might have been friends for the past twenty years. It's about the dead, Catrin. A death has done this to us. It pushed us apart and now it's pulling us together.'

'I thought you were taken to London because your parents divorced. Not because Hazel died,' says Catrin.

'The point still stands,' Nina replies. 'The question is, what are we going to do about it?'

Catrin shakes her head. 'There's nothing *to* do. We can't change the facts.'

'But we can change how we deal with them.' Nina pulls her chair closer to the table, an idea taking hold. 'Don't show Roz that photograph, Catrin. It's not going to help her. We only have a short time here together. I think Roz could really do with a friend right now.'

'But the photograph is important, Nina. The *truth* is important. Roz wants the truth.'

Nina sighs. 'If the truth is going to hurt Roz, then what's wrong with a lie?'

Catrin looks aghast. 'Because . . . because. I can't believe you're saying this, Nina.'

'If it turns out that the people in that photo turned up here and took Hazel away – murdered her, even – how is that better than thinking she fell? It would open up a whole other can of worms that could take years to resolve – or it might never be resolved at all. It could be your father in that picture, Catrin, and then what would you do? That photograph throws up more questions than answers. Roz is looking for answers right now. She's desperate for them. And you might not like what you dig up.'

'If I don't show her this photograph, it's lying, right?'

Nina throws up her hands in exasperation. 'You told me how wonderful I look when you met me this morning, how well dressed. I just learnt to cover up my flaws. That's a kind of lying, isn't it?'

'Come on, Nina . . .'

'I tell lies every day! I tell strangers who write in to me that they are going to be OK, that everything will work itself out. And they need that. They need to be told that lie. I have no idea if they're going to be OK, a lot of them probably aren't. I don't know them. But they think they know me. It's all an illusion, Catrin. But it works. It makes people happy. And isn't happiness more important than the truth?'

Catrin looks confused and, for the first time since their reunion, uncertain. Nina feels she is slowly winning her over. 'What good will it do, showing Roz that photograph?' she urges. 'It's only going to cause more heartache for her. Whoever those people are, it doesn't change the fundamental fact that Hazel is gone. Knowing the identity of the people in the picture won't bring Hazel back, and it might make matters worse between you and your father. It will cause more pain. That's the truth of it, Catrin.'

There is a beat when Nina's words land and strike, one by one. She can feel Catrin's resolve crumbling. A dark look crosses Catrin's face.

'I'll think about it,' she says. 'But I don't like hiding things. It's not in my nature. It's not in Stella's nature either.'

'Stella isn't in charge here. We are. It's important to present a united front when she arrives, or she'll have us all for breakfast.' Nina looks around the room. 'Now, what about that wine? Shall I cobble together some nibbles for us all?'

'Yeah, go ahead,' Catrin replies, sounding distracted. 'I want to take a few pictures before the light goes.' Catrin finds her camera bag and assembles her camera, taking a spare lens with her. Nina hears the front door close and, at last, the only sounds remaining with her are the wind, the waves, and the gulls.

Nina stops what she is doing and listens for a little while more, in case Catrin decides to come back. But after a few minutes, there is a settling in the house that tells Nina she is alone. She tiptoes into the hallway and over to the library, her heart beating thickly in anticipation. The Turkish rug is still there. She walks across it and a familiar squeak moans into the damp air. The large bookcase is the same, its legs akimbo, a smooth wooden ball under each clawed foot, looking as if it would scuttle off if it wasn't for all the books it was carrying. Nina breathes through her nose, trying to control the prickly feeling that is spreading across her chest. She kneels in front of the bookcase and murmurs a little prayer.

Gingerly, she reaches her fingers underneath the base of the bookshelf. The gap is only a couple of inches, she hopes she won't have to reach far. The floorboards are dusty and there is a web in the corner, running underneath the bookcase and into the space she must explore. She is frightened of spiders and hopes there isn't one there, crouching in the darkness. She musters her courage and pushes her fingers a little further, trying not to graze her fingertips through the dust. She feels what she hopes is a dust ball, and not another spider web. She is just about to withdraw her fingers when her nails brush against something solid. She feels the shape of it, flat and slim, and breathes, finally, a sigh of relief.

Chapter Twenty-Four

CATRIN

Catrin returns after taking as many photos as she can before the light goes, letting the comfort of focusing on something she does well settle her. By the time she is back at The Old House she feels calmer, ready for the next conversation. Roz doesn't come back until after the sun has set. The crisps and nuts that Nina emptied into bowls have been eaten and the bottle of wine is half empty. She and Nina have danced around polite small talk, even stooping low enough to compare the weather in Africa to England. Catrin watches Roz warily as she comes back into the house, looking paler and much younger than her thirty-three years.

'How was your walk?' asks Nina, leaping up to fetch Roz a glass and pouring a measure of wine.

'I know you think I'm mad.' Roz sits down heavily, accepting the glass of wine from Nina. She sighs and takes a sip. 'I suppose I am a bit mad. I'm sure Simon would agree. And Willow.'

'I wouldn't listen to your ex,' says Nina. 'He's bound to have an angle.'

'We got married for the wrong reasons. It's more my fault than his.'

'You said earlier that you got married because you needed someone to love you,' says Nina. 'What's been going on, Roz? Did things really get that bad?'

Catrin sees Roz blink away tears as she takes another sip of wine. 'Things weren't great to begin with. My parents were always overly protective. You know what they were like.'

Catrin and Nina nod to one another.

Roz continues, 'But after Hazel . . . things just went up another level. They blamed me. Of course they did. I deserved it.'

'Roz . . .' Nina begins.

'Their grief . . . it became anger. Catrin's family felt most of that.' Roz turns to Catrin. 'And I'm sorry about that, I really am. For me, it was more subtle. They turned towards one another, my parents, blocking me out, as if I didn't understand what they were going through.'

'That must have been very lonely,' says Nina, her voice soft and understanding. In that moment, Catrin can see why so many people trust her, sending in their problems, hoping to get a sincere response.

'When I met Simon, it felt so good to be the centre of someone's attention again. We got married fairly quickly, I was barely twenty. I wanted to leave home so badly. I thought if I had a child with him, that feeling of security I'd found would last forever. I couldn't wait to start a family, surround myself with more people who loved me. But it didn't work out like that. When I had Willow, all the feelings around Hazel's disappearance came back, and I knew how untrustworthy I'd been as a sister.'

Nina shakes her head. 'You did everything you could for Hazel.'

Roz ignores her and lets out a hollow laugh of despair. 'What was I thinking, trying to be a parent? I couldn't do it. I couldn't trust myself to look after Willow properly. I don't have the confidence Simon has. The only reason she isn't living with him permanently is that his job is so full on, he's never there. But she'll be twelve soon, and off to secondary school. She'll be able to get herself to school and back without me. And I think . . .' Here, Roz's voice wavers. 'I think she'll choose to live with him instead of me. I think she'd prefer it.'

'Have you explained to Willow why you're like this?' says Catrin.

'I haven't told her about Hazel,' Roz replies.

'Why?' Catrin asks, surprised.

'Well, at first I convinced myself it was because I didn't want to burden her with such a sad story at such a young age. Then, when she got a bit older, I knew it would upset me to talk about her, because it was my fault . . .'

'It wasn't your fault!' says Nina with exasperation, bringing her wine glass down with a thump. A spatter of red spills on the table and stays there, wet and shiny.

'I broke a promise. If I'd just woken her up . . .'

Nina gets up and finds a box of tissues on the Welsh dresser. She wipes up her spill, then she leaves the tissues at Roz's elbow. Roz takes one and blows her nose.

'What about Simon? How much does he know about Hazel?' queries Catrin.

Roz sighs. 'Only the basics. He found me very tragic when we met at seventeen. He loved the pathos and the mystery. But when I didn't change, when I couldn't get over it, and I still refused to talk about Hazel in detail, he just lost patience with me. The way I am with Willow, it just tipped him over the edge. When she was a baby, I used to call him all the time at work, because I didn't know how to keep her safe, I was terrified I was doing the wrong thing. He nearly lost his job, I phoned him so much. He deserves to be with someone who's confident, and carefree. I just . . . drag everybody down with me.' Roz pulls out another tissue and holds it to her eyes.

Catrin looks at Nina, who looks stricken by Roz's story. Nina asks tentatively, 'What about your parents? Are they still . . .'

'Difficult? Yes, they are. I've kept my distance from them. I phone them on Hazel's anniversary, and birthdays, that sort of thing. It's all I can do.'

'What about your daughter?' says Catrin.

'Willow has no relationship with them. They only have space for Hazel. And Willow looks so much like her. It tore them up, to see her.' Roz describes her childhood home, every scrap of available space taken up with Hazel: files containing information about her disappearance, all the flyers they got printed and then updated over the years with a face that aged into a woman Roz couldn't recognise any more.

'The thing is . . .' Roz says, thinking it through, 'everything about Hazel's disappearance is bound up in blame. And when that blame comes from your own parents . . . the shame of it . . . it's impossible to discuss that with anybody else.'

Until now, Catrin realises with a jolt. She can feel there is something happening here. Some kind of magic the three of them had together that has lain dormant for twenty years. As the conversation opens up before her, Catrin can feel little shards of light filter their way through the darkness of the past. And a fleeting thought crosses her mind: that the arrival of Stella might ruin it all, that her gamble might not pay off. She quietly watches Nina and Roz talk together, and wonders if the fragile thing she can feel between them will survive the next forty-eight hours.

'When Willow was born,' Roz continues, taking a breath, 'I thought it might be a turning point, that some kind of magic reset button might be pressed when I gave them a granddaughter.

But . . .' Roz hesitates, remembering. 'Willow looked so much like Hazel . . . I suggested staying with them once. Bringing Willow. But they told me they couldn't have anyone sleeping in Hazel's room. They'd kept it exactly as it was, in case she came back. There wasn't any point reminding them it was my room too.'

Roz looks at Nina and gives her a rueful smile. 'I was always so jealous of your relationship with your mum, Nina. You were so close. Are you still?'

'Yes,' says Nina quietly. 'We see each other most days. For lunch, or whatever.'

'That must be so great, to have that kind of relationship,' says Roz, looking deflated.

'It's a double-edged sword,' concedes Nina. 'Howard, my ex-husband, he never really appreciated why we were so close. She can be a bit— overbearing, I suppose. She did a lot of things with us – holidays, Sunday lunch. He used to joke he was married to both of us.'

'Did she like Howard? Did they get on?' Roz asks.

'She tolerated him. She doesn't like coming second. I don't think she understood why my attention diverted away from her when I married him.'

'Sylvia was one of the strongest women I knew,' says Catrin, remembering, unable to imagine what it must be like, to have a mother so invested in her life. 'I loved her for that. Did she never meet anyone else after your dad left?'

'No. I think she devoted her entire life to me, and she never left her post.'

'Wow,' says Catrin. An unfamiliar feeling spreads across her like ink in water. Self-pity.

Nina notices. 'We never spoke about your mother when we were little, did we, Catrin. Are all children self-absorbed, or was it only us?' she says, her voice edged with sympathy.

Catrin smiles a wan smile, traces a mark on the table with her fingertips. 'I don't remember her. Only what James told me. It's not like you and Roz, having a close relationship with a parent and losing it suddenly.'

Roz turns to Nina. 'Oh! Did your dad die?'

Nina nods. 'Yes, shortly after I moved to London.'

Roz frowns. 'I'm surprised I don't remember that,' she says.

'He moved, after he married his very pregnant girlfriend.'

Roz's eyes open wide. 'I didn't realise, Nina. I'm sorry. You have siblings then.'

'A sister, I'm told.'

'You're *told*? You mean you haven't met her?'

'No,' says Nina quietly. 'They were in Hong Kong when my father died. They're probably still there, for all I know.'

'Aren't you desperate to find out?' Roz urges.

'It just felt a bit too late to play happy families after he'd gone. I'd started a new life in London, I was just getting acting roles. It was exciting and my old life seemed just that. Old.' Nina takes a sip of wine and looks, steadfast, into the glass.

'Yes, but your sister . . . your little sister.'

'Look, Roz,' says Nina evenly. 'My situation is very different from yours.'

'But she's your *sister*.'

'I'm aware of that. But it's not like I'm a hard person to track down. I'm on TV every weekday morning.'

'Surely you have a responsibility to reach out.'

'Things are never as black and white as they appear to others. Life is full of grey areas and families are one of the hugest grey areas you can find.'

'If I had a sister out there . . .' Roz trails off when she sees Nina's face.

'Please don't use your situation to judge mine. It's not fair.'

Catrin feels the tension rise in the room. 'I think we could do with another bottle of wine. And some proper food. Is everyone OK with beans on toast?'

'I'll get the wine,' says Nina quickly.

There is an uneasy atmosphere in the air when they eat together. The conversation see-saws between small talk and silence. Catrin looks at her watch. Tomorrow afternoon, Stella will be here. If she shows Roz the photograph, she should do it before Stella arrives. But the question that Nina put into her head won't go away. It keeps popping up, like a cork in water. Is it really worth showing Roz that picture? She is no longer convinced the truth is the ally she thought it was. It would cause Roz such grief, wondering if someone was responsible for her sister's death. And if it *was* Roz, or her own father, in that image, there must be an innocent explanation. There must.

Chapter Twenty-Five

Roz

They all know when Stella is going to arrive because of the tide. Catrin decides to walk out to meet her in the cove, while Roz and Nina cower in the house. The day has a freshly laundered feeling about it. The clouds are fluffed up and white, the sky is a milky blue and there is a sweet smell in the air. Even so, everybody has slept badly, and Roz is dreading meeting Stella.

'Nina,' she says, finding her in the library. Nina looks up at her and smiles, gestures for her to take the armchair opposite. Roz sinks into it, grateful that somehow, overnight, the tension in the house has dissipated.

'What are we going to do?' Roz says. 'I don't want to get dragged into this podcast, not after what you said.' The old feeling comes back as if it had never left. The hope that someone else is going to take charge and make everything all right.

Nina takes a sip from her coffee cup. 'I'm not saying this Stella woman is a bad person, I'm just saying her interests aren't aligned with ours. She wants drama. We don't.'

'I'm worried I'll say something, and she'll twist it into something else. They always do that kind of thing, don't they, journalists?'

Nina smiles reassuringly. Roz can see she has left a stain of lipstick on her coffee cup. A perfect red smile on the white porcelain. She looks composed, in control, everything that Roz isn't.

'It depends,' reflects Nina. 'The problem we have is that Stella has all the balls in her court. Catrin won't take us back to Eider until we've given Stella a chance. Before we know it, we'll be spending another night here.'

'But what can we do? Nothing,' says Roz, resigned.

Nina talks to herself, staring into the empty fireplace between them. 'We want to know what she's got, but she won't show us until we give her what she wants. It's a conundrum, unless . . .'

'What?' Roz asks, sensing a resolution. Nina looks at her with those cool grey eyes. Roz had trusted those eyes, once, implicitly. A memory of them both, ten or eleven, the summer before they all transferred to the big secondary school and they were nervous about it: *I'll look out for you,* Nina had said. *Don't worry.*

'Well, we could try and find out what she has before she's ready to show us,' Nina says.

'How do you think we should do that?' Roz cannot tear herself away from Nina's eyes. She has a hunch the knowing look, the slow, certain nod of her head, must be something Nina has perfected for television, but she feels the power of it, lifting her up. It is real.

Nina considers something. 'She'll suspect me. But you . . .' Again, those eyes turn to Roz, as if she is the most important thing in the room. 'There's something innocent about you. Why don't we just play along with her, pretend we're giving her a chance, and then, in the early evening, you say you need a lie-down or something and then you just . . . go through her bags while I keep her busy. Whatever she's found, she's probably brought it with her

175

so she can bring it out for maximum impact. If we stole it from her, she'd lose all her leverage.'

Roz takes a deep breath, feeling her heart beat like a little bird. She doesn't like being a thief, but to find out the truth she can make an exception. And in this moment, just like her younger self she trusts Nina implicitly, she wants to impress her. 'OK. I think I can do that. But what am I looking for?'

'Hopefully, you'll know what it is when you find it. If it has something to do with Hazel, you'll be the one to know, surely?'

Roz swallows. There is a big lump in her throat. 'Yes, OK,' she says.

'Catrin's made up the bedroom next to ours for Stella. Let's make her feel welcome – she can stash all her bags there and we can ply her with wine. Hopefully, she drinks alcohol.'

'What if she catches me?'

'Listen, Roz. Whatever she's taken, it doesn't belong to her. You have just as much right as her to take it. More, probably, because Hazel is your sister.'

Roz remembers this, this feeling of being enveloped in the absolute certainty of Nina. It felt safe back then and it feels safe now. 'You're right,' she says, feeling much more confident. 'You're absolutely right.'

The door blows open and Roz can hear the voices of Stella and Catrin in the hall. Nina looks at Roz, holds her in that penetrating gaze and whispers, 'Remember what I told you. Make her feel as if she's going to win us over, make her feel welcome. Then she'll let her guard down.'

Roz nods, grateful she has an ally, and she turns to the library door as Stella and Catrin walk in to give them her brightest smile.

Stella is not what Roz expected. She thought journalists were smartly dressed and had an intellectual air about them. But this woman is in cut-off jeans and a T-shirt with what looks like a band logo sprayed across it. Her eyes have black kohl around them, and her hair is bleached white; it stands in stiff peaks above her head, like whipped meringue. Her ears and nose are pierced and filled with little silver rings of varying sizes. She even has tattoos. A fat snake coils up her left arm, its head at her bicep, its tail at her wrist.

'Hi. I'm Stella,' she says, giving the room a generous wave. 'It's so great to meet you face to face. I know this must feel slightly weird for you all.' She turns to Roz, offers her hand and says, 'I'm going to do my very best to give Hazel's story the time and space it deserves.'

As Roz shakes Stella's hand, a little piece of her resolve melts. She finds herself nodding along without really meaning to.

'And you, Nina,' Stella continues, 'it's wonderful to meet you again. I love what you're doing with *Rise*. I've followed your acting career, which is incredible by the way, all that work under your belt before you were thirty. Amazing! And the way you deal with the public. You're an absolute natural. Sorry! I sound like I have a crush on you! I suppose I do in a way.'

The laugh Stella gives is unselfconscious and infectious. Nina laughs, self-deprecatingly, bats off the compliments and offers Stella coffee.

'I brought a few things, in case you needed them.' Stella puts a tote bag on the long table under the window. There are a couple of bottles of expensive-looking wine, which Nina falls upon; a selection of Japanese rice crackers Roz adores and some very good coffee that impresses Catrin. But Stella hasn't finished. She pulls out some dark chocolate, several Indian mangoes, a punnet of large red strawberries, some plump blueberries and a large pot of thick Greek yoghurt. The memory of beans on toast for dinner and toast again for breakfast is still fresh and they all fall upon the fruit. Roz pops a strawberry in her mouth and is engulfed by its fragrant sweetness. Stella reaches for another bag and reveals all the makings of a simple meal that won't need anyone to prepare it, beyond opening several boxes with the Selfridges logo on the stickers keeping them shut. Stella shrugs. 'I thought we could all use a treat,' she says.

Catrin herds them all into the kitchen and busies herself brewing the coffee, chatting to Stella about her journey over, while Roz finds a bowl for the fruit. As she reaches into the Welsh dresser, she glances back at Nina, who is sitting, elbows on the kitchen table, her hands folded underneath her chin. There is a big smile on her face as she joins in the conversation. And suddenly, Roz recognises that smile, she understands the meaning behind it. It is like hearing a language that hasn't been spoken for years. She knows, with a certainty she cannot fully explain, that Nina has not been taken in at all.

The afternoon turns into evening and wine, once more, is opened and drunk. Roz is enjoying herself so much, she forgets the task she has been set by Nina, until a foot kicks her under the table and Nina shoots her a glare. Then her heart races, and she feels a bit sick.

'Are you OK, Roz?' asks Nina pointedly, loudly.

Roz touches her head. 'I think I have a migraine coming. It's probably the wine.'

'Why don't you have a lie-down and we'll call you when dinner's ready?' says Nina. 'You look a bit off-colour. I have some painkillers on the cabinet between our beds. Take what you need.'

'Thanks, Nina,' mumbles Roz, excusing herself from the table. She walks up the stairs, which ascend into gloom. The light is beginning to leave the sky but there is plenty enough to see. She creeps into the bedroom that Stella has been given and sees she's left her bags on the floor. There is a leather holdall and what looks like a laptop case. She decides the holdall is the best place to start and gently unzips it. Below her, she can hear Nina change the gears of the conversation and begin a story involving a well-known celebrity, which is already making Stella laugh.

Clever Nina, thinks Roz.

Her hands search around the edges of the holdall, which contains a change of clothes and a small spongebag. There are no papers or hard objects that seem out of place. Her fingers brush up against plastic. It feels smooth and doesn't crackle like a supermarket bag. Roz grips it and tries to slide it out from between Stella's clothes without disturbing anything. It looks like a folder, the size of an A4 sheet of paper. It is semi-transparent, and Roz realises it is one of those nice food bags you might put sandwiches in, or food for the freezer, with a seal at the top that can be pulled apart. Roz holds the bag up in front of her face, wondering what she is looking at. She hasn't switched the lamp on in the bedroom and the light is dim through the small windows. It looks like an item of clothing. Something flip-flops in Roz's stomach. The item is black, and Hazel never wore black. It is bunched up in a way that prevents Roz from recognising what it is, so she gently prises open the bag, and as she does so she is engulfed by a powerful smell.

It is earthy, and salty, and aged, and damp. It smells of something that's been in the ground for a very long time. Feeling nauseous, Roz opens the bag wide and peers in. She can see soil and sand and little bits of stone. Threads of something fraying and split apart. Even as she pulls it out of the bag, she still doesn't realise what it is. But when the object unfolds itself and she finds herself staring into that singular glass eye, Roz realises it is Goggin.

Chapter
Twenty-Six

NINA

They all hear Roz's cry. Nina stops mid-sentence, wondering what
it is she has found.

'That headache must be a bad one. I'll go and see if she's OK,'
she says, getting up from the table. Catrin and Stella make a move
as well, but Nina waves them back down. 'I'll call if I need help,'
she says. She runs up the stairs. She opens the door to Stella's room
and Roz is sitting on the floor, rocking gently as she cries, holding
something to her chest. It looks like a small animal and something
about it makes Nina afraid.

'What is it, Roz? What did you find?'

Roz offers her the thing in her arms and Nina recoils when
she takes it. The smell of it is enough to make her feel sick. Its eye
stares at her sightlessly. Its limbs dangle, stiff with salt and earth.
Some of its innards hang out of its body cavity. She hands it straight
back to Roz.

'It's Goggin,' whispers Roz, her eyes wide, her face a mixture
of wonder and shock.

'I can see that,' says Nina uneasily. It creeps her out, to see this bundle of limbs with one eye. There is something malevolent about it. But Roz pulls it to her chest as if it is a baby.

'What do you think this means, Nina?' whispers Roz, her face streaked with tears. 'Hazel would never be parted from Goggin. Never. Why did she drop him?' Roz looks around the room wildly, as if she will find the answer there. 'If she'd fallen, she would have held on to him, tight. I know it.' She gives Nina a pleading look. 'Maybe my parents were right all along. Maybe she was taken, and she dropped him . . . or maybe she left him behind as a sign and we just missed it somehow? I wonder where Stella found him.' Roz talks quickly, her teeth chattering.

There is a thunder of footsteps on the stairs and Stella's voice sounds out from behind them. 'Are you in my room?' she asks. 'Oh, I see.' Stella stops when she understands what has happened. 'I honestly didn't think you'd do that,' she says. 'Stupid me.'

'Where did you find him?' asks Roz. She looks like a child, sitting on the floor, cradling Goggin.

Something in Stella's face changes. She stops looking annoyed. 'I found him on the cliff path,' she relents.

'How far up?' asks Catrin.

'About two-thirds of the way up to the cairn. I marked it.'

'How could the search party have missed him?' asks Roz.

'They were looking for a little girl,' Stella replies. 'From what I understand, the search party was mainly villagers. Amateurs, really. I only found him because I fell over when I was walking. He was underneath a gorse bush.'

'I want to see,' says Roz. 'Right now.'

Nina, Catrin and Stella look outside. It is getting dark. Catrin looks at her watch. 'I think we have about an hour's worth of light.'

'That's enough time.' Roz is already leaving the room.

'I'll grab a couple of torches,' says Catrin, with a grim face. 'And my camera.'

The wind has picked up and the gulls are leaving the sky to find places to spend the night. The colour is leaking out of the pretty yellow flowers that carpet the grassland around the house, and everything slowly loses its warmth as the sun turns its attention to other places. Nina is afraid to go up to the cliff, but she is more afraid of being left alone in the house when the sun sets, so she puts a jacket on and follows.

They have to walk in single file, Stella at the head, followed by Roz, still holding Goggin. Catrin is behind Roz and Nina trails at the back. She takes a moment to look around her. Forty-eight hours ago, she was getting ready for an early night. She had a movie lined up and a nice Barolo. It seems impossible she is here, searching for clues on an island with a bunch of amateur detectives.

'This is insane,' she says to Catrin's backside. 'We'll probably all go over the cliff at this rate.'

'Roz needs to see where he was found,' says Catrin, her voice heavy with the exertion of climbing and talking. 'She'd be out here by herself if we hadn't come with her. It's safer this way.'

'Really,' replies Nina with heavy sarcasm.

The sun sinks lower, setting the skyline on fire, bathing the landscape in an eerie orange glow. Stella disappears through a hole in the scrub and switches from the path inland to the old path by the cliffs. Nina's heart races as they near the edge. 'This isn't safe,' she pants.

'It's safe enough. You can wait here, if you like,' says Catrin. But again, Nina feels very certain she doesn't want to be left alone. So she follows them until, finally, Stella stops.

'Here,' she says, out of breath. 'I tied a piece of ribbon to the gorse.' Stella walks past the waving red ribbon to allow Roz access.

'This is the ribbon you found, the day you arrived,' says Catrin to Roz, her voice full of understanding.

'I thought . . . I thought that . . .' Roz doesn't finish the sentence. She sounds dejected.

Nina can't see much, so she says nothing. She is happier hanging back.

'Just here,' says Stella, indicating a dent in the earth where Goggin has been pulled out.

Catrin leans over to take a look. 'It's close to the edge. Hazel could easily have dropped him if she slipped or something.' She takes a couple of pictures, the flash of her camera temporarily blinding everyone before she adjusts the settings and takes more pictures with a long exposure.

Roz kneels down in the dust.

'Stay back, Roz,' says Catrin. 'Don't touch anything in case the police need to check it out.'

'It's a bit late for that,' Nina mutters under her breath. 'We've all handled Goggin and we're all trampling around the place he was found.'

Catrin turns to Roz. 'Maybe we should get out of here. What do you think, Roz? Have you seen enough?'

Roz looks crestfallen as she gets up and backs away from the dent in the ground. 'Hazel could have fallen and flung him back. It doesn't mean anything, I suppose. We should still give Goggin to the police tomorrow, just so they can check—'

'Except it does mean something,' interrupts Stella, and even in the fading light Nina can see that Stella is about to drop a big reveal. Something she's prepared already, maybe even rehearsed in the mirror for exactly this moment. 'I didn't tell you this earlier, but when I found Goggin, he was buried.'

'Twenty years of dirt being flung at you by the wind and the waves will do that, I'm sure,' dismisses Catrin. 'He's bound to be covered in silt and stuff after such a long time.'

The sun has moved beyond the sea and Stella's face is cast in silver shadow, making her look like a ghost. 'He wasn't just covered in silt. He was under a rock. Even if Hazel had thrown him to the ground, it takes a human to lift up a rock and cover him, doesn't it?'

'Which rock?' asks Nina, edging forward.

'Um, wait. Here, this one,' says Stella. She points to a large flat rock, not quite big enough to cover Goggin but big enough to pin him down for two decades.

Roz stands up. Nina can see her profile in the dimming light. Even in monochrome, she can see the stress on her face. 'What are you saying?' Roz cries. 'Are you saying somebody took her? Pushed her? What?'

Stella looks down to the depression in the ground. 'I'm saying it's something we have to talk about. Catrin – I know we should get the police involved, and of course we need to do that, but tomorrow morning, before we can sail back to the mainland, I'd like to have a forensic look through the house and see if there's anything else the police missed. Did they do a proper search of the house at the time?'

'I can't really remember,' says Catrin.

'Well, if they'd done it properly, they would have had every stick of furniture upended, every drawer emptied, that sort of thing.'

'No,' says Catrin slowly, 'I'm pretty sure that didn't happen. I'd remember that.'

Nina looks over the cliff to the sea. It has lost its orange glow and is becoming silvered in the burgeoning moonlight. A tardy gull swoops across her vision, looking for somewhere to rest for the night, and Nina feels a fervent desire to be like that bird, able to simply take off and leave all of this behind.

Stella looks at each of them, one by one in the dying light, as if to make sure she has their attention. 'If Hazel was so attached to that toy, and she'd slipped and fallen, it would have gone over with her. But it didn't. Even if she fell or dropped it on the way, toys don't pin themselves under a rock on the ground, do they? Another person has to do that.'

Chapter Twenty-Seven

NINA

The journey back down to the house is slower in moonlight. Catrin and Stella have turned on their torches, Nina uses her phone light and Roz, who has lapsed into silence, allows herself to be ushered down the hill to the house, shuffling and stumbling like a child who has missed bedtime.

Nina's stomach is empty, and she can feel it growling uncomfortably, but even the thought of the decadent food parcels from Selfridges makes her feel nauseous. 'Are you OK, Roz?' she asks, waiting for her to catch up.

'No,' says Roz miserably.

'No,' agrees Nina. 'That was a stupid question.'

Catrin and Stella are a little way ahead of them now. They are talking together in animated voices. 'Do you think she's right?' asks Roz in a small voice. 'That it wasn't an accident?'

'I think something doesn't feel right.'

'What? What do you mean?' Roz's voice is anxious now. Her step picks up, and now the path has widened there is room to walk side by side as they have the house in their sights.

'She's whipping us all up. For one thing, we only have her word she found Goggin there. It's definitely Goggin you found, right?'

'It's him,' whispers Roz in a fearful voice.

'And she discovers him – what – hidden under a rock? It seems a bit odd. If he was hidden, how did she see him? It feels a bit convenient, that she fell at the exact place he was buried.'

Roz shakes her head. She looks exhausted.

Nina places a hand on Roz's arm, stopping her, and looks around to make sure Catrin and Stella aren't watching them. 'Roz, what do you remember about that morning? Are you sure you didn't see anyone else on the cliff path when you came back down to the house?'

Roz shakes her head. 'I can't remember. It's not a blur exactly, it's just . . . not in sequence, and some things I'm not sure if I just made them up.'

'Tell me what you remember. Everything.'

'I remember trying to wake you up first thing in the morning, when it was still dark. Catrin had left the bedroom to pack her camera. She said she'd wait for me in the library. I shook your shoulder, but you didn't want to be woken up. You said you were tired. So I left. I don't remember much about the journey up. I just remember sitting next to the stone cairn. Catrin had gone. And then I got really creeped out. I can't remember where that was, though. Only that I was by myself. I started thinking about Catrin's dad and the stories he told us.'

'What stories?'

'Oh, you know, we had that fire the night before. He was trying to freak us out with folk stories about evil fairies.'

'What fairies? Oh yes,' Nina remembers, 'the . . . what was it?'

'The cold-eyed fairy folk,' Roz supplies. 'I got the feeling I was being watched, and then I thought I was being chased. Anyway, I ran most of the way down the cliff path. Then I remember going into the kitchen and Mum and Dad were there. I was so relieved to be back. But then . . .'

She doesn't need to finish the sentence because they both know how it ends.

'So you don't remember anything about your journey back down the path?' Nina asks.

'Only in snatches. I remember running and feeling scared. But not anything in detail.'

'But you didn't see anybody? Or hear anybody?'

'No, I don't think so. The gulls were noisy, I do remember that. I told you, my memory is jumbled. I have tried, over the years. But it never really came back.'

'OK. Here's what I think,' Nina says. 'I think we need to get off this island as soon as we can. We just have to hold off talking to Stella until tomorrow afternoon and then we can put this place behind us.'

'What about Goggin? Do you think we should take him to the police?'

'I don't know. I guess so. But I honestly don't know what good it's going to do.'

Roz gives Nina a pleading look. 'I don't want to give him to the police. They'll just shove him in an evidence bag for years. I want to take him home and clean him up and look after him. He's the only thing of Hazel I have left.'

They begin to walk towards the house once more and when they reach the entrance, Nina guides Roz through the front door. 'I wouldn't blame you if you wanted to do that. And if Stella doesn't have Goggin, she can't really do much with her podcast, can she.'

The meal they share at the kitchen table in The Old House is a quiet one. Stella tries her best to get Nina and Roz to talk, but they are both too tired, and too reluctant. Nina derives a quiet pleasure from the fact that Stella has spent so much money on good food and drink and it has all gone to waste.

Nina takes Roz up to bed when they have finished. Roz is so exhausted, she goes to sleep straight away. But Nina lies there, listening to the sounds of the house settling for the night. She knows Catrin must be tired because none of them slept well the night before, and Stella has had a long drive from London. Lying awake, Nina hears them clear plates away, listens to them wishing one another goodnight. She feels the beat of her heart, the blood that pulses through her body; she feels her breathing even out and become shallow. She sleeps for one hour, maybe two. When she wakes, it feels as if she is underwater. The room is blue with shadow, the house motionless, cold and silent. She listens to the silence, then she listens some more. When she is sure she has the house to herself, she eases her body out of bed, puts her hoodie on and creeps slowly down the stairs.

The light from the moon shines through the picture window, and Nina can see the silhouette of black, immovable land against the restless silver sea. She reaches the bottom of the stairs and stops, listening for any noise, and she gets a feeling the house is listening too. The house, she thinks, must remember what occurred here all those years ago. It must wonder how all of this is going to play itself out.

The door to the library is ajar and Nina is grateful she doesn't have to turn the handle, which squeaks. Once again, she kneels in front of the large bookcase against the wall, but this time she doesn't whisper a prayer. Her hand finds it almost immediately, and she tries not to think about what else might be crawling in that space. She pulls the book out, and dusts it off. It is slim with a plain cover, the kind they used to get in school to write essays in. A corner has been chewed away by mice, but otherwise it is the same as she remembers. The light from the moon is bright through the window and she takes it there, for a moment of reflection. There is her name, still legible on the cover in bold, black capitals.

ROZ RICHARDSON! Do Not Read This On Pain Of Death!

Nina knows she should take the book to the wood burner, which should still be hot enough to do its job, but her curiosity overtakes her impulse, and she opens the book, reading the secrets of a thirteen-year-old girl, feeling the emotion in between those pages. Nina doesn't cry very often, but she does tonight. Her tears spill on to the pages as twenty years roll back and all that pain, fear and grief seem as fresh now as they did on that day. When she has finished, she takes the book to the kitchen and opens the door to the wood-burning stove, where the charred logs are still glowing at their heart. Nina imagines Stella tearing the house apart in the morning and finding nothing. By the time everybody gets out of bed, this will all be ash.

But she can't do it. She cannot destroy the account of what happened that day. It is so compelling, so brutal, so utterly heartbreaking, it seems a monstrous thing to do, to throw it in the fire. It is the only thing in this whole mess that is true. As she rips out the pertinent pages, quarters them and puts them into her hoodie pocket, she burns the rest of Roz's book, thinking how proud Catrin would be that she rescued these words. But one thing Nina is certain of, she won't be sharing them with anyone else. As she watches the paper char and burn, she feels she is back in control. She will be out of here in twelve hours' time. Roz will be protected, and Stella will have nothing.

She jumps when she hears a bedroom door opening, the sound of footsteps coming down the stairs. 'Nina, what are you doing up?' asks Catrin as she comes into the kitchen. 'It's barely morning.'

'I couldn't sleep. I thought I'd build up the fire and get warm. Those rooms are freezing up there.' Nina takes in Catrin and sees she is fully dressed, with her backpack over her shoulder and a frantic look in her eye. 'Are you OK?'

'No. My phone pinged and woke me up. James has been texting me. There must have been a window of reception, and they've all come through at once. Something has happened to Dad. He's on his way to hospital. James wants me to meet him there. He sounds upset.' Catrin looks at her watch. 'If I leave now, I might be able to make it out. I can't wait until tomorrow afternoon because he needs the Land Rover to get back to Chapel Farm.' She puts a folded piece of paper on the kitchen table. 'This is a note to explain where I am. I wasn't expecting to bump into anyone.'

'I'm coming with you,' says Nina, getting up. 'And so is Roz. I just need to pack my things.'

'Nina, I have to go right now. I'm already cutting it fine. There's no time to wake people up and pack your bags. I'll try and come back in the afternoon to pick you up, but I can't promise anything. If I don't come back this afternoon, it'll definitely be tomorrow.' Grim-faced, Catrin runs out of the house, ignoring Nina's protests.

Shocked, Nina assesses the situation. Her plan to leave with Roz looks impossible now. She has no idea how long Catrin will be at the hospital. Maybe they can get Adam to come and fetch them, he might do that for Roz. She realises she hasn't told work where she is, that if she doesn't turn up there will be hell to pay. Then, with a sinking heart, she realises Catrin has taken her phone, the only one that works in this godforsaken place.

191

Chapter Twenty-Eight

CATRIN

It is still dark when the boat leaves the island. Catrin feels her way out of the cove, trying to understand if the tide is with her or not. She hears the rocks scrape against the wooden hull and remembers Arvis telling her that these boats could withstand all sorts.

It can sound worse than it is, he said to her once when she was learning to navigate the route. *This boat is one of the good ones. It's tougher than most.*

Catrin hears another scrape along the hull, and it feels like fingernails on a blackboard. She swears loudly and prays that Arvis was right. Grabbing an oar from the floor of the boat, she fends off the rocks that lie stubbornly close. She can smell them, their wet and jagged skins giving off a salty, feral odour. They glisten in the moonlight, their oily surfaces crusted with barnacles and limpets that would tear her skin if she used her hands. Catrin angles, awkwardly, out of the cove, and after a small time when it looks as if she is stuck fast, the boat suddenly frees itself and a ripple of energy pushes the vessel out to open water. She has the island behind her now, cutting a silver arc across the water as she finds the path that she must take, racing to the east, towards the lightening sky. She ties the boat up at the wooden jetty in Eider and runs to the Land Rover, which is still parked outside the Bed and Breakfast, dumping her bag on to the back seat, barely stopping herself from squealing away into the high street.

The car cuts through the countryside swiftly, following the curve of the single carriageway that twists through the heather. The road is dark, there are no other lights, save the reflective eyes of a couple of deer she captures on her way through the valley. It will take her more than an hour to get there. She grips the steering wheel and stares into the beam cast by the headlamps, her mind roiling with questions about her father.

Twenty years ago, she did not really understand the stories in the papers. Like a bad smell, she knew something was rotten, she just didn't know which direction it was coming from. People started looking at her in a funny way when she went into the village. Did they believe her father had done something wrong? She had nobody to talk to. James staunchly defended their father, but he wasn't on the island when Hazel disappeared, and he never told her what he was defending him against. *He's done nothing wrong*, was the mantra, repeated over and over until the words lost their meaning. At the height of her confusion, Catrin stopped communicating with Roz and Nina. She could only take the temperature of the local community. The village was her second family. They had closed ranks when her mother died, she'd been told, they had formed a cushion of protection around Chapel Farm. But every time Catrin set foot in the grocery store or the post office, instead of sympathetic looks and kind words, the reception was decidedly muted. Questions began to swirl in her mind. Doubts. Until, after many months of not talking about it, she had a row with her father about something trivial. It turned nasty, and when he asked if she believed the rumours that were being spread about him, she fell into a sullen, stubborn silence. The look in his eye told her she had done something unforgivable.

Catrin has never apologised to him for the betrayal. Part of the reason she was so keen to have Stella involved was to be able to prove, once and for all, that he had nothing to do with Hazel's disappearance. It would be she, Catrin, who would clear his name. She would bring her father proof, like a cat dropping a mouse at the foot of its master. But now Goggin has been found, covered by a tell-tale rock, and she has seen that photograph, the truth looks murkier than she would like. Catrin wonders if she will ever be able to put an end to their unspoken feud.

Eventually, after what seems like a long time, the lights of the town blink and reveal themselves in between the shoulders of the hills, illuminating the darkness with starry points of light in red, white and orange.

It is the early hours of Monday morning, and the hospital is in a semi-conscious state. The only area that is humming with quiet activity is the Accident and Emergency department. The dregs of the bank holiday revellers are waiting to have their injuries seen to. A pale and silent child is ushered into a room with his worried-looking mother. As Catrin walks across the emergency department, she sees a flurry of activity burst through the door, a patient on a trolley being wheeled swiftly into a cubicle. She looks away as he is hidden behind a hastily drawn curtain, and searches for her brother. She sees James in the waiting area looking lost, clutching a bag. He is in joggers, a T-shirt that looks slept in, his bare feet in trainers.

'What happened?' she asks, her adrenaline rising.

'I don't know,' James says, running his hand through his hair. His fingers are shaking. 'He said he didn't feel well last night. I've never known him to admit to that, so I was worried. I tried to call you, but I know there's never any reception in The Old House. I got up in the night and I saw his bedroom light was on. I went in and he was on the floor.'

'Was he unconscious?' Catrin tries to keep her voice steady for James's sake.

'No, not completely. I think he had a stroke.' James looks at her. She has never seen him afraid. 'Cat, he couldn't stand up. I couldn't get him off the floor. I was too worried about hurting him.'

Catrin groans. 'And I have the Land Rover.'

'It wouldn't have made any difference last night. I came in the ambulance. But I need it to get back to Chapel Farm today.'

'I should have been there for you. I should have helped.'

'It's fine,' James says, attempting to regain his composure and shaking his head. 'You're here now. He's one floor above. I just came from there and I'm desperate for coffee. You go, I'll catch you up.'

Catrin stops at the nurses' station and asks how he is.

'It's early days,' says the nurse on duty. 'He can talk, but he's lost some movement on his right side.'

'Will he get it back?'

'We don't know. We can't give you any firm answers.'

Catrin thinks about the repercussions of her father being unable to move. It would kill him, not to be able to stride around the estate. She walks into the ward and looks left and right, trying to locate him. She reaches the end of the room and still cannot see him. Then she realises she has walked right past him.

He is unrecognisable. His features have fallen. Like a rockslide, the familiar contours of his face have slipped and altered into a new landscape. And he looks so *old*. Catrin tries to hide her shock.

'Dad . . .'

His left arm rises, weakly, and then drops down on to the sheet. He doesn't move his head from the pillow.

'Can I get you anything?' she asks, feeling helpless.

'No. Sit,' he slurs.

Catrin is momentarily so grateful to receive an instruction from him, she breaks into a smile. She sinks into the chair that James must've previously occupied.

'You need to help James. With Chapel Farm. Make it permanent.' His words blur into one another, and she has to strain to hear him.

'I want to help, of course I do . . . but I have to go back to work at some point. We'll have to hire some help at Chapel Farm to tide us over until you get better.' She looks at his broken face, his helpless body, hardly believing there is a chance he will get back to normal.

'Fruit needs picking now. It won't wait.' He looks stubborn.

The familiar irritation wells up. It has been a long time since she was ordered around by him, but she hasn't forgotten the resentment it generates. 'I have my own life, Dad. My own career. I can help for a bit, of course, until you're back on your feet.'

He looks at her with an intensity she is unfamiliar with. After a long pause, he says, 'You should have stayed, Catrin.'

She knows he is not talking about her recent trip to Little Auger. 'Let's just focus on getting you out of here,' she says.

A desperate look comes into his eye. 'You were wrong to run away from us. You should have stayed. You need to come back now.'

Catrin tries to curb her annoyance. Even here, helpless in a hospital bed, he can still rile her up. She responds with the truth. 'You never wanted me, Dad. You wanted a son to run Chapel Farm, remember?'

'You should have stayed and proved me wrong. You're very good at that, Catrin. Proving people wrong. Why not for me?' There is a plaintive note in his voice. Something she hasn't come across before.

Catrin shakes her head, taken aback. 'I . . . I don't know. You didn't make it easy for me, Dad, remember? You never spent time with me. You were always off on the estate. You didn't take an interest in what I wanted to do. I felt like I hardly knew you.'

'I expected you to follow me. Like James.'

'I guess I expected you to follow *me*.' Catrin smiles, despite the tone of the conversation. 'We are very similar, you and I.'

He nods, a small gesture, but she recognises it. 'I made a mistake with you,' he says.

Catrin isn't sure if he is accusing her of not being good enough.

'I should have been . . . I can see now, it is important, what you do.' A slow tear tracks its way down his left cheek.

She has never seen her father cry. Ever. It makes her feel slightly panicky and embarrassed. She waits for him to draw himself up, as best he can, and recover.

'But it's not the sort of thing a woman your age should be doing any more. It's dangerous. It's a job for a young person. A person without a family.'

'That's simply not true,' Catrin counters. 'Why do you always have to assume women aren't as good as men? Why are we always second best in your eyes?'

'Don't you miss your roots? Your family?' he presses.

Catrin considers the past few days, reconnecting with James, with Nina and Roz. 'Maybe. But my job is important.'

'Family is more important.'

'Then you should have thought about that before you treated me as second fiddle to James.' She cannot help the cruelty of her words. They rush out in a torrent. He is a captive audience and still knows how to push her buttons.

'Chapel Farm needs you, Catrin.'

It needles her, this attitude that he always knows best; that he hasn't asked nicely, that he hasn't said it is him that needs her. It's always about the estate.

'So now I'm valuable,' she says. 'I'm supposed to put my life on hold, my career, because of a business I have no part in? I'll help for a few days, but my time is limited and precious, just like yours. Try and understand that, will you?'

A look of discontent crosses him. He turns away from her, his face half hidden in the pillow. A signal she is to leave. She is overcome by exasperation at this childish move and flounces out of the ward, feeling like a kid again. Why does every conversation with him end in an argument? Why can't she be the grown-up if he cannot? They are always reduced to adversaries; they can't ever seem to meet in the middle.

Still frothing with annoyance, she finds James in the hospital canteen and tells him of their father's demand. James offers her a bag of crisps, which soothes her mood.

'I'm not gonna lie,' he says to her carefully, 'it would be a godsend to have an extra pair of hands on the estate. Who knows?' he adds with a small grin. 'It might be fun.'

Eventually, she agrees to help while their father recovers. 'But I'm doing this for you, James,' she says begrudgingly. 'Not him.'

James nods, blows out a breath of relief and cradles his empty cup between his hands. 'I hoped that going back to Little Auger and meeting that journalist might help smooth things over between you and Dad.'

'I . . .' Catrin doesn't know how to answer this. She doesn't want to tell him that the things she's discovered have not helped, that they have complicated everything. 'Stella only arrived yesterday. Give it time.'

'Can I ask you something?' James says. 'If you had evidence, incontrovertible evidence, that Dad had nothing to do with Hazel's disappearance, would you still be so hard on him?'

'Well . . . I . . .'

'Wouldn't you, right now, be falling over yourself to help with the family business while he recovered?'

'I don't know,' says Catrin, the image of the photograph she took and Goggin, weighted under a rock, uppermost in her mind. 'I don't know what to think any more. But I'll help. Of course I'll help.'

'OK,' says James. 'We should get back to Chapel Farm. The dogs will want feeding soon. Dad needs new pyjamas, a toothbrush, that sort of thing. And I'll write you a list of jobs that will need doing while Dad's in here.'

Catrin looks at her watch. She must help James, and she needs to sleep. There is no way she will be back in time to pick up everyone from Little Auger this afternoon.

James gets up. 'I'll go and tell Dad what the plan is. We can come back this afternoon with his things. Hopefully, it will soothe him.'

'Do you mind if I tell him?' Catrin says, a wave of regret for their earlier conversation breaking over her. 'It'll mollify him, to know I'm going to stick around and help.'

'Can you promise me it won't end in another row?'

'I'm giving him what he wants. Of course there won't be a row. If he could just learn some manners and ask nicely . . .'

Catrin walks next to her brother, enjoying this back and forth, this feeling of partnership that is emerging between them. It's refreshing to be able to talk to someone about the work that needs to be done, instead of having an internal conversation and ticking everything off in her head. But when they reach the ward, the curtain is drawn around her father's bed, and a nurse prevents them from going in.

'I'm so sorry,' she says. She looks flustered. 'Can you wait here a second? The doctor is busy with him right now.'

'Why can't we see him?' says Catrin, looking over the nurse's shoulder to the curtained-off bay.

The nurse looks over her shoulder. 'I'm sorry. He had another stroke.'

'Is he going to be OK?' asks James.

'Let me get a doctor for you. Wait here,' the nurse says, turning to go.

'Just tell us what's going on,' says Catrin, her voice rising.

The nurse looks around the ward, as if someone else might be coming to help. When she realises she is on her own, she turns to them both and tries to explain. 'Sometimes, it happens like this. Another stroke after the first one. We did everything we could . . .' the nurse begins. She looks from James to Catrin, and from Catrin to James, willing them to understand.

Chapter
Twenty-Nine

Roz

After several attempts to wake Nina, Roz decides to go down for breakfast by herself. Stella is finishing a bowl of the fruit and yoghurt she brought with her.

'Want some?' she says, eyeing Roz, sliding the yoghurt pot towards her. 'Did you sleep OK?'

'Sort of,' says Roz. 'Is Catrin still asleep?'

'She had to leave. Her father is ill, so she took the boat to the mainland. There's a note on the table.'

Roz takes the note and reads it, feeling uneasy. 'So we're stuck here?' she says.

'Well, we've always been stuck here, technically, ever since Adam dropped me off. Hopefully, Catrin'll come back on the afternoon tide. But if she can't, we can call Adam again.'

'My phone doesn't work here,' says Roz, panicking.

'Oh yeah,' Stella replies. 'Mine doesn't either. I forgot about that.' She doesn't look bothered at all.

Roz sits down with resignation, scooping a large dollop of yoghurt into the bowl Stella has laid out for her, throwing a handful of blueberries on to it.

Stella gets up and rolls up the sleeves on her denim shirt. 'I have lots to do today. I want to poke around the house. See what I can find. And I'd like to start interviewing you and Nina.'

'I don't think Catrin would like that, would she? Poking around the . . . um . . . house, I mean,' queries Roz.

'I asked her last night. She said it would be fine.' Stella gives Roz a big smile.

Roz wills Nina to wake up and join her. She feels cut adrift without Nina. She had forgotten how much she relied on her friends when they were younger. The feeling of wanting their protection has resurfaced so quickly, Roz wonders if the need for it ever really went away.

'I'll start in the library,' says Stella cheerfully.

'What are you looking for?'

Again, that smile that Roz doesn't trust. 'I have absolutely no idea,' Stella beams. 'But if there's something hiding here, I'll find it.' She picks up her coffee cup from the kitchen table and drains it. The snake tattooed on her forearm writhes its way underneath the sleeve of her shirt.

Roz eats her breakfast, listening to books being removed from the bookshelf across the little hall, their pages skittering through Stella's quick fingers. Stella sneezes several times as the dust gets into her airways. Finally, to Roz's enormous relief, Nina comes down the stairs, looking weary and anxious.

'What's she doing in there?' Nina asks in a low voice. Her hair is curlier than ever and for some reason, she smells of wood smoke.

Roz blinks. 'Apparently, Catrin said it's OK that she goes through the house before we leave this afternoon.'

'Fat chance of that,' says Nina, yawning and filling up the kettle. She sets it on top of the wood burner. 'Catrin's not here to take us back.'

'I know,' says Roz, 'and we can't call Adam if Catrin doesn't show up.'

Nina makes a face. 'I'm supposed to be at work tomorrow morning. I need to let them know I'm stuck here.'

A little surge of hope lights up inside Roz and she leans towards Nina and whispers quietly, 'I don't think Stella knows about the hill.' Roz gestures to the back of the house, in the direction of the hummock that rises up behind it, and then she points to Stella's phone, which is face down, peeking out from under a tea towel. 'Maybe we could . . . ?'

Nina's mouth breaks into a wide smile, and she puts her finger to her lips. Then she picks up Stella's phone and, straight away, a look of displeasure wipes the smile from her face. She replaces the phone gently, shaking her head. And then she says in a bright voice, 'I think we need some more firewood first. Look, it's running low. Come and give me a hand.'

Perplexed, Roz shrugs. 'OK.'

They have to cross the open doorway to the library as they emerge from the kitchen. 'Where are you off to?' asks Stella. She is standing before the large bookcase, putting back several books she has clearly just rifled through.

'Have you found anything interesting?' asks Nina sweetly.

'Not yet,' replies Stella. 'Are you off somewhere? I thought we could start some interviews now you're both up.'

'Nope, just getting wood. If we're going to be here for another night, we'll need to stock up. We won't be long.'

'OK, I guess I'll make a start in the kitchen then. It's just maps and history books in here.'

Nina leads Roz around to the side of the house, which is more sheltered. There is a wooden structure to keep the rain off and, underneath the slate roof, a large pile of logs that look as if they have been lying there for a very long time. Roz begins to select some logs to take back inside when Nina stops her. 'She's recording everything we say,' she says in a furious whisper.

'Who? Stella?'

'Yes. Her phone has some kind of recording app on it, and it was running when I looked at it. She must have been doing it all along. I wondered why she hadn't press-ganged us to do interviews until now. She must be recording us on the sly.'

Roz thinks back to the night before, when they went to the cliff path. Stella had been quiet, allowing her, Nina and Catrin to speak with one another. She'd assumed it was out of respect. Now she realises it was because her phone was doing all the work. 'That's sneaky,' she says.

'Don't let on to her that we know, OK?'

Roz shrugs. 'Sure. But what do you think we should do?'

'Bide our time,' replies Nina, looking into the distance, thinking. 'Let me figure something out.'

'We should get some logs, so she isn't suspicious,' says Roz helpfully.

'Urgh, they're probably full of spiders and woodlice. I don't want to touch them,' says Nina.

Roz laughs. 'Are you still afraid of spiders? After all these years?'

Nina screws up her face in disgust as Roz loads some logs into the crook of her arm. When they come back to the house, Stella is sitting at the kitchen table. She has cleared the breakfast things away and laid out a selection of photographs on the table. Her phone is still underneath the tea towel, Roz notices, still in the same position.

'Look what I found,' says Stella, clearly pleased with herself.

'What are they?' asks Roz, dumping the logs in the empty basket, angling her head so she can make sense of what she is seeing.

'Some pictures that Catrin must've taken during your holiday. Look. This is you, right? You haven't changed much. And this must be Hazel.'

Roz steps nearer and is confronted by several pictures of her sister. 'Oh,' she cries, her fingers flying up to touch her lips, as if they need to check the emotion in her voice. 'Oh my God.' She sits down. The pictures are beautiful. But they are tragic and awful at the same time. There is her sister, her long curly hair flying in the wind, her arms outstretched like a bird about to take off, her face tilted to the sun. She looks so happy, so vibrant.

'Catrin was already a photographer when she took these,' declares Stella. 'Look how she's captured the island, and look at you all. I wonder if she'll let me use these on the website.'

Roz looks up, horrified at the thought that her sister might be used in some kind of advertising campaign.

'Maybe that's something we can talk about later,' says Nina, breaking in. She gives Roz a meaningful look, and once again Roz is filled with the certainty that Nina knows what to do, and how to act.

'Do you know when these were taken?' asks Stella.

'At the beginning of the holiday, I think,' says Nina lightly.

But as Roz leans closer, she understands that Nina is mistaken, or is obscuring the truth from Stella. She picks up each photograph and examines them, very closely, drinking in the image of her happy, healthy sister. There is a shot of her and Hazel, sitting in a pebbly cove. Their faces are filled with the certainty that they will have a great week. The fact it could all go wrong never even entered their heads. She picks up the next set of images, some shots of the cliff path, and of her own face, smiling in the half light, and she realises with a sickening jolt that this must be the morning she left with Catrin to see the sunrise. Roz looks at each image in turn, with the notion that she is travelling backwards from a time in the present when Hazel is dead to a time when she was very much alive. Catrin has taken each moment in sequence; the cliff path angling up to the cairn; the cairn itself; the view to the mainland. In each image, the sun is a little higher, the shadows a little shorter, the space of time between Hazel's life and death narrowing in each shot.

Roz doesn't want to look any more, but she can't help herself, she must finish what she has started. When she gets to the last few images, she sees this is the point in time when Catrin left her by the cairn. Taken below the cliffs, there is a vertiginous shot back up to the sky, where the bright yellow gorse traces the line of the precipice. The quality of the early morning light is extraordinary, and Roz is so wrapped up in the colour of the sky, the burnished bronze of the cliffs, that she doesn't immediately notice the two people standing at the top. Roz squints to see who they are, trying to understand. But when she scours the next image, where there is a gap in the gorse and one of the figures is exposed, she knows who she is looking at, and exactly what it means.

Chapter Thirty

NINA

Nina watches Roz as her face betrays her emotions. She can see that Roz understands the significance of the photographs and she can see her struggle to contain her sense of what it all means. She watches Stella, too, who is leaning over with interest and asking questions. Nina does her best to answer in as bland a way as possible, because Roz is mute.

'Tell me about the day you all landed here,' says Stella in a conversational way. She nudges the tea towel a little closer to Roz, and Nina can see the corner of her phone poking out from underneath it. 'What was the weather like? Tell me about the journey over here with Adam. Presumably he brought you all over?' Stella looks from Roz to Nina, a look of expectation on her face, and Nina's stomach turns over.

'Well, it was OK weather, as far as I can remember,' says Nina, scrabbling around for something uninteresting to say. She glances at Stella, whose face is alight with desire for information, and the woman's greed for a good story repulses her. But Roz has other ideas, it seems. Trance-like, she points her finger to the photograph she is staring at. She is glassy-eyed, like a sleepwalker.

'This,' she says, touching the photograph of the gap in the gorse. 'This is Hazel. Can you see this? Nina?' She looks horrified.

Nina leans over and tries to make light of it. 'I can't really tell,' she says, feeling nauseous. 'It could be anyone. I think Catrin was trying to capture the beauty of the cliffs in that one. Look at the colour of the gorse.'

'It's Hazel,' declares Roz in a defiant voice.

But Stella has caught the significance in Roz's voice, like a hunter sensing prey. 'How can you tell?' she asks, looking to Nina with the gaze of a hawk.

'Here,' says Roz, her finger moving to the gap in the gorse. 'Can you see? There's something dangling from her hand.'

'That's just a shadow,' says Nina dismissively.

'We were there to look at the sunrise coming over the mainland, that morning. The shadows would be behind these figures, not in front. That's not a shadow.'

Stella's eyes linger on the photograph, wanting more. 'Hang on, are you saying that this photograph was taken on the morning that Hazel disappeared?'

'Not necessarily,' says Nina cagily.

'Yes,' declares Roz. 'It was. This must have been the last few minutes of her life. Look – it's her.'

'How can you be so sure?' says Stella, a feral expression on her face.

'The shadow here, it isn't a shadow at all,' Roz repeats, her fingernail tracing the dark shape hanging below the arm of the person standing in the gap. 'It's Goggin.'

Nina squints at the image, and now it is explained, it is very hard to un-see what Roz has deduced.

'This must be where I found him, on the cliff path,' says Stella in wonder. 'So who is that with Hazel? There's someone else standing with her, slightly behind.'

All three of them are now poring over the image. Nina is so close, she can feel Roz's hot breath come out of her nostrils and move the curls on her head. 'What if . . . what if that's not a person,' Roz breathes.

'What?' Nina asks, turning to her.

Roz is gripping the photograph, hard. 'I told you. There's a reason why this house is covered in witches' marks.'

'Not this again, Roz,' says Nina with a warning note in her voice.

'Let her speak,' says Stella. 'Tell me what you mean, Roz.'

Roz looks up from the photograph and her face is full of fear. But there is something else there, too. A hardness, a stubbornness that comes from thinking you are right, against popular opinion.

'I was up there, that morning, by the stone cairn,' Roz begins. 'I had a feeling I was being watched. When I went down the cliff path, I felt it again. I don't know how to describe it – it was a presence, and it scared me so badly I ran all the way back to the house.'

'I thought you couldn't remember much about that morning, Roz?' says Nina.

'I can remember that feeling. It was horrible.'

'Talk to me about the witches' marks, Roz,' urges Stella. Nina watches her face light up with desire, a barely controlled lust for the information she wants to prise out of Roz.

'You've seen them,' says Roz, gesturing wildly around the room. 'They're here for a reason. Witches are embedded in Welsh culture. Witches' hats originate from traditional Welsh hats. The person standing behind Hazel, they have a hat on, see? Or a hood. It's pointed.'

'This is insane,' says Nina, standing up and pushing her hair out of her face.

'Then where is she?' shouts Roz, her voice rising with hysteria. 'Where's my sister? And if that's a human being, then who is it?'

There is a silence while all three women consider the implications of this question. And as each one of them wonders what to say next, Nina notices a smell fill the room. It is a dirty smell, heavy with the mineral stench of salt and earth; a smell of something deep underground that hasn't seen light or life for a long, long time. She looks around the room to try and trace the origin of it, noticing that Roz and Stella can smell it too. As the expression on their faces turns from confusion to alarm, a sound comes from the bedroom above, a small sound of something hard hitting the floor and bouncing across the stone flags.

'What was that?' Stella asks in a quiet voice. 'Did you hear that?'

'It came from our bedroom,' says Roz, looking up to the ceiling.

Nina, who wants to get away from the smell and put an end to the eerie feeling in the kitchen, volunteers to find out.

'Let's go together,' says Stella, and Nina notices that she grabs her phone and puts it in the top pocket of her shirt.

Nina goes first, the sound of three sets of footsteps on the stairs a comfort. She reaches the bedroom door and it is open already, but she can't see anything different about the space. There are two single beds separated by a bedside table with a lamp on it. She walks further into the room, around the bed nearest the window, and there, on the floor, tied by fishing twine, is a stone with a hole going right the way through. Nina picks it up and Roz gasps when she sees it.

'It's Hazel's,' Roz says in a whisper, as if she is afraid of disturbing whatever is in this room. 'Where did it come from?'

'It was just here, on the floor, by the bed.' Nina points to the ground, before handing Roz the stone. Then she peers around the room, checking the space behind the open door, to see if there is someone in there with them. She knows that nobody could possibly enter the house, unknown to them, but she cannot help herself, and she sees Stella do it too.

Roz walks over to the bed to see where Nina found the stone and crouches down. Stella follows her. 'Adam gave Hazel this stone,' Roz says. 'It's called a hag stone – some people call it a witch stone. He gave it to her for protection.'

'Did she ask for it?' says Stella. 'Was Hazel frightened of something?'

'I didn't think so,' replies Roz, hanging the stone around her neck. 'But now, I can't be sure. Ever since I landed on this island, I've felt Hazel, all around me. And now this.' Roz touches the hag stone reverently.

'This doesn't mean anything, Roz,' Nina reasons. 'Anybody could have left it here. Hazel could have left it here herself. She was in this room as much as we were. We could have dislodged it when we made the beds up.'

'Do you know what I think?' says Roz, with that stubborn look on her face. 'I think that you'll cling to any logical explanation because the alternative terrifies you. There are things in this place that we cannot control or explain. For the past twenty years, I have believed that Hazel's death was an accident because it was what I was told. But being here, I have to be open to the possibility that something else happened to Hazel. Something not easily explained. Someone or something else was involved, and that photograph on the kitchen table is the key to it all.'

Chapter Thirty-One

CATRIN

Catrin is too shocked to drive, so James eases the Land Rover out of the hospital car park. Exhausted, she dozes for most of the way, her head bobbing on to the window, surfacing her from sleep briefly. She only wakes up properly when the car swings into Chapel Farm.

Her childhood home takes on a greater significance as they pass through the gates. The lime trees arching over their heads seem to be bent in sadness. The house itself slouches, depressed, the windows sagging, the roof hunched. She is an orphan now, she understands. She is the grown-up, no longer a child.

She stands, with James, in the entrance hall. Neither of them moves for a moment, overwhelmed by the things that need to be done.

'Right,' James says eventually.

Catrin turns to her older brother, looking for answers. 'What are we going to do?'

'I . . . I don't know.' His face crumples and he sobs, dips his face into his hands. 'When Mum died, Dad took care of it all.'

Catrin takes her brother in her arms and holds him, adrift in unfamiliar waters. 'Let's not do anything tonight,' she says into his hair. 'Let's just get something to eat. We can make lists tomorrow. Tonight is just for us to get our heads around everything, OK?'

James pulls away, nods, wipes his eyes. 'I thought he would live forever,' he says, looking like the boy she remembers.

'I know,' Catrin replies. 'So did I.'

The dogs, one black and one white, come slowly, wagging their tails. They are both old, but their gait seems to reflect uncertainty rather than age. They can tell something is up. James drops to his knees and cuddles them, burying his face in their fur, talking to them in a low voice.

'I'll feed them, shall I?' Catrin asks, ushering them into the kitchen. 'Why don't you have a lie-down? You must be exhausted and hungry. I'll make something.'

She watches James walk slowly to his room. He is diminished, somehow. The size of the hole their father has left in the fabric of their lives is already gaping.

After dinner, when they have talked each other round in circles, Catrin sends James to bed, early, while she clears the plates, thinking about the time that led up to her leaving this place, and the years that have separated her from her family. She had badgered her father to bring her friends to Little Auger. He was reluctant, but she had insisted. It was her idea to go to the clifftop at sunrise. Hazel was left behind under her direction. She distinctly remembers telling Roz not to wake her, she had been so set on reaching the top in time for the sun. Catrin and her father are one and the same. They are both leaders, not followers. She is guilty of paying little heed to others' needs, in favour of her own better plans. She has led a selfish life, putting herself at the centre, and the price her family have had to pay for that has been dear.

When she, Nina and Roz returned to school that September after Hazel's death, what happened next was also her fault. Instead of begging her friends for forgiveness, admitting she had been wrong, she'd turned her back on them both. She couldn't bear to deal with someone else's pain. It embarrassed her, to see the destruction she had inadvertently caused, and this realisation embarrassed her more. Instead of closing ranks with her family, as James had done, she had pulled away, building a photographic portfolio that would provide her with a ticket out of Chapel Farm, and away from the trouble she had created. Catrin acknowledges, with shock, that she has spent her life documenting other people's problems in order to distract herself from her own. And now it is too late. Her father is dead. And she will never have an opportunity to take back the words she threw at him, minutes before he died. It is only now that she realises how hard it must have been for him in the shadow of his wife's sudden death. To run a business, and bring up two children, alone. She never once heard him complain.

Catrin recognises she has a choice. She can run away, leave James to it. Or she can do what she should have done all those years ago and step up.

As she surveys the house that has now passed to her brother, she has an urge to do something. If she couldn't honour her father in life, she will do so now, in the only way she knows how. She will document everything before the day closes, while it still contains a trace of him and the life he left behind. The summer light is low and waning, but she sees that this makes the room close in, the colours richer and heavier, the textures appear like the brushstrokes in a Dutch master. She remembers a weekend she spent in Holland, documenting the flooding of a housing estate; a free afternoon in a gallery absorbed in the paintings of Clara Peeters. She saw a parallel, there, with her own work. The way the ordinary was elevated into something filled with beauty.

She sprints to the Land Rover and pulls out her bag. Her camera, the only thing she has shown any loyalty to in her life, is charged up, waiting. Still thinking about the quality of those paintings, she sets up a still life, the loaf of bread she and James have just shared, the butter still bearing the marks of his knife, the glass of red wine she could not finish, the curve of an orange peel, pitted with shadows. She works quickly, spending a few more minutes in the kitchen, and then she walks upstairs to her father's room.

It still smells of him. The bed is unmade, the pillows dented, the corner of the blanket pulled to the floor. She touches the mattress, searching for the heat of him, then takes pictures of the impression his body left behind. The dwindling sun slants through the window, creating a landscape of light and dark. She takes more shots: his fingerprints on the windowpane, his glasses folded neatly on top of a book. She wanders over to his dressing table, touching the things he used every day: a hairbrush, silver backed, inherited from his father; a shoehorn made of tortoiseshell and a pair of oval cufflinks. She arranges them into still lifes. She records the shadows drawing over them, the light leaving the room.

She opens his wardrobe and touches his clothes, the rough and smooth of cotton and wool. At the end of the bed is an old wooden chest. She opens the lid, the hinges squeak, a drift of cedar wood reaches her nose. And sitting on the top of a pile of folded towels, a thick folder bearing her name. She pulls it out, sits cross-legged on the carpet, tips out the contents over the floor. They are all the photographs she has taken. Every picture reproduced by a British publication. Each one labelled by date in his unfussy, old-fashioned hand. A document of her life's work at the foot of his bed.

Chapter Thirty-Two

CATRIN

By the time Catrin is ready to leave Chapel Farm, it is dark. She has slept for a couple of hours and drives through the night to Eider, to catch the early morning tide. James has agreed to lend her the Land Rover once more, now there is no reason to go back to the hospital. He will be bound to the farm for the next few days. The estate won't give him time to grieve.

The village of Eider is asleep. As the car rolls down the hill towards the sea, it passes the church, its steeple picked out in moonlight, the gravestones huddled together like crooked teeth. There is a light on in the bakery, the owners getting ready to warm the ovens and fill the village with the smell of rising dough. The roof of the Bed and Breakfast, one of the tallest buildings in the village, stands out as a shadow against the mercury sea. The window in the dormer is wide open, welcoming in the night air. Catrin turns into the car park and picks up her bags, relieved to see her boat is still there at the end of the small wooden jetty. She doesn't need to use the lights on the boat, because the moon is large and clear and crisp, filling the sea with tiny points of starry light, a reflection of the sky. The surface of the water looks like stippled glass, and further out into open water, the stipples turn to waves. Catrin stops for a moment to take it all in, thinking of her father and all the things she will never be able to ask him, all the things she will never be able to say. Whole galaxies open up ahead of her, and the beautiful vastness of it makes her feel even more alone.

As the boat reaches Little Auger, she slows the engine, feeling the mood of the tide. She finds the cluster of rocks she must align herself with, the gap that looks impossible to pass through, and she angles the boat accordingly, hearing the gentle slap of water on the wooden hull. She fancies she can smell the dark; the wet, metallic cool of it, clinging to her hair.

To navigate at night is to give oneself over to trust. What looks like an impassible route suddenly opens at the last possible moment. Just when it seems like the boat will be splintered on the rocks, it finds the space between them that will safely take her in. But as Catrin approaches the cove, the light from the moon is dulled by cloud, and she becomes disoriented. She switches on the search lights at the front of the boat and a powerful beam illuminates a small area of rocks to the exclusion of everything else. It temporarily blinds her, and she immediately shuts off the lights, realising her mistake. She waits, hoping she will know what to do as soon as she can see once more. But the feeling doesn't leave her. She feels her body freeze up, a physical sensation, her hands unable to urge the boat forward because they are stopped by fear. She cannot turn back because the passage is too narrow. The only way is forwards, but which direction? Catrin shuts her eyes tightly and takes a deep breath, hoping this feeling will pass, willing her eyes to adjust to the darkness once more. When she opens them again, she sees a figure, waiting for her, standing in the cove ahead. The way he leans slightly to the right, his weight on a slim wooden walking stick painted in moonlight, is familiar and comforting.

Don't be ridiculous, Catrin, he seems to say. *You've done this a million times.*

Catrin balls her hands into fists and opens them again, waggling her fingers like a pianist warming up. She places them lightly on the controls as she urges the boat gingerly towards the figure. She knows it is not her father, that this is a trick of the moonlight on her sleep-starved brain. But she is grateful for it as she sees the slab of stone with the rusted rings reflecting the dim moonlight, and she moors the boat safely. Now she uses her torch to find the goat path leading to the house, and as she follows the curve of scrub, she sees there is a light on in the kitchen. She looks at her watch. It is 3.30 a.m.

Nina is sitting in front of the wood burner as if she hasn't moved in the twenty-four hours since Catrin left. 'Am I glad to see you,' she says, getting out of her chair. 'I thought for a minute you weren't coming back. I haven't been able to contact work to tell them I'm not going in today.' She looks at her watch. 'Though I guess they'll find out soon enough. Not that I can bring myself to care. How's your dad?'

Catrin can't find the words. Exhausted, she drops her bags on the floor where she stands and shakes her head. Nina crosses the floor and gives her a tight, fierce hug.

'I'll get some coffee on, shall I?' Nina asks.

Catrin shakes her head once more. 'I just want to sleep,' she says. 'How have you been and what are you doing up?'

'My body wants to get up at this hour. And I wanted some peace from those two.' Nina nods her head towards the stairs.

'Stella and Roz?' asks Catrin, intrigued.

Nina indicates a flat package on the kitchen table. 'Stella found your photographs and showed them to Roz.'

'Ah.' Catrin is too tired to care that Stella has been poking around her belongings. 'And what did Roz say?'

'Roz identified one of the people on the cliff as Hazel.' Nina pulls out the photograph from the package and shows Catrin. 'She's holding Goggin. See?'

Catrin whistles, looking at the image. 'I don't know how I missed that. And what about the other person, did she identify who that was?'

Nina lets out a big breath. 'Catrin, I think Roz is unwell. She's convinced something weird and witchy is going on. Being here has tipped her over the edge. Stella is egging her on.'

'How is she egging her on?'

'She's hanging on her every word, encouraging her deluded train of thought. Recording everything. I'm not sure Roz even realises the consequences of talking to her. Her whole narrative of Hazel's death has been upended. Just as she's trying to make sense of it, there's Stella, eagerly holding her phone up. They were talking together all afternoon and there was nothing I could do to stop it.'

'Well, surely it's up to Roz to decide what she wants to do?'

'I don't think she has the capacity, honestly, Catrin. She's always been a bit away with the fairies, but this is a new level of crazy.'

Catrin looks at Nina with curiosity. 'What was her reaction when she saw the picture? Was she genuinely surprised?'

Nina considers the question. 'Yes, I'd say so.'

'So you don't think the other person in the image is her?'

Nina shrugs, looking uncertain.

Catrin crosses the floor and sits at the table, motioning for Nina to do the same. 'Look, Nina, I know you two were close. But don't you think there's a possibility that Roz is putting all of this on?'

'What do you mean?'

'The amnesia, all of that hocus-pocus rubbish. If the other person in that photograph is Roz, it's very convenient for her to say she can't remember anything and that something witchy is going on. It's a smokescreen, surely.'

'That's a big accusation, you know.'

'Well, it would make sense, wouldn't it? She was up there at the same time as Hazel. We have proof of that now. She's delivered it herself by identifying Hazel in the photograph. Her explanation – that it's some kind of supernatural being – is ridiculous. We have to go with the most logical explanation and that means the other person in that photo is Roz, and she's covering it up. So the next question we have to ask ourselves is *why* she's covering it up.'

'I don't know, Catrin. There was one weird thing that happened. There was an incredibly powerful and horrible smell in here just as we were discussing it.'

Catrin chuckles. 'When the wind blows in the wrong direction, it can come back through the chimney here.' Catrin motions to the range cooker and the opening of the old chimney above it. 'The wind carries smells from the island and they're not always nice.'

Nina suddenly looks a little happier.

Catrin sits back in her chair. 'Why would Roz deny meeting Hazel that morning? What other explanation do you have for me?'

'Roz would never harm Hazel. You must know that. She's vulnerable.'

Catrin narrows her eyes. 'Nina, do you know something? Something about Roz?'

'I just don't think that Stella is a good influence, that's all,' says Nina.

'Why are you protecting her? You always took her side over mine.'

'Roz isn't as strong as you are, Catrin. She's been through a terrible ordeal. She needs our protection! Can't you see that?'

'What about me? My poor father? He was made out to be a murderer in some of the papers. If Roz knows what really went on that morning, the fact she never lifted a finger to help my family . . .' Catrin cannot bring herself to finish.

Nina shakes her head, looking stricken. 'I'm sorry, Catrin. I forgot how awful it was for you. You always seem so . . . together. And Roz always seems so . . . not.'

'I don't make an art of dumping my problems on to other people's laps. But I still have them.'

Nina looks at her with a strange expression on her face.

'What?' says Catrin.

'You reminded me of my mum. Which is weird, because I always assumed you were the polar opposite. I'm sorry if I haven't been there for you. You do such a great job of being self-sufficient, I just . . .'

'I know. I know how it looks. But yesterday . . . I don't know what to do any more. He died, Nina. My dad died before I could find the words to tell him I was sorry.'

Catrin tells Nina about the argument that was never fully resolved.

'He will have known, Catrin. Parents always know what their kids really mean, don't they?'

'Do they? Neither of us has kids, so I don't think we're the experts here.'

Nina suppresses a giggle. 'Ignore me, I don't know what I'm saying.'

'Yeah,' says Catrin, with a thoughtful look. 'What I really need right now is a qualified advice giver. Like an agony aunt or something . . .'

Nina snorts. 'Well, don't ask me. I'm terrible at my job. Really awful. I have an assistant who basically tells me what to say. I'm a divorced, fatherless, childless woman. What the hell do I know about other people's problems? I can barely walk straight in the shoes they make me wear.'

'Well,' says Catrin. 'You're a pro compared to me. I'm an orphaned, childless, homeless person who can't hold down a long-term relationship.'

Nina's snort turns into a laugh that she tries very hard to keep quiet, and Catrin remembers this feeling, of trying to make Nina lose it, the pleasure she took in pushing all the right buttons so she could make Nina's pretty face stream with tears as she tried not to wet herself.

'I will kill you,' Nina says, breathless, clutching her stomach. 'My pelvic floor is not what it once was.' She tries to straighten her face and fails, letting out a huge snort that dissolves them both.

After a while, when the giggles have left them, Nina yawns. 'I need to go back to bed. My abs are going to be sore tomorrow, thanks to you. You look shattered, Catrin. You should get some sleep too.'

'I think I'll stay up for a while. I want to wallow in self-pity for a bit longer.'

Nina hugs Catrin again before she leaves the kitchen, promising not to wake her in the morning if she sleeps in. Catrin hears her tread the stairs, the creak of the house as she gets into bed. She admits to herself that she feels resentful about the careful way Nina treads around Roz and not her. *Maybe that will change now*, she thinks. It felt nice to be hugged, given sympathy. It felt good to be vulnerable.

Catrin looks over to the chair Nina has vacated. A grey hoodie hangs over the back, and poking out of the side pocket is a sheaf of folded pages. Catrin can make out the handwriting on the pages. It's odd to see so much handwriting on one page these days, when most people type everything. She leans in a little closer and sees the writing is not adult, that these are the words of a child. There are little circles that dot each *i* and *j*. The writing is large and rounded. There is something familiar about it and with a jolt she realises who this writing belongs to.

Catrin pulls out the folded sheets and begins to read.

I thought secrets were fun. But now I have a horrible one that I can't share. So I am writing it here because it's the only place I can talk about it.

Chapter
Thirty-Three

CATRIN

It takes Catrin several minutes to read through the pages. Then she reads them again, not quite believing what she sees. She feels the weight of the paper, the weight of the words it contains, and an unfamiliar feeling steals over her. She wonders what to do. For a moment, she has an urge to fold the paper and put it back in the hoodie pocket, pretend she hasn't seen it.

'What have you got there?' says a voice behind her. Stella.

Before Catrin can react, Stella takes the paper from her hands and begins to read the words out loud.

> *I took the wrong path on the cliff. I didn't realise where I was until it was too late, and I couldn't get back. I didn't realise it was Hazel, at first. I thought it was Catrin. Her face was red and sweaty. Not from running, like me, but because she was Angry at being left behind.*

'What is this?' she asks, her eyes fixed on the paper, scanning the words. She has a look on her face, like a predator tracing a scent.

'I didn't hear you come in,' says Catrin weakly. 'Maybe you should give that back. It's private.' She tries to keep her voice light, tries to give the impression that the writing is of no consequence.

But Stella continues to read, out loud.

And then she told me she'd been reading my journal, which is the Worst Thing one person can do to another. When she said my own words back to me, words I had written In Private that were Not for others to see, I felt something cold slice through me. So I did the most Horrible Thing I could think of. I took the one thing she truly loved. She wasn't expecting me to do that. I was quick. Quick as a rabbit. And it made me feel big to have Goggin in my hands. She begged me to give him back, and instead of feeling sorry for her, I held him away, high above her head.

Stella looks at Catrin, her face alive with understanding. 'This is a confession. This writing . . . it's a child's writing. A kid has written this. Oh my God, Catrin, this is it.'

I cannot forgive myself for doing that. Her face, dirty with tears.

She continues to read from the pages, uttering the words out loud when she comes to something important, shaking her head in disbelief at what she has in her hands.

I held Goggin above my head and before I could stop myself, before I could tell myself it was a Very Bad Idea,

I threw him as far away as I could. But he didn't go over the cliff, like I wanted him to. He landed on a gorse bush and stayed there, bouncing up and down in the wind. I could see his eye looking at me.

'Oh my God,' says Stella, her fingers flying up to her lips. The next few sentences she says in a rush. But Catrin has already committed them to memory.

Then Hazel made a noise, like a crying noise and a choking noise but all done at the same time. And then I realised what was going to happen. And then I realised I wanted to take it all back.

I tried to stop her. I told her I would get him for her, that I was sorry.

'This is it! The evidence I've been waiting for,' says Stella, a look of triumph on her face. 'I knew there would be something else if I just dug a little . . .'

'What do you mean?' asks Catrin, confused.

Stella doesn't answer Catrin, she is too busy looking at the pages, reciting the words written there quickly, without drawing breath.

And then the earth disappeared. It gave way under her feet, like she was standing on a trapdoor. It was so quick I thought I had imagined it. I looked around me, like maybe she was playing a trick. But when she didn't come back . . .

I knew she would never come back.

Stella sighs with contentment, as if she has eaten a beautiful meal. 'This is amazing. So powerful.'

And I knew it was All My Fault, and that I would never be forgiven, and I would never forgive myself.

'God, it's just . . . it's perfect. Listen to this, Catrin . . .'

I can't understand how an argument can end like that. I thought you had to be sick or old before you died.

Catrin feels as if she is in a moving vehicle she cannot get out of. 'Wait, listen to me,' she says, feeling dizzy and sick. 'I don't think . . .'

But Stella has taken her phone and is photographing the pages, one by one.

'I don't think Roz would . . .'

Stella swings around and looks at Catrin. 'This is Roz's writing? You recognise it?'

'Well,' Catrin begins, realising what she has said. 'Look, stop. Stop that. I need to get my head straight. I've barely slept the past twenty-four hours.'

Stella has finished photographing the pages. She puts them on the kitchen table. She checks herself, nods once and swallows. 'Of course, of course, this must be a huge shock. I'm sorry, I just went into work mode there for a moment.' Stella's forehead creases with concern, and Catrin can see the physical effort it takes her to stop herself punching the air. 'This must be a lot for you to process. Here.' Stella sits down at the table, and she slides the pages between them, her hands vibrating with excitement. She sets her phone, face down, on the wood.

'Roz's family did nothing to dissuade the press from what they said about your father, did they?' Stella asks gently.

Catrin is silent.

'This must feel like such a betrayal. At least you can let your father know you have the truth, here, right? Some good can come from this.' Stella reaches for Catrin's arm and squeezes it firmly.

Stella's words land on Catrin and shatter like glass. Her touch feels like a burn. The knowledge that she never made the apology she planned, that she never found out the truth before he died. That he died thinking she believed those awful things. The tears that she couldn't shed in the hospital, at Chapel Farm, they come now in a hot, wet torrent and she gasps for breath. Stella gets up and searches for tissues.

'What's going on?' Nina is standing in the doorway of the kitchen, her face pinched and drawn. She sees Catrin, crying, and looks visibly shocked.

Stella looks at Nina, and then she looks at Catrin. 'I think you'd better explain,' she says quietly.

Catrin sniffs, blows her nose, and pushes the pages towards Nina. 'Roz . . . she knew what happened to Hazel all along. She was there. And her silence has destroyed us all.'

Nina sits down, hard, on the chair next to Catrin, her eyes scanning the pages. Her fingers move to her mouth as she reaches the end. She turns to Stella, her expression hardening. 'Did you take this from my hoodie?' she asks.

'No,' says Catrin. 'It was me. Why have you been protecting her, Nina? When you know what her family did to mine.'

'Her parents did that, not Roz,' counters Nina. She looks at Catrin pleadingly. 'You can't let Stella use this. This is a terrified young girl. Please, Catrin.'

Stella clears her throat. 'It's a bit late for that, I'm afraid. The cat is well and truly out of the bag. I mean, I don't want to sound insensitive, I know it's a really big thing we have here, but

Catrin's family will benefit hugely from knowing this. Her father for one . . .'

'My father is dead,' says Catrin with a sob. 'He died yesterday. That's why I had to leave. I can't believe the timing of this . . .'

'Oh, Catrin, I'm so, so sorry,' says Stella. 'I had no idea.'

'You're loving this, aren't you?' says Nina suddenly, to Stella. 'This is gold for you, isn't it? Watching us all wallowing around in misery.'

'I'm just looking for the facts, that's all,' Stella says evenly.

'Isn't finding Goggin enough?' continues Nina. 'These are my *friends*. This is the lowest point in the life of a thirteen-year-old girl. Her absolute lowest ebb. And you want to parade that in front of *everyone*.'

'Well, I thought you, above anyone, would understand how valuable—'

'Valuable? You see our emotions as something to be bought and sold.' Nina turns to Catrin now. 'Catrin? I can't believe you're going along with this. You can't tell me you want this to be aired online. Or worse. She'll have this all over the television if she has her way. Is that really what you want?'

Catrin turns to Stella, her brain in a fog. 'What did you mean, earlier, about needing more evidence? Isn't Goggin enough? Couldn't we keep this out of the podcast? You already have a lot of material without this.'

'Nobody is going to take a toy that I found inside a gorse bush seriously! Come on, Catrin. This is dynamite. There's no way—'

'I knew it,' says Nina, banging the table and making them all jump. 'You didn't find Goggin buried, did you? You made that bit up. You absolute—'

'Sometimes, the truth just needs nudging in the right direction,' replies Stella with a shrug. 'It's not going to be enough, finding Goggin. That was never going to be enough.'

Catrin feels sick. 'You lied about someone burying Goggin?'

'I just needed a reason to get you all back here, talking together. Look at how you've rekindled your friendship . . . we have the truth now, Catrin. That's what we were after, right? That's what matters.'

'Catrin, can't you see what she's doing?' says Nina, a note of desperation in her voice. 'She made us believe there was someone else involved, someone who did something bad to Hazel . . . She let you suspect your father . . . How can you think—'

'Stop it! I don't know what to think,' moans Catrin, feeling trapped. Her heart hammers in her chest and she feels as if she might throw up.

'I think we should let Roz have her say, don't you?' asks Stella. 'She can tell us why she let her parents ruin Catrin's father, his business—'

'No!' Nina says in a shout. 'She's blocked everything out. Leave her be.' She looks at Catrin, desperately. But Catrin, still feeling the sharp edge of jealousy that Nina is protecting Roz, knows there is only one way this can end.

'I think Roz needs to know what we've found,' she says, making her decision. She snatches the pages from the kitchen table. 'Stay here,' she says to Stella. 'This is our business, not yours. Nina, come with me.'

Chapter
Thirty-Four

CATRIN

Catrin walks up the stairs, opens the door to Nina and Roz's room and sees Roz lying in bed, asleep.

'Catrin, please . . .' Nina whispers.

'It's time we got this straightened out,' says Catrin in a grim voice.

Their words wake Roz up. She turns over in bed, and her face is hard to read. She looks confused and pale. 'What's going on?' she asks, her voice thick with sleep.

Catrin walks into the space between the two beds, switches the lamp on, making Roz flinch, and sits down near Roz's feet. She shows her the pages. Nina is silent and absolutely still.

Roz turns the pages over in her hands. 'Is this my handwriting?' she murmurs, rubbing her eyes with her fingertips. 'Where did you find it?'

'It doesn't matter,' says Catrin, wondering if she is faking or genuinely amnesic. Roz struggles to sit up in bed, but when she manages, she looks directly into Catrin's eyes. She looks so innocent.

'Why don't you read it?' says Catrin, searching Roz's face, wanting some kind of recognition.

'Don't,' says Nina in a pleading voice. But Catrin ignores her.

Roz opens the pages and begins to read. Curious at first, perhaps, at what her younger self has written. Then her face changes to incomprehension. 'Who wrote this?' she asks in a bewildered voice.

'Don't you remember?' asks Catrin gently. 'It's your handwriting, isn't it? You always dotted your *i*'s like that.'

'Well, yes, but . . . I . . . I don't understand.' Roz looks so utterly lost, her hands are shaking. Catrin hands her the photograph she took on the morning of Hazel's death.

'See,' she says, as if she is talking to a child. 'This is you and Hazel, isn't it? This photograph was taken just a few minutes before she died. That's you. Standing on the headland with your sister. She followed you, just like you thought. And when I went down to the beach to take these photographs, Hazel caught up with you, angry because you hadn't woken her up. You had an argument about it, didn't you?'

'Where . . . where did you get these pages?' asks Roz, turning over the papers in her hands. Looking from front to back as if she is missing some vital message.

'I told you, it doesn't matter,' says Catrin firmly, wanting to get to the truth. She can feel its presence, like a stone in a peach. She just needs to press a little deeper to get to it. 'Why did you lie to us, Roz?' Catrin says. 'Why did you say you hadn't seen Hazel that morning, when you had?'

'Is that me?' says Roz in a tremulous voice. The look of incomprehension on her face is so pure and without guile, a needle of doubt pricks Catrin's resolve.

'Well, isn't it?' Catrin asks, a note of exasperation in her voice.

'I didn't see her, Catrin, I swear.' Roz looks at the pages, then the photograph, scrutinising them with an intensity that wavers Catrin's conviction.

'How can you be sure it isn't you? You said you couldn't remember much about that morning.'

'I know that I didn't write this.' She looks across the bed at Catrin, shaking her head. And then she opens her mouth as if to say something, before a look crosses her face. Then she turns to Nina. Roz's face slowly fills with horror. It is like witnessing someone watch a car crash. Roz puts her hand in front of her mouth, as if she is about to vomit. 'Oh God,' she moans. 'It was you, wasn't it. I gave you my journal to write in. At the beginning of the holiday. This is *your* writing, Nina. We both wrote like this, because I copied you at school.' Roz drops the pages, and the photograph, and leaps out of bed. She grabs Nina by the wrist. 'Is this some kind of sick joke?' Roz looks from Nina to Catrin, trying to understand.

Catrin is completely thrown. 'I don't get it. This isn't you, in the picture? This isn't your writing?'

Now the bleariness in Roz's face is replaced by a grim determination. 'I brought two journals with me that summer and I gave one to Nina. She was upset, and she couldn't tell me why, so I said she could write it down. I gave her a spare journal. I hadn't written anything in it, apart from my name on the front.'

Roz is still holding Nina's wrist tightly, and Nina squirms to get out of her grip. Roz has heavy rings on her fingers, and they grind against one another every time Nina moves.

'I don't understand,' Roz continues, looking at Nina intently. 'How were you there? You were asleep when I left you and asleep when I came back. *How were you on the cliff path without being seen?*' The anger rises sharply in her voice. Roz holds her ground, not letting go of Nina's wrist. The pages fall to the floor and Catrin crouches down to pick them up, feeling her world tilt suddenly once more.

Nina makes a noise, somewhere between a cry and a gasp. 'I wasn't asleep when you came back.' Her voice is high and thin, her words strangled and halting. She has stopped trying to get out of Roz's grip. 'I woke up as soon as you closed the door. I tried to get back to sleep but I couldn't, so I decided to catch you up. But I met Hazel on the old cliff path. She was coming back down to the house. She was upset about something. We had an argument, and she told me she'd read my journal. I'd written about my mum and dad, and how it made me feel, about fancying Adam. It wasn't meant for anyone else to read. She made fun of it. So I became very angry.'

Nina is shaking, visibly. 'She wouldn't listen to me. The cliff gave way before I had a chance to stop her. Please . . . please believe me.'

Roz lets go of Nina's wrist and for a moment there is a stillness in the air when anything could happen. Then Roz draws herself up and slaps Nina across her face, quickly pushing her away with both hands before Nina has a chance to regain her balance. Nina falls sideways, hitting her head on the bedpost before she lands awkwardly on the floor. And there is a moment of stillness when it seems she is dead.

'Nina? Nina!' Catrin runs over to her, crouches down and realises she doesn't know what to do. Just as she is about to panic, Nina moans and curls into a ball.

When Nina struggles to sit up, Roz moves towards her.

'Stop it!' Catrin shouts, holding an arm outstretched like a referee to prevent her from coming any nearer. 'Roz, please! Please stop!'

Roz is unexpectedly compliant. She falls back on to the bed, weeping, and gives a sidelong glance at Nina, who is still on the floor, curled up on her side.

'Nina, are you OK?' Catrin touches Nina's shoulder gently, moving her hair so she can see her face. There is a cut above her eyebrow, which is bleeding freely. The rest of her face is smothered with a mixture of tears, saliva and snot.

'I can't see anything,' she says, her voice devoid of emotion. She sounds wiped out, her voice is slurred.

'Your eye is bleeding. We should clean it up.'

'Why didn't you say anything?' cries Roz. 'Why didn't you tell anybody?'

Nina's voice is stony with shock. 'I expected you to come and haul me out of bed. I assumed somebody saw me or realised where I'd been. But the longer I stayed there, the more paralysed I became. The longer the silence, the harder it was to break. When Catrin's dad was out looking with your parents, I saw his mobile phone in the library. He'd left it on the table. I took it outside and called my mother and confessed everything to her. She told me if I said anything to either of you, I'd lose your friendship forever and nobody would speak to me again. She said I would get into trouble with the police. She made me promise not to tell.'

Roz turns her face away to weep. 'You killed her. You killed my sister and never said a word.'

Nina begins to cry, quietly. 'It was an accident. I made a promise not to tell. If I could take it all back, I would.'

But Roz is not listening. 'You've made a career out of helping other people,' she observes with venom. 'What a hypocrite. I wonder what your trusting viewers would think of this confession?' Roz holds up the pages. 'That's why you came back here, isn't it? To keep hold of your precious career.'

'At first, yes,' confesses Nina. 'I wondered if Stella had found the journal. As soon as I wrote it, I hid it under the bookcase in the library because I was scared you would find it in our room. I never got the chance to get it back. I thought Stella might jump to the same conclusion that Catrin did. Your name is all over the front cover. I burned the whole thing the other night, but I couldn't bring myself to destroy those pages because . . .' Nina sobs, '. . . I don't know . . . because maybe I wanted to show you and make you understand.'

Catrin looks at Nina's face and a swell of panic rises up in her stomach. She checks her watch. 'I think I need to get you to a hospital, Nina. You've banged your head. I don't like the look of that cut. We need to get off Little Auger and into the boat, right now. There's still time to get to the mainland.'

'Well, I'm not coming with you,' says Roz in a dangerous voice. 'I'm staying here.'

Catrin glances at Roz on the bed, and then at Nina, on the floor. She grits her teeth and makes a decision. 'OK, stay here if you want. I'll come and get you tomorrow afternoon. But Nina needs help, right now.' She leans down to pull Nina up off the floor and puts her arm over her shoulder to walk her out of the room. As she turns to the door, she sees something on the floor, right on the threshold, and when she lurches towards it, she sees it is a phone. Stella is sitting on the floor in the hallway, just outside, her knees drawn up to her chin. She looks up at Catrin as she comes out of the room, and her face is a mixture of fear and triumph.

'Don't tell me you just recorded that,' says Catrin, her voice dripping with derision.

'That's what I'm here to do,' Stella replies in a businesslike voice, snatching up her phone.

Nina takes her arm away from Catrin. 'It doesn't matter any more,' she says, her voice wet and slurred. 'But at least get it right.'

She turns to Stella. 'I'll talk to you in the boat. But after that, I'm not ever talking to you again.'

Stella leaps into action and puts on her coat, helping Nina with hers. Catrin gathers up her own coat, her chest fizzing with fear. The tide has already turned, and she prays she isn't putting Nina into more danger, but her cut is wide open and her face is a mess. She finishes dressing Nina as warmly as she can, and puts on a head torch to light their way to the cove. The scrub-lined path that leads them there is a stunted, wild, clawing version of the driveway at Chapel Farm in this light. It has taken her whole life to notice this. She puts her arm around Nina, who is walking like a drunk beside her.

'I tried to burn it,' says Nina, as the darkness swallows them up. 'We could have been happy again, the three of us. But I just couldn't do it. And now look at where the truth has got us all.'

The tide is at the turning point between coming and going, its energy no longer linear, but tumbling upon itself as it gathers strength to turn around. Hopefully, there is still time to travel back without getting caught in the rocks. As Catrin tries to manoeuvre the boat out of the cove, Nina takes the phone from Stella.

'Don't ask me any questions,' Nina says, not looking at Stella. 'I'm just going to talk into this thing as if you aren't here, and then I'm done, OK? You never contact me again.'

Stella nods, and Catrin can see she is barely able to contain her delight at how this morning is turning out.

With one hand clutching the side of the boat, Nina grips the phone to her chest with the other, as if it is soothing a pain she feels there, *and perhaps it is*, thinks Catrin, as she feels the teeth of the rocks scrape the hull of the boat. She prays the water is still deep enough to get them out safely. As she steers towards the mainland, she hears Nina repeat the story she wrote down, each painful detail magnified by her voice, which falters under the strain of exposing herself so brutally. *She is a good storyteller*, Catrin thinks to herself; it is as if she is back there with Nina, making all the mistakes she made that morning twenty years ago, feeling the devastation of what she had done.

When they are almost at the jetty, but still in deep water, Nina lifts her head and says, 'I don't think I have anything else to add. That's it.' And then, in a blur of movement that neither Stella nor Catrin predicts, Nina throws Stella's phone out of the boat, through the darkness, and into the black of the sea.

'What the . . .' Stella begins.

'Like I said in my journal,' says Nina, a hint of grim triumph in her voice, 'I'm as quick as a rabbit.'

Chapter
Thirty-Five

ROZ

Roz's teeth do not stop chattering for a long time. She cannot move from the bed. Her limbs are stiff, and her eyes are raw and salty. With great effort, she makes herself sit up. She won't sleep now. There's no point trying. She picks up the pages from the floor, takes a moment to look at the words, allowing them to sink in once more, feeling each one make its cut.

Nina had changed over the weeks leading up to the holiday, Roz recalls that now. She had turned from a bubbly extrovert into a quiet, secretive friend. Neither Catrin nor she had the right words to check that Nina was all right. They already knew there was trouble between Nina's parents. It didn't matter to Roz or Catrin, but the shame Nina obviously felt created a silence that was hard to penetrate. Giving Nina a book to write in was probably the closest Roz had come to sympathy.

She continues to read the words that Nina wrote. They tumble off the page, sometimes illegible and incoherent. Some of the pages are stained with tears. The agony of her mistake is still vivid and sharp through the blur of ink pen. Roz remembers the exchange they had when she gave Nina this book.

'What's a journal?' Nina had asked.

'It's like a diary but you don't have to write in it every day, just when you feel like it. And nobody is allowed to read it, unless you want them to, so you can write what you like without getting into trouble.'

An uncomfortable thought enters Roz's head. Could she be responsible for some of this? She is certainly responsible for Hazel's bad mood that morning. She remembers, now, a conversation she had with Catrin about it at the stone cairn. She knew Hazel would be annoyed with her for leaving her behind. Roz had called her a baby. She had meant it in an affectionate way, but if Hazel had followed her, if Hazel had overheard her saying it . . . The reason Roz felt she was being watched that morning was because, surely, Hazel had been there. She must have found herself on the old cliff path, standing behind the scrub, listening to Roz's every word, unable to protest, unable to cry, lest she prove herself the baby that Roz had declared she was.

The idea that Hazel died angry and upset, unwilling to go to her big sister for help, is something Roz cannot get over. The possibility she was responsible for her anger and distress is unbearable to think about. She carries on reading the pages until she has reached the end, a horrifying realisation settling over her that Hazel was dead by the time she came back to the house.

And how had Roz lived her life in Hazel's absence? Not to the fullest, that was certain. She had met a man whose affection she had stretched and broken. She had borne a daughter and clipped her wings. She had lost her friends. She would probably lose her clients, and then she would lose her house.

Roz lets the pages flutter to the floor, puts her head in her hands and wails. She doesn't know how long she gives in to self-pity, but after a while her emotional reserves wane. Then an understanding presents itself among the tangle of thoughts, clear and uncomfortable. Nobody is going to help her out of this. Hazel is not coming back. She will never have the kind of mother that Nina has. Simon is gone. She can change none of these facts. She thinks about the sketches of Hazel she made the first night she got here. *They are good*, she thinks. *They are very good.* There is still something inside of her that she can control. She hasn't lost her creative spark. She has just neglected it.

Roz looks out of the window. The light is beginning to touch the sky. She goes downstairs. In the kitchen, she snatches a permanent marker pen from the table and strides outside, in her pyjamas, tracing the old cliff path up to the cairn. She finds a large flat stone, one she can carry, and she writes Hazel's name and dates on one side, and on the other she draws her sister's silhouette, with Goggin dangling from her fingers. She carries the stone to the top, a weight that becomes hard to bear. When she reaches the summit, she doesn't try and lift the stone above her head. She is too short to reach the top of the cairn, and the stone is too large. She finds a space in the middle, sheltered by other stones. She slots it into the space, like a book into a shelf. She likes the idea of Hazel being protected by others. As she settles the stone, the pain in her arms beginning to ebb, the light from the east strikes the cairn. Roz curls up on the grass, her back to the stones, closing her eyes to the sunshine, allowing it to warm her skin.

She is still asleep when she feels someone approach. She opens her eyes, just a little, for the sun is bright now. It's already a beautiful day.

'Roz?' the voice says. 'Rosalind?' It is Adam. He kneels before her, taking her hands and sitting her up, slowly. Her head spins a little. 'Why are you in your pyjamas? And your hands . . .' Adam says. 'What happened to your hands?'

Roz looks down. Her hands are covered in ink and earth. She thinks back to the early hours of the morning. The quick violence of it. She is calm, now. Serene, almost. She's had a good few hours' sleep, here on the clifftop. Her face feels tight with sunburn.

'What's going on?' asks Adam. He cannot keep the concern out of his voice.

'Why are you here?' she answers, feeling she is in a dream. Adam looks very strange. He is dressed in a sleek black wetsuit; the top half is unzipped and rolled down to his bare waist. His skin is wet, his hair is wet. He looks like a surfer who has lost his board.

'Catrin called me and asked me to check on you,' Adam replies, squatting down next to her. He smells of the sea. 'She's at the hospital.'

Roz looks at her watch. 'I thought you couldn't land a boat here so early.'

'You can't. I dropped anchor and swam the rest of the way. And then, when you weren't in the house, I hiked up here.'

'Isn't that dangerous? Swimming over here?'

'I was worried about you.'

Roz looks down at her hands, the kindness of his words rendering her mute.

'What's happened here?' he presses.

'Will you sit with me for a moment?' she asks him, and he complies.

He lowers himself next to her, close to her, his legs bent like hers. She can feel the heat of him from her ankle to her shoulder. The hike has made his bare skin warm against hers. It doesn't feel odd. It feels comforting, familiar, right. He doesn't say anything. She feels him breathing, she feels her own breath, the silence between them as significant as words. Roz closes her eyes and lets her head rest in the curve of his shoulder. She feels his head tilt in return and touch the top of hers, not minding the damp of his hair. They stay like that for a long time, listening to the sea, feeling their bodies fill with air, feeling their lungs expel it, the same sound as the waves drawing up and back again.

After a length of time she cannot measure, Roz stirs, picks up the marker pen from the grass beside her. 'Take me down to the house,' she says. 'I need to eat something.'

Adam washes her hands in the kitchen sink, while she stands, compliant. He looks as if he belongs here, in this house. The morning light shines through the kitchen window, lighting up his sun-bleached hair. She takes in his tanned face, the lines that are forming around his eyes where he has squinted into the wind. The muscles formed by his work on the shore. It feels to her as if he is shaped by the landscape around him. The water is cold and smells faintly peaty. He slices some bread and slathers it in peanut butter, cutting it into triangles for her, and she eats it, obediently, at the kitchen table as they wait for the kettle to boil on the stove.

'Are you going to tell me what's going on?' he asks when she has finished eating. He is standing, leaning against the worktop, drying his hands with a tea towel.

'Catrin didn't say?'

'She said nothing. She just told me that she and Nina were at the hospital.' He slings the tea towel over the arch of the kitchen tap and folds his arms. She notices a scar on his forearm, a long, elegant line tracing the muscle, whiter than the rest of his skin.

Roz looks around for the pages, finds them on the floor. 'Read this. It should tell you all you need to know. Nina wrote it on the day Hazel died.'

Adam takes the pages from her and reads them carefully. Roz watches his face. His expression gives away nothing. At last, he folds them up. For a second, her doesn't look at her and just continues to stare down at the folded paper. Then he sits down opposite her at the table.

'Is this true?' he asks, eventually looking up.

'Yes. She admitted as much last night.'

Adam looks as if he is choosing his next words carefully. 'That must have been a hard thing to own up to.'

'She's lied to us all for twenty years.'

'Yes. That's a painful thing for you and your family.' He opens the pages once more. 'What are you going to do about this?'

'I could make it public. Ruin her life with it, like she ruined mine.'

'Would that make you feel better?'

Roz considers the question. 'Maybe. Yes, I think it would make me feel better.'

Adam nods to himself.

'What is it?' Roz asks, needing validation. 'Don't you agree with me?'

'It's your decision,' he replies.

'Why don't you tell me what you're actually thinking?' she says.

'Well, it's a story I'm thinking about. Everyone in Eider knows this story. It's told to most of the kids that grow up here, on the water.' Adam scratches his head and begins. 'There were two friends, boys. Known each other since nursery school. They egged each other on a bit, but they were good boys really. One of them, the older of the two, his father owned a boat, a little dinghy. The younger boy wanted to go out in it, but the father told them no, it wasn't safe to go out alone, they were too young. He promised that when he was not so busy he would go out with them both and teach the younger boy how to sail, just as he had taught his son. Well, the

244

boys got sick of waiting. The older boy could sail already, and he decided he was just as equipped to teach his friend as his father. So, on a nice calm day, with a gentle breeze just right for sailing, they took the little dinghy and launched it, unseen, into the sea. They had a wonderful time together. The older boy was a good teacher, just like his father, and they had fun, until the breeze became a bit too lively and the older boy realised he wasn't experienced enough to get them back to shore under sail. The boys lowered the sail and tried to start the outboard motor, but they couldn't get it going. So the older boy took the oars out, as his father had taught him, and instructed the younger boy how to row back to shore.'

Adam shifts in his seat and looks away from Roz and out of the window. 'The wind was an easterly and it blew them back out to sea. The older boy tried again to get the motor started, but it was no use. A current held the boat back and they drifted further out. Then the wind picked up even more, and the boys began to get really frightened. The waves got choppy, without warning. The sun became covered with cloud. It was like a switch had been turned off – a completely different day. The little boy lost the grip of his oar and as he reached over to catch it, it fell into the sea, and the boy tumbled with it. The boy could swim, and he had a life jacket on. But the current began to take him in a different direction. He got separated from the boat. The waves grew taller, and soon they were lapping the boy's head every time they passed him. The older boy knew if he left the boat to be with his friend they would both be taken by the current, so the only thing he could do was reach out with the remaining oar, in the hope that his friend could grab it. He spent a minute or two trying to do this, but it's very hard holding on to a rocking boat with one hand while holding the length of an oar out over the side with the other. He grew very tired.' Adam clears his throat and swallows, hard. 'And then, by some miracle, a freak wave pushed the little boy straight to the boat. He grabbed the oar and the older boy was able to pull him up. But in doing so, he dropped the second oar into the waves.'

'So now they had no oars and a broken motor,' Roz says, not understanding why she is being told this story, but sensing that Adam isn't completely on her side by telling it.

'Yes. The older boy tried once more to fire the motor, but it was unresponsive. Then he remembered his father always had a flare stowed away in case of emergencies. He found the flare and fired it, it was seen by most of Eider, and after what seemed like a very long time to both of those boys, they were rescued and towed back to land.'

Roz looks at Adam expectantly. 'So,' she says, nonplussed, 'it has a happy ending, your story.'

'Yes, it does,' he replies. 'But I think, if it hadn't been for that freak wave, the one that pushed the little boy back to the boat, the ending would have been quite different. Instead of everybody being pleased they were back home, safe . . . the older boy would have come back, alone, and he would have been blamed for the death of his friend.'

'So which one were you?' asks Roz. 'The older boy or the younger?'

'The older,' Adam nods. 'I knew what I was doing, I was a good sailor. But I think about the line we nearly crossed, my friend and me. It was so . . . random, that wave. Yet it was a rubicon. I wonder what my life would have turned out like if it had gone the other way. People aren't very forgiving in a small community like this. The family of my friend were very well liked. Their Eider roots went back generations. My father moved to Eider as an adult, from Latvia. It's taken him many years to gain the trust of the community here.'

'Do you still keep in touch? With the little boy?'

'I was best man at his wedding.'

'Nice.' Roz bows her head, feeling tired. 'That's nice.'

'I suppose what I'm trying to say is . . . I was a good kid. I just did a stupid thing. Still, now, I dream about it, and I see it go the other way. His hand misses that oar, and I wake up in a cold sweat.'

'But he didn't die. He's fine. He had a life, fell in love, got married. He did all the things he was born to do. Things that Hazel should have done.'

'Reading this,' – Adam lifts the pages up briefly – 'you can see how affected Nina was. She must still be affected by it.'

'You wouldn't know it to look at her. She's living her best life.'

'But below the surface,' Adam persists. 'I know how I am, sometimes, underneath, when I think about what might have happened. Never mind that it didn't.'

'Listen, Adam. My whole life has been coloured by the death of my sister. My marriage has failed. My daughter doesn't want to live with me any more . . .'

'I can only imagine what you've been through,' says Adam gently. 'It's a terrible thing. But, if you don't mind me saying, I don't think Hazel has coloured it and I don't think Nina has either. You've done that all by yourself.'

Chapter
Thirty-Six

NINA

Nina holds her breath while her eyebrow is stitched. She can feel the thread pulling through her skin. It is a strange sensation, being sewn back together like a broken doll. The staff at the hospital have been lovely. She is cooed at and joked with. Nina wonders if it would be the same if she wasn't a celebrity.

'What have you done to deserve this?' laughs a friendly nurse.

If only you knew, thinks Nina.

She is moved to a ward and left for periods of time when nobody talks to her. It is early morning, and the hospital is in a lull as it moves into the first working day after the bank holiday. A hushed mood infuses the room, conversations are murmured and indistinct. Footsteps are swallowed by the rubber floor, and there is an old lady snoring lightly in the bed next to her. The air is warm. It smells clinical and cosy, the effect of windows bolted shut against the emerging sunshine. There is no sign of Catrin. Nina is not sure where Catrin has gone. Perhaps she has been abandoned. Perhaps Catrin has done her duty, delivering Nina here, but feels she is as hateful as Roz does. Either way, Nina has time to think about what has happened to her, and what might happen next. Her life is about to go in a different direction. If Roz or Stella decide to make that confession public, things could get very sticky indeed. The police might get involved. Would they prosecute her for something she did, aged thirteen? She is not sure, and the uncertainty worries her. Her phone is still on Little Auger. She won't be able to return to *Rise* looking like this. She wonders if there is a clause in her contract that forbids her from getting her face damaged. She has already decided on the lie she will tell them. Unless Roz gets there first.

Catrin crosses the ward, looking for her, and a sliver of light slides into the gloom that has settled upon Nina's thoughts. She raises her hand, ridiculously glad she is being sought out. 'How are you feeling?' Catrin asks, sitting in a chair next to Nina's bed.

'I'm fine,' says Nina, trying hard to look it.

'They did a good job, patching you up. Are they letting you out soon?'

Nina nods. 'One of the nurses called my mum for me. She's going to pick me up tomorrow, when I'm allowed to go home. They want to keep me in overnight.'

'Did you tell them what happened?'

'I said I had a boating accident. But Roz might decide to enlighten everyone, so I don't know how long that story will stick.'

Catrin looks worried. 'It could get messy.'

Nina nods. She has an irresistible urge to ask Catrin if she still likes her. If they are still friends. She feels as if she is thirteen again. But she can't bring herself to beg.

'How did you do it?' Catrin asks her. 'How did you manage to keep something like that to yourself all this time?'

'I'm a good liar,' replies Nina. 'One of the things I inherited from my mother.'

'What do you mean?'

Nina has had time to think about this. She has thought about nothing else since she landed in this hospital bed. 'My mum always maintained that she moved me to London to protect me from what I'd done. She said if I blabbed the truth – which I would have done, eventually – all hell would have broken loose. She was probably right, but really, I think she wanted me to come with her so my dad couldn't have me. She wanted me all to herself. She's a good liar, my mother. I learnt to lie from a very young age, and I've been perfecting it ever since.'

'That sounds a little extreme, Nina.'

'Shall I let you into a secret? I have no idea who I am. I spent so long trying to fit in, trying to be liked and accepted, I've forgotten who I was supposed to grow up to be. Sometimes I wonder what would have become of me if Hazel hadn't died. If I'd returned from that holiday a happier child, gone back to school, kept my friends. If I'd ended up doing an ordinary job that involved meeting everyday people. A job that didn't rely on what I looked like or how I sounded.'

Nina smooths the bed sheet around her lap. 'I have spent my whole life believing that if I told you and Roz the truth, I would lose your friendship forever, but the irony is, I lost it the day I left for London. And I never found acceptance from anyone else.' A fat, wet tear runs from her good eye and on to her lap.

'Nina, Nina.' Catrin leans over and squeezes her arm. 'We all had a part to play in the death of our friendship. We all managed to ruin it, in our own way.'

Nina looks up at Catrin. 'Do you think that children are better at friendship?'

Catrin looks surprised. 'I don't know . . . how would I know that?'

'Because we were children, once. I think we were better at it. We gave ourselves completely to our friendship. We took risks. We told each other things when we were little that I wouldn't dream of saying now. What is it that makes us so trusting? And what makes us lose that trust when we grow up?' Nina says sadly.

Catrin thinks. 'Maybe, when we get older, we understand what the risks are, and we don't want to open ourselves up in that way, so we begin to close down.'

'I think it's because we start to pretend we're someone we're not. When we're children, we tell the truth. When we're adults, we learn how to lie.'

'That's a depressing thought, Nina.'

'I'll never have friends like you and Roz. I thought perhaps . . . but Roz will never forgive me.'

Catrin hesitates. 'Was it just as you wrote down?'

'Pretty much.' Nina nods.

'I've been angry with Dad for a long time, and with Roz's family. All for no reason. I never got the chance to make things up with my dad. I'm not going to make that mistake again.'

Nina looks over at her friend, and for a moment Catrin looks as if she might cry. She has never seen Catrin cry, until last night, not even when they were children, she realises. Catrin has always been the steady one, the one who battles through. But she looks different now. She has lost her arrogance.

Catrin takes a big breath, nods to herself and gives Nina a heartfelt look. 'Then it was an accident, wasn't it?' she says, with conviction. 'An awful, horrible accident. The world is full of them.'

'It doesn't make it any easier to live with.'

'Would it help if Roz forgave you?'

'She's not going to do that. I'd like to know what she's going to do with those pages though. She still has them.'

'We'll have to wait and see what shape she's in when she gets back to Eider.'

'What about Stella? Is Stella still around?'

'Stella is staying in the next town. She tried to book into the Bed and Breakfast but it's full. Adam is going to bring Roz and everyone's bags back to Eider. When I take Stella's belongings back to her, I'm hoping that will be an end to it.'

'I'm not so sure. I know she doesn't have any of her recordings, but Roz might give her Goggin and my confession. It might be enough to finish her podcast.'

Chapter Thirty-Seven

Roz

The Bed and Breakfast is full. There are no more vacancies for another week.

'I should just go home,' says Roz. She takes her bag from Adam, who has carried it back to his jeep. 'Can you drop me off at the train station?'

'It's too late in the day. You won't find a train to take you home until tomorrow. You'll have to stay with me for tonight.'

'I can't do that.'

He grins at her. 'Won't be the first time.'

'Are you still at your parents' house?'

'No, I have my own place now and I have a spare room, so nobody will be made to sleep in the boatyard this time.'

Roz remembers the time she stayed in Eider, when she'd slept in Adam's bed. It was still the height of summer, and the Bed and Breakfast was, once more, fully booked. Adam's parents had kindly given their house over to Roz and her family so they could be near while the police and the coastguards were searching for Hazel. She hadn't thought, until now, where Adam and his parents had stayed for the week.

'You slept in the boatyard?' Roz asks.

'Mum didn't. She went to stay with her sister. But Dad and I slept in a boat he was working on. The owner didn't mind. It was quite luxurious, as I recall.'

'OK. I'll stop for the night. If that's all right with . . . Are you married? Do you have kids? I never asked you.'

'No. I lived with someone a while back, but it didn't work out.'

'Sorry,' says Roz.

He shrugs, hauling her bag into the back of his pickup. 'I like my own company. I keep very early hours, and I have to work the weekends when the tourists are here. I'm not often at home, and that doesn't suit some women, unfortunately.'

Adam's house is not what Roz was expecting. He has taken over an old fisherman's cottage on the shingle, on the outskirts of Eider. The wooden clapboard is painted a deep matt black, and the window frames are a striking acid yellow. There are flowers, in pots, everywhere. They hang from the roof in baskets, they adorn the windowsills, and they line the pathway that leads to the front door.

'You have green fingers,' she says, intrigued. She sees lavender, geraniums and marguerites. The colour stands out, sharply, against the black of the building.

'I like flowers. You can't grow much in the shingle here. So I put everything in pots.'

'Does it survive the winter?'

He laughs at the question. 'Of course not. It's far too exposed here. But it gives me a new challenge, every year, to try something different. I make mistakes and then I get to write them all off when the spring comes. I get a new chance to start again, every year.'

'I like the sound of that,' admits Roz.

254

Adam leads her into the house. 'Just dump your bag in the spare room here,' he says, indicating a small, simple room with a double bed and side table. The bed linen is white, and there is a bright-yellow throw at the foot of the bed. A set of photographs detailing the boatyard and several local seascapes fill the raw wooden walls. They impart the room with a restrained colour palette, echoing the exterior views.

'I think you missed your calling as an interior designer,' Roz says, surveying the room. It looks like a boutique hotel. When she enters the living room, she stops in her tracks. The wall that runs the length of the room has been replaced with glass. It overlooks the bed of shingle that eventually reaches the sea. Roz draws breath, is still for a moment, captivated by the view. She can see Little Auger in the distance, a smudge of black among the sea spray, a full stop underneath the clouds. It should disturb her, she thinks, to be confronted with the place her sister died. But now she knows for sure that Hazel is not alive, it gives her a strange comfort. She feels looked after, watched over, by Hazel.

'I can't get over that view,' she says. 'How do you leave this place every day?'

'I just exchange it for the view from the boatyard, it's pretty similar,' he laughs.

There are more photographs in the sitting room, detailing the older houses in Eider, the hills that rise inland, and the valleys between them, verdant with colour. 'Did you take these pictures yourself?'

'No, that was my ex. She let me keep them when she left.'

Amicable split. That's a good sign, thinks Roz, before she can stop herself.

Adam looks at his watch. 'Are you hungry? I thought I'd nip out to the chip shop before it shuts. I'm not great at cooking. Make yourself at home and I'll be back soon. There's beer in the fridge.'

'Ah, so you aren't perfect, that's good,' Roz jokes. For a second, she wonders if that sounded like flirting. And then she wonders if it matters.

When Adam has gone, she stands at the window in the sitting room and calls Simon.

'How's Willow?' she asks.

'Do you want to talk to her? I think she might be ready.'

A wave of relief breaks over her. Willow's voice is monosyllabic, but it is a start.

'I'm sorry for shouting at you,' Roz says. 'I'm sorry I didn't tell you about Hazel. I promise I'll answer all your questions when I get back.'

'OK,' Willow mumbles. It is such a short word, but it says everything Roz needs to hear.

'Tell me what you've been up to, Willow. Let's talk about something else.'

'We went to the estate agents,' Willow says.

'You don't mind the idea of selling the house? Moving to a different one?'

'As long as I can still see my friends and I get my own bedroom.'

Roz can't figure out the disconnect. She doesn't understand why Willow doesn't share her attachment to the house, but she stops herself from sharing her misgivings. Roz has a harder task ahead of her: winning back her daughter's trust.

They end the call with Roz reluctantly agreeing to look at a flat Willow has picked out for her. *I bet it won't have a view like this*, she thinks, as she looks out to sea. Her eyes scan the horizon. Hazel is out there, somewhere. Her body has been scattered by the water and absorbed by the land. She is part of the landscape right in front of her. It's strange, but it's not a horrible thought.

When Adam returns with fish and chips, they spread the food out, still in its paper, and he hands her a bottle of beer. The light has drained from the sky and the whole house fills with the deep red of a cloudless sunset. It feels unearthly, being plunged into a singular colour, as if she is on Mars. But as soon as the thought enters her head, the red weakens to orange, and the windows, which were lit with warmth, slowly turn black. Roz begins to feel maudlin and finds herself telling Adam about being forced to sell the family home.

'I feel like all those years of being a family in that house mean nothing to Willow.'

'Surely that's better than dragging her out of there kicking and screaming? It's good that she wants to move forward.'

'I suppose that's my problem. I hold on to the past too much,' Roz says gloomily.

'From what I can see, the past hasn't done you any favours so far,' says Adam. 'Anyway, it's people that matter more than houses, surely?'

Roz thinks about the pots full of flowers outside, optimistically blooming in the darkness, in a climate they are not built for. She thinks of Adam, knowing they will need to be replaced next year, relishing the act of doing that, instead of mourning their loss.

The train out of Eider leaves early in the morning. Adam has to be at the boatyard, so he gives her a lift on his way to work, and when he drops her off, he hesitates.

'You know, I wrote to you after you left here,' he says.

'You did? I didn't receive anything.'

'I never posted the letters. Postcards, really.'

'Postcards? You wrote more than once?'

He smiles sheepishly. 'I wrote to you every week, for a time. Not a long time, but up until the new year, I think.'

'What did they say?'

Adam looks embarrassed. 'Stupid things. Trivial things. I didn't talk about what had happened. I didn't think you'd want me to. It was more day-to-day stuff to distract you. I didn't think you'd want to read about the place that Hazel died. I think I listed the local football scores on some of them. God.' He shakes his head, grimacing.

But Roz is touched. 'How come you never posted them?'

'Because I thought that the connection we made . . . it was a bad thing, the reason I got to know you that summer. And . . . I thought you wouldn't want to hear from someone who reminded you of that time.'

Roz thinks back to her life after Hazel died. The loneliness she felt. 'Thank you for thinking of me. That would have meant a lot.'

'Well, I see that now. I wasn't going to mention it. But having you back here, it brought some of that stuff up again, and it seemed weird not to. I suppose . . . I suppose I wanted you to know that I was thinking about how you were doing, even though I never reached out.'

Roz remembers what the old man said to her on the beach. *We all lost Hazel that day. The whole village grieved.* She stands on her tiptoes and throws her arms around Adam's neck, taking in the smell of soap and sea.

'I didn't think about how hard it was on you and your family. The village,' she whispers into his neck, her voice breaking.

'But not as hard as it was for you,' he replies, stroking her hair. 'Text me your email address,' he adds. 'I'll write to you, and this time I'll press *send*. How about that?'

'That sounds perfect,' she says, wishing they had more time to talk.

'Don't be a stranger, OK?' he says finally. 'You're welcome to stay, any time.'

'Thanks, Adam. For everything.' Roz shoulders her backpack, waving at him as he drives out of the station car park.

When he turns the jeep towards the coast, she is suddenly filled with things unsaid. She wishes she had talked with him about the days just after Hazel's disappearance. They had avoided it, discussing their own adult lives instead. Now she yearns to relive the strange days they spent together as children. She should have told him that she still remembers how to tie a fisherman's knot, that for some reason those few minutes he spent teaching her outside The Old House were minutes she returned to, often, even now. She turns to the train station with a sense of loss she can't shake off.

She doesn't have to wait long until the train draws into the station. A few people disembark, families mostly, wanting to make the most of the day. She gets on and finds a seat next to a window, settles herself down and watches the landscape slide past. It feels as if history is being left behind her, it is such a physical sensation watching Little Auger and the sea that surrounds it dissipate into a blurred swathe of pine trees, and eventually into dry land.

Chapter Thirty-Eight

CATRIN

Catrin pulls up in the car park of the hotel. It is a cheaply built concrete-and-glass box, devoid of personality, positioned just off a busy ring road, the kind that caters for jaded businesspeople passing through. She enters the lobby, texting Stella a message to say she is there, before she remembers that Stella's phone is at the bottom of the sea. Catrin goes to the reception instead and asks them to relay a message to Stella's room, before finding a soulless lounge area to wait in.

'Hi,' Stella calls breezily as she approaches Catrin. 'Is that my bag? You didn't have to do that. I was planning on coming back to Eider this afternoon.'

'I thought I'd save you the trouble,' says Catrin. 'You can be back in London before rush hour this way.'

There is a brief pause while Stella swiftly rearranges the expression on her face. 'I was actually hoping to get back to Little Auger this afternoon. I really need to talk with Roz. I still have some bits and pieces I need to finish up.'

Catrin sighs. 'It's over, Stella. Your project. I thought you knew that?'

'Just because Nina destroyed most of my research, it doesn't mean the project is over. Roz still has the diary, and Goggin. I can make it work without Nina's involvement.'

Catrin takes a breath. 'Roz gave me the diary. She's made it really clear that she doesn't want to speak to anyone. She's traumatised by what happened and she's already on her way home.'

'Do you think I could take a look at those pages again?' asks Stella sweetly.

'No,' says Catrin. 'I destroyed them.'

'What?' The mask of kindness drops for a moment, and Catrin sees irritation.

'Nobody wants this podcast to go ahead apart from you, Stella. As I understand it, you need my cooperation for it to work and I'm withdrawing it.'

'I don't think it's as easy as that, Catrin,' says Stella lightly. 'We've set something in motion here, and I think it's going to be very hard to stop it.'

'Well, let me give you some reasons why you might want to try.' Catrin counts on her fingers. 'One, you've trespassed on my family's land. Two, you've withheld evidence from the police. Three, I know many colleagues who would feel very let down to hear that you quite happily fabricate evidence and lie to the subjects who trust you with their stories. Journalists are curious people. They might want to dig around some of your past work and double-check you haven't done it before. You have nothing, Stella. No diary, no photographs, no Goggin, and nothing on record from any of us. We will deny you ever had permission, and I will personally guarantee I will ruin your reputation if you continue with this project. Do you understand?'

Stella draws herself up and tries to look nonchalant. 'Perfectly. Can I ask you a question?'

'Yes.'

'Did you know she was going to do that? Nina. Throwing my phone overboard?'

'No,' says Catrin. 'It was as big a surprise for me as it was for you. I take it the lack of reception on Little Auger meant none of your work was backed up?'

'I think you must know the answer to that question.'

Catrin tries to suppress a smile. 'One more thing. I want you to contact Roz's parents and tell them you found absolutely nothing. Tell them there's no evidence that Hazel was taken, that in all likelihood she fell and died instantly. Can you do that for me?'

'Why can't Roz do it?'

'Because they'll believe you. And it might give them some peace.'

Stella picks up her bag. 'You know, this is really unprofessional. I would have thought that you, above all, wanted to air the truth.'

'Sometimes,' Catrin says, thinking of Nina, 'happiness is more important than the truth.'

Stella looks at her, aghast. 'You can't mean that, surely?'

'Believe me, I surprise myself. But in this case, I do.'

Catrin gets back into her car, but she doesn't drive off. She waits, thinking about her visit to Adam's house the night before when she called to pick up the bags. Adam's house had smelled of fish and chips. The screwed-up papers were still on the table.

'Beer?' Adam offered, as he ushered her into the house.

'No, thanks, I just need to speak to Roz,' said Catrin, feeling awkward. There was an atmosphere in the room she couldn't get to grips with, a sense she had interrupted something. She looked around his house. It was small. There would be no privacy. 'Maybe we could walk?' she'd said to Roz, indicating the beach beyond, which was now bathed in moonlight.

'I have to pack the jeep up for tomorrow,' said Adam, grabbing his coat off the hook near the door. 'I'll leave you to it.'

When the door clicked shut, Catrin sat down at the table, opposite Roz. She wished she'd accepted the beer.

'You've been with Nina?' asked Roz.

'Yes. She's still in hospital. She needed stitches, and they want to keep her in overnight, because of the bang to her head.'

'I didn't mean to hurt her like that. It was . . .' Roz paused then, and gave Catrin a look. 'It was an accident. Is she going to be all right?'

'She'll be fine.'

'When are you going back?'

'I'm not sure. I need to see Stella, first thing tomorrow. She's in a hotel out of town. Then I'll probably make sure the house on Little Auger is properly shut down before I go back to Chapel Farm. There's so much to do over there.'

'I'm sorry about your father.' Roz reached over the table between them.

Catrin took her hand. Then she shook her head. 'I'm sorry I doubted you. I honestly thought that person in the photograph was you. I thought the amnesia you had was . . . selective. I was just trying to get to the bottom of what happened.'

'Well, you got what you wanted.' There was something in Roz's voice. Regret? Acceptance? Catrin couldn't quite make out what it was.

'So did you. You found out what really happened to Hazel. I hope it brings you some peace, Roz. Are you going to tell your parents the whole story?'

'I honestly haven't thought that far.' Roz sounded wiped out.

'No. Of course not. Do you still have those pages? Did you bring them back with you?'

'Yes, why?'

'What are you going to do with them?'

'You're asking me questions I can't answer right now, Catrin. I'm still trying to get my head straight.'

'Please don't give them to Stella. Or make them public. It doesn't seem fair on Nina.'

'You and Nina were always in cahoots.'

Catrin laughed. 'I said the exact same thing to her about you. She protected you when I thought you knew more than you were letting on.'

'Only because she wanted to protect herself.'

'I think she came back here, partly, to protect you. She knew your name was on the front cover of that journal. She knew Stella would have jumped to the same conclusions as me. Nina didn't have to confess anything. She could have stayed in London and let you take the blame. But she didn't. Doesn't she deserve some credit for that?'

'I don't feel like giving her credit for anything right now.'

'Will you at least give me those pages?'

'You could use them to clear your father's name, you know. By exposing Nina, you could save his reputation.'

'Don't think I haven't thought about it. But it's too late for my dad. It's not too late for Nina.'

'Are you going to be friends with her after this?'

'Yes,' Catrin said firmly. 'And I'd like to be friends with you, too.'

Roz nodded. 'I'll be in touch,' she said. 'But I'm not ready to give those pages up just yet. I need some time to think.'

Lying does not sit comfortably with Catrin. It has surprised her how easily the words rolled off her tongue just now. Suddenly, she sees the white-blonde hair of Stella Cox emerging from the hotel, moving above the roofs of the vehicles in the car park. She watches Stella get into her car and drive off, holding her breath as the car draws up at the crossroads, not knowing if Stella will turn left for Eider or right for the motorway that will take her back to London. When she sees the indicator pulse and the car turn right, Catrin breathes a sigh of relief. Her gamble will pay off. Roz will not seek Stella out to give her those pages and Stella will not ask.

Chapter Thirty-Nine

NINA

Nina folds herself gingerly into her car. Sylvia has taken the train from London and picked up Nina's car from the Bed and Breakfast at Eider before driving to the hospital to collect her. Getting public transport always puts Sylvia in a bad mood and Nina is already exhausted from trying to transform her mother's ire into something manageable. Sylvia is angry with Roz for what she has done to Nina's face, angry with Catrin for running back to Chapel Farm and abandoning Nina here. Nina knows she should be grateful for her mother's protection, but she feels suffocated before she leaves the ward. Several hours in a car isn't going to improve things.

Sylvia drives as she moves through life: fast and full of purpose, carried along by her own version of truth. Nina waits until they hit the motorway, the landscape of the west brimming with green.

'Roz has a right to feel the way she does, you know,' she says.

'She hurt you, Nina. She's cut your face. Have you spoken to work?'

Nina shakes her head. In a moment of cowardice, she asked if one of the nurses could leave Curtis, her director, a message, but she knows she needs to face him soon. 'They can't fire me because of this,' Nina says wearily. 'You can't sack someone because they aren't pretty any more. Anyway, once the stitches are out you'll barely see it.'

'They told you that you shouldn't wear make-up until it's fully healed. How are you going to work if you can't wear make-up? I could swing for Roz Richardson.' Sylvia's voice takes on a venom that is hard to stomach in such a small space.

Nina turns to look out of her window, the fields and hedgerows zipping by. 'Try and see it from her point of view,' she says to her own reflection.

'That's not my job, Nina. My job is to protect *you*, not her.'

'I appreciate that, you know I do. Sometimes, though . . . I wish you wouldn't, Mum,' says Nina carefully, looking down at her nails. The pretty pink polish she had applied last week is beginning to flake and chip.

'What's that supposed to mean?' Her mother turns to her and the car slides towards the edge of the lane before she corrects it, swiftly, with a jerk.

'Hazel. If I'd just come clean . . . people might have understood it was an accident. And things would have been better by now.'

'Did you really think I was going to take that chance? They might have thrown you in jail.'

'I was only thirteen. I don't think they do that to kids.'

'Well, I wasn't going to sit back and hope for the best. You needed protecting.'

'And look at me now.' Nina gestures to her face.

Sylvia taps her long fingernails on the steering wheel. 'If I see her, I will kill her, Nina. No doubt about it.'

'Where does it come from, all this malice?' Nina asks her suddenly.

'It's what mothers do for their children.' Sylvia shakes her beautiful hair and the smell of her expensive shampoo fills the car. 'Good ones, anyway.'

'And what about fathers?' says Nina quietly, her heart speeding up.

There is a pause. 'I don't know what you mean.'

'Where was Dad in all of this? Did he agree with you? About the move to London? Did he agree we should hush it all up?'

'I didn't give him a chance to pass opinion. He lost that privilege when he went off with that woman. He didn't want to know about you.'

'You didn't tell him what happened to me while I was away on that island?'

'He'd already moved out by the time you got back.'

'You must have had some communication with him. You had to sell the house, get divorced. Didn't he pay child maintenance?'

'I didn't want anything more to do with that man.' The way Sylvia says this, like a sulking child, makes Nina think she is lying to her.

'What about me? I really could have used having my dad around that year. I had no idea our time together was so limited.'

The car wobbles on the carriageway as Sylvia turns to her. 'Haven't I been enough for you?'

'You are above and beyond my mum. There's no disputing that. But I would have liked to have had some contact with Dad before he died, that's all I'm saying. It doesn't alter my relationship with you.'

'If I'd let him see you, he would have poisoned you against me.'

The words take a second to sink in. 'If *you'd let him see me*? You told me he was the one who didn't want contact.' Nina thinks about the night she thought she heard his voice, the banging on the front door. 'Are you saying he tried to see me?'

There is a silence while Sylvia says nothing, her mouth a hard line.

'Mum? You always said to me there were no secrets between us, but I think you might be lying right now.'

Sylvia thumps the steering wheel. 'Why do you have to bring all of this stuff up, anyway? It happened ages ago.'

'Because it matters! Don't you think it matters? I thought he didn't want to see me because of what happened to Hazel. That's a hurtful thing to feel, don't you get it?'

'Have you stopped to think about me? It's hurtful to me, too, Nina. How could you say you wanted contact with him after what he did to us?'

'He did that to you, not to me.'

'They had their own daughter, Nina. I wasn't going to give them mine.'

Nina turns to Sylvia. 'Mum, why did we go to London? Was it because of what I did to Hazel, or was it to get me away from Dad? Did you do it to protect me, or to protect yourself?'

Sylvia says nothing. She drives, too fast, down the motorway. They sit in silence for the rest of the journey, both of them looking at the road in front of them, and Nina understands that something has changed. The wall of silence that her mother built around them to protect her has been shifted. It now sits between them, keeping Nina out.

When she closes the door of her home behind her, she waits in the hallway, the cat winding himself around her legs. She listens as her mother gets into her own car and revs the engine, and waits until she hears the crunch of gravel fade away. So much has happened since she left this house. She has relived her childhood and lost it, all over again. She doesn't know if she will see Catrin, if Catrin wants to stay in touch. She doesn't know what will happen with Roz. So many uncertainties, so many questions.

Nina goes to her bedroom and gets her journal out of the side table. She writes, the words tumbling on to the page, making sense of the last few days, trying to untangle the web of thoughts that crowd in. When she has finished, she reads what she has written. It is a full account of the weekend, but it doesn't soothe her to read it. She gets off the bed and walks to the wardrobe, where she stores the rest of her journals. There are twenty years of them, bundled together, the stories of her life. She wonders what the point is, all of this writing, all of her wounds opened up before they are stored away. What is it all for? She knows how she feels. It is others who need to know.

She thinks back to Howard, his breach of trust when he read her journal, and realises she would have done the same. He just wanted to get to know her, but she was afraid Sylvia would disapprove. She gets her phone out, texts his number.

Hi, she writes. Feel free to ignore this message if you don't want to talk to me any more, but I've done some growing up. I think I'm ready for you to read my journals now.

She presses *send*, and several seconds later, three tell-tale words announce *Howard is typing*.

Chapter Forty

Roz

Roz gets a taxi back from the train station. As it pulls up outside her house, she realises the number of times she is going to pass through this particular door is dwindling. Has it really only been a few days since she left? In that space of time, her whole perception of the past has been upended, old friendships resurrected and extinguished in the space of a long weekend.

The first thing she does is take Goggin out of his plastic bag and fill the kitchen sink with warm water and laundry soap. She washes him, lovingly, as if she were bathing a toddler. As she squeezes his little body, twenty years of mud, silt and salt bleed into the milky water. Roz rolls him up into a towel and gently presses until he is damp, then settles him in the airing cupboard to dry in a warm space.

Simon drops Willow off in the evening, and Willow runs straight up to her room. Roz lets her, not wanting to push things.

'Do you want to come in for a bit?' she asks Simon.

Simon looks surprised, glances at his watch, and then nods. 'Sure, why not.'

They talk about the things he and Willow have done over the past few days, the plans they have made. She realises they work well together, without her. She tells him the truth. Where she has been, what she has seen, what she has done.

'What are you going to do?' he asks. 'About Nina, I mean? Is there any point in telling the police?'

'I wanted to ruin her for about twenty-four hours. Now . . . I don't know what to think. I suppose I want to try and focus on the future.'

'I thought this was a work trip, anyway,' Simon says, confused.

Roz tells him about the brief for the children's book she has been given. The trouble she has had putting pen to paper, the creative block she has suffered, and how she thinks she may have begun to move past it.

'I think these new studies I made while I was away might be the beginning of something.' She shows them to him, and he looks at them thoughtfully.

'They're good,' he says. 'But I wouldn't submit them as part of this brief you've been given. Why don't you develop Hazel and Goggin as characters in their own right? You could do a lot more with them then, and you could control the whole narrative if you wrote everything yourself.'

'Well . . . I'm not sure. I'm an illustrator, not a children's book writer.'

'You're good at writing, Roz. You should nurture it. You have plenty of contact with publishers, I'm sure they could help you if they think it's got legs. You could turn the loss of your sister into something positive. Plenty of families have suffered what you've been through, it might be nice for them to see a way forward. It's a compelling story, if you're ready to talk about it.'

'Yes,' she says, looking at the images with a fresh focus. 'Maybe I am ready to talk about her. It will help me explain everything to Willow too.'

'Listen, Roz. I've been meaning to tell you. I met someone. Actually, it's one of the reasons I want to sell the house. We – Kelly and I – want to move in together.' He looks sheepish. 'Sorry, I should have told you sooner. You just seemed like you had a lot on your plate before you left and now you seem . . . well . . . so much better.'

She is not expecting this news to hit her as hard as it does. For a second, she is numb, not knowing what to say or do. 'Wow,' she says, trying to sound cheerful. 'So we really are moving on.'

'It won't affect my relationship with you, or with Willow. But Kelly will be living with me when I find somewhere bigger.'

Roz turns away from him to make some more tea.

'I'm sorry, Roz,' says Simon once more.

'It's fine,' she says, surprised at her urge to cry. 'I'm happy for you. Really. It's just . . . the end of an era, I suppose. I should have realised you wouldn't stay single forever. Does Willow know?'

'I mentioned it. Not that we want to move in together. Just that I'm seeing someone, and it might be a long-term thing.'

'And what did she say?' Her voice is flat and dull.

'She seemed to be cool with it. Kelly would like to meet Willow. Obviously I'll arrange that with you first.'

Roz grips her cup. 'Do you want another cup of tea?' she asks him, hoping he'll say no.

'Um, nah. I better get off.'

She hears the chair scraping back on the wooden floor. 'OK,' she says, turning around with the biggest smile she can muster. 'I'll see you out.'

Simon turns to her before she closes the front door. 'She won't take your place, you know. You do . . . you do know that, don't you?'

Roz tries to smile. 'Thanks. I know that. I'm happy for you, honestly. I just wasn't expecting it, that's all.'

She closes the door, returns to the kitchen and hears Willow come down from her room. Roz washes up her cup at the sink, unable to trust herself to face Willow without crying. Willow comes towards her cautiously. 'Did Dad tell you about Kelly?'

'Yes,' Roz says, trying to sound breezy, putting the wet cup on the draining board.

Willow gives her a hug from behind, her skinny arms encircling Roz's waist. 'I bet she's not as nice as you.'

Roz turns and hugs her back, kissing the top of her daughter's head, smelling the familiar scent of her shampoo. It is such a gift to be able to do this, she realises, to be loved and hugged by your child. For a moment, the sadness she felt at Simon's news is completely erased by the comfort that Willow gives her. She doesn't know if she would feel it so keenly had she not lost Hazel, or if the feeling would be just as strong for the simple fact that Willow is her child. She doesn't care. She just feels so lucky to have her, the pressure of her touch, the sincerity of her love.

'Do you know what?' she says into Willow's hair. 'I think it's time we sold this place.' The image of Adam and his pots of flowers have not left her. If he can start fresh every year, knowing things might not work out, then she can at least try. 'Shall we put it on the market next week? Then Dad can buy his house, and you can decide where you'd like to live.'

'You're going to let me choose?' Willow asks, looking uncertain.

'I'll be honest with you, Willow. I'm not sure I can afford a place really near to your new school. If I moved a little further away,

I would understand if you wanted to live with Dad during the week and come to me for weekends.'

'Wouldn't you be upset if I did that?'

Roz swallows her grief. 'I'd miss you, of course I would, but I'd understand. Sometimes we need a change. Dad would like to see more of you, I'm sure. And he wants you to meet Kelly.'

'Maybe. I'll think about it.'

Roz tries to make her voice light. 'You're so grown-up! I can hardly keep up with you.'

'Mum?'

'Yes?' Roz looks into Willow's eyes, and she sees Hazel there, looking back.

'Even if I decide to live with Dad for a bit, and Kelly's nice, you'll always be my mum.'

'Thanks, my gorgeous girl,' Roz says, her throat closing up. 'You don't know how happy that makes me feel.' Roz clings on to her daughter as if she is a life raft in a rough sea. And for the first time in a long time, she feels as if they are on the same side.

Chapter
Forty-One

Roz

Roz wakes feeling optimistic. She lets Willow sleep in, and when she finally gets out of bed, Roz makes pancakes for them both. She lays the table with care, using the good cutlery and plates that match, and she picks a small posy of flowers from the garden and puts them in a jam jar. Then she retrieves the photo album and sketchbook from the bottom of her wardrobe and places them carefully on the kitchen worktop. When Willow eventually comes downstairs and takes in the effort Roz has made, sees the album and sketchbook, she looks apprehensive.

'I thought the best way of saying sorry was to your stomach. I've even made hot chocolate.'

'Um, OK,' says Willow, allowing herself to be served, eyeing the photo album on the worktop.

The atmosphere is quiet at first, but when Roz begins to dish up the pancakes and allows Willow to pour a steady stream of golden syrup over hers, things relax, and they stop treading carefully around one another.

When Roz clears their plates, she takes a leap of faith and tells Willow where she has been, and what happened on Little Auger before Willow was born. Then she shows her the photo album.

'Ask me anything,' she says, and she lets Willow turn the pages.

The conversation lacks the drama she imagined it would contain. Willow doesn't really understand what it means to lose a sister, though she nods thoughtfully when Roz tries to explain. She takes Goggin, who is now dry, out of the airing cupboard and places him on the table between her and Willow.

'This is Goggin,' she begins. 'He was given to Hazel when she was born. He went everywhere with her. Can you see how loved he's been?'

Willow looks at Goggin with curiosity and nods, slowly.

'I thought you might like to have him. Hazel was eleven when he lost her, and it seems like a nice thing to be looked after by another member of the family, close to her age.'

Willow says nothing.

'What do you think?' says Roz.

Willow looks at Roz, her eyes full of compassion. 'No offence, Mum. But he's a bit gross. And creepy.'

Roz looks at Goggin through Willow's eyes. A giggle bubbles up inside her as she understands exactly what Willow means.

'No offence taken,' she laughs.

'Can I see my friends today?' Willow asks her. Her plate has a thin pool of syrup over it, and Roz offers it to her before she takes it away so she can run her finger over the surface. 'Melissa said she was allowed to have a sleepover at her house tonight. Her mum will be there.'

'Actually, yes,' says Roz, an idea brewing. 'I'm going to go out today and I'll be back late tonight, if you don't mind me going away again.'

'Sure,' Willow says, sliding off the kitchen chair, already reaching for the phone and dialling Melissa's number.

Roz drops Willow off, arranging with Melissa's mother to pick her up the next afternoon. Then she gets into the car and drives for the two hours it takes to get to her parents' house. She has not called them to tell them she is coming. She didn't want to give herself an excuse to change her mind.

When she pulls up on the kerbside, she has to steel herself to enter a house she tried so hard to get away from. Her parents never moved. Just in case Hazel came back. She is sure Hazel's school photos still adorn the mantelpiece, that the bedroom they shared is still a shrine. As Roz approaches the front door, the same colour, the same knocker, the same pot of red geraniums on the step, she wonders if this was also for Hazel, this lack of change, that her little sister would find comfort in a house that never altered in her absence.

'Rosalind!' exclaims her father as he opens the door, clearly shocked to see her in person, unannounced. 'Is everything all right?'

He is smaller than she remembers, a shrunken version of himself. Roz has sent photographs of her, and Willow and Simon, over the years, but there was never any reason for her parents to do the same. The years of grief have curved his spine. His hair is grey. She feels a pull of tenderness.

'Yes, everything's fine,' replies Roz. 'Are you busy? I wanted to talk with you both. Is Mum in?' Roz peers into the dim hallway; the wallpaper is as she remembers, a steady supply of scattering leaves falling across the walls towards a deep-red carpet that covers the floor, worn in the middle from the shuffled footsteps of a grieving family.

'Yes, she's in the garden, weeding. I was about to cut the grass.'

Roz glances into the sitting room as she passes, which is neat and tidy, the tired sofa a little paler, bleached by the light of ten thousand sunsets. It looks like the home of an unremarkable family. She wonders what went wrong between them all, why Hazel's death pulled them apart instead of pushing them together. Roz follows her father out into the back garden, where her mother is weeding a border. She, too, is smaller, less significant, the colour leached out of her hair, her skin. The garden is the only thing that has not respected their loss. It has swollen with exuberant growth. The crown of the cherry tree at the foot of the garden blots out the sky. The borders jostle with greenery that has been left, unchecked. A buddleia, smothered in butterflies, has burst out of the ground like an exploding firework.

They sit, like an ordinary family enjoying a sunny day, sharing a jug of home-made lemonade. Roz had no idea her mother made that sort of thing. She wonders how many other things she hasn't understood about her, and she feels a pang of regret for the lost years between them. And then she realises. The box files piled up in the hallway, the papers scattered over the sitting-room table. They have gone. Every detail of Hazel's death – the police reports, newspaper cuttings, legal documents, every scrap of paper that her parents have collected, read and reread. They have all been tidied away.

'Where are all the files?' she asks them both.

'Stella got back in touch,' says her father. 'She said she wasn't going to go forward with the podcast. She said there was no evidence to suggest Hazel had been taken. We decided we'd had enough, it was time to stop. It's been twenty years. We've had our hopes raised one too many times.'

She sees it then. The resignation. She understands that the sentence they have been serving for the past twenty years has been lifted, that the passing of time has reduced them to shadows. Suddenly, Roz feels protective, a need to reach out and build them back up.

'Did Stella tell you I met her there?' asks Roz. 'On the island?'

'She didn't say very much at all. Seemed desperate to get off the phone. I couldn't get much sense out of her. I thought she'd found something.'

'She did, Dad,' Roz begins carefully. She takes a breath. 'She found Goggin.'

Her mother puts her fingers to her lips, as if to stifle sound. Her father closes his eyes, tight, and says nothing.

'I brought him here with me. Would you like to see him? I have him in my bag.'

'Yes, of course,' her mother whispers, nodding.

Roz gently lifts Goggin from her bag and her mother cries as she folds him to her chest.

'How?' her father asks, shaking his head. 'Where was he?'

'He was on the old cliff path. Under a gorse bush. Nobody else would have realised what it was, he's so tattered.'

'It's a miracle he stayed there all this time.'

Roz smiles at her mother. 'He's had a wash. He looks a lot more respectable now than he did when he was pulled out.'

'Did you see anything else?' her dad asks, hardly daring to hope.

'The whole cliff is very crumbly, Dad.' Roz swallows hard, careful not to raise their hopes again. And then a deeper, more complicated part of her decides not to involve Nina. 'It seems certain that she fell there,' Roz concludes, knowing this is for the best.

She had expected her mother to protest, to deny the truth that Roz has offered. But she doesn't. She holds Goggin as if he is a precious baby and nods, not looking at Roz, preoccupied with arranging Goggin's arm, gently pressing some of the contents back into his stomach.

'Well, that's that, then,' says her father.

280

'I think you were right. Hazel did follow me, that morning,' says Roz, finding it hard to say the words, but knowing she must. 'I'm so sorry I didn't do a better job of looking after her.'

Her mother says nothing, but her father reaches over to her. 'We all feel guilty over Hazel.' He looks at his wife. 'We got a bit muddled after it happened, didn't we? And then it seemed impossible to get ourselves on a different track with you. We know how we were, your mother and me. We know how it annoyed you and Hazel, to have us fussing over you both when you were younger. We both owe you an apology.'

Roz bows her head, unable to trust herself to speak. The feeling of his hand in hers is something she thought she had forgotten, something she thought was in the past.

'I'll get some more lemonade,' says her mother, patting her shoulder, still cradling Goggin. 'And maybe something to eat?' she asks him, lifting his knitted face to hers and planting a kiss, lightly, on his head.

Her father continues, 'We made a mistake, blaming you. I told your mother that, but I think . . . I think that when you're angry and sad, there's nowhere for it to go. So it turns to blame. And then when Willow was born . . . it was very difficult, especially for your mother.'

'Why? Because she looked like Hazel?'

'Yes,' her father admits. 'It was very hard to get over the fact she wasn't Hazel.'

There is a lapse in the conversation, where there are no words to carry on. They both look to the garden, the lawnmower waiting to be plugged in, the bucket filled with weeds standing on the grass.

'Rosalind,' her father says eventually. 'Do you remember the witches' marks in The Old House on Little Auger?'

'Of course. They're still there.'

'Do you remember Hazel had one, on her neck?' He touches the nape of his own neck to show her where.

'Yes. I remember that.' Roz thinks back to the crescent shape on her sister's skin, how she'd trace it sometimes, very lightly, to make Hazel giggle. She had forgotten that game, until now.

'We didn't talk about it at home. It was covered by her hair at any rate.'

'Why are you calling it a witch's mark?'

'Because that's what some people called them, birthmarks like that. Your mother became quite taken up with their meaning when Hazel was born with it. A long time ago, people used to be ostracised from their communities if they had birthmarks. People thought they brought bad luck. Your grandmother, she was sure it was something your mother had done wrong. Eaten the wrong thing, picked up something too heavy. Not said her prayers properly. She even said she'd been cursed. She was a superstitious lady, your grandmother.' Her father waves his fingers dismissively in the air. 'She was critical too. She died before you got to know her, and I'll tell you now because your mother can't hear, but it was a blessing she did.'

'Is that what Mum thought about Hazel's birthmark? That it would bring bad luck?'

Her father nods. 'When we went to Little Auger and stayed in the house, your mother saw the marks on the doorways and windows, and she made a connection between the shape of them and the shape of Hazel's birthmark. When Hazel disappeared, your mother got it into her head, for a while, that Hazel had been taken by whatever those marks were warding off.'

Roz remembers being so certain there was something otherworldly about the house and the island before she found out the truth of Hazel's death. And she remembers the gnawing hunger for knowledge that would never be sated. 'When something as

282

awful as that happens to you, you seek an explanation. No matter how wild,' she says softly.

Her father nods and looks into his empty glass.

'Dad, do you think it was a bad idea, bringing Goggin here?'

'No, I think finding Goggin might go a little way to helping her understand she isn't cursed, we were all just terribly, terribly unlucky.'

'What if I took you both there . . . to Little Auger?' Roz asks.

Her father shakes his head. 'Oh, I don't know about that. We have no yearning to go back to that place.'

'It might be helpful to see where Hazel fell, where Goggin was found. It's a beautiful place, really.' Roz tells him about the cairn, the stone she decorated with Hazel's name, the hazelnut she pushed into the ground.

'What do you think?' says her father, looking up, and for a moment Roz thinks he is talking to her. But close behind, she hears her mother's voice, feels her hand rest lightly on her shoulder.

'I'd like that, Rosalind,' her mother says. 'I think that would be a nice thing to do.'

Chapter
Forty-Two

NINA

Nina has only agreed to this meeting because the idea of going into the studio is worse than having Curtis show up on her doorstep. Her body is still sore. It has taken a few days for her muscles and bones to stop complaining about their mistreatment, and she moves around the house stiffly. She has tender parts on her body from where she fell against the bedpost and on to the floor. While the cut above her eyebrow is healing nicely, an impressive bruise has bloomed, like ink in water, on the side of her forehead, staining her skin with purple and yellow. It doesn't hurt. But it looks dramatic enough to skive off work. Especially if she exaggerates the head injury. Which she has.

When the doorbell rings, she checks herself in the mirror and gives herself a nod before she opens the door to let Curtis in. He is carrying a large basket of fruit and a bouquet of flowers. They are blousy, ostentatious, and not Nina's style at all.

'A little get-well-soon gift, from all of us,' he says. Then he does a second take. 'Wow. You look . . . have you had a perm?'

'No, Curtis. This is what I look like. I have naturally curly hair.'

'I never knew that. You look completely different. And your face.'

'I'm not wearing any make-up. This is what women look like without it.'

'Yeah . . . yeah.' He nods, thoughtfully.

Nina takes in his confusion. 'I suppose you don't see women looking like this, do you, in your line of work?' She thinks about the models and actresses that Curtis dates. Then she thinks about all the female television presenters she knows with naturally curly hair and realises that every single one of them has their hair blow-dried and straightened before they are allowed on camera. 'This is me *au naturel,*' she says, feeling defiant.

'Au . . . what?'

Nina suppresses a smile. 'Never mind. Come in.' She shows Curtis into the kitchen. She motions for him to sit at the breakfast bar. The stools are uncomfortable after a while, and she hopes this will speed up their meeting. She busies herself by dividing the flowers between several vases so they look less pretentious, making coffee for them both, making small talk with her back to him, delaying the moment they will sit, face to face.

'Once the bruising goes down, you'll be right as rain,' says Curtis, accepting the coffee. 'Though it would have been *mega* if that scar was bigger. And permanent. Not that I'm wishing that on you, or anything. God forbid. We could have made something of it, that's all. You know, *my journey to recovery,* that sort of thing. Do you have oat milk?'

'What? No,' says Nina. She pushes a black coffee towards him. 'You've really thought about this, haven't you.'

'What?'

'My accident. It's just a cut and a bruise. It will heal.'

'Yeah, I know, but I need to increase the diversity on the show, and it would have been good if . . .'

'If I had the kind of facial injury that permanently blighted my life?'

'Well, I wouldn't put it like that . . .'

Nina shakes her head, takes a sip of coffee. 'Sometimes, working with you is like being in a parallel universe. In fact, it *is* a parallel universe, I suppose.'

'I don't get you.'

Nina thinks about going back there. Pouring herself into clothes and shoes that pinch and push her body into shapes it doesn't want to occupy any more. She has loved slouching around in joggers this week. Even if they are double-lined and made of silk.

'Curtis, I'm not coming back to the show,' she says, before she loses courage. 'I thought about what I want, and about what you need, like you said. And I don't think I want to give you what you need.'

'Seriously?' His gaze slides towards the expensive flowers.

'Seriously.'

'What are you going to do?'

'I don't know. But I don't want to present any more. I'm sick of putting on a fake smile and pretending all is well with the world.'

'You're so good at it though. People really love you. The team, I mean. They've really missed you. Even the cleaner, what's her name?'

'Marguerite.'

'Yeah, Marguerite. She said the place was very quiet without you around.'

'I didn't realise that. Thanks for telling me.'

'You have a knack for being friendly without getting too close. You'd make a good producer, actually. I could put you in touch with a few people if you don't want to be in front of the camera any more.'

Nina looks at Curtis with surprise. 'Would you do that?'

Curtis shrugs. 'Of course. Why wouldn't I?'

She sees him with fresh eyes. 'I don't know. I thought that maybe resigning from the show would annoy you. That you'd take it personally.'

'Nah. I don't take things personally. And it won't be hard to replace you. No offence.'

'None taken.'

He smiles at her, exposing large, even teeth. 'And I can take credit for reinventing you if the production thing works out. Women make good producers. They're more organised than men.'

Nina feels she has misjudged Curtis, somehow. 'I'll think about it. Thanks, Curtis.'

'But don't leave it too long, yeah? Who was it that said, *A week is a long time in television?*'

'Nobody said that, Curtis. Wilson said: *A week is a long time in politics.*'

'Wilson who?'

'If I could roll my eyes at you, without it hurting, I would. Now, get out of my house, I'm tired.'

As Nina shuts the door, she feels she has just received an education. She had no idea how much she was liked by the staff at the show. She had no idea Curtis could be insightful and loyal. A small shiver of optimism runs through her. It's been a rough few days, wondering whether Roz would go public with her journal, but since Catrin got in touch to tell her what she'd said to Stella, she has felt reassured. She still can't quite understand why Catrin would protect her like this, over clearing her father's reputation, but she has. For the first time, Nina allows herself to wonder if there might be a way through this with Roz, if she might be forgiven. If she might retrieve the family she once had.

She misses her father. The thought catches her out. She doesn't think about him often, because she was only – what – fourteen, when he died? She doesn't remember him clearly as a person, but she still remembers how he made her feel. Safe. Loved. Then another thought catches her out. The sister she knows she has is out there, somewhere. She would be a teenager now. Bound to have a social media account. Nina has never been curious about her half-sister, because her mother told her not to be. But since her return from Little Auger, she's realised that several things her mother has said to her over the years haven't added up. She was told never to confess about Hazel, but now she feels better, lighter. What if she contacted her father's other child? Would that make her feel better, too?

She goes into her office, opens the laptop. She knows her sister's name. *Laurie.* She types it in and pairs it with her father's surname, the one she used to have – another thing her mother told her she didn't need. The list of names is long and depressing. There is no way of knowing which one might be her sister.

Unless she has my eyes, thinks Nina. Unusual eyes. Her father's eyes. She switches the search to images only, and adds in the words *Hong Kong*. But the women she sees on the screen don't bear any kind of family resemblance or they're too old, too young. Nina wonders if they moved back to Wales, or even England, after her father died. They moved out there for his work. It would make sense that his widow might want to come home. Nina narrows the image search to UK only, and then, in a flash of inspiration, she remembers Laurie's mother's name and adds that in too. She doesn't have to look for long before she sees something that takes her breath away. It is a family picture of a teenager, a distorted version of Nina, but with the same curly hair and the same grey eyes. She is standing between two adults, who have their arms around her. The girl, Laurie, is named. She has a medal around her neck. *Hornsey*

5K Fun Run. Laurie Edwards, winner of the under-eighteen girls, with her mother, Marion, and father, Julian.

Her father. Nina's father. He is older. But it is him. Nina looks at the date of the photograph. It was only taken last year.

Nina never searched for her father's name because he died in a foreign country, and he didn't have any social media accounts, according to her mother. It didn't occur to her to look for him in the digital world. But now she types, obsessively, like someone falling into a pit of madness, gathering every scrap of information she can about him. She holds each morsel up, gulping it down like a hungry dog. As she trawls Laurie's social media profile, the picture she builds of her father seems idyllic. Holidays in the South of France. School plays, sports events, fundraisers for Laurie's school, all attended faithfully by a man who didn't find Nina interesting enough to keep in touch with. A man who pretended he was dead.

As she scrolls through a life he has led without her, a life shared with a different daughter, she wants to scream, *What about me? Didn't I matter to you?* There is nothing of her in his life. Nothing in the background images taken in his family home, where he stands, on numerous occasions, his arm flung carelessly around Laurie's shoulder, around the narrow waist of his wife, the sunburnt necks of his golfing buddies. Nina touches her own neck, reflexively. Sylvia has always abhorred outward shows of affection. A peck on her dewy cheek is all she allows.

And then Nina sees something odd.

LOLZ, writes Laurie. *My dad just won this!* There is a picture of Julian accepting an award, a link below that takes her to some kind of organisation that dishes out prizes for sustainable business leadership. There is a Q and A with him, snippets of his life. She learns he lives in a sustainable house, that he doesn't fly any more, he always takes the train. That at work, he only allows vegetarian food to be ordered for business events. He is a man with a conscience, with principles. Which, somehow, makes everything worse. Nina scrolls down the column, scanning through his favourite ways to relax, his favourite books, favourite movies. And she pauses, then, because his favourite movie is a film she is very familiar with.

I've watched it hundreds of times, he says in the interview. *I watch it every Christmas. It has huge sentimental value for me.* The movie he names is one Nina took a leading role in when she was a child. It wasn't very good. The script was clunky, and the plot was thin. But she was in it from start to finish. Something that never happened again.

Nina closes the laptop, trying to understand. Why would he say this in an interview if he didn't want anything to do with her? Is it a signal for her? Is it a signal to Sylvia?

Sylvia. Several times, Nina glances at her phone, picks it up, looking at the button that will speed-dial Sylvia's number. Nina has called it so many times she could do it with her eyes shut. But as her finger hovers over the glass, something stops her from pressing it. Each time she thinks of Sylvia, remembers things she has said, it stops her. Slowly, quietly, her memories of her mother take on a different hue. Nina goes over the journey back from the hospital. The wobble of the car when Nina questioned Sylvia about her father. The pause in conversation. The silence.

Something inside Nina unravels. Is it possible – is it actually possible – that it is not Julian who is at fault here, that it could be Sylvia? Could she have done something this monstrous, this devious, to keep Nina close? There are only two people she can talk to about this. Her mother, or her father. But which one is the liar, and which one is telling the truth?

Chapter Forty-Three

CATRIN

Catrin and James breakfast early. There is much to do, before the service. As Catrin is spooning cereal into her mouth, a bell rings through the house. It is loud, insistent. More like a buzzer.

'What's that?' she says.

'It's the gate bell. It's probably the villagers.'

'It's barely eight,' says Catrin, looking at her watch.

'They wanted to help with the funeral breakfast. You don't tell people round here they can't help,' he says.

Catrin joins James as he buzzes the gate open and walks to the front door to welcome them in. Several cars trundle up the driveway, and when they reach the top, Catrin sees they are full with people and produce. When the cars disgorge their contents, men, women and children begin to distribute boxes and bags into the kitchen and out into the walled garden at the back of the house. Catrin follows them, her arms filled with plates covered with foil and clingfilm.

In the kitchen, there are cakes that are waiting to be cut. Loaves of sliced bread and giant tubs of butter are spread out on the countertops. Children are sent to collect eggs for hard boiling. Outside, in the garden, trestle tables are unfolded and set up, tablecloths laid out and weighted with stones. Jugs borrowed from the local primary school are lined up, waiting to be filled with large bottles of cordial. Catrin has only experienced this kind of community spirit halfway across the planet, in dusty villages and war-torn cities. She hadn't appreciated it existed right here, where she grew up. She listens to them talking with one another, exchanging memories of her father. The affection and respect they have for him runs deep. A realisation unfolds. The silences, the awkward words after those awful articles in the papers – she wonders, now, if these people felt just as she did: embarrassed, awkward, not knowing the right words to say to a confused thirteen-year-old, settling on the decision to say nothing.

Later, when everybody has done as much as they can, they get back into the cars and go home to change. Catrin wonders what she will wear to the service, which is early this afternoon. She goes into her father's room, thinking about borrowing a suit. He is more her size than James. Was.

His room is tidier than it was when she found it; she has made the bed and put away his clothes. There are two wardrobes either side of a large, draughty fireplace; the left one belonged to her father, the right to her mother. She hasn't opened her mother's wardrobe because she assumed it would have been cleared, but now she does, knowing she has been wrong about her father before. Sure enough, every stitch she wore is still here, and Catrin feels a pinch of shame for thinking he wanted to erase her memory. She touches the clothes, neatly hanging, proving her wrong, and she wonders what else she will discover about him to make her regret herself.

There is a knock on the doorframe. Catrin turns to see who it is and is surprised by Roz.

'What are you doing here?' Catrin asks.

'My parents called to say the whole village was buzzing about your dad's wake. Why didn't you tell me the funeral was today?'

Catrin apologises. 'I haven't had a chance to think, I'm sorry. This place has been . . . nuts.'

'Is Nina coming?' Roz looks around the room, as if Nina might be hiding in the wardrobe.

'I didn't want to drag her back here. It's so far away. And she's having some issues of her own.' Catrin explains the revelation concerning Nina's father. They have been on the phone most evenings, hashing it out.

Roz visibly relaxes and then a look of uncertainty clouds her face. 'How is she, otherwise? Her face, I mean.'

'She's healing. I think she's worried about what you might do with the information you have.'

Roz walks over to the large antique bed and sinks down on the mattress, the weight of her mood making her slump. 'I've never hit anyone in my life.' She gives Catrin a pleading look.

'It was a huge shock for you,' Catrin replies. She joins Roz and sits next to her on the bed.

Roz turns to Catrin. 'I keep going over that morning. Nina was in bed when I came back. She seemed fast asleep. She pretended I'd woken her up when I came into the bedroom, even though she must've made it in there by the skin of her teeth. That's what I can't get over. Lying about it like that. Why didn't she just say something?'

'She was only thirteen. She must've felt like a rabbit in headlights. And her mother is a force to be reckoned with. Nina promised her she'd keep quiet.'

'Had you any idea? Is that why you stopped being friends with us when we got back to school?'

'No,' Catrin replies, her voice full of regret. 'That was my own stupid teenage reaction to everything.'

Roz shakes her head. 'I can't get over it. I can't forgive her for what she did.'

'She's not asking you to, Roz.' Catrin feels caught between the sympathy she feels for Roz and the sympathy she feels for Nina. She wishes she could work some magic and reconcile her two friends, but she knows life is never that straightforward.

Roz rubs her forehead as if trying to clear a thought. 'Maybe that's the problem. I kind of wish she would.'

'I don't understand,' Catrin says.

'I don't know. For a few hours when we were together, it was so . . . comfortable. I don't have any friends that knew me before I had Willow. They all see me as a mother, or a wife – ex-wife. It's different when you're with friends who knew you as a kid. I can't describe it. It's like wearing an old cardigan.'

'Nina said that children make deeper friendships. That you can't do it when you're a grown-up.'

'Huh,' says Roz. 'I know exactly what she means. It's simpler when you're a kid, somehow.'

'Did you tell your parents, by the way?' asks Catrin.

'Stella got there first. But I backed up her story. I think they're relieved they don't have to go on wondering any more.' She turns to Catrin. 'They just wanted someone to blame. I'm sorry it was your family that took the brunt of it.'

Catrin does not anticipate the comfort Roz's words bring. 'And how do they feel now?' she asks.

'I think they're coming to terms with it. But there is something I'd like to do for them.' Roz tells Catrin about the plan to go back to the island, just for the day.

'You'll have to be quick,' says Catrin. 'James and I just put it up for sale.'

'What?' Roz asks. 'Why?'

'We want to do things with Chapel Farm. We're going to plant a vineyard and we need a cash injection to do it. Little Auger is in the past, for both of us. I thought, perhaps, the three of us, being there together, it might heal something, but it just made everything worse. I think it's time someone else took it over. We've already had some interest.'

'But what about the cairn? It's a memorial.'

'James already put something in the contract of sale about preserving it. It won't be touched.'

'So would you take us? One last time? You don't mind having my parents there, after what they did to your family?'

'If there's one thing I've learnt documenting other people's misery, it's this: when you hold a grudge, the only thing that it hurts is you.'

Chapter Forty-Four

Roz

Roz drives Catrin and James to the crematorium. The service is short and businesslike. James reads a eulogy he has written himself and Roz holds Catrin's hand as she weeps silently, her tears sliding down on to her lap. When the crowd scatters to head back to the house, Roz sees Adam and his father, Arvis, both dressed in suits, looking handsome and unfamiliar. She feels a squeeze of pleasure to see Adam. She should have realised he would be here, but she hadn't. She walks through the crowd to reach them before they get into Adam's jeep.

'You scrub up well,' she says cheerfully. 'I hardly recognised you.'

Arvis gives her a hug, holding her at arm's length to get a good look at her. 'You haven't changed at all, Rosalind,' he says in his strange lilt.

'Are you both coming back to the house? I think there's enough food to feed the county.'

'Yes,' says Adam. 'We closed the boatyard, just for today.'

The journey back to Chapel Farm is slow, the guests causing their own traffic jam on the country road. Roz parks the car as best she can and walks the rest of the way with Catrin and James up the driveway to the house. The sun is shining, the air is warm. There is a party atmosphere to the wake, which has been set up in the walled garden at the rear of Chapel Farm. Roz talks to several people she went to school with, who have now grown up and have families of their own. She wanders around the estate, seeing some of the changes Catrin and James have already wrought on the place. She can't find Adam, though she has glimpsed him through the crowd, several times; she has been stopped by so many people who want to know how her parents are doing, how she is doing. The time slips by and eventually she realises she needs to get a move on, it is a long drive home. She looks for Catrin, wanting to tell her she has to leave soon. Roz passes through the house, where there is still an army of women in the kitchen, making tea and slicing cake. She hears Catrin's voice. She is in a sitting room, talking to Arvis. Roz says her goodbyes to both of them.

'Adam went looking for you,' says Arvis. 'Make sure you say goodbye to him. He'll be disappointed if you don't.'

Roz wanders back through the house and walks beyond the walled garden, letting herself out through a warped wooden door. There is a large, fenced area for the chickens, who are scratching and pecking the earth, and beyond it, a wide grassy path that runs between two long herbaceous borders. The path rolls down to a lake that is partly obscured by a row of silver birches, and in a gap, sitting on a bench, is Adam. He has his back to her, looking over the water. She walks towards him, enjoying watching him without him being aware.

'Hi,' she calls eventually, unable to resist. 'You're a hard man to find.'

He turns to her and smiles. He has taken off his tie, and the top button of his shirt is undone. 'I've been looking for you. But when I saw this,' he nods to the lake, 'I couldn't resist. I can't be away from water for long.'

She sits next to him, looking over the lake. The water is a mirror, reflecting the sun, which is bright but low in the sky. A couple of ducks fly over their heads and water-ski into the lake, rippling wakes behind them. She can hear them calling to one another and it sounds like laughter. 'It really is a perfect day,' she says. Then she puts her hand to her mouth. 'Oh, that sounds *really* bad,' she giggles. 'You know what I mean.'

'I don't think the old man would care. It is a perfect day. Look at that sky.'

'Pity I have to drive back now. If I lived a bit closer . . . but it's going to take me a couple of hours.'

He turns towards her, looking concerned. 'You're leaving already?'

'I should get back to my daughter. And I just had an offer for the house. They want a quick sale because it's in a catchment area for the local school and they have to apply soon, *blah blah blah*. I haven't even found anywhere to live yet. I need to get my skates on.'

'What if you can't find anywhere?'

'I can rent. I just . . . I don't know. It's hard to find a place I can work. Somewhere I want to be creative. It sounds ridiculous, I know.'

'It doesn't,' says Adam. 'It really doesn't.'

'It's been so nice to see your father again,' she says, remembering Arvis's warmth, the fact he was so pleased to see her, making her feel she mattered. 'He's looking really well.'

'He was right about you, you know. You haven't changed in twenty years.'

Roz laughs. 'Yes I have,' she replies. 'I've changed a lot. Haven't you?'

He turns and glances at her, then he sits back, blowing a big breath of air as he puts his hands in his pockets. 'When I look at you, I think I haven't,' he says quietly to the water.

'What do you mean?' she asks.

He turns to her once more and looks embarrassed. 'When I look at you, I'm sixteen again.' He shakes his head. 'Such a weird feeling. I never had it with anyone else. I don't think I ever shook you off, Roz.'

'Adam, I had no idea.'

He shifts awkwardly on the bench. 'I take it you don't feel the same, then.'

Roz thinks about the little jolts of pleasure she has experienced every time she sees him. *But it's all caught up with Willow and Simon rejecting me*, she thinks. And the death of her sister.

'I'm not sure,' she says carefully. 'When I first met you, it was such an awful time. You rescued me, really. You were the only person who helped. I remember you teaching me how to make a fisherman's knot. It was the kindest thing anyone has ever done for me, I think. You took me away from a terrible situation. For a few minutes, I forgot what was going on. I can still tie one, you know. I do it sometimes. And it's you I think about when I do.'

Adam draws his hand out of his pocket. Fastened to his keyring are two pieces of twine, one the colour of butter, the other the colour of sky. They are joined together in a knot that hasn't been undone in twenty years.

Roz is speechless, just for a moment, as she turns the knot over in her hands. 'I can't believe you kept it,' she murmurs.

'It was a piece of you,' he says simply. 'How could I throw it away?'

Chapter
Forty-Five

NINA

Nina didn't want to have her father come to her home, and she didn't want to go to his house. It feels too much. Meeting in public is worse, so they agree on a compromise, and Nina drives herself to her father's office, which is in central London, not far from the studio she used to work in. They could have passed one another on the street, hundreds of times, she thinks, as she weaves her way across the capital, glad she has tinted windows when she stops at traffic lights and pedestrian crossings. She wonders if they have brushed shoulders, when she watches the melee of strangers cross her vision; if he has recognised her in the street and fought the urge to shout her name.

She is buzzed into a car park under the building, which is several storeys high, the typical glass and steel of newer developments in Moorgate. She takes the lift to the top floor, checks her appearance in the mirrored glass. Her skin has lost its discoloration. Her stitches have come out. When her curls fall over the left side of her face, as it does now, she looks intact.

They have not spoken yet. She didn't trust herself to unravel the mess her mother has made of their lives on the phone. Once she knew where he worked, it was easy to get an email to him. They have exchanged several long messages before this meeting. Hers have been formal. His have been affectionate. She could feel his delight through the screen, the restraint he has had to apply to keep himself sounding sane.

When the lift doors open, she is faced with a long, curved desk adorned with a tasteful floral display. The company logo is above, cleverly lit from behind by a soft yellow glow. A woman in a well-cut suit welcomes her, showing no sign of knowing who Nina really is, and ushers her into her father's office like any other client as soon as Nina has confirmed her name. The door closes quietly behind her, and she is left with her father.

'Look at you . . .' her father begins. And then he stops, unable to continue. He is crying, Nina realises.

'Hello.' She feels numb, looking at him, crying in front of her. She doesn't know what to do, but she feels still, composed. It is the same feeling she sometimes gets on set, just before the cameras roll. She takes a few steps to a chair on the other side of his desk, to sit, just for something to do.

'Can I . . . is it OK if I give you a hug?' he asks.

She shrugs, gets up, feeling very much the grown-up. 'Yes, of course,' she says, her voice steady and clear.

He takes a few steps across the room and envelops her in his arms. When he pulls back to take a look at her, he sees her injury. 'How did that happen?' he asks, his eyes wide with concern.

Nina has spent the past few days thinking about what she is going to tell her father, how much of the truth of her life she will share. She has the story of falling in a boat well practised and smoothly told. But she is very conscious that she wants to do things differently now.

She takes a big breath and tells him everything, every detail laid bare. She has planned it like this, because she has acted in too many movies to know that secrets come out at the most inconvenient times, particularly when you are trying to impress someone you love. She has reasoned with herself that this must be done in their first meeting, before any promises are made, before connections become stronger. If she is going to be a disappointment to him, she wants it to happen right away, so she can go back home and pretend they never met. But as her story unfolds, he listens with sympathy. The regret her father feels is that he wasn't there to help, that Sylvia never told him of the part Nina played in Hazel's death.

Throughout the morning, Nina sets her father a series of tests, which he passes, one by one. He looks his female secretary in the eye and treats her respectfully. He says please and thank you. He doesn't talk about himself unless Nina asks for details. They talk about Laurie, and he explains he does not love Nina less because she has been out of his life.

'Laurie wants to meet you,' he says. 'She's desperate to meet you, actually.'

'One thing at a time,' replies Nina.

Everything she throws at him, he catches with deftness and skill. He is open about his mistakes, honest about his regrets. He lays bare his own failings as a father and doesn't blame Sylvia. The only time he loses composure is when Nina tells him she was under the impression he was dead.

And then he drops his own bombshell. 'So you have no idea we meet sometimes.'

Nina fights an urge to swear, loudly. But she keeps her composure because she doesn't want this meeting to be hijacked by Sylvia, and the poison she has spread. 'How often do you meet her?' Nina asks.

'Whenever she or you need anything. We met a lot in the first few years. Then less regularly. Maybe once a year.'

'Why are you still financially supporting her?' says Nina.

'I felt guilty about what I did, and she needed the money to have a comfortable life with you in London.'

'Not now though. You've been divorced for almost twenty years.'

'She gave up work to look after you. My business became successful, and she thought both she and you were owed. It's a small price to pay. I used the meetings to hear about what you were up to, and to try and persuade her to put us in touch again. If I'd stopped meeting her, I would have lost the opportunity to re-establish contact.'

'But when I was an adult, you didn't have to go through Sylvia to see me.'

'Believe me, I tried. I didn't realise she'd changed your surname for a very long time. I did have some contact with your agent, eventually. But I think they thought I was a stalker.'

Nina has had a few stalkers in her time. Verity has done a good job, over the years, fending them off.

'If you'd done any theatre I would have hung around the stage door, but you didn't.'

He clearly has no idea she has been working on *Rise* for the past few months, that the studio is a stone's throw from his office.

'Anyway,' he continues. 'Sylvia led me to believe you very much did not want to be in touch, and I didn't want to be a pest.'

'Mum doesn't know I'm here,' she says. 'She doesn't know that I found out you were alive. I'm not sure I want contact with her any more. She's done so much damage. To both of us.' Nina stops herself. 'Look, I don't want to spend this time with you talking about her mistakes. Let's go over that another time.'

He looks hopeful. 'So there'll be another time? You'll meet me again?'

'Yes,' she says. 'Of course.'

Somebody brings in lunch, an assortment of things that make no sense, and far too much for both of them to eat.

'I wasn't sure what you liked, so I got every dietary requirement covered,' her father says.

The heavy, life-changing questions turn into something lighter, less important, and Nina relaxes a little, doesn't feel so stiff. As they part, her father hugs her once more. This time, he doesn't ask her permission. When she is in his arms, she allows her body to remember the force of him, the sensation of being treasured by him. And when this happens, she feels the transition from grown-up to child.

Chapter Forty-Six

CATRIN

When Roz and her parents walk up to the cairn to look at Hazel's memorial stone, Catrin stays behind in The Old House. But before she packs the things she wants to take back with her, before the removal company arrives and boxes up the house, she takes her camera out and documents the interior, just as she did for her father in Chapel Farm. It is a memorial of past lives, past holidays, past troubles, and past mistakes.

The meeting with Roz and her parents, in Eider, started awkwardly. Catrin met them all in the boatyard, where her boat was moored. They tried to apologise, and she did not want to hear it. She understood why they had put some of the blame on her for Hazel's death. She still blamed herself. Instead, she changed the subject. Then she escorted them all into the boat and took them across the water, all of them silent.

The sea was flat and quiet, too, choosing this day, of all days, to be the smoothest crossing she had ever had to make. Catrin felt as if the island was holding its breath, waiting to see what would transpire. When they landed and tied the boat up, Roz suggested going into the house first, but her mother refused, wanting to walk to where Goggin was found and go to the cairn as quickly as possible.

Catrin watches them take the cliff path, Roz's parents holding hands. Roz has packed a picnic, on Catrin's instruction. It's a selfish request because Catrin wants the house to herself for a few hours, knowing it will be the last time she sees it, that it will probably be razed to the ground in a matter of months.

She starts in the library, the autumn sun nourishing the room with a yolky light. She sets up her still lifes on the long table: the island map her father pored over every morning before his walk; the stone paperweights he used to weigh it down, a pair of brass binoculars she knew her mother loved, the leather strap cracked and worn. She documents the books on the shelves, stacking them haphazardly with candlesticks dripping with wax from long-extinguished candles.

Moving into the kitchen, she clears the table and puts together a tableau of all the domestic items she associates with this house: the flat-bottomed kettle, black with heat; the silver toast rack, still dainty and bright; a sprig of dried heather that has always hung over the stove. They take on a life of their own, tell their own stories, the identity of the house and its past inhabitants revealed through her camera lens. As she takes the photographs, capturing moments in time, she imagines the heat of a thousand pots being stirred by a thousand women, cooking in this space over hundreds of years, while the wind and the sea did their best to devour them all.

When she has finished her still lifes, she documents the witches' marks in every doorway, window and chimney breast, their circles, lines and letters soon to be pulverised to dust. Then she begins to pack the few things she would like to take home. She pauses, her arms resting on the edge of a box, pondering that notion. She doesn't know what home looks like to her any more. Chapel Farm is getting back on its feet, now the money has come through. James has made it clear what his wishes are: he wants her to stay on, as an equal partner, building Chapel Farm back to its former glory, sharing their father's legacy and creating something of their own. It goes against every instinct she has had for the past twenty years. That burning need to move, to be among strangers, documenting their tragedies, has dwindled to embers.

She thinks about the photographs she has taken over the past few weeks. Her still lifes, the absolute opposite of all she has done before, they have taken hold of her, somehow. She has been working on the collection she took on the day her father died, and she has surprised herself by the emotion they carry. She has contacted a gallery, who are interested to show them. But she will need to set up a studio, buy a printer, become static – a word that hasn't been in her vocabulary, until now.

The door opens, a suck of air breathes through the house. Roz and her parents are coming back in.

'How did it go?' Catrin asks. She knows the question is difficult to answer. She can tell by the look on Roz's face.

'Fine,' Roz says. It is what she doesn't say that fills the room.

They sleep in the house, all four of them, because the tide will not allow them to leave. And it seems right to Catrin that they should come here on the island's terms, not on their own. It does people good to be reminded they are not in charge.

When they leave the next morning, Catrin clicks all the switches on the control box to *off*. She takes one last look at The Old House, making sure the windows are shut, the fire is out, she has everything she needs. Then she navigates the boat through a passage she will never forget, a complicated set of twists and turns, all the while fighting the invisible push and pull of the current below.

When she reaches open water, she takes a moment to turn around and see what she is leaving behind. Little Auger belongs to somebody else now. She has asked the estate agent not to tell her who it is, or what they want the island for. She will not come back here. She couldn't bear to see it change.

Chapter
Forty-Seven

Roz

Roz looks around her empty house. She can still hear the slow, deep rumble of the removal truck in the distance making its way to the storage depot, and she is reminded of the constant rumble of the sea that has filled her ears in her dreams. She has dreamt a lot, these past few weeks, about Hazel, about Little Auger, even Adam and his house. The conversation she had with him by Chapel Farm lake has changed the course of her life. They talked for more than two hours together. She can remember every detail.

'I wanted to tell you something a while back, but it felt too soon, but now you just told me you've sold your house, it might be too late if I leave it,' he said.

'What do you mean?' she replied, confused.

He took a breath. 'There's a fisherman's cottage, like mine, a short way down the shingle. It's for sale. I saw your face when you walked into my house. You were like a kid at Christmas.'

Roz put her head in her hands and groaned. 'That's impossible,' she said. And then she said, 'I don't know.' But she felt her heart quicken, and in her head, before she had time to stop herself, she imagined living in a house like his, facing the ocean. Close to Hazel. It was the first time, the only time, she had felt enthusiastic about moving since her house went up for sale. A small voice in her head said: *Do it.*

Adam continued, 'I'd ask you in a heartbeat to move in with me, but I can see that would be too much.'

'Yes, that is too much. Way too much.'

'But think about it. You'd be happy there. I'm not around all the time. I'll keep my distance. But you'd have a friendly face nearby, someone to call on.'

Roz's head spun with possibility. 'This has come out of nowhere . . . I . . .'

'It's not come out of nowhere, Roz. You're connected to Eider.'

'Willow – she's starting a new school. I need to be there for her.'

'Oh. Sorry. I thought she lived with her dad. I didn't realise.'

'She's moving in with him, it's true.' It was hard to explain how she couldn't quite believe Willow wouldn't be with her soon, during the week. That she would be with her dad and a woman she had only met once.

'I'm going to have her at weekends,' Roz explained.

'She'd love the sea. I could teach her to sail. It's an easy train journey.'

Roz groaned again. 'You're tempting me too much, don't.'

'Because it's right. It feels right, doesn't it? All you have to do is trust yourself.'

She looked at him then, his eyes a clear blue gaze into hers, and she knew, with a certainty she couldn't fully understand, that her future lay with this man in it, that the friendship they had embarked on, twenty years earlier, would somehow run its course.

It has been hard, packing away her life here, leaving behind memories of Willow as a baby, Simon as a husband and father. Saying goodbye to the optimism they all had. The loss of it all seems too much to bear sometimes. And she feels very alone, today. Her parents would have helped her, she is sure, if she had asked them. They are longing to turn their attention to a project, but she didn't want to ask. Their distance from one another is an old habit that is hard to break.

The fact that Willow has chosen to spend more time with Simon is a disappointment Roz has tried hard to conceal. Willow has already moved in with him. He now lives near her new school. Roz has tried very hard not to mind the ease with which her daughter has let go of her. This house is already in the past for Willow, and Roz marvels at the ability she has to shrug off history and look forward to the future. She walks through the building, now an empty shell, remembering the years she spent here as a couple, a part of a trio, and then a half of a whole.

She stops at a doorway that leads into the kitchen and runs her fingers over the notches she has made through the years, documenting Willow's height. Of all the things she has found hard to leave behind, this is one of the hardest. She mentioned it to Catrin, and she offered to photograph the house before Roz began to pack. Catrin spent two hours making photographs of the things that made up their lives here. She has promised to make the pictures into a book, so she has some kind of record of the three people that briefly passed through here, adding to the history of the house.

Roz runs her fingers over the numbers she has scratched into the wood, recording Willow as a toddler to Willow as an eleven-year-old. She is reminded of the witches' marks in The Old House on Little Auger, and suddenly those marks don't seem to be imbued with such menace any more. She has done more reading into the making of those marks, discovering that often they were made as a gesture of luck and good fortune. Maybe the marks in that house were carved with optimism, not fear, like the marks she can feel now, under her fingertips.

She has made several trips up to Eider, to slowly move her things into her new house on the shingle, and each time she sits down at a table facing the ocean, she can feel her fingers itch to draw. It is the only thing that has pulled her through her divorce, and her separation from Willow. Last week, she took several cuttings from the hazel tree in the garden and planted them in pots. Two of them are in Eider, under Adam's care, and two of them she has left with Willow, who has promised to water them and keep them safe. Even if only one cutting survives, it will be enough.

Before Roz shuts the front door for the last time, a childish urge comes upon her. She slips her house keys out of her pocket and climbs up on to the kitchen counter to access the top of the wooden window frame. There, she carves her own initials, and those of her daughter, in a corner she hopes will not be disturbed.

I have lived here, she wants to say. *I was happy here. I want to leave my mark.*

Chapter Forty-Eight

NINA

Nina takes a deep breath before she rings the bell. Her mother's house is pristine, with closely clipped box hedging guiding her feet to the front door, a black-and-white tiled path that never seems to get dirty, and windows that never see dust. Sylvia opens the door and is dressed in a silky cream jumpsuit that was designed for a twenty-year-old but looks fabulous on her. Discreet gold earrings and a thin gold bracelet contrast with her lightly tanned skin. Her clothes echo the colour palette of her house: cream, caramel, chocolate and gold. The colours of comfort and indulgence. As she steps into her mother's house, Nina realises, with a jolt, that her father has probably paid for most of this. She cannot understand why she hasn't thought about it before. Her mother's lifestyle has always been at odds with the clerical work she did. Nina has given Sylvia a monthly allowance ever since she gave up her part-time job. But it's not enough to cover this.

Her mother kisses her on the cheek, briefly holding her upper arm as she does so, in a restrained show of affection. They have not spoken for weeks. Before she arrived at Sylvia's front door, Nina made a pact with herself not to mention Howard. She is surprised she doesn't feel the old urge to consult Sylvia about what is happening between them. This time round, her relationship with him will be Nina's to govern. Howard will not be shared.

'You've let your hair curl,' her mother says, and Nina can't work out if she can hear a note of disappointment in her voice.

They sit in Sylvia's lounge, the low October sun slanting through her perfectly clear windows, sipping green tea.

'I know a plastic surgeon who could correct that scar,' Sylvia mentions.

'I don't want it correcting. I like it.' Nina feels belligerent.

'How are you going to find work? I worry about you.'

'I'll get a job that doesn't rely on what I look like.'

Her mother looks genuinely puzzled. 'Like what, exactly?'

Nina sighs, aware they are not talking about the thing she has come here to talk about. But she has all morning, and she won't leave here until it is done. 'I'm setting up a production company. Working behind the scenes for a change. I have plenty of contacts.'

Her mother sits primly on her cream leather sofa. '*How* can you not mind, Nina? Look what that woman did to you. She *damaged* you.'

'What I did to her was worse. A lot worse.'

'*That* was an accident.'

'I wasn't talking about that. I was talking about the lying. I lied to her. We lied to her parents, to everyone.'

Sylvia's mouth draws itself into a familiar line of disdain.

Nina cocks her head. 'Mum, lying is bad. You know that, right? People hate being lied to. It's a basic human need, to want to know the truth.'

'That lie protected you. Your life wouldn't have turned out the way it has if it wasn't for me.'

'Sometimes, I wish we hadn't left. Don't you? You must have left friends behind, just like me. Haven't you been lonely, here?'

'I have you,' Sylvia says simply. 'At least, I thought I did. I don't know what's happened to us recently. I told you not to go back to that place and meet those girls.'

'Women. They are women, now. And so am I.'

'You're different, Nina. So spiky. I don't recognise you.'

Nina takes a deep breath. 'I am angry. Because you lied to me, as well, didn't you?'

Sylvia looks up. 'What do you mean?'

'You told me my own father was dead. How could you do that? That was absolutely unforgivable.'

'Nina . . .'

'You met him at Easter. Apparently, you meet him every year.'

Sylvia sits up. Nina realises she has finally got her attention. 'Have you met with him?' Sylvia asks, looking afraid.

'Yes, I have. Of course I have. We have twenty years to catch up on. And I have a sister who has grown up without me. I could have been a force for good in her life, and you took that away from both of us.'

Sylvia puts her cup down, carefully. 'This is very hurtful to me. Very hurtful.'

Nina feels like screaming. 'Can we just, for a minute, not make this about you?'

'I suppose you're going to play happy families with him now?'

Nina can't help a drop of spite whet her words. 'Of course I will! Why would I not? At least they're honest.'

Sylvia looks incredulous. 'You'd turn your back on me, just like that? You don't know what he did to me.'

'Tell me, then. I'm listening.' Nina puts her cup down and folds her arms.

315

Sylvia looks away. 'What's the point of talking about it? It happened so long ago.'

'There's plenty of point,' Nina says firmly. 'You're obviously still very angry.'

Sylvia looks away and out of the sitting-room window. There is a gust of wind, and it blows a flurry of leaves up against the glass. She turns to Nina. 'She was my friend, first, you know. Marion. I met her at the gym. I always had difficulty making friends in that village. I was too pretty. I don't mean that in a vain way. It's a fact. A lot of women don't like it if you're too good-looking. Anyway, the women in the village, they didn't like their husbands talking to me. They kept me at arm's length. But Marion was different. We got on straight away. Soon, we were working out together, having coffee together. And then I started inviting her over for dinner. She became my best friend in such a short space of time. I broke a cardinal rule and confided in her. Your father and I – we weren't getting on very well. I told her a few things.' Sylvia looks away, masking her shame.

'Anyway,' Sylvia continues. 'She used the secrets I told her about our relationship. She used them to make the gap between your father and I a lot wider. And then— well, you know what happened. He left us. For her. All those secrets I told her, all those confidences. She just threw them back in my face.'

'Mum, that must have been awful.'

'I couldn't complain about it because I had no other friends. The only other person I could talk to about things like that was your dad, and he was part of the problem.'

'Why do you want to still see him?'

Sylvia looks away.

'Is it about the money? I know he still gives you some.'

'No. Not really.'

'Then why do you see him?'

'I love him,' Sylvia says with defiance. 'It's not a tap you can turn off, just because that other person doesn't want you any more.' Sylvia swallows, hard. 'You'll prefer him, I know it. And then I'll lose you, too.'

Nina can hear the fear in her voice, but it doesn't alter the facts. 'Mum, you lost me the day you told me my father was dead.'

Sylvia looks like a child afraid of being left in the dark. 'And what about me? When you're off with them all? Where does that leave me? How is this going to look?'

'You need to build your own life, away from me. Things are going to be different now. Don't call me. I'll be in touch when I'm ready. *If* I'm ready.'

Nina stands up and grabs her bag and her car keys. For a moment, she thinks her mother will crumble. There is something in her expression that falters, a tremor in her lip. But she straightens her back, looks away, and brings her cup to her lips.

Chapter
Forty-Nine

Nina

At first, Nina doesn't know why she doesn't point her car towards her own house. She finds herself pulling into a petrol station, filling the tank up, even though it is already half full. She finds herself driving, with a quiet, deliberate force, towards the outskirts of London. She cuts in and out of closely packed traffic on the ring road smoothly, efficiently, until she finds herself speeding down an elevated slip road, building up speed like a ski jumper until she lands on the outside lane of the motorway, where she plans to stay until she takes the exit for Eider.

There is something deeply relaxing about the absolute certainty she feels right now, when she has spent so much of the past few weeks feeling unsure of herself, flailing about in a sea of her own misgivings. It is a powerful feeling, her own sense of right. She wants to capitalise on it. She doesn't know how long it will last.

Normally, she would have consulted Sylvia about making this trip, debated the pros and cons. But now she is acting on her own instincts and she likes the clean efficiency of it. She likes the absence of uncertainty, the feeling there is no one to answer to from now on.

Nina adjusts the button on her steering wheel that activates the cruise control and sets it just above the legal speed limit. Fast enough to get her there before nightfall. Slow enough so she won't get pulled over. Over the hours it takes her to reach the borders of Wales, she has time to talk herself out of it, but she doesn't. Her sense of conviction only deepens. It feels as if several things are clicking into place, like a machine that has been switched on after a long time dormant.

She opens the window and lets in the evening breeze as she approaches the coast. She doesn't like the smell of the sea, she doesn't like the greasy moistness of the air, with its metallic taste and briny scent, but she needs to be alert. Catrin has told her Roz now lives in one of the fishermen's huts on the shingle. There are several small black cottages made of clapboard scattered along the beach, like charred building blocks from a children's game gone wrong. Nina drives the length of the coast road, slowly, looking into every lit window, trying to ascertain which one is Roz's. The road skirts the back of each house; they are close enough for Nina to see inside each one. Eider is the kind of place where people only close their curtains in the bedroom. There is no other reason to block out the view.

The car slides through the darkening sky. Nina can see ahead of her that the road will soon swerve to the right, to avoid the cliffs that rise swiftly like a dark, motionless wave. The last house on the beach is lit from within. Nina has a view straight through the house to the sea beyond it. Beyond that, she can just make out, under the brightening moon, the shape of Little Auger crouched on the horizon like a closed fist. Framed by the lit window is a figure, bent over a table, focusing on something Nina cannot see. The figure reaches, without breaking their gaze from the paper in front of them, pulling a paintbrush out of a jar of water on the corner of the table. Nina gets out of the car, stretches her legs, and walks over the shingle towards the house.

Roz answers the door, her gaze still pulled by the paper on the table. When she finally focuses on Nina's face, it takes a second for her to understand.

'What?' Roz says, looking confused. 'What do you want?' She looks at Nina as if she is a creature that has broken out of another, forgotten world into hers.

'I want my writing back, please.' Nina looks at Roz directly, without expression. She is glad she dressed well for Sylvia this morning.

'What writing?' Roz searches Nina's face, trying to make some kind of sense of the situation.

'The pages from my journal. I'd like them back.'

'You mean my journal?' Roz draws herself up a little, but it is a weak gesture.

'You gave it to me.'

There is a moment while Roz considers the request. Nina can see her turning it over in her mind, examining the angles for something discordant. 'Why do you want them?'

'Because they are mine. They belong to me,' Nina states.

'What are you going to do with them?'

'Do I have to have a reason? I just want them back,' she says.

Nina debates with herself whether she should share with Roz this feeling she carries inside her. It is as if a crashing wave has come down on her, scattering her emotions into something hard to hold on to. And now that the wave has gone, something has solidified, like wet sand after a high tide.

'How do you know I have the pages?' Roz asks.

'Catrin told me.'

Roz lifts her chin a little. 'So you're in touch still?'

'Of course. We're friends. It means something.'

Roz nods, briefly.

'Look, Roz,' says Nina. 'If I could take everything back about that day, I would. I've gone over it a million times, just the same as you must have done. I'm sorrier than you will ever want to know. If I could give you Hazel back . . .'

Roz looks at Nina for a long time. She can see her eyes travel across her face, taking in the damage she has inflicted on her. The scar above her eyebrow, now a thin swoop of red. The silence stretches between them until it must snap.

'Wait there,' Roz says, and she disappears into her house.

Nina waits, her heart beating fast and strong. The wind blows in her face, powerfully, pushing her curls away from her forehead and neck. She breathes in the air, takes it down deep into her lungs, and breathes it out when Roz returns.

'Did you read what I wrote?' Nina asks. She cannot help this question. She wants to know.

'Yes. Yes I did,' Roz replies.

'It's the truth. I was close to Willow's age. Just bear that in mind.'

Roz nods and says nothing. Nina can see her swallow, the movement under the thin skin of her neck, taking away the words that have begun to form in her mouth. She hands the pages back to Nina, and Nina hugs them to her chest.

'Do you want to come in?' Roz asks neutrally. 'You must be tired after such a long drive.' She moves slightly, angling her body as if to let Nina come past.

'No,' says Nina. 'I want to go home.' And then she says, 'Maybe another time.'

'OK,' says Roz. She crosses her arms, drawing her cardigan around her body.

The shingle traces Nina's departure as she leaves the beach behind her. It is only when she reaches her car that she hears the sound of Roz closing her door.

Sunset

There is a clifftop path, in Eider, that winds up from the shingle to the headland, giving whoever cares to follow it a bird's eye view of Little Auger. Roz walks the path most evenings, when the weather permits, as the light leaves the sky. It is the thing she looks forward to, after sitting at her desk, submerged in her work. She has nearly finished her children's book, and she is pleased with what she sees. She works on it through the young hours of the morning, until they wane at night. It keeps her mind off the absence of Willow and answers an urgency that has opened up inside her since she moved here, deep as a wellspring. To create something purely out of her imagination means to live it. It takes a special kind of concentration. She draws the day in her mind's eye, seeing the images unfold as she sketches them out on the paper. She doesn't know where the stories originate, only that they are coming as a torrent bursts its bank. It is something to do with this place and the way the forces of land and sea gather and conspire to do what they will. It can be frightening, trying to sleep through a storm, but this fisherman's cottage has stood here for one hundred years, so Roz supposes she is safe.

The hag stone she found on the beach at the boatyard hangs over her bed on its own piece of twine. The stone Adam gave to

Hazel is back in his possession. Roz remembered what Adam had said, that they only bring luck to the person who finds them. It felt like the right thing to do. She has walked the beach many times with Willow, who is growing her own collection of stones and shells. They line the windowsills of Roz's house, reminders that her daughter will come back, that their time together is sweeter because of the time they spend apart.

As Roz pulls her coat off the hook in the hall, she pauses, looking at the cards displayed on the narrow table under the mirror by the front door. There is one from her parents, wishing her luck in her new home, and a promise to visit her and Willow soon. Catrin has sent a photograph of the vineyard she is planting, row upon row of furrowed earth in the dawn light.

Here's to new beginnings! says the scribble on the back.

She received a card from Nina, too. A short message, wishing her happiness. But it is a message Roz reads over and over, tracing the perfect circle Nina has drawn over the *i* in her name.

For a housewarming present, Adam bought her a pair of binoculars. At first, she poked fun at him and his middle-aged gift. But he is the one who is laughing now. She has been known to leap across the room for them so she can learn the identity of a bird, or a shape in the ocean, or a figure on the shoreline. They have become an invaluable tool for her illustration work. She is getting very good at drawing wading birds and herring gulls wheeling in the sky.

The front door clicks shut behind her, and the binoculars bounce on her chest as she climbs up the cliff, the sun slowly dropping under its own hot weight. Roz finds the place she always stops at: a low, smooth rock, right at the peak. On a day like today, out of season and far from the warmth of the sun, the cliff path is empty. The rock is wet, so she stands on it to gain more height, keeping her eyes and her binoculars trained on Little Auger.

The island is undergoing renovation; the new owners want to build a hotel and a golf course, but the process has been frustrated with setbacks. The inhabitants of Eider talk about it with raised eyebrows. If anyone had bothered to ask them, they would have explained it could never happen. Little Anger will not allow it. Somebody – nobody knows who – has written to an influential heritage group, alerting them to the historical importance of The Old House. The witches' marks are particularly fine; apparently, some of them quite rare. A set of photographs has been sent as evidence and reproduced in the press. Even if there hadn't been a national outcry over its demolition, the building work will still be halted. Human remains have been found during excavation, a great many of them, lending truth to the folk tales about the Sallows and the Thorps. No work can continue until all the bones have been exhumed, examined, dated and catalogued, and there are far too many to count. Some say the owners are having second thoughts, that the island is proving too much trouble. Against all odds, The Old House still stands, and Roz is under no illusion why. The witches' marks are working their magic, keeping unwanted visitors out. Keeping the rightful inhabitants of the island safe.

The sun sinks lower, drawing the light from the sky, flooding the western horizon with fire. Roz holds her binoculars steady, focusing them on the headland of Little Auger, scanning the ridge of the eastern cliff. As the sun slowly sinks behind the island, there is a trick of the light that is easy to miss. Shadows flicker and are not what they seem. They take on their own shape, their own movement. If she looks very hard, holds her breath, and doesn't move, she can sometimes see the figure of a little girl, running along the headland through the gorse. Her long curly hair streams out behind her, her paisley pyjama bottoms a blur of red. Often, she is not alone. There are shadows of other children, some bigger, some much smaller than her, racing through the scrub, weaving in and out in some nameless, breathless game. On a windless night, when the waves are low, and their rhythmic murmurings are hushed and soft, Roz thinks she can hear laughter echoing over the water. She shouted, once, and the little girl paused. She turned and waved, a bundle of rags dangling from her hand.

AUTHOR'S NOTE

I am half Welsh, on my father's side, and I spent many school holidays as a child, visiting family in South Wales and exploring the coast. I nearly drowned on Ogmore Beach when I was about five years old, and now, into my third book, I wonder if this event has had a bigger influence in my life than I realised.

My Welsh grandparents died when I was a teenager, putting an end to those long car journeys, and my father passed away in 2011, severing another connection to the area. It is only recently that I have begun to reacquaint myself with this beautiful country through an old school friend who invited me to join her on the isle of Anglesey when she was holidaying there with her family. I cannot resist an island. And when I discovered there was another, much smaller island a thirty-minute drive from where we were staying, I knew I had to visit it.

Ynys Llanddwyn (Llanddwyn Island, in English) is a tidal island, measuring less than half a square mile, off the coast of Newborough National Nature Reserve. It can only be accessed at certain times of the day on foot – it becomes cut off at high tide – and this fact charmed me when I read about it. When I visited, I knew I wanted to set a book on an island that became impossible to reach during certain times of the day, so it formed the inspiration for Little Auger. Little Auger grew into a much larger, rockier, more sinister place, and bears little resemblance to my original muse. If you do happen to visit Llanddwyn, though, look at the rocks that rise from the sand as you approach. There is something distinctly reptilian about them. And the island would soon lose its charm if you became cut off by the tide and the wind started to blow.

Between the Waves is dedicated to my father, who was a great reader, and who died before I became an author. He would have been delighted.

BOOK CLUB QUESTIONS

1. Do you think that happiness is more important than the truth?

2. Was Stella a force for good?

3. Do you think that Roz was an unreasonable parent?

4. Do you think Willow had a right to be angry with Roz for withholding information about Hazel?

5. Is not telling somebody something to protect them the same as lying to them?

6. Adam suggests that it is Roz who has ruined her own life, not Hazel's disappearance. Is he right?

7. Each of the three women blame themselves for Hazel's death. Do you think one person is more to blame than the others, or do they share the blame equally?

8. Nina believes that children are better at friendship because we lose trust when we grow up. Is she right?

9. Do you think that Sylvia's intentions were good or bad?

10. It is inferred in different ways that Nina, Roz and Catrin are selfish: Catrin for deserting her family, Roz for withholding information from her daughter and husband, and Nina for concealing what she knew about Hazel's death. Do you think this is a reasonable accusation?

ACKNOWLEDGEMENTS

Thanks to my editors, Victoria Pepe and Victoria Oundjian, for their insight, patience and their invaluable collaboration. Thanks also to my agent, Rebecca Ritchie, for always being in my corner and to all the staff at Lake Union who spend time making the words on the page sparkle, and who champion my work long after it has been published. From Jenni Davis and her forensic copy edit to Nicole Wagner and her marketing team, to Jonathan Pennock at Brilliance, there are so many talented people who work away behind the scenes to make a book better, and I am grateful to each and every one of them for their help.

I continue to write about friendship because, for me, friendship is the foundation of happiness. Deepest thanks to Elizabeth Walton, my oldest school friend, for inviting me to share her Anglesey adventures and to her husband, G, and her son, Rex, for showing my family a thoroughly good time over the years. Love and appreciation, always, goes to my mother, Gill, who I also count as my friend, and who continues to support me in ways too numerous to count.

To Rosie Ruddock, who gets me out of bed in the morning to swim or run, and to Sian Hurst, who gets me into the woods for walks and talks, thank you both for your precious friendship. Thanks also to Anna Wise because we agreed this would happen, didn't we? Simone Sorrell, you are here because of your cheery support, and the kindness and generosity you have shown me and my children over the years. Nicola Fox, a cheerleader from the very beginning, thank you.

David Shah is someone I have worked with for many years and another person who has enthusiastically supported this diversion in my career. It has been such a pleasure collaborating with you, your team and your beautiful family. Thank you for the trust you place in my creative work.

Thanks to all the people who make me a better writer: my brother, Jim, who worked on a very early plan of this manuscript with me, I am grateful for your time, support and help. The North London Writers' Group read an early draft of this novel, and I am indebted to the time and energy they spent reading it and providing feedback. Also to Fran Littlewood, just because we never run out of things to say.

Lastly, my family. Myla, as I write this, you are on the cusp of leaving home, changing our family dynamic forever. I cannot wait to see you make a new life for yourself and wish only good things for you in the future. Thank you for the education you have given me over the years and the humour and energy with which you navigate life. To Ruby, who may leave us next year, I am so grateful for your positive, sweet nature. Thank you for your endless cheerfulness and fabulous fish tacos. I'm so glad we have a little more time with you. To Satish, who I met as a student, discovering London together, it feels as if we have come full circle now we prepare to wave our own kids off. Thank you for your support, humour, wisdom and patience over the years. You wanted an island, and I've given you one.

If you loved *Between the Waves*, turn the page to discover another gripping novel from Hilary Tailor, *Where Water Lies*.

Out now!

Chapter One

Winter, 2015

It is not yet light, and it's so cold the mist that hung low on the ground last night has turned to a hard, stubborn frost. I pass the sign that says: *WOMEN ONLY. MEN NOT ALLOWED BEYOND THIS POINT* and I walk down the narrow path between oak and willow. The little blackboard sign that hangs outside the changing room tells me the temperature of the water is two degrees. If it gets any colder, the ice must be split. Yet still I return like a spawning salmon, unable to resist a ten-year habit scored into the surface of my life.

I stand on the platform, absorbing the peace, my bare feet used to the cold. The water stretches like a long shadow in front of me, and I step towards the railings where the ladder reaches down into the dark. Tied to the railings by a narrow red ribbon is a heart made of willow branches, arched and fastened with twine. My own heart sinks. I had forgotten the date. When I go to work today, the school will be filled with giddy teenagers exchanging Valentine's cards. No matter how hard I try, I still can't conjure up my own, youthful optimism. It remains in 1995 on a hot summer's day, crushed under the weight of a single sentence.

I touch the willow branches, bent into submission. The days here are marked by things like this. A basket of rose petals on midsummer's morning, a chalked message encouraging us to make a wish as we take a handful and throw them into the water. On All Hallows' Eve, strings of ghosts and rubber spiders are tied up around the lifeguards' hut to twist in the chilly air. Some women come in fancy dress, shrieking in pointy hats and wigs. These are the days I find difficult. It is the everyday, the average, I crave, the days without decoration and seasonal greetings.

I climb down the ladder and lower myself in, my limbs becoming ghostly as they fade into the gloom. The breath that leaves me returns in a hard, raw gasp. I push my body through the water, slow and thick with cold, urging myself to breathe. Something within me appreciates the brutality of it all. I can feel it stirring my thoughts, a creature waking after a deep sleep. As I swim, it talks to me, driving me on to the farthest reach of the Ladies' Pond.

The pond is an open secret, a sacred space for some, tucked away behind the ancient greenery of the Heath. Any woman can come here to swim, but, during the winter months, few do. Especially at this hour. In the summer I've seen kingfishers and dragonflies here, skimming the water so near to me I could close my fist around them if I was quick enough. But now is the time I like best. The insects are gone, and the trees are stripped to their bones. The population of swimmers dwindles to a hard core of fanatics. There's something about this colourless state of affairs that appeals to the voice in my head because it's always more vocal when the mornings are dark, and the nights darker still. I can hear it now as I move through the black of the water, urging me to duck under the boundary rope and swim to the murkiest corner, where we are not allowed to go. It tells me it wouldn't matter if I didn't turn back, that nobody would miss me. When I go home, at the end of the day, there will be no cards on the doormat, no messages on the phone. It will be a day like any other.

I swim behind a curtain of willow branches, reaching through the skin of the pond. There, I tread water, my breath caught in clouds, feeling the sly creep of cold move through my limbs. There are two worlds here: the one above and the one below. The world above is for the living. Below the surface, it's not the same. This is a place for the things we don't like to think about: the shadows that slide beneath our feet, the tangle of weeds we try to avoid. It is a quiet, dark place, secretive and slow. When the water closes over me and my ears fill with silence, the voice in my head becomes muffled and I am, finally, left with my own thoughts. If I'm patient, if I hold my breath for long enough, I can see what I came here for. Sometimes they are memories, circling like fish, half-remembered images, hard to reach. But every now and again, I see his face.

A hand, hard on my shoulder, fingers digging into my flesh, pulls me roughly out of the water, back to daybreak.

'Hey!' A woman's voice cuts through my sluggish thoughts. 'You've been in too long.'

She shakes me out of myself, her voice an insistent, buzzing insect.

'You need to turn back right now,' she scolds, 'and . . . as if you didn't know already . . . you're on the wrong side of the rope.'

I squeeze my eyes shut and ignore her, willing her to leave me alone.

'What you're doing is incredibly stupid.'

I open my eyes, orientate myself, then duck under the rope and swim hard and fast back to the ladder, leaving the woman behind me, riddled with indignation. When I get out, Carole the lifeguard is waiting and gives me a telling-off, threatening me with a ban. It's not the first time. I apologise and try to look contrite. My lips are blue, and I'm sent to the changing room to get dry.

It is still early, and the room is empty. I ignore the showers, preferring to strip off and dry myself as quickly as I can, my fingers stiff and non-compliant. When I'm slowly folding my towel into my backpack, she comes in.

'What was that all about?' The indignation has gone. She's curious.

I recognise her as one of the regulars. She could be in her fifties or her seventies, it's hard to tell. Her hair is grey and her body lean and strong, the softening of age kept at bay with a swim routine as punishing as my own.

'Nothing,' I say. 'I lost track of time.'

'Not the first time though, is it? I've seen you do that before. Cross the rope. It's there for a reason.'

'I know.' I pull the contents of my bag out onto a wooden slatted bench, blackened with damp, to find my hat. She looks at me carefully and, for a moment, I stop what I'm doing, feeling exposed.

'That's what worries me. The fact that you know.' She turns away and begins to towel herself. 'The boundary rope across the pond,' she continues, 'I know it's tempting to swim beyond it, but it's dangerous in these temperatures. A few minutes more out there and you might not have had time to get back. It's very easy for the lifeguard to miss you in that spot. You were lucky I saw you.'

I pull the hat low, scooping up the contents of my bag and stuffing them quickly back in. She notices my book, which has landed on the wet floor. 'You enjoying that?'

I nod, stooping to retrieve it, wiping the cover on the front of my coat.

'Then we have something in common. I don't know anyone else who could finish it.'

I know what she means, and a smile escapes me before I can squash it down.

'I set up a small library in the lifeguards' room. It's for the regulars. You can borrow any of the books there. Do you know about it?'

'No.'

'All the books I bring in never get taken away. Maybe that'll change if you go and have a look. You can take as many books as you donate.'

I hesitate, suddenly shy.

'Iris.' She extends her hand towards mine and our fingers find each other in an icy embrace. 'And you?'

'Eliza,' I reply, not quite meeting her gaze. Her hair is short, like mine. My body is thin and muscular, like hers. We could pass for sisters, or mother and daughter.

'Nice to finally meet you.'

I know what she's implying. Mine must be the only name of the winter cohort Iris doesn't know. It's different in the summer when the fair-weather swimmers come; the changing room fills with noisy chatter and the water churns with women. The year-round swimmers look forward to autumn when the tourists leave, and the pond thickens with leaf mould. They relish the early morning, the dead flat of the black water shrouded in a dank mist. They are bound together by it all. It's a bond I have never understood. They swim because it makes them feel good, they are energised by the cold. I swim because it blunts the sting of life. It is the only thing that makes me numb.

ABOUT THE AUTHOR

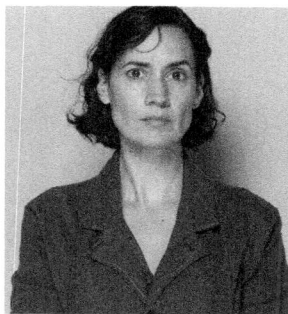

Photo © 2024 Tom Willcocks

When she's not writing fiction, Hilary Tailor runs a design consultancy specialising in colour and trend forecasting. She has worked with Adidas and Puma and sits on the Pantone View colour committee. Hilary was raised on the Wirral Peninsula and graduated from the Royal College of Art. Her debut novel, *The Vanishing Tide*, was published in 2022 and has thousands of five-star reviews, and was followed in 2024 by *Where Water Lies*. *Between the Waves* is her third novel. She can be followed on Instagram @hilarytailorwrites and has a website: www.hilarytailor.com.

Follow the Author on Amazon

If you enjoyed this book, follow Hilary Tailor on Amazon to be notified when the author releases a new book!
To do this, please follow these instructions:

Desktop:

1) Search for the author's name on Amazon or in the Amazon App.
2) Click on the author's name to arrive on their Amazon page.
3) Click the 'Follow' button.

Mobile and Tablet:

1) Search for the author's name on Amazon or in the Amazon App.
2) Click on one of the author's books.
3) Click on the author's name to arrive on their Amazon page.
4) Click the 'Follow' button.

Kindle eReader and Kindle App:

If you enjoyed this book on a Kindle eReader or in the Kindle App, you will find the author 'Follow' button after the last page.

Printed in Great Britain
by Amazon